Will & Patrick

Wake Up Married serial
Episodes 1–3

Leta Blake
&
Alice Griffiths

An Original Publication From Leta Blake Books

Will & Patrick Wake Up Married, Will & Patrick Meet the Family, Will & Patrick Do the Holidays

Written and published by Leta Blake and Alice Griffiths
Cover by Tiferet Design
Copyright © 2015 by Leta Blake
All rights reserved.

ISBN: 979-8-88841-039-4

Other Books by Leta Blake

Any Given Lifetime
The River Leith
Smoky Mountain Dreams
The Difference Between
Heat for Sale
Stay Lucky
Stay Sexy
Omega Mine: Search for a Soulmate
Bring on Forever
Angel Undone

The Home for the Holidays Series
Mr. Frosty Pants
Mr. Naughty List

The Training Season Series
Training Season
Training Complex

Heat of Love Series
Slow Heat
Alpha Heat
Slow Birth
Bitter Heat

'90s Coming of Age Series
Pictures of You
You Are Not Me

Co-Authored with Indra Vaughn
Vespertine

Cowboy Seeks Husband

Co-Authored with Alice Griffiths
The Wake Up Married serial
Will & Patrick's Endless Honeymoon

Gay Fairy Tales
Co-Authored with Keira Andrews
Flight
Levity
Rise

Audiobooks
Leta Blake at Audible

Free Read
Stalking Dreams

Discover more about the author online:
Leta Blake
letablake.com

Gay Romance Newsletter

Leta's newsletter will keep you up to date on her latest releases and news from the world of M/M romance. Join the mailing list today. letablake.com

Leta Blake on Patreon

Become part of Leta Blake's Patreon community in order to access exclusive content, deleted scenes, extras, bonus stories, rewards, prizes, interviews, and more.
www.patreon.com/letablake

Acknowledgements

The authors would like to express their gratitude and appreciation for Vanessa North for her input and advice, and Keira Andrews for speedy-yet-thorough editing. Thank you to Jenn for the diabetes information. Leta would like to thank her friends and family for their endless support. Alice would like to thank Leta for being a wonderful and giving writing partner and for all the laughs. Leta would like to thank Alice for the same. It's been a blast!

Dedications

This trope-based serial goes out to the Girls Who Cried Havoc and their beautiful ilk in celebration of the community playpen in which we joyfully cut our teeth and exercised our creativity.

Will & Patrick

EPISODE ONE

Wake Up Married

BY

Leta Blake & Alice Griffiths

About This Book

Join the fun in this vibrant first installment of the new romantic comedy serial by best-selling author Leta Blake and newcomer Alice Griffiths!

After a drunken night of hot sex in Vegas, strangers Will Patterson and Dr. Patrick McCloud wake up married. A quickie divorce is the most obvious way out—unless you're the heir of a staunchly Catholic mafia boss with a draconian position on the sanctity of marriage.

Stuck between a rock and a hard place, Will and Patrick don't like it, or each other, but they have to make the best of it until they can find another way out of their marriage. To ensure the trust fund Will's charitable foundation relies on isn't revoked by his mobster grandfather, he and Patrick travel to Will's hometown of Healing, South Dakota, posing as a newlywed couple in the throes of true love at first sight.

Complicating their scheme are Will's unresolved feelings for his all-too-recent ex-boyfriend Ryan, and Patrick's desire to get back to the only thing that really matters to him in life: neurosurgery. Will they fool everyone? Or will the mafia get wind that their marriage is a fake? Throw their simmering attraction into the mix and all bets are off!

Episode 1 of 6 in the Wake Up Married *serial.*

EPISODE ONE

Chapter One

WILL SQUINTS AGAINST the bright light streaming in through the open curtains. His head is pounding and his mouth tastes of liquor and come. It's hard to breathe. The panic is the same every time Ryan breaks it off, but this time feels different. More final. And Will still can't breathe. This cannot be happening. This *can't* be happening. The mantra plays on a loop in his head.

"If it can't be happening, it's not. So could you shut up?" mumbles the heavy weight against Will's chest.

Will looks down. Lying there, drooling onto Will's pecs, is a man, perhaps thirty-five or so, with short auburn hair that curls. A man with long wiry muscles, and trim shoulders and hips.

A man he definitely does not know.

And he's naked. They're both naked. Together.

Will jerks up, dislodging him. "What the hell…?"

The guy groans and flops over onto his back, shielding his eyes with his hand.

Will looks around frantically. White sheets, curtains, a hotel room. He remembers Las Vegas, a medical conference he's attending to woo doctors to Healing's brand-spanking newly renovated hospital, the sound of coins rattling out of slot machines, a phone call from Ryan, and a hotel bar with a lot of very appealing liquor.

This cannot be happening.

The man lifts up on his elbows, rakes his eyes over Will's nakedness appreciatively, and smirks.

"Who are you? How did you get in here?" Will yanks the sheet up to his neck.

The man rolls his eyes, and when he speaks his voice is a low-pitched purr that sends shivers up Will's spine. "This is my hotel room. I think you should be asking yourself how did *you* get in *here?*"

"I—I don't—I don't remember," Will says, swallowing hard. He scoots as far away from the man as possible. His ass twinges, making him catch his breath.

He stares at the stranger next to him. The stranger stares right back without shame or any apparent concern to find himself here post-coitus with Will. No, he can't have done this. He would never.

"Did you—did you roofie me?" Will asks.

"Are you asking if I *raped* you?" The man looks as violated as Will feels. "Uh, no. I don't need to chemically incapacitate someone to get laid. I can assure you, Mr. Whoever-the-Hell-You-Are, that this was completely consensual." He frowns and adds, "Drunkenly consensual. On both sides. We were both plenty blasted."

Will isn't sure if he believes him, but he's too woozy to think about it properly. He needs to check his blood sugar, and he needs a do-over button to push immediately. God, did they even use condoms? Given how his body aches this morning, he's obviously had a lot of sex with this guy, and he doesn't even know if they've been safe. Panic and nausea swell inside until he's sure he's going to spew.

"Could you see if there's any water?" Will asks, nodding toward the minibar. "And could you find my clothes?"

The guy snaps, "I think I serviced you enough last night. Get them yourself."

A memory flashes through Will's throbbing head of being fucked as he clawed at the sheets. His neck and cheeks heat, and he rubs his hand over his face, trying to wipe it all away.

"I'm sort of naked under here, and my pants are on the other side of the room. Yours are right there." Will points at them, and the movement makes the room spin. He's definitely going to be sick.

The guy stares at him with really intense blue eyes. Will hears the unspoken thought radiating loud and clear: *A little late for modesty, isn't it?*

But after a moment, the man shrugs, throws the sheet off and walks naked to the fridge. Will flushes, looking away, but glances back when the man bends over. His small ass is perfectly formed, and his balls swing low between his thighs. Blue-black dots swirl in Will's vision.

The guy tosses a bottle of water at Will before cracking open one of his own to take a long drink. And then he just stands there. Completely naked.

Will opens his bottle and lets the cold water soothe his parched throat. He averts his gaze, focusing on the very white bedclothes, but his eyes keep straying back to the guy's chest, abs, and the bush of sandy-auburn pubic hair around his…

Oh God, this *cannot* be happening.

More dots crowd his vision.

"Not that I really care, but I'm trying to remember what the hell happened last night. So what's your name?" the guy asks.

Will stares at him dumbly. He can't shake the idea that this hasn't happened—that he's not naked in this bed with this man staring at him. But he is. He just keeps on being here. It just doesn't stop. He wants to be home in his apartment with Ryan.

And oh God, Ryan will never forgive him for this. Not even if Will can convince him that breaking up was a mistake. No, if this is real, and he's actually slept with this stranger, Ryan will never take him back now.

"Seriously. Do you have a name?" the guy asks with so much impatience that Will flicks him an angry glance, but then looks away fast because he's still standing there naked with absolutely no shame.

Will focuses on the water bottle and takes another drink. "Will Patterson." He hesitates, but he probably should know too. If waking up without knowing the guy's name is bad, not asking now has got to be even worse. Blood rushing in his ears, he asks, "What's yours?"

"Dr. Patrick McCloud."

A doctor. He's picked up and had sex with some doctor from the conference. What the hell is wrong with him? "Oh my God…" Will scrubs at his face.

"Hey, that sounds familiar." Patrick sits on the edge of the bed with one leg tucked underneath him. "I remember you chanting that last night."

"Could you put some pants on?" Will begs. "Please."

Patrick smirks, shifting on the bed so his groin is even more prominently displayed in Will's line of sight. "It's starting to come back to me. We had sex. Lots and lots of sex."

Will takes a deep breath. "It was a mistake. All of it. I don't *do* things like this!"

"I know you don't." Patrick turns serious. "I remember you telling me your ex was basically your first. Your only."

"Ryan," Will whispers, shaking his head. "He'll never forgive me." He bites his lip so he won't cry.

Patrick says his name like it's a dirty word. "*Ryan* is an asshole."

Will's head snaps up. This man, this *Dr. McCloud*, has seduced him and ruined his life, and now he's talking trash about Ryan? "You don't even know him."

"He dumped you. Over the phone. Hate to break it to you, but I think he's just not that into you."

Will shifts uncomfortably, the world goes a little topsy-turvy again, and his stomach lurches. He forces himself still until it passes and keeps his eyes averted. "He needs some space—that's just how Ryan is. You don't know him." He clutches his sore head. "You don't know anything about Ryan and me."

"Oh-ho, yes I do. You're a mouthy drunk. You spilled all the sordid details last night."

Will jerks backward.

"Oh, yes." Patrick shifts and scratches at his thigh. Will stares at Patrick's long fingers, suddenly remembering them shoved in his ass. Jesus, it had felt incredible.

Patrick lips quirk as though he can read Will's mind. His left hand comes up to scratch idly at his chest and flakes off what appears to be dried come.

Will is mortified to realize that it's probably his, or maybe a mixture of theirs, and then his eyes are arrested by the gold, shining band on the guy's left ring finger. "Oh my God. You're married." Vomit starts up his throat and he chokes it back with a swallow of water.

Patrick startles and stares at his hand.

Will scrubs at his face again. "This can't be happening. I'd never do this. I'd *never* sleep with a married man. This is a joke. Don't tell me, let me guess: you're married to a woman. Does she even know you're gay? Are you that deep in the closet?"

"I'm *not* married to a woman," Patrick says, and his voice is so serious and low that Will goes silent and still. "And either you're being more than a little hypocritical, or…"

That's when Will notices the unfamiliar weight on his finger. He holds his hand up and the room tilts sideways.

"Oh my God." In a whoosh of tumbling horror, Will remembers it all. *No, no, this can't be happening.* "We got married."

Patrick presses the palms of his hands against his eyes, shaking his head furiously. "For the love of—oh, you've got to… For the record, *this* cannot be happening."

Patrick is finally on board the panic train and Will's ready to ride it with him, but his vision goes spotty and his mouth numb. He moans. A rushing noise hits his ears, and then there's darkness.

For a day that started out pretty great, what with waking up with his face buried in a hot guy's furry pecs, it's all going downhill fast. Bullet train fast.

First, said hot guy freaks out and accuses him of rape. Patrick remembers clearly how Will had *begged* for it last night, and, sure, drunken consent is basically no consent, but they'd both been smashed out of their minds, so if anything they'd raped *each other*. Over and over. And enjoyed it the entire time.

Then the guy turns out to be a total prude when sober. A prude who freaks out about an even more prudish ex-boyfriend who sounds like an utter asshole. And Patrick knows from assholes, being one himself.

And then Patrick finds out that he's gone and *married* the idiot. *Why?* Why would he do such a thing? He doesn't know. He hasn't remembered that part yet. Surely there's a good explanation, like someone held a gun to his head. If anyone was roofied here, it was clearly him. He's categorically opposed to marriage, in all its forms and guises.

He doesn't even have a pre-nup signed. This pretty piece of ass could take him for everything he's worth. And he's a neurosurgeon, so he's worth a lot. At least they'd used condoms. He remembers rolling them on, and a quick glance toward the trash can shows that, yes, there are six in there. Christ, no wonder his balls are killing him.

A sharp memory takes his breath away.

Will's bent over the bed, taking Patrick's slamming cock, saying, "Everyone says married sex is boring, but this…this is amazing!"

Patrick fucks Will even harder then, grunting at the tight grip of his ass and the slap-slap of their sweaty skin. "Yeah, who knew?" And he comes, bending down to bite Will's shoulder as he shoots his load.

Now, as the cherry on the crap-cake, his new spouse has suddenly gone gray and passed out.

The medic alert bracelet Patrick finds on Will's right wrist indicates he's a Type 1 diabetic and the binge drinking his blushing bride had engaged in the prior night was a fool's move. A cold prickle races over Patrick's skin. He'd been too drunk to notice the bracelet either. Sure, it's an expensive, fancy one, designed to be unobtrusive unless there's an emergency, but he's a goddamn doctor. He should have noticed.

"Hey," Patrick shouts, tapping Will's cheek. "Hey. Wake up."

Will opens warm brown eyes and looks just as shocked as the first time. He starts to move, and Patrick encourages him. "Sit up."

Will does as he's told. "Did I pass out?"

"For a few seconds. Where's your kit?" Patrick looks around the room for anything resembling a glucose test kit. "You need to test your blood sugar. Is the meter in your room? Since I didn't see an insulin pump site on you last night, I guess you take injections."

"Yeah."

"Okay. Do you take your long lasting insulin at night or in the morning?"

"Uh, night."

"Did you take it last night?"

"I think so? I don't know."

Patrick sees a small bag on the floor by the unfamiliar jeans, wadded-up buttoned shirt, and boxers. "Is that murse yours?"

"What?"

"That man-purse. It's yours. Do you keep your meter in it? Test strips?" Without waiting for an answer he crosses over and opens it. "Bingo." He tosses the bag on the bed. "Test yourself."

"Leave me alone. I'm just tired. Need a nap. I'm fine."

"Ain't that just jolly news? The last thing I need is a strange guy I'm married to collapsing into a coma in my hotel room due to diabetic hypoglycemia."

Will doesn't reply but does get the meter out of his bag and test himself. "I'm low. Thirty-five." He looks like he's going to slip unconscious again.

"You need some glucose. Drink this." Patrick grabs a bottle of juice from the mini fridge and watches as Will drinks half of it down.

Giving the benefit of the doubt isn't something that Patrick does often or well, but maybe Will doesn't know that binge drinking is off-limits for him. After all, the clowns-to-competent-doctors ratio is pretty high; it's possible that Will is unfortunate enough to be seeing a Bozo.

"You need to test again when you've finished that. See if you need more glucose or if it's time to stabilize you with some fats and protein." Patrick heads to the fridge, pulling out a second bottle of orange juice and tossing it to Will. Then he grabs a fancily wrapped block of cheese from the fridge and the carton of whole-wheat crackers from the basket of snacks.

"Thanks," Will murmurs.

Patrick nods toward the medic alert bracelet on Will's wrist. "Drinking like you did last night is dangerous."

Will takes a large swallow of the orange juice. "Tell me something I don't know."

So, benefit of the doubt is unnecessary. As usual.

Using a knife to cut small hunks, Patrick quickly builds a few cracker sandwiches. He watches Will test again and is relieved when the number is significantly improved.

"I shouldn't drink for a lot of reasons."

Will's color is getting better and he's more lucid. Patrick hands him the cracker sandwiches. "Eat up. Chug-a-lug."

Will remains silent, obviously panicking as he chews and swallows the last bite of cracker and cheese. Patrick sits beside him on the bed, and, taking Will's left hand, tests him a third time just to be sure. "Eight-three," Patrick mutters. "Good. Crisis averted."

Will sucks on his pricked finger, not making eye contact while Patrick takes in the evidence of Will's workout regimen—firm abs and strong shoulders, v-ing down to slim hips. His short hair glows gold in the light from the windows, and his nicely formed pecs are liberally dusted with blond hair. Will strikes him as pretty, even though he's taller and larger than Patrick. He can't be more than twenty-six, farm fed and, if memory from the night before serves, normally rosy cheeked. He isn't rosy cheeked now.

Patrick cuts to the chase. "FYI, I don't have any STDs. And condoms were used. I know what you told me last night about your ex being your only. But you also told me about the shady meet-cute with his new boyfriend."

"He's not with Hartley like that."

"That's not what you thought last night."

"Shut up."

"All I'm saying is if he's been dipping the wick in some other pot of wax, it's possible you might be carrying something you're not aware of yet."

Will's eyes blaze. "No. That's impossible."

Patrick lifts a brow. "Oh, right, because your ex wasn't much of a lover, right? It's been, what did you say? Six months since you last got any?"

Will shakes his head but says nothing as he blushes.

It's this Ryan idiot's loss, really. Will's a great lay. "Regardless, we should both keep an eye out for any difficulties down below, like pain or blood in the urine or—"

"Let me guess, you're a urologist?"

"No, I'm a neurosurgeon."

Will snorts and rolls his eyes. "Yeah, right."

Patrick's not sure why he's offended. Maybe because now that they both remember all the ways Patrick made Will come, he expects a little respect?

"What? I don't look like a neurosurgeon to you?"

"You look...you look..." Will evaluates him. "Like you still aren't wearing any pants." He covers his face again like he hasn't been at the receiving end of the cock he's so scared to look at. "Please. Hand me my clothes. I have to get out of here."

"You need to eat the rest of that food before you do anything else. I'm a doctor."

"That means I have to do what you say?" Will snaps.

Patrick takes pity on him and pulls on his boxer-briefs and jeans before tossing Will's clothes over.

"There. Since you're so uncomfortable with nudity, maybe this will cheer you up and we can figure out the first step to extricating ourselves from this mess."

Will drains the bottle of OJ before he wriggles under the covers to pull on his underwear and pants in prudish privacy. "I'm sure you noticed my bracelet last night. Why didn't you seem concerned about my drinking then?"

Will's on the bed on his hands and knees. Patrick pounds into him as he rubs up and down his back over and over. A strange, possessive thought fills him: he's mine now and I have to take good care of him.

Patrick shrugs the memory away and answers Will. "You wear one of those dangerous, fancy-pants bracelets instead of the traditional medic alert. If you weren't so vain and trying to hide your disease, I'd have noticed instantly and none of this," he gestures between them, "would have happened. As for last night, I drank too much and wasn't thinking clearly." Patrick holds up his hand, waggling his ring finger. "Obviously."

As Will stews, Patrick focuses on how to resolve their predicament. Hopefully they can do it quickly. If they can get married in Vegas in less than fifteen minutes, it can't take much longer to get a divorce, right?

"Look," Patrick says. "Don't beat yourself up. You're a good person—even I know that much after one night. We'll get a divorce, you'll go back to wherever the hell you're from. I'll go back to Atlanta, and we never have to see each other again."

Will eyes go wide at the word 'divorce.' "What? No. Oh, no. No, no." He's hyperventilating again. "I've ruined everything. Oh my God, it's over. It's all over."

Patrick isn't pleased to be married either, and he's going to freak out about it as soon as Will gives him a turn, but he really doesn't think that what's happened between them is the worst thing imaginable. Sure, he's never drinking again, because this is so far outside of his comfort zone that he's shocked he's not on fire. But no one's *dead*.

And, while looking on the bright side of things is far from his forte, the sex was amazing, and he's not been that big of a jerk to Will yet, and that Ryan guy is good riddance. So Will's level of distress can be taken down a notch as far as he's concerned. At least until it's his turn to start the apoplectic hijinks.

"Come on, chin up." Patrick hates that he's giving a pep talk here. "Pull it together."

"You don't understand," Will says, his eyes wide. "We can't get divorced."

"The hell we can't." Patrick's voice rises a few octaves. "What are you? Catholic? They're not that fond of the whole gay marriage thing in the first place. I'm sure they'd fully support a gay divorce."

Will rises and starts pacing. He's bowlegged from being fucked and there's a hitch in each step. Patrick surges with pride. There's something incredibly satisfying about any job well done, of course. Except that he's gone and *married* this particular job-well-done, which zaps the pleasure from it just like that.

"No, it's…" Will shakes his head. "It's Good Works. I'll lose Good Works!"

"What the hell are you talking about?"

"The Healing Foundation for Good Works." Will runs his hand through his hair. "I run a charitable foundation. I started it with money I inherited from my father's family."

"O-kay. So?"

"My father is Tony Molinaro."

Patrick stares. "*The* Tony Molinaro? Mafioso boss?"

Will nods.

"Wait a minute. You said your name was Patterson."

"It is. It's my mom's maiden name. I don't really have anything to do with the Molinaro family."

If the Molinaro family is involved, who knows what elaborate and illegal scheme might be in the works here? While he has no idea what they might want with him, or why they'd want him to marry and screw the brains out of Will, Patrick's back to wondering if he *was* roofied by this baby criminal. Maybe he's about to be dragged away at gunpoint into some nefarious and twisted plot of international crime and neurosurgery.

"Great. So, I've married into a world-renowned family of criminals. Why don't I see this ending well?"

"I told you, I'm not part of that," Will protests. "My mother left Tony when I was just a baby. She raised me alone. Tony, he's just…he's…"

"A very terrifying sperm donor?"

"It's complicated."

"Whatever." Patrick shakes his head. "You haven't explained why we 'can't get divorced.'" He air quotes it.

Will's hands are shaking but his voice is steady. "A few years ago, I came into a trust set up by my Molinaro great-grandfather."

"Blood money. Nice."

"It's not like that." Will rubs his eyes, his cheeks flushing again. "You don't know what I've done to try to make something good out of my family's past."

Patrick shrugs. "I'm not here for story time. I just want a divorce. But apparently the mob says I can't have one, so hurry and tell me why."

Will's jaw clenches but he goes on. "I inherited the trust money when I turned twenty-one, but I've never used it for myself. I started a charitable foundation."

"Great. Bully for you."

"Shut up and listen, will you? There was a caveat. If I ever marry, it has to be for good. If I get a divorce I lose access to the money. It all goes back to the family."

"What?" Patrick laughs. "That's insane. Every second person gets a divorce these days."

"I know!" Will throws up his hands. "The problem is Great-grandfather Molinaro was a strict Catholic—"

"A strict Catholic who runs a crime family. So, the best kind."

Will flashes another angry glance. "He got tired of everyone disregarding the Church's stance on divorce. He said it made it impossible to instill the Molinaro family's value system—"

"The value system of murder and mayhem?"

"—in the kids born of broken marriages. He cracked down especially after this last generation. See, my mother divorced Tony, and since then he's been married twice more. And Tony's cousin Mario divorced three wives, and his other cousin Evelyn divorced her husband, and then another cousin, Gino—"

Patrick holds up one hand. "Please. Stop, for the love of God."

Will glares. "I can't get a divorce or my foundation, Good Works, will lose the money. It's as simple as that."

"You expect me to believe this?"

"Yeah, I do. Because it's true."

Patrick stares at Will, measuring him up, and concludes that he looks far too horrified to be making it all up. Still...

"How much money are we talking about here?"

"Millions. Hundreds of millions. The kind of money that can change the lives of thousands upon thousands of people."

Well, at least he doesn't have to worry about the lack of a prenup. He's gone and married Richie Rich. "Too bad," Patrick says. "You'll lose the money. If you think I'm going to agree to—"

"Of course we won't stay married forever. We just need to figure out a way around the caveat. I can't lose Good Works. You don't understand. That money can't go back to the Molinaro family. I'm doing so much good with it!"

Will slumps back down on the side of the bed, and Patrick sits beside him. Heat radiates from Will's bare torso.

"Okay, listen." Patrick begins gently. "Don't freak out. We'll just get an annulment. That won't break the rules, right?"

"I'm not sure. I hope not." Will stares across the room for a long moment but then takes a deep breath and nods. "Yeah. That might work."

"There. Problem solved. It'll be like it never happened."

There's a knock at the door. Patrick's stomach growls, and he hopes he had the sense to pre-order breakfast at some point during their drunken debauchery. He jerks the door open. Alas, no.

"Chief."

"Dr. McCloud." Laurence Schaeffer, his chief of staff, nods. He wrinkles his nose, looking Patrick up and down. "Long night?"

"Something like that."

Schaeffer taps his watch. "It's after ten, Dr. McCloud. I came to accompany you to today's lectures, which, for the record, began two hours ago."

"You don't say?"

Schaeffer steps into the room uninvited. "I know you wouldn't *dream* of missing the rest of them, doctor."

That's exactly what Patrick had been planning to do, actually. He's still pissed at Schaeffer for dragging him here in the first place. He'd tried to get out of it, of course, but once his chief had played up Dr. Andrew Morris's interest in the conference, Patrick was screwed. He couldn't let Morris get the upper hand in the upcoming bid for head of department. When Patrick thinks of it like that, this mess with Will is all his chief of staff's fault for manipulating him into coming to this damn conference in the first place.

"Oh." Schaeffer pulls up short when he spots Will sitting on the rumpled bed. "I didn't know your, uh, *partner* was meeting you in Las Vegas, Dr. McCloud."

"Oh-ho," Patrick says. "He's not my partner. He's a one-night stand gone awry."

Schaeffer chuckles as though Patrick's made a joke. "Ah, yes, well, that's how it is in this day and age. Or so my children tell me. Things were different in my time. How long have you and your partner been together, Dr. McCloud? I feel remiss in not knowing more about your personal life."

Patrick stares at Schaeffer, trying to decide if the man is really that stupid or if he's becoming senile in his old age.

"Less than a day," Patrick says, and Schaeffer looks confused. What's so hard to get about hooking up with someone in Vegas? Isn't that what Vegas is *for*? "He might as well be a rent boy," he adds. Sometimes being crass does the trick like nothing else can.

Will's eyebrows shoot up to his hairline, but Schaeffer looks like he's missing the joke and will hunt until he finds it. Will smiles politely at Schaeffer.

"Hello." He stands up and holds out a hand. "I'm Will Patterson."

"Dr. Laurence Schaeffer." He shakes Will's hand. "Ah ha," he says and laughs jovially. "*Less than a day.* I get it now. Dr. McCloud, I can't help but notice you're wearing a wedding ring." He looks back at Will. "You too, Mr. Patterson. Congratulations!"

Patrick sputters. "I don't know how to make this more plain to you, Chief, but beyond the Biblical sense, I don't know this guy from Adam." Why is he explaining this at all? It's not Schaeffer's damn business, anyway.

Schaeffer holds up his hands. "Excuse me, but are you or are you not married?"

Clearly the man could not be denser. "We met in the bar last night, had a little too much to drink, and apparently decided it was a good idea to tie the knot."

"Funny story, huh?" Will chimes in, shoving his hands in the pockets of his jeans. Patrick notices how that makes his still-bare chest look deliciously strong and his shoulders broad.

"Hilarious," Patrick deadpans.

Schaeffer looks anything but amused. "Dr. McCloud, are you telling me you and this young man got married on a whim? While drunk?"

Patrick sighs. "I'm as appalled as you are."

"I hardly think that's true, Dr. McCloud." Schaeffer turns to Will. "Are you…?" He looks back to Patrick. "Is this young man a hooker?" He spits it out.

"If he was, that would be none of your business." Patrick fumes. Who does Schaeffer think he is? What does any of this have to do with neurosurgery?

"I am *not* a hooker!" Will scrambles to add.

"Let me get this straight," Schaeffer barks, and Patrick's on the verge of forcing him out the door. He is already so *done* with explaining himself today. "You married a stranger while intoxicated?"

"That sums it up." Patrick shrugs. "We're getting it annulled. No need to worry your little head about it, Chief. All's well that ends well, and all that."

"You can't get the marriage annulled, Dr. McCloud. Correct me if I'm wrong, but it appears the union has been consummated." Schaeffer looks pointedly at Patrick's chest, still flecked with dried come. Will slaps a hand over his mouth, his face turning bright red. "And I can't imagine that you have any other sustainable grounds."

"Fraud, for one," Patrick says.

"There was no fraud!" Will gasps.

Patrick grabs Will's wrist and points at his bracelet. "Withholding information about a major disease surely counts as fraud. And there is the question of sound mind at the time of the marriage, and given the extent of our intoxication, neither of us can claim that. And, if it comes down to it, I'll happily fudge on the definition of consummation to get out of this mess. What the assholes in charge of handing out annulments don't know won't hurt them. I'd say we have plenty of grounds."

"Dr. McCloud." Schaeffer sounds more appalled than Patrick's ever heard him. He's surprised that's even possible. "Are you telling me you intend to lie to court officials?"

"Well, I can hardly stay married to some trust fund brat I met in a bar, can I?" Patrick's flabbergasted by the idiocy. Though why that is, he can't say. Nearly everyone is stupid. Life only proves that to him again and again.

Schaeffer's eyes narrow, and Patrick is reminded of why he's a formidable Chief. He's got opinions and annoyingly uptight morals and he's not afraid to stand by them. *Crap.*

"Dr. McCloud, I must say that I find your cavalier attitude on this matter quite reprehensible."

"Well I find the idea of some sort of *sanctity of marriage* to be equally reprehensible," Patrick replies, pissed now.

"I'm not talking about the sanctity of marriage, Dr. McCloud—though, yes, I'm disturbed by how lightly you seem to take that revered institution as well. I am *extremely* uncomfortable with your attitude toward taking responsibility for your actions, and your willingness to perjure yourself for your own benefit."

"Excuse me? This was a drunken mistake, not a—"

Schaeffer talks over him. "If your moral fiber is so weak that a little alcohol and a night in Las Vegas are enough for you to give into poor decision making, and *then* you are willing to compound that lack of morality with a premeditated lie to a court of law to get yourself out of the resulting consequences of those actions, I can only imagine the lies you might tell the Georgia Medical Review Board to maintain your license."

Patrick goes cold. "If you're saying what I—"

"Oh, yes, I am, Dr. McCloud. If you're willing to try to take a shortcut out of owning up to your responsibility here, I see no reason to believe you wouldn't do the same during your recent disciplinary hearing regarding the death of Jake Taylor."

Patrick can barely see through the fury. The cold helplessness that swelled in him when he realized he was losing the boy had haunted him for months. "I did everything I could to save Jake. His death was unfortunate, but not malpractice. I stand by my work and my choices that day. The board agreed with me at the hearing."

"So you say, Dr. McCloud. So you say. We both know the rumors amongst the staff—"

"Are you really going to believe sordid gossip from a nursing staff that has it in for me over the findings of the board?"

Schaeffer shakes his head and then glances toward Will. "Frankly, I can't see how someone who baldly admits to being so untrustworthy could possibly be expected to head up any department in my hospital. I believe you've just helped make my decision about who the new head of neurosurgery will be."

"You have *got* to be kidding me," Patrick shouts. "Do you have rocks for brains? My personal life has no bearing on my performance as a surgeon, and you can't seriously consider Andrew Morris for that position. You may as well hire the local butcher."

Will's hand squeezes his arm, and over the rush of blood in his ears, he hears Will say his name warningly, like he's trying to get Patrick to shut up.

"Morris is a fine surgeon, Dr. McCloud, and while he might not be as talented as you, at least I can trust him."

"Trust him to what? Kiss your ass and bring malpractice lawsuits raining down on your head?"

"Patrick," Will hisses again.

"Dr. McCloud, I will consider this conversation your resignation." Schaeffer turns to the door. "I will not be willing to offer a letter of recommendation on your behalf, but somehow I suspect you won't need one. Your reputation precedes you. God help the hospital that's willing to take you on. They'll need it." He pauses and looks back at Will. "A prostitute? Absolutely disgusting."

Patrick slams the door behind the pompous bastard. He stands staring at the bed in stunned silence for several seconds. Across the room, Will puts on his shirt, fingers clumsily fumbling with the buttons.

"Do you realize what just happened here?" Patrick points at Will. "I had that asshole in the palm of my hand until you seduced me into marrying you." He knows that's not even close to true. Schaeffer's always been suspicious of him and the hospital staff has always wanted him gone. Getting the position of department head was going to be the ultimate fuck you to them all. Looks like the joke's on him.

"What?" Will asks incredulously. "*You* seduced me."

"Oh please," Patrick scoffs. "You were throwing yourself all over me at the bar. You practically pulled me to the wedding chapel by my dick!"

That's not even close to true either. Flashes of dragging Will toward the stairs that lead to the chapel while Will followed, flushed and laughing, burn in his mind.

Maybe Will remembers it all too, because his mouth opens and closes a few times, but no sounds come out. He stands there gaping like a fish. A very hot fish. With an attractive glow from arguing staining his cheeks.

"Screw you," Will finally says, tucking his shirt into his pants and stalking toward the door. "I'll meet you in the lobby in thirty minutes and we *will* go down to the courthouse and get this marriage annulled. Do I make myself clear?"

Bossy Will is sexy. Patrick salutes. "Sir! Yes, sir!"

Will scowls and slams the door behind him.

"Well, all righty then."

Chapter Two

STANDING UNDER THE shower, Will soaps up. His ass throbs insistently, thrusting memories of the night before into his head. The most horrible thing is how the memories aren't horrible at all. He remembers Patrick sitting down beside him at the bar, and the initial rush of annoyance at the interruption in his drinking. But that was immediately overshadowed by Patrick's flash of a smile, like a hidden thing Will uncovered by accident and then desperately needed to see again.

He'd *liked* Patrick last night. He'd leaned against him early in the evening just to feel his body, tight and firm against his own, and plummeted into rash, drunken affection that seemed so real at the time. So intense and hilarious, yet calm beneath its craziness.

He reaches around to wash his ass, touching his tender hole with his fingers. He shudders as a memory courses through him of Patrick's tongue teasing him there. Patrick had been so gentle, commanding, and in control. Will shakes his head, dunking it under the spray of the water. He works to get the dried come out of his chest hair and pubes, and ignores his hardening cock.

Lightning-quick smiles and great bedroom skills don't change the fact that Will's screwed a stranger, who's turned out to be a complete jerk in the light of morning. Patrick isn't charming at all. Or funny. Or even very nice. If Will needs a reason to recommit to staying sober, he's married it.

With luck, the 'til-death-do-us-part vow is something he can delete like a drunk email he composed but never finished, passing out before clicking send. He gets out of the shower, shaves, brushes his teeth, and pulls on a pair of nice pants and a responsible-looking pale yellow, button-up shirt.

When his room service breakfast arrives, he checks his glucose levels again, calculates the amount of carbs he's going to consume, and injects the right dose of insulin. He chokes down the food without any pleasure and then paces the room. Yanking open the curtains, he gazes down at the Las Vegas Strip. It looks less glamorous in the daytime: dusty, sun-pale, tired. Finally, he sits down on the bed and, with shaking fingers, digs his cell phone out of his bag to call his attorney, Owen Marsh.

"Will, I wasn't expecting a call from you today. How's Vegas? You haven't gotten yourself into any trouble out there, have you?" Owen laughs, but Will can hear the worry behind his joke. It's not as though Will hasn't relapsed before and Vegas is a risky place for a drunk.

Will swallows against his shame. "That's why I'm calling actually."

Owen's chuckle dies out softly. "Oh no."

"Yeah. It's bad. Please don't lecture me, Owen. I need your help."

Owen is silent for a long moment before asking, "What do you need?"

Will's stomach tries to crawl out of his throat, but he manages to sound somewhat calm. "I need you to look up my great-grandfather's trust stipulations regarding marriage, or, well, I guess divorce or annulment too? I can't remember the particulars."

Owen is silent for a very long time, and Will can just picture him, balding, rumpled in his suit, turning away from his computer and pushing his glasses up his nose. Will wishes he could be there with him now, safe in Owen's staid, fussy little office in the Good Works building, surrounded by Owen's leather furniture and boring law books. He would feel less ashamed if he could look into Owen's calm, gray eyes while they talked.

"Give me a moment, Will. I'll have Marcy grab the file."

"Thank you."

He's put on hold for a second, but then Owen's back. "Marcy will have what we need in just a few minutes."

"Great."

"Do you want to talk about it?"

Will shakes his head even though Owen can't see him. "I can't. Not yet."

"Are you sober right now?"

"Yeah. Hungover as hell, but I'm sober."

Owen's soft sigh filters over through the connection.

There's silence for a good forty-five seconds, and hot tears press against Will's eyelids. His whisper is raw. "You're not going to ask why I slipped?"

"You know I don't ever ask that question. In all the years I've been your sponsor, when have I? You slipped for the same reason any alcoholic does. You wanted to drink. It seemed like the only option to make it through whatever moment you found yourself in. All the context around the decision is, for all intents and purposes, excuses." Owen never bullshits. That's one of Will's favorite things about him. Owen sighs. "Also, I know you well enough to hazard a guess. Ryan again?"

"Yes."

"Another break?"

"Yeah."

"I know we've discussed this before, but Ryan can't be your definition of recovery. It's too much to put on him, and a dangerous place to put yourself. Your recovery should be defined by something you can control, Will. And you can never control another person."

Will's throat aches. "I know, I know. It's just that I love him."

Why does love hurt so much? Why does it never lay soft and easy against his skin like a comfortable sweater? It's unfair that love is so hard.

"Is it because of that young man I've seen Ryan going around town with?"

Yes.

"No, it's me. It's always me. I'm weak and too needy." His list of flaws and failures is long, but weak and needy is always at the top. "Ryan says if he stays with me I'll drag him into addiction again. He's been sober so long. Nine years this past fall. He can't risk it."

Owen's silence speaks volumes. But he's Will's sponsor, not Ryan's, and his loyalties are clear. "All right. Let's talk about our first priority here: getting you to a meeting. Can you make it to one today? I can look up locations in Vegas. There have to be dozens of groups."

"I can't. I've got something else going on."

Owen's voice is like the granite steps of the public library in Healing after a day in the sun: warm but rock solid. "I feel strongly that a meeting is what you need most right now."

"There's no danger of me drinking again any time soon, Owen. There's a bigger problem to solve."

"The marriage problem," Owen says with a twist in his tone that makes Will's heart break with shame.

"Yes," Will whispers. "I got drunk and married someone last night."

"Dear God, Will." Owen's voice is raspy. "Who?"

"A doctor. A neurosurgeon I met, actually."

"Was he someone Don encouraged you to ingratiate yourself with?"

Will wishes he could say yes. "No, I didn't even know he was a neurosurgeon until this morning. Well, I don't think I knew."

"Were you drunk when you met him?"

"Already on my way."

"I see."

"Yeah. One thing led to another." Will makes a helpless noise.

"Will, this is… I don't know what to say. The consequences of this could be immense. You know the stipulations of the trust are ironclad in the legal sense and as rigid as they are absurd."

"I know, I know." The light from the window falls harshly over the hotel room carpet, illuminating the swirls in the design.

For a moment Owen sounds just like a real father when he asks, "What were you *thinking*?"

"I wasn't. Obviously. I'd gone into the bar to look for a few of the neurologists on my list. I figured they'd be drinking in there and I was ready to be strong and just have club soda."

Owen sighs.

"Then, while I was sitting there trying to put names with faces, Ryan called to break up with me. The next thing I knew I'd downed four shots of whiskey and was working on a cocktail of some kind or another. It's all a blur."

"Will, hold on. Yes, Marcy, thank you. Please close the door again behind you."

Will hears Owen shifting the papers around. "There can be no divorce, not even one instigated by your spouse, or the money reverts back to the Molinaro family."

"I know."

"The criteria for annulment are tight. No fraud, no immoral grounds of any nature. We can discuss them in more detail, but there's another stipulation that surely you haven't forgotten. It's the strictest of all. And, I have to admit, I've never understood how the Molinaros could possibly prove or disprove it, but it's a doozy and a huge problem in your situation."

Will's throat is dry, but he manages to swallow. "Just tell me."

After Owen spells out the terms in excruciating detail, Will sits on the bed, his chest tight and even his blood is screaming.

"I can fly out this afternoon," Owen says. "You shouldn't be alone."

"No, I'm coming home today. I can't stay here. I know that."

"What will you tell Don? I take it you didn't recruit any neurosurgeons for the redesigned unit? Or even discussed the hospital with any of them?"

"Other than the one I married? No." Will remembers mentioning Healing Regional briefly while he and Patrick were flirting, but things went so far afield after that.

"How can I help you, Will?"

"I need all of this to be confidential. You know how much rests on this playing out perfectly. Don't tell anyone anything at all, Owen."

"As your attorney, I'm legally bound not to. As your sponsor, I wouldn't jeopardize your trust that way. And, when it comes to Good Works, I'd lie if I have to in order to make sure we don't lose everything."

"Thank you. If we can get this annulled on the only grounds open to me, then it won't be a problem. If we can't, then I honestly don't know what's going to happen."

Owen makes a soft, worried noise and Will wishes he could hug the man and gather strength from him. "You need to call your grandmother. Eleanora will know what to do."

Will shivers at the thought. "Maybe. If I can't resolve it myself."

Owen's silence communicates his disagreement, but he only says, "Call me if you think about drinking again. I'll be worried until I see you face-to-face."

"Thanks, Owen. I'm so sorry about this. When I get home, I'll get back to working my program."

"You work a program every day, Will. So work your program now. But remember, it can't take you any further than your definition of recovery, and so long as your definition of recovery is Ryan, then it will take you only as far as your relationship with him goes. That's not something you can bank your life on."

"I wish I could."

Owen's breath was soft in his ear. "If wishes were changes…"

"I wouldn't be in this mess."

"Amen."

Forty-five minutes later, Patrick saunters into the lobby. The Christmas carols piped in overhead are annoyingly cheerful, and the massive Christmas trees dominating the already ornate lobby are gaudy as hell, but he's full of room service breakfast and therefore in a much better mood. Somehow food fixes a lot of things for him.

He smirks when Will half stomps and half limps over.

"You're late." Will glares.

Patrick shrugs. Will's showered and changed his clothes. He has the sleeves of his shirt rolled up and the top three buttons undone, exposing tantalizing glimpses of that chest hair Patrick woke up with his face nestled against this morning. Patrick has to tilt his head back a little to meet his gaze. "Beauty can't be rushed."

Will runs his eyes over Patrick and then swallows, looking away. "Whatever. I have to tell you something. It's important."

"Hit me."

Will looks down at his toes. Patrick can see shame looming up inside him. "It's a problem with the annulment," Will murmurs. "I called my attorney and it turns out there are a few more stipulations in the trust than I remembered before."

"You better not tell me we can't get one."

He doesn't meet Patrick's eyes. "We can. Probably. But it can't be for any reason we qualify for. Not if I'm going to keep Good Works. There's only one reason we can possibly give for the annulment."

"Oh, I beg to differ. I've got nothing to lose here. So I can give any reason I damn well please."

"But you don't have to, is the thing. We can make this happen without Good Works losing anything at all."

"Great. Spit it out. I'm brilliant, but I'm not a mind reader." Patrick taps his fingers against his leg. Catching himself, he shakes out his hand to stop his nervous tick.

Will's hot, desperate gaze pierces Patrick. "If I ask for an annulment based on any quote-unquote immoral reason, such as fraud or due to intoxication or drug use, then the trust money reverts back to the Molinaros immediately."

"This bizarre focus on marital morality from a crime family is more than a little hypocritical, don't you think?"

"It doesn't matter, does it? It is what it is. It still means we're screwed."

"What happens if the money goes back to the Molinaros?"

"I'm not sure. I think it gets put back into the pot to be divided out amongst my great-grandfather's other descendants. Not all of them are good people, Patrick."

Patrick stares at him. "This isn't real. Where's the camera? I thought *Punk'd* was canceled a lifetime ago."

Will shakes his head.

"Dammit, you're serious?"

Will presses his lips together and looks at his shoes again.

"What about lack of consummation? Is it immoral not to screw your spouse on the wedding night?"

"No, that's still open to us."

"Fine. I already told you and my ex-boss that I'm ready and willing to lie about our activities last night. I'll happily deny ever touching you if that's what we need to do. So let's get this over with. I need to start looking for a new job since apparently I'm out of one."

"Sounds good," Will says tersely, leading them outside. Patrick admires Will's ass in his well-fitting pants, then mentally chastises himself. He's in enough trouble as it is.

THE LINE AT the courthouse isn't nearly as long as Patrick expects it to be.

Doesn't everyone get drunk-married in Vegas? Like as a rite of passage or something? That's what he's been telling himself during the entire cab ride over in between absolutely *not* admiring how hot Will looks in the daylight, all blond and glowy (which is a description that is just…ugh).

He's also been studiously ignoring the self-congratulatory comments that come completely unbidden to his mind, like: *Damn, Patrick, that guy you married last night? Super fine!* Or, *See that ass? I plowed it, thank you very much!* Or, *Take that, Dean Wellington! Bet your scrawny butt never landed anything as hot as this one!* Or, most disturbingly, when Will turns his face just a certain way and the sun comes in the cab window, *You've got good taste, Patrick. Too bad you can't keep him a little longer.*

It's the last one that pisses him off again and makes him wish he'd brought an extra room service muffin or two, because this idiot he keeps admiring is the reason he's currently out of work. He really should be on the phone to Johns Hopkins right now, or Vandy, or the Mayo Clinic to let the bidding wars begin. Every moment wasted is another he's not saving a life.

Once at the courthouse, though, he puffs up with misplaced, ridiculous pride again. At least his idiotic bungle hasn't led him to be trying to divorce one of the crying women repeating how their parents are going to kill them. Thank God his cock is gay no matter how drunk he is. And that his biological parents are far too dead to care about his marital status.

After twenty long minutes of Will looking annoyingly attractive while he shifts anxiously from foot to foot, he starts asking nosy, annoying questions.

"So, is your chief of staff on target? About what he said?"

Patrick has no clue. "He said a lot of things."

"I mean about you lying during a malpractice hearing?"

Heat rises up his neck. "Mr. Patterson, just so we're clear, I would lie about any number of things in order to keep my medical license. But no, I did not lie about that boy's death. I'm a brain surgeon. Patients die. It's crappy, but it's inevitable."

"Yeah? Then why are you rattled?" Will crosses his arms over his chest and gets up in Patrick's personal space.

"If you get much closer to me, we might actually merge, and I think we did enough of that last night, don't you?"

Will doesn't step back. If anything, he invades Patrick's space even more. "You were angry when he accused you. And now you're angry at me for bringing it up."

"Can we focus on what we're here to accomplish? Getting an annulment? Let's not turn my former chief's assholery into an Agatha Christie novel."

"Okay, I won't." Will pauses. "But only if you spoil the ending for me. So, whodunit, Dr. McCloud?"

"Cancer. Cancer and a brain hemorrhage during surgery. Nothing—and no one—else is responsible for Jake Taylor's death. And that's all. I'm not going to discuss my patient with you."

Will cocks his head and studies him. "Are all surgeons this cold? Do you have an on switch so you can actually feel things, or is this it for you?"

"What you see is what you get." Patrick remembers how very warm he'd been last night. If Will considers that cold, then God help the man Will manages to get hot.

Will eyes are narrowed and suspicious.

Patrick sighs. "Really, Mr. Patterson, why do you care? Hopefully, in the next ten minutes we can clean up this mess and never see each other again."

"Accidentally marrying a murderer's probably acceptable grounds for an annulment don't you think?"

There's an audible gasp from one of the weepy women behind them, and Patrick glares at her. "First, I think your precious Molinaros aren't too concerned with murder. And second, I think that falls under the category of fraud, which you've already told me is out of the question due to your family's little morality problem."

Will cracks his first smile in a while, nudging Patrick with his shoulder. "Lighten up, Dr. McCloud. Or can't you take a joke?"

"Not when it's not funny."

Will's brows draw low and his lower lip tucks between his teeth. "Yeah, sorry. My sense of humor's a little out of whack right now. Seems I went and married a stranger and I could lose everything important in my life."

"Huh. I can relate," Patrick mutters.

Will shoots him a half grin.

"Cheer up. Looks like we're next. In just a few interminably long minutes we'll be free."

Five minutes later, a clerk stares at them with his eyebrows disappearing beneath a pink and white Santa hat. "Are you two *really* trying to tell me your marriage wasn't consummated?"

"That's right," Patrick replies.

The clerk wears a badge that reads *Santa's Favorite Elf*, which makes Patrick want to laugh, cry, or puke. Maybe all three. "You expect me to believe that?"

"Yes," Will says, leaning in to read the clerk's nametag and smiling winningly. "Yes, Joe. Dr. McCloud and I did not have sexual relations after our otherwise entirely consensual and above-board marriage."

Joe snorts. "Oh, honey, the way you limped in here, I'm guessing you two had sexual relations *all* over the place."

Will's face falls and Patrick can't help but snicker. Of course they've ended up with a gay clerk. That's how their luck is running today. Clearly, the jig is up.

"You are correct, Joe," Patrick states proudly. "We did it lots of times, in many different positions. I was fantastic."

"Patrick, you're such a jokester!" Will fake laughs and kicks Patrick in the shin unsubtly. "What are you doing?"

"Oh give it up, Will. Joe here's not buying what we're selling, are you Joe?"

Patrick's disappointed too, but the sooner they get out of here, the sooner he can eat. He's hungry as hell. They can always come back later when there's another clerk behind the desk. And if that doesn't work out, then it's divorce at any cost. Will's money be damned.

"Nope, not at all," Joe agrees. "Sorry, honey," he tells Will with a sympathetic smile. "But you're not a very good liar."

"Do you know who I am?" Will changes tactics and Patrick groans, squeezing the bridge of his nose. Just his luck to marry a cute-as-a-button wanna-be thug.

"You're Guglielmo Michael Patterson-McCloud, according to your marriage certificate," Joe waves the piece of paper in the air.

"Gugli-what-mo?" Patrick hiccups out a laugh.

"My father is Tony Molinaro." Will ignores Patrick, pausing as though allowing Joe to feel the gravity of offending a scion of the Molinaro family. "I'm sure you recognize that name."

"I don't care who your daddy is, honey. There are no grounds for annulment since 'changed my mind' isn't on the list and you've already said you were of sound mind, not intoxicated, and there has been no fraud."

"Oh my God." Will finally snaps, his voice rising hysterically. "We don't want to be married anymore! What do you not understand about that?"

Joe shrugs patiently. Clearly this isn't the first time he's dealt with a hysterical bridegroom wanting out of his vows without consequence. "Them's the breaks. Speaking of, it's my lunch break. Oh, and just in case you thought you might come back later and try this on a different clerk? I've put a little note next to your names in the computer." Joe winks at them.

"Why, thank you, Joe," Patrick says. "You're an ass."

Joe grins good-naturedly. "You should get some diaper rash

cream for your husband's ass. It'll help with that ache." He winks again and puts up a *CLOSED* sign.

Patrick and Will don't look at each other as they retreat from the courthouse and flag another cab.

Back in Patrick's hotel room, Will paces back and forth. "What are we going to do now?"

"We're going to get a divorce," Patrick says matter-of-factly from where he's sprawled on the bed. He's got his laptop open, and he's found no fewer than five sites that guarantee a divorce in Nevada within two days. He's already fired off an email to one of them, and their automated reply gave them an appointment for the next morning.

In the meantime, he's got room service on the way, and he needs to get the word out to his shortlist of prestigious clinics about his availability. He can't wait to start poaching patients from Schaeffer, Morris, and the whole Atlanta team. As far as he's concerned, now that he's decided to move ahead without concern for Will's issues, everything's set. It amazes him that he can solve a problem in ten minutes when it takes other people days and gobs of worry to never solve the problem at all. Being a genius in an idiotic world is either very tedious or very awesome. Most days he can't tell which.

"I cannot *get* a divorce, Patrick," Will grits out, long fingers tugging at his blond hair in frustration.

"You need to learn the difference between can't and won't. And, lucky for me, you don't have a choice in the matter." Patrick tracks Will's progress along the strip of floor between the bed and the window. His ass looks marvelous, and on his way back across the room his broad shoulders and dimpled chin command Patrick's attention.

Will glares. "What do you mean?"

Patrick shoves the laptop his direction, showing him the email he's just sent off to Three Step Divorce dot com.

"Oh my God, what have you done, Patrick?"

"I've started down the path to freedom. I'm getting rid of my ball and chain. What do you mean, 'what have I done'? Do you really expect that I'm going to just stay married to you? Because of some *money*?"

"It's not just *some* money, Patrick. It's hundreds of millions of dollars that can go to charities like Doctors Without Borders, or to help kids with leukemia, or to provide the research grant for a scientific breakthrough that can save thousands of lives. It provides healthcare for hundreds of Native Americans on the reservations in South Dakota, and it's building a whole new neurology unit in Healing, which is upgrading our hospital to a regional facility to benefit the residents of four states. Doesn't that mean something to someone like you, Dr. McCloud? Or are you really so cold that you'd rather see all that money go back into the hands of a crime family, where it'll be used to pay the salaries of assassins, or to set up drug cartels, or—"

Patrick holds up his hand. "Fine, fine, fine. You can stop before you get to the part where you turn on the waterworks. What exactly do you want from me?"

"Time." Will steps forward, his hands in his pockets, and he's obviously put on his big boy pants, because he's sounding reasonable for the moment. "Look, I need a little time, that's all. I'll figure out a way to get around the rules and then I will *happily* grant you a divorce."

Patrick is more convinced than he wants to be by the strangely compelling expression on Will's face. "And what am I supposed to do until then? I have a life to get back to in Atlanta."

"Do you have a boyfriend?"

"No." Patrick's offended at the suggestion. "I wouldn't have picked you up if I did. I'm not that kind of guy."

"Well you don't have a job anymore, and you don't have a boyfriend. So there's nothing urgent you need to get back to."

"Logic is clearly not your strong suit." Patrick scowls. "You know, I could say that you owe me compensation. Loss of income."

Will stares at him incredulously. "You have *got* to be kidding."

"Hey, I lost my job because of this marriage. How am I supposed to pay my bills?"

"You lost your job because of *you*. If you'd been at all civil—"

"Civil? Who needs civil? People with nothing to do with their time, that's who. I'm a busy man and this whole thing is wasting my time. I want out of this marriage and I want on the first plane back to Atlanta. But if I can't have both, I'll settle for one. So consider me out of here."

Patrick snaps his laptop closed and stands up, deciding to call a cab and get to the airport as fast as possible. He's not going to spend another second with Will. Nothing good is going to come of it. "I'll have my lawyer contact you." Patrick opens his suitcase and throws in his socks and underwear.

"Wait." Will sounds conflicted. "Just hear me out."

"I think I've heard enough from you to last a lifetime."

"You can't leave."

Patrick doesn't understand why he's still discussing this. He doesn't want to care about the money or the people Will claims to be helping with it. He just wants to get back to where he feels safe: an operating room. "Oh yes, I can, and I am. Get out my way."

"Dr. McCloud—Patrick, I'll lose Good Works. People will die because of this choice. People who could be saved with medical treatments funded through my foundation. Can you really live with that?"

Patrick sighs. He doesn't know if he can, actually. It's just that without his job, without work to do, and patients to save, he doesn't know what to do with himself. If he doesn't get a new position soon, *feelings* might crop up. He hates feelings. Especially the old ones lingering from his childhood. Memories. Fears. It's best when he's too busy to think.

"Mr. Patterson, I'm still going to be married to you for at least three days, and probably more, no matter if I'm in Atlanta or Antarctica. My immediate departure from the hell of this hotel room and your endless angst about our mutual mistake isn't going to affect your precious money just yet. You can have that time you asked for with me in Atlanta, and you in…wherever you hillbillies like to call home."

"No—I can't."

"Yes. You can."

"But there's something else I didn't tell you."

Patrick looks up to the ceiling. "Oh, for the love of… Fine, what now?"

"The Molinaro rules. They don't just cover the divorce or the annulment, but the circumstances of the wedding too." Will swallows hard. "We need to have married for love."

"What?" Patrick asks, like that makes any kind of sense at all. Like any of this does.

"No other reason is acceptable. Lack of consummation was our only out."

"I hear you speaking, but it's all nonsense."

"Patrick, my great-grandfather insisted on a love match."

Patrick rubs the bridge of his nose. Dear God, he's saddled himself with a lunatic.

Chapter Three

IT TAKES A few more minutes of explanation while Patrick stares at him with his mouth open and eyes wide before Patrick yells, "You have got to be kidding me! Who the hell is this demented Molinaro patriarch? The Mob-qui de Sade?"

"Well, he's dead now, but he strongly believed marriage should only be for love and divorce should never happen." Will knows it's ridiculous. He agrees it is. Well, kinda. He sort of values the same things too. Not that anyone would know that after last night.

He closes his eyes and takes a long, deep breath. *God grant me the serenity to accept the things I cannot change, the courage to change the things I can, and the wisdom to know the difference.*

He's not sure he's ever had a conversion experience, the mythical moment that changes everything for an alcoholic and opens the path to true and lasting sobriety, but he suspects that the clarity of purpose he's experiencing now might be close. He has to find a way to keep Good Works and he needs a way out of this marriage. Drinking will accomplish neither.

"What I hear you saying is that not only do I have to stay legally bound to you for you to keep all this money, but you want me to act like *I'm in love with you*? For how long?" Patrick's twitchy all over as he stares at Will.

"As long as it takes?"

"That's insane! Do you know how ludicrous this sounds?"

"Yes, of course I do." Will reaches his hands out, hoping that if he stays calm, Patrick won't jump ship. "But it doesn't change the reality of our situation."

"*Our* situation? No. *Your* situation—"

"I know, I know," he says soothingly. "You're right." He hopes he can placate Patrick, because he's not sure he's physically strong enough to restrain him if he tries to leave the room. He might be bigger, but Patrick's wiry and more powerful than he looks. "Look, seriously, this will all go so much more smoothly if we just work together."

Patrick stares at him like he's grown two heads. That's good in Will's book. At least he's not slamming out the door with his suitcase.

"So," Will says. "Let's work together. What should we do next?"

Patrick's eyes trail down Will's body and back up again. He says nothing for a long moment, his right hand tapping against his pant leg in a nervous staccato. Will holds his gaze and tries to appear open, ready to listen to Patrick's ideas.

"We could recreate some of last night's activities?"

"You can*not* be serious."

"Why not?" Patrick shrugs. "After all, we're *married*. No sin in it any which way you slice it. And I could stand to blow off some steam in a healthy, athletic, orgasmic way. Frankly, so could you. You were pretty relaxed after we screwed. Limp even. And you liked it."

"No! No way. Oh my god, what are you doing?"

Patrick is unbuttoning his shirt.

"Stop that!"

"Oh come on," Patrick scoffs. "I had you spread out on the bed last night begging me to lick your ass. You can stop with the false modesty now."

Will's burning up with mortification, but can't deny it's true. He remembers it vividly. Patrick's tongue on his hole had been amazing. Rimming was something Will had always wanted to try, but Ryan had been reluctant, saying ass play was too much of a trigger for his drinking. Patrick wasn't squeamish about it at all, though. He'd loved it. And, yes, Will had begged him for more, and then begged him not to stop, until he'd finally screamed for Patrick's cock inside him. Oh yes, Will remembers. His body does too apparently, because his dick is hard.

Will discreetly turns to face the window, taking a deep breath and staring at the silver, red, and green Christmas decorations all along the sun-drenched Strip. "Okay, this is what's going to happen. We're going back to South Dakota. My grandmother will know what to do."

"I'm not going anywhere with you—"

Will whirls around. "But you're willing to go to bed with me?"

"Well, yeah, we're husband and husband. May as well get a little something out of this marriage."

"No."

Patrick rolls his eyes, but leaves his shirt unbuttoned. "Looks like what they say about married sex is true after all."

Blood rushes to Will's cheeks. He stares out the window again, gritting his teeth until he's able to talk without even a hint of waver to his voice. "My grandmother will be able to help us, but this isn't the sort of thing I can talk to her about over the phone. I'll need to meet with her in person."

"Pray tell, what will some little old granny in South Dakota be able to do about Mafioso business?"

"She's my father's mother. Eleanora Molinaro, widow of Max 'the Ear' Molinaro."

"The Ear."

"Yes. Do you know why they called him that?"

"I have a feeling you're going to fill me in."

"Because he was so highly placed and valuable to the bosses back in Brooklyn that he was never mentioned by name. They tugged their ear instead and that gesture was enough to terrorize a man."

"Such a proud heritage." Patrick wipes a pretend tear from his eye.

Will clenches his jaw. "The point is my grandmother may have left the mafia world when Max went to prison, but she still has connections."

"Fascinating. Do tell."

"God, you're an ass."

"No really, go on. I want to hear all about it."

Will takes a deep breath. "Fine. My grandmother and my father, Tony, came to South Dakota when Max went to prison, and that's how my parents met. As soon as the government's attention turned from RICO laws to terrorism, Tony got back in, became a made man. My mom left him and my grandmother disowned him—ostensibly. But she's still a powerful woman in her own right. She has money, connections, and if anyone can find out who has the power to change the rules of the Molinaro Trust, it's her."

"I see. So I'm supposed to put my future in the hands of a woman I've never met because of her supposed mob connections and good will towards her grandson?"

"I'm her favorite grandchild," Will says softly. "She'll help me. And she's trustworthy. She knows how to keep secrets."

Patrick shakes his head. "I don't see how this is the best solution." But his tone is no longer strident. Will is fairly sure he's going to cave. He just needs to quell Patrick's growing panic over his suddenly floundering career.

"We've already established you have no job in Atlanta, no boyfriend, and no reason at all to return, really. In other words, you have nothing better to do than come to Healing, all expenses paid of course—"

"I'm not going to Helling or wherever you're from."

"Healing." Will wheedles, "Come on, that's a name that's got to appeal to a doctor, right?"

"I need to contact hospitals and let them know I'm available. They'll all be scrambling for me."

Will scoffs. "Full of yourself much?"

"I am the finest neurosurgeon in the country. That's a fact. But you know what? It isn't just about me. It's about my patients. Many of whom have waited months to see *me*. Not Dr. Morris or anyone else. They're in dire straits. Some are near death, and each requires the kind of help that only I can give them. Until I'm installed at a hospital, they won't get well. You speak of lives ending if you lose your money, but I have patients who will lose their lives immediately if I don't work. We're not talking about hypothetical future deaths, but real ones. People who have jobs and children, and whose faces I've seen with my own eyes."

"We can solve that problem. I promise."

"How?"

"I'll get to that in a minute. All I know is we can't split up now. It'll look suspicious."

"And what? The Molinaros are gonna swoop in and take all of your money because we're apart for a few days?"

"*Maybe!*" Will flings his hands up in exasperation. "I have no idea! They could do anything! That's what I've been trying to tell you!"

"This isn't *The Godfather*, you know. They aren't watching your every move and I have my own problems to worry about."

Will grabs fistfuls of his hair. God, Patrick could *not* be more impossible. Why did he have to marry someone so entirely obnoxious and stubborn? This situation isn't exactly a picnic for Will either, and things will go so much more smoothly if Patrick will just stop fighting him on everything.

A wave of dizziness hits him, and he bends over. "Oh," he breathes. "I think I'm going low again."

Patrick helps him down to the bed. "Test yourself. What's the number?"

Will sticks himself again, groaning as he reads the meter. "Thirty-eight."

"It's the stress and activity from last night." Patrick raids the snack bar again, pressing fruit snacks into Will's hand. "I'll order something now. Burgers for us both."

It surprises Will how quickly Patrick shifts into a caretaker mode.

He still crackles with energy and mild irritation, but now it's all focused on Will as a patient. He places the order and then sits next to Will on the bed, observing as he eats the fruit snacks. He takes Will's blood glucose again and touches Will's clammy forehead with gentle, cool fingers before taking his pulse. "You'll be fine. Keep eating."

Will smiles. "Gee, doc, didn't know you cared."

"I don't." Patrick gets up, grabs another orange juice from the mini fridge, and tosses it to him. "It's just…" He stares at Will, his lips and eyes going soft for a moment before he frowns. "What kind of idiot drinks himself into a getting-hitched-in-Vegas stupor when he's diabetic anyway?"

"The kind who's an alcoholic who's just been dumped. What's your excuse?" Will stuffs fruit snacks in his mouth to keep from saying more.

Patrick's eyes flicker. Will's not sure if it's compassion or disgust, but Patrick only says, "This morning, how was your urine? Did it smell fruity? Sweet? Any discolor—"

"I'll be fine."

Patrick narrows his eyes and presses his long fingers to Will's forehead again like he's feeling for a fever. He gets his medical bag and pulls out his stethoscope.

"Just lie back. I'm going to listen to your heart. After you've eaten the burger I ordered, you need to test your glucose levels. It's important—"

"Patrick, I'm fine. I appreciate your concern, but I'll be okay."

Patrick shrugs and throws his stethoscope back in his bag. "When's the last time you saw your Endocrinologist?"

"Last month."

"And your last A1C?"

"Not that it's your business, but it was five-point-nine. I'm pretty sure this adventure's going to blow my next one, though."

Patrick seems like he's trying to decide if Will's telling the truth.

Will sips more juice, eats another fruit snack, and then tries to get their conversation back on track. "Look, I should have thought of this before, but I didn't realize the urgency in helping your patients. Good Works has funded an amazing neurology department in Healing. It's going to be state of the art. A neurosurgeon's dream come true. We have a lot of the equipment already in place and we're cleared to start surgeries as soon as we have a surgeon on staff." He smiles in a way he hopes is winning. "Why not come to Healing for a few days on my dime and check out what we've built? We'll pay you for consulting with us. You can see if what we have is suitable for your work and maybe perform surgeries for whatever patients you feel our facility can handle. Then, before you know it, we'll be divorced or annulled, and you can move on if you decide you don't want to stay."

"I don't—" A knock on the door stops Patrick mid-sentence. "That was fast. Great, I'm starving." Patrick opens the door with gusto.

"I'm looking for Dr. and Mr. Patterson-McCloud," a man with dark hair and wearing a suit intones in heavily accented English.

Patrick's face turns red and he sputters, but he steps back to allow the man to enter the room. The dark man smiles, crosses to where Will sits on the bed, and hands over a gigantic bouquet of brilliant red roses.

"This is for me?" Will asks.

The man bows his head and leaves again without waiting for a tip.

Patrick's brow crinkles and his blue eyes cloud with confusion. Will's sure his own expression isn't much different. Maybe the flowers are from Ryan? Will's heart skips a beat. Maybe he wants to make up after all? Still, this is extreme for him, and not his style. And wait, the delivery guy had said Dr. and Mr. Patterson-McCloud.

And this isn't Will's hotel room.

Heart thumping, he pulls out the card nestled among the flowers.

"Who are they from?" Patrick asks.

As Will reads the note, the blood drains from his face.

Congratulations on your marriage, Guglielmo.
We hope you and Dr. McCloud enjoy a long, happy life together.
The Molinaro Family.

PATRICK'S GOTTA HAND it to himself. He's married well. It turns out, aside from being terrifyingly small, private jets are the schiznit. No lines. No security. Just walk right on up, get on the plane, and fly away. Patrick should ask for alimony in their eventual separation and demand full use of the Good Works jet for the rest of his life. No wonder his Little Lord Fauntleroy is afraid of losing his bucks. It would suck to give this up.

The pilot provides them with soft drinks and snacks. Will takes a sensible packet of cheese and crackers. Patrick takes three bags of chips and a cellophane-wrapped muffin. Then the pilot, whose name Patrick didn't bother to catch, excuses himself to the cockpit. Patrick popped a Xanax earlier when he saw the tiny tin can they were going to fly into the sky, and it's doing its job. He gets another journal out of his briefcase and takes a sip of Sprite before stuffing a handful of chips in his mouth. "There's more where this came from, right? Because I don't want to run out."

Will cocks his head and looks at Patrick with a you've-got-to-be-kidding expression. "You ate before we left the hotel. It's a four-hour flight. You'll be fine."

"So? I don't like heights. Food comforts me. Unless you want to see me re-enact a scene from *The Exorcist*, you'll keep me in chips and soda."

Will's eyebrow goes up. "Does the almighty Dr. McCloud suffer from human weaknesses?"

Patrick says nothing, turning to his journal.

He's surprised when Will lets it drop. In the short (and yet epically disastrous) time they've been together, Will's basically been like a dog with a bone about everything. Now he's letting this go. Patrick can't help but be a little suspicious.

Will leans forward, elbows on his knees. He drops his head into his hands and stays that way. Patrick looks down at the article—*Prioritizing neurosurgical education for pediatricians: Results of a survey of pediatric neurosurgeons.* Boring. He's not in education. He does cuts, not talks. Still, Aldana, the primary author, is someone he doesn't altogether despise, and he likes to keep up with his work. A survey, though? Please. Give him real science.

Will makes a noise that sounds suspiciously like a sniffle.

Patrick flips to the next article. *Passive range of motion functional magnetic resonance imaging localizing sensorimotor cortex in sedated children.* Ogg is a good scientist, and Patrick would usually be a lot more interested in this. Pediatrics isn't his primary specialty, but it's a subspecialty that he's taken on willingly since he has the balls for it. Not many people have the confidence to cut into children's heads.

Will sits up, wipes a hand over his face, and if there aren't tears on his cheeks, then Patrick's sure there are some standing in his stupidly pretty brown eyes.

He's not asking. He's reading. About MRIs and children.

Will sniffles again.

"Are you okay?"

"I'm fine." Will leans back in his chair, crossing his arms over his broad chest, and stares out the airplane window. His face is splotchy, and Patrick's throat goes dry. Will should look ugly with his eyes red rimmed and his mouth all wobbly. Instead, Patrick fights an irrational urge to kiss him.

Grabbing the water bottle from Will's armrest, he tosses it at him. "Drink. Airplanes are notorious for dehydration. So are tears."

Will shrugs, his face all twisted up, and takes a big gulp of his water. He whispers, "Don't see the point anyway."

"Excuse me? Don't see the point of what?"

"This," Will says, shrugging his mouth up and shaking his head tightly. "The water, dealing with my diabetes, staying sober, any of it."

Patrick stares at him. "What are you saying exactly?"

"Nothing. I'm just being stupid and weak." Will's chin wobbles.

God, Patrick has no patience for this kind of thing. Except he does apparently, because he waits for more words to spill out. He's pretty sure he'd wait even if he wasn't trapped on this airplane.

"It's just—" Will begins. "Ryan. You know, I can't… How can I make this right?"

"I'm pretty sure you can't. I'm also pretty sure he dumped you. So, why does it matter? He's free; you're free. Get over it."

"Easy for you to say."

Patrick rolls his eyes. "What's that supposed to mean?"

"I just mean, you don't seem to have real feelings at all. You probably don't even know what love is."

Patrick sits back in his seat, keeping his gaze away from the sun glinting on the clouds outside Will's window. "Did you think saying that would hurt me? You'd be wrong."

Will leans forward again and presses his forehead into his hands. "No. I'm sorry. I didn't mean that."

"Sure you did."

"No, it's just—he'll never love me again. Not after—" Will motions at Patrick.

"Not after I polluted you."

Will shrugs again like that's mostly accurate, but then he says, "It's my fault, though. I let you—"

Patrick snorts. "Let me? You begged me. Listen, Will. I don't know this guy, but everything you told me last night and now this? Come on, he's a jerk. Get some self-esteem. You're worth more. And I test drove the goods. For hours. So I know what I'm talking about."

"Test drove?" Will's voice is still wavering. "You bought the car."

"Exactly. And I'm not an idiot. Usually. But if I bought the car then it was something special. You've got nothing to worry about. Someone besides your precious Ryan is gonna wanna take you out for a spin."

Will doesn't look comforted by that. "I don't want to be taken for a spin. I want Ryan back."

"*In vino veritas*, Will. And last night? You didn't want Ryan."

Will presses his hands to his eyes like he can block it all out by force.

Patrick tries again. "I've known you less than forty-eight hours, and so far you've managed to get a sworn bachelor to marry you and then screw your brains out. In that order, which is unthinkable in this day and age. You've talked him into flying across the country with you instead of insisting on an immediate divorce. And now you have him trying to cheer you up. I get the impression you get what you want. If this asshole Ryan means that much to you, I'm sure you'll get him back too."

"You really think so?"

Patrick rubs a hand across the back of his neck. "You know, whatever. He's a piece of crap. If that's what you like in a guy, maybe you deserve each other."

"Gee, thanks, Dr. McCloud. Now I feel all warm and fuzzy."

"Whatever." He turns his attention to his journal again.

"Maybe I won't even have to tell him. Maybe we can get this all taken care of before he ever knows. But no. If it's ever going to work between us, I have to be honest. I have to tell him the truth."

Patrick doesn't really care one way or another so he says nothing.

"What was I thinking? I'd been working my steps, staying sober. I'm so tired of relapsing; so tired of starting over. I screwed everything up. Again."

Patrick remembers his father sitting at the cracked, old wooden table in the kitchen of the apartment he lived in for the first fifteen years of his life. He remembers the rough texture of his dad's hand as it curled around the back of his neck, still damp from holding a bottle of beer. He shivers against the sick roll in the pit of his stomach.

"Why?" Will whispers to himself.

"You experienced an extreme stressor. Your brain secreted CRH, a hormone which releases corticotropin. Long story short: the chances of an addict relapsing or having a slip go up exponentially in the presence of corticotropin."

Will clears his throat and looks his way. "In English?"

"You couldn't help yourself."

"Do you know a lot about addiction?"

"Some." He can almost smell his father's beery vomit spreading over the sofa cushion. "I studied it from the neurobiological point of view, mainly."

"Are you—I mean, do you have personal experience with alcoholism?"

"I don't drink often. I prefer to be sober for a lot of reasons, including being on call a lot."

"Oh." Will's eyelashes fan down against his cheeks.

The note of shame in his voice keeps Patrick from saying more. It won't do any good for him to hear about Patrick's father. There's no joy in that tale and there's nothing good to come from telling it.

"I guess it is my fault we got married," Will says. "If I wasn't an alcoholic—"

"Beating yourself up for your disease won't solve anything. It's as much my fault as it is yours. The truth is I advocated strongly for our marriage last night."

"Yeah?" Will turns to him, the sun lighting up his blond stubble and golden lashes.

"Yeah."

Will smiles. He's damn gorgeous in that moment—tears, blotchy skin, and all. Patrick forces his attention back to his journal. He can't process a single word.

Chapter Four

"SWANKY," PATRICK NOTES.

Will glances around the Tallgrass Hotel lobby. There's a tasteful Christmas tree in the corner next to a baby grand piano and lots of greenery lining the oak doorways. The Meadowlands restaurant is off to the right and features one of the best menus in town. The bar is to the left, and Will hopes he forgets it's even there. Down the hallway are the elevators that go up to the four floors of rooms and down to the basement exercise facility and indoor swimming pool.

Everything is top-notch. It's new after all, recently built to lure doctors and travel nurses to staff the expansion of Healing Regional. The success of the hospital depends on it. The town has plenty of old motels, some of them nicer than others, but they needed a long-term facility with an air of class to make things easier on medical staff who might decide the balmy beaches of South Florida are a better fit than the freezing cold plains of Healing.

"I suppose it is," Will agrees.

"Why are we here anyway? Don't you have your own place?"

"I can't go back there. Can we talk about it later?" He's exhausted and really doesn't want to deal with anything more than getting them checked in right now. Especially not with an audience, even if it is just an audience of one.

Patrick shrugs and wanders over to the piano, inspecting it closely and then running his fingers over the keys lightly. He shudders like he's cold and returns to the front desk to stand beside Will.

"What time is it, Beth?" The hotel clerk on duty is a young, blond woman Will's known forever. He used to babysit her younger siblings sometimes when he was in high school.

"Almost nine." Beth gives him a significant look and adds, "Congratulations on your marriage. It's certainly a surprise!"

"You can say that again," Will mutters.

"I mean, a Vegas wedding. To someone who isn't Ryan. Wow."

Will nods. It's Healing. Everyone knows everyone's business, and when he'd called to book the room, he'd made sure to do it as a couple, just in case the Molinaros are looking in on him. He needs to keep up appearances, but it's still embarrassing that Beth, and soon everyone else, will find out about Patrick.

She leans forward, blond hair falling in her face. "Does Ryan know?"

"No."

He will soon.

This gossip will spread like wildfire. Will's got to tell his family first thing in the morning before they find out from anyone else. As for Ryan, well, what can he say to him? He doesn't even know if he can look at him right now. What he wants most is for Ryan to take him into his arms, hold him close, and tell him everything will be all right. But Ryan hasn't done something like that in a long time, and he sure as hell won't do that now.

Beth doesn't seem too worried about the fact that Will's married a stranger and brought him home, or that it's over between him and Ryan. "Was it love at first sight?" she asks.

"No," Will answers just as Patrick leans against the counter and says, "Yes."

"Did you know each other *at all?*"

Will rubs his face. "Listen, Beth, I'm sorry, but we're really tired."

"Oh, sure. I'm sorry. You should hit the sack." She winks at him and then smiles brightly again. "But surely after your husband, uh…I didn't catch his name?"

"Patrick."

Patrick stops rifling through the small bowl of red and white striped peppermints. "You can call me Dr. McCloud. I reserve Patrick for friends."

Will sighs.

Beth is obviously perplexed, but, after a pause, she grins again. "Sure. Of course, Dr. McCloud." A sappy romantic bloom returns to her cheeks as she rattles on. "Falling in love in Vegas? It's like a story. Or a movie. Or a made-for-TV miniseries."

"More like an Adam Sandler film," Patrick interjects.

Beth finishes entering Will's information into the computer and hands back his credit card. "You have to tell me everything soon, okay? How you met! What you were wearing! What he was wearing too! What you thought when you first saw each other!"

"Sure," Will says. *Shoot me now.*

"What we were *wearing?*" Patrick scrunches up his face.

"Elopement is so dreamy. And kinda hot."

"So's the sex." Patrick wraps his arm around Will's shoulders. "How much longer, Will, honey? I'd like to get back to that, actually."

Beth eyes go wide and bright, like Patrick just gave her the world on a platter. She gives Will the plastic keys to their room. "I've signed you up for the honeymoon breakfast. It'll be delivered to your door at eight-thirty, unless you put out the Do Not Disturb sign." She winks and then giggles. "In that case, they'll bring it up whenever you want. Chocolate sauce for strawberries, heart-shaped muffins, and wonderful warm rolls with a custard filling." She holds up her bare left hand. "Not that I've been lucky enough to eat it myself. I'm trying to talk Cody Elk Eagle into buying me a ring, though."

"You're still young," Will says. "Don't rush it."

She breaks into a gale of laughter. "You're one to talk!"

The reminder of his new ring makes Will touch it with his thumb, spinning it, a surge of weird emotions coursing through him. He'd always thought it'd be Ryan's ring residing there.

"Chocolate sauce?" Patrick asks. "I can think of other things to dip in that."

Beth blushes as red as the Christmas bows lining the edge of the front desk.

"*Patrick*," Will grits out. He elbows him and turns on his heel, leading the way.

Patrick's thankfully silent on the ride up in the elevator, but as soon as they walk into the room, he starts up again.

"You sprang for a suite." He looks around at the large, fluffy bed, and the sofa and chairs surrounding a low coffee table across from a massive TV. "Is there a Jacuzzi tub? Are the sheets silk? Shall we pop open some fizzy water for a toast before we christen the room?"

"What's your problem?" Will asks, swinging around to glare at Patrick. He doesn't understand why Patrick's being such a dick now. On the plane, he'd been sweet. Or as close to sweet as Patrick apparently gets without being drunk. "I'm exhausted. I'm in pain. My ass is *still* sore from last night and I just rode two hours on a plane. I'm married to *you* of all people. To say I'm on the brink of *losing it* isn't that far off. I've had a *very* bad day. So back off."

Patrick taps his fingers against his pant leg, but he says nothing for a few moments. When he does speak, it's in a softer voice. "Fair enough." After another few seconds of silence, he goes on. "Do you want to tell me why we're staying in a hotel instead of going back to your place?"

Will's trembling with exhaustion and the flash of anger. He sits on the edge of the bed, elbows on his knees, and presses his face into his hands, taking some deep, focusing breaths. "Because I lived with Ryan, okay? I have off and on since he moved with me to Healing after we graduated from college."

"Before you left for Vegas, you were 'on,' I take it."

"I'd been living there again for a few months."

"I see. Where do you live when you're 'off'?"

"With my mom."

"I guess you can't show up at your mommy's place with a surprise husband."

"Not this late at night, no. It'd be too much to explain, especially with my little sisters and brother around. But I guess I can't keep this from her either. Not if this is going to work." He swallows thickly. "Patrick, everyone's going to know."

"Yep."

He shakes his head, glancing up between his fingers. "I'm so embarrassed."

Patrick leans against the desk and picks up a pen, twirling it restlessly in his fingers. "I don't know why. You did pretty well for yourself."

"Don't pick on me."

"C'mon. I did pretty well too. We're both hot, both loaded, both smart. I'd say that for drunken, horrific mistakes, we did okay."

"Except for the part where we're stuck this way."

Patrick shrugs. "For now." His voice is slightly wary, but mostly just gravelly with exhaustion. "You said your grandmother could take care of this for us."

"She can. I'm sure she can." Will's throat goes tight again. He presses his fingers against his eyes, holding very still to ride out the waves of humiliation.

He's always been Eleanora's favorite grandchild. Despite the drinking, despite the hospital scares, she's always forgiven him every wrong and mistake. But this... She's going to be so disappointed in him. And the rest of his family is going to be upset too. His mom, Uncle Kevin, Grandma Betty. Oh God. What will his little sisters and brother think?

He hears Patrick moving around, but at least he's not saying anything, so Will ignores him. He looks up when the bed beside him dips. Patrick's putting his stethoscope in his ears. Will sighs, but sits up and takes some deep breaths as Patrick listens to his heart through his thin dress shirt.

"Good. Now lie back and let me listen to your stomach."

Will hesitates, but does as he's told. Patrick's fingers are gentle as they lift up his shirt and slide the cold stethoscope against his skin. Then he puts it aside on the bed, touches Will's stomach, and presses down.

"We were rough last night. I'm feeling for any internal swelling," Patrick murmurs, pushing a few more times and then moving his hands away. "I don't suppose you'd let me check your anus for damage?"

Will hesitates, but he's been in pain all day and Patrick *is* a doctor. "Okay, but no funny business."

"Cross my heart." Patrick makes the motion, his blue eyes tired and sincere.

Will unbuckles and kneels on the patterned hotel-room carpet, leaning over the bed. He works his pants and underwear down over his hips, aware of the soft duvet pressing against his hot cheek as he squirms to expose his ass without dropping his pants all the way.

Patrick has retrieved a pair of thin surgical gloves from his bag along with a penlight. "Relax. I'll just have a look." His voice sounds a little shaky, but he puts on the gloves and kneels behind Will. "I'm going to need you to hold your glutes apart, okay?" he says softly.

"Sure," Will agrees, but his voice squeaks.

"Then there'll be a soft touch once I can get a look, just to make sure I don't feel any distension," Patrick murmurs, and Will swallows, squeezing his eyes closed as his cock starts to rush with blood.

They don't speak as Will spreads his ass cheeks and Patrick leans in to look at his hole. Will's stomach flutters and he's lightheaded. The hangover and a sharp rush of arousal lend a fuzzy lack of reality as he squeezes his eyes shut.

Patrick's gloved finger is gentle on his sensitive pucker, and Will inhales sharply. There's a breathless moment when Will knows they're probably both remembering Will making that sound last night. Then Patrick pulls away. "You look fine. Just a little puffy and tender. Nothing a good night's rest won't cure."

Will releases his hold on his ass and looks over his shoulder. Patrick's usually pale skin is a little flushed, and he doesn't meet Will's eye as he snaps the gloves off and tosses them in the trashcan. He glances at his watch. "You need to eat some good carbs and protein before bed, though."

Will stays on his stomach for a few seconds, hoping his erection isn't obvious when he shifts back over and fixes his pants. Relieved to see it isn't, he takes calming breaths as Patrick puts the stethoscope and penlight back in his bag.

Patrick starts on the buttons of his shirt. "Call room service or raid the snack bar here. And test your blood sugar. After that, we should hit the hay. You can call your sweet, little, mafia-connected Granny tomorrow."

After Patrick disappears into the bathroom, Will tests his blood sugar. It's surprisingly decent given the way it's been behaving all day. Then he pulls a pre-packaged ham and cheese sandwich out of the mini fridge. He calculates the carbs, does the algebra for his insulin dose, and sticks himself. He's started to shuck his clothes when Patrick comes out in boxer-briefs, a t-shirt, and smelling like toothpaste and the hotel's soap. "Patrick?"

"Mmm."

Will grabs pajama pants from his suitcase and yanks them on over his boxers. He'd normally remove his undies, but Patrick is observing him closely. He pulls on a comfortable T-shirt. "Even if my grandmother can help us, we aren't going to have this resolved tomorrow. Or even this week."

"I know."

Will sits on the sofa. "So, do you mind if we get to know each other a little? Since we'll have to be in close quarters and pretend to be in love, it'd be good to know something, wouldn't it?"

Patrick shrugs. "I guess it wouldn't actually kill me to know more about you. What the hell? Sure."

Will's surprised by a laugh that works its way through the tightness in his chest. "Great. And I want to learn about you too."

Patrick frowns and looks away. "I'm a neurosurgeon. That's all there is to tell."

Will pulls Patrick toward the sofa. "Come on, I let you check out my asshole. You can open up for me a little too, can't you?"

"Are you propositioning me? If so, the answer's yes."

Will ignores that. "Let's talk. Can you trust me?"

"What do you want to know?"

"Where you're from, your parents' names, what your childhood was like, your hobbies and interests. A little bit of everything."

"Oh, goodie. All the stuff I've been just dying to share with someone! Girl talk at the sleepover! How did you know?"

"Lucky guess."

Patrick laughs and sits beside Will on the sofa. "All right. I was raised in Alabama, did pre-med at UK, med school at Yale, and I've been in Atlanta for the last five years."

"UK? Like Kentucky?"

"Duh."

"So what's your specialty? In neurosurgery, I mean?"

"I'm a generalist, which means I can operate on kids, adults, the spine, and the brain. But I have a preference for brain trauma in peds. Those are my favorite."

"Creepy."

Patrick yawns. "Let's see, what else? You wanted to know about my parents. My mother's name was Sandra and my father's name was Gerry. They're both dead."

"Oh God. I'm sorry."

Patrick shrugs. "It's fine. My mom died when I was eight and my father died six years ago."

"That had to be rough. Who raised you? After your mom, I mean."

"My father." Patrick's mouth thins. "We weren't close." He clears his throat. "Now for the quid pro quo."

"Hit me."

"All right. First things first, what's your sign?"

Will laughs. "Libra. Yours?"

"Aries. Aquarius rising."

"That explains everything," Will says sarcastically.

"It really does." Patrick doesn't sound like he's kidding, and Will cocks his head trying to gauge whether the self-proclaimed genius surgeon really believes in astrology. Patrick asks, "What's your mother's name?"

"Kimberly."

"What do I need to know to fake it as your loving husband?"

"Well, I'm really close with my family. There's my mom, like I said. And I have two younger half-sisters and a little half-brother: Caitlin, Olivia, and Connor."

"Ew, too many kids." Patrick doesn't sound serious, though. Maybe he's starting to see through Patrick's bullshit.

"Um, there's my Nonna, Eleanora—"

"Your mafia grandmother."

"Yeah, and my other grandmother, Betty—I call her Grandma. She and my Uncle Kevin, my mom's twin, live out on the old family farm. Kevin's always lived there. He's gay too. The family joke is that I resemble him that way." Will laughs softly. "He's a horse trainer. Grandma says he was born in the barn—literally."

"Classy."

Will scratches at his chin. "Kevin doesn't like to leave Healing. He traveled a little now and again back when his partner, Roy, was still alive. But he didn't enjoy it."

Will mainly remembers Roy as a skinny man, coughing and trembling on the farm sofa with an oxygen tank at his feet. But he's seen pictures of Kevin and Roy from before, and he'd been handsome, with black hair, green eyes, and a smirky, wise-ass smile. Will's mom always says Roy was funny, but Will just remembers being afraid of him because he was so sick.

"Roy died of AIDS. My uncle's never really been the same since."

Patrick grunts. "Anything else I should know about? Traumas you'd have shared with me?"

"I had a stepfather pass away." Will shoots Patrick a glance. "We weren't close."

Patrick's lips curl up in acknowledgement of the code established for 'no sympathy needed.'

"Then there's Ryan, but hopefully you won't even see him."

Patrick's head tips back against the sofa and his eyes slide lower. His tight, always twitchy body relaxes a little. "So tomorrow. What's the plan?"

They outline the next day as Will does his final blood glucose test and injects his long-lasting insulin according to his nightly schedule. As they talk, Will shares some more tidbits of his history and life that Patrick will need to know to make a believable husband out and about in the town. He learns a few more things about Patrick too. Patrick is pretty tight-lipped about his life and Will surmises from his body language that his childhood was pretty grim.

But Patrick's eyes light up when he talks about neurosurgery, and Will stops listening for meaning because it's all beyond him. But the rambling excitement underscoring Patrick's words, the intensity of his delivery marking his passion, and the vibrant, richness of authority, is enough to stir Will's blood with vicarious enthusiasm.

"I'm excited for you to see our new neurology department. I think you'll be impressed. We consulted with some of the best—"

Patrick snorts.

"Maybe not as good as you, but some very good surgeons gave input to our design team."

"I'm sure. Regardless, all that matters is that it's functional enough for me to do my work. I've got a waiting list a mile long. If I could see the hospital tomorrow and meet the chief of staff, that'd be great. What doctors do you have on staff already? Anyone I might recognize by name? Or are they all first-year-out-of-med-school putzes?"

Will bristles. "That's why I was in Las Vegas, remember? I was supposed to chat up some neurosurgeons and neurologists. Drum up interest. We're grossly understaffed at the moment, though we have some good applications from some promising—"

"They aren't promising."

Will rolls his eyes. "Should the hospital run every resume past you before setting up an interview?"

"Sounds boring as hell, but yes. If you want to keep from hiring butchers. I'll be honest with you about their abilities."

Will considers. "It would be up to Don, our chief of staff, but he might want to take you up on that."

"Sure, whatever." He stretches. "That's enough chitchat for tonight. If you're right about this situation not being resolved in a day, we'll have plenty of time for more charming tête-à-têtes."

Patrick rises from the sofa and stretches high. His boxer-briefs and T-shirt separate, displaying the trail of hair below his bellybutton. Will remembers the way it felt against his cheek the night before. He blushes and coughs. Patrick doesn't notice, though. He walks to the bed, pulls off his T-shirt, slides under the sheets, and snaps off the lamp on the nightstand.

As tempted as he is to slip in beside Patrick and reacquaint himself with the firm press of his body, Will stays put.

God grant me the serenity…

Chapter Five

Will wakes up in an unfamiliar room for the second time in two days. He sits up and rubs at his neck. In his sleep, he'd been happy. He closes his eyes, searching for that dream place again, and he jerks fully awake when he realizes he'd been dreaming of Patrick, of their hands laced together, and their bodies moving in a slow rolling fuck.

Why are even his dreams betraying him?

"I'm ordering extra room service," Patrick announces from the bed.

Will swallows and stares at the floor.

"You need to eat something too." The phone by the bed clatters as it's dropped and then picked up again.

Will wishes he could take a few minutes to fall apart, but that won't solve anything. So he stands up and rubs his hands over his hair. "I'll have cottage cheese, eggs, and whole wheat toast. Hold the jelly."

Patrick nods absently as he studies the room service menu in his hand. "Sensible choices."

"I'm going to take a shower." Will wishes he had time to hit the gym too. Exercise always makes him feel better. "Then I should head over to Nonna's. I need to get it over with."

"Agreed. Procrastination is for the weak." Patrick dials the phone.

Will shuts the door against Patrick's seemingly endless breakfast order. He doesn't understand how the man can apparently eat like he does and still be so fit. He turns on the shower, testing the water. He's not going to think about Patrick's body or the sex they've had.

He climbs into the shower and takes a few minutes to just be. The water beats against his back and he rubs the soap over his body, gently touching a tender hickey under his collarbone. He presses the bruise and shudders. When was the last time he had a hickey? He remembers it'd only happened once. There are a lot of things— sexually and otherwise—that Ryan only gave him once.

Ryan.

A stab of fear in his gut makes his knees go weak. How can Ryan turn his back on their relationship? After six years? And for what? Hartley's calm, black eyes?

Will soaps his hair and forces himself back to the present. *First things first! Get out of this marriage mess and then get your boyfriend back.*

There's a knock on the door followed by the click of it opening. Will covers his crotch with his hands even though he's blocked by the shower curtain.

"Gotta use the facilities," Patrick says, pushing the door open a little further.

"Uh, sure. Go ahead." Will can *feel* Patrick on the other side of the curtain. Hear him lifting the toilet lid and see Patrick's hand with its long, neat fingers press against the wall. Patrick's sigh of release is followed by the splashing rush of piss.

Will's been in locker rooms, shared showers with other guys, and he's used urinals his whole life. Yet standing on the other side of the shower curtain while Patrick obeys nature's call feels different. Those fingers pressed against the wall were on him and *in* him. *Patrick* was on him and in him. Growing half hard from the memories, Will's heart pounds. What if he's ruined now? Sex with Patrick so surpassed his prior experience that…that…

That what? You'll never want Ryan to touch you again?

He shakes the thought away. Because of course he'll let Ryan touch him. If he's ever lucky enough to get Ryan back. He loves

Ryan, and it's like Ryan always says: sex isn't about pleasure. Sex isn't even necessary. Not when you really love someone; not if the other person doesn't like it.

The toilet flushes. "Nothing like a good piss in the morning."

Will grunts in agreement and listens to Patrick wash his hands.

"Hurry up, Starshine. Room service should be here any second." He throws back the curtain, and Will jolts away, hands going back to cover his half-hard dick. Patrick tosses a towel and Will reaches to catch it.

"Out." Patrick shucks his underwear.

Will's towel is more than half wet, but he wraps it around his waist and leaves the shower running as Patrick brushes by him. The places where their bodies touch tingle even after Patrick jerks the shower curtain closed again. Will rushes through his morning testing ritual.

There's a knock on the hotel suite door, and Will holds the wet towel around his waist as he rushes to answer it. "Coming!"

Of course it's Perry, an acquaintance from Will's high school days, standing outside with a laden room service cart. Will's smile aches as he greets him. Perry's aged nicely enough over the years, filling out admirably, but he's always had a ratty look to his face, and that hasn't changed at all.

Perry gives Will a cool once over but then silently and professionally delivers the honeymoon breakfast, along with Will's order, and about four other items that Patrick has apparently requested.

"Thanks, Perry. Everything looks great."

Perry takes the five Will presses into his hand. "Heard the news this morning. Married in Vegas. Can't say I'm entirely surprised. You always did have a wild hair in you." He winks.

Oh God.

"Yeah, I guess."

"You and Jack Linton. Always sneaking flasks into class, going out into the woods behind the gym to get drunk. Remember that?"

Will does remember it, but they weren't drinking in the woods. Will was sucking Jack off. Hungrily, eagerly, hoping he could get himself off too before Jack blew his load and shoved Will away again. As far as Will knows, Jack never came out. Less than a week after graduation and a final blow job in the back of Will's car, Jack'd left to go play ball for Indiana State and never came back.

Will also remembers how Jack and Perry used to taunt him, calling him Willy the Whale and slipping Jenny Craig ads into his locker. Once Will left Healing and arrived in Vermillion for college, he started working out daily, replacing alcohol with exercise for his stress outlet. He's trimmed down and pumped up. If Jack was still around, he wouldn't have anything to taunt Will about, except for being gay. And Jack's dick had spent too much time in Will's mouth for Jack to ever tease him about that.

Perry chuckles. "Those were good times, man."

"Yeah."

The shower turns off. Will tries to steer Perry to the door, but it's too late. Patrick steps out in just a towel, still wet and glistening from the shower. His muscles are thin but strong. Will's heart swells with misplaced pride at how handsome his husband is.

Perry grins like he's got a fish on the line and he can't wait to reel it in.

Patrick wraps his arm around Will's shoulders. A frisson rushes where their wet skin touches. "It's about time our breakfast arrived. I was thinking I might have to eat *you* again."

Will's face flames, and Perry's eyes go wide.

"Oh, uh. Yeah." Perry coughs, calling over his shoulder as he opens the door, "Have a good day, and if you need anything at all, just call." The door shuts a little too hard.

"*Patrick.*" Will clutches his towel harder. "What the hell?"

He pulls away, shrugging. "I'm just trying to keep up appearances."

"No, you're trying to humiliate me."

Patrick frowns. "Actually, I'm not. Believe what you want about me, but I don't get off on that. Breath play, spanking, sure, but not humiliation."

Will's cheeks heat and his breath catches. Trying to hide the way those words line up with his own shameful kinks, he grabs his last clean pair of pants and a decent-looking shirt from his suitcase and puts them on. Glancing toward Patrick's suitcase, Will realizes it's full of clothes intended for a week in the desert, not for winter in South Dakota. He needs to take Patrick shopping for a winter coat and some warm gloves at the very least. Hell, probably an entirely new wardrobe if he's going to be here long at all.

"Look," Patrick says, taking the shiny, metal cover from the first room service dish and pulling up a chair. "You wanted me to act like I'm in love with you. That's what I'm doing." The scent of bacon and eggs fills the room.

"This is how you behave with men you're in love with?" Will flashes to their night in Vegas. Patrick had been so solicitous then, and protective of Will's modesty when he'd been embarrassed for the room service guy to see him naked.

"I don't know." Patrick pops a sugary, glistening doughnut hole into his mouth. "I've managed to avoid that particular affliction so far."

Will calculates his carbs, does the math, and injects his insulin.

"So I was right? You've never been in love?" Will sits at the small table to eat his much less appealing breakfast. He wishes he'd calculated for a few doughnut holes in his dose, but he really doesn't feel like sticking himself again.

Patrick makes a happy sound of agreement. "Never. Love is a pointless emotion. It leads people to make terrible choices and limit their options." He stands, takes the plate of doughnuts with him, and flops down on the bed. His towel slips a little and shows the length of his inner thigh.

"Oh, like you're such a free spirit that you need limitless options in your life? Come on, we both know you live to work." Will rolls his eyes, trying to ignore the flex of Patrick's muscles in his abdomen and arms every time he reaches for another doughnut hole to stuff in his mouth.

"Exactly. Loving someone would just get in the way. Besides, there's something to be said for having options even if you don't use them."

"Well, I guess you'd know. But did you have to be so rude?"

"Why do you care? He's a room service guy."

"I know everyone in this town. I've lived here my whole life and I plan to live here for a long time to come. Could you be a little more circumspect? A little less of an asshole?"

"Could you be a little less ungrateful?" Patrick snaps.

"Excuse me?"

"You heard me. I could end this charade in a heartbeat. I'm going along with it so far out of kindness. Something about the idea of being responsible for removing funding for kids with cancer chills the depths of even my black soul, but I'm not a fount of endless patience." Patrick bites into another doughnut hole, punctuating the next sentence. "So, darling husband, maybe you could show a little gratitude for the fact that I have any patience with you or our predicament in the meantime. Understood?"

Will swallows. He's been kind to Patrick, hasn't he? Let him know how much he appreciates what Patrick's doing for him? He tries to remember, but he's not sure. Maybe not. He can't remember if he's ever said… "Thank you."

"Whatever. Just get our divorce so I can get back to my life."

Will holds back a retort that they've already established that Patrick doesn't have a life to get back. Instead he asks, "Are you going with me or not?"

"To see Granny? Hell, no. You deal with it. It's your mess."

Will narrows his eyes. It's *their* mess. It's not like he married Patrick all by his lonesome. "What about the Molinaros? Won't it look strange if I'm going around town without you? Shouldn't I be, I don't know, introducing you proudly? Especially to my family?"

"First? This is not *The Godfather*. Well, maybe part three, but definitely not part one or two. Second? You *want* me to pretend to be in love with you in front of your grandmother? You didn't seem pleased with my performance a minute ago."

The idea of Patrick saying something like he'd said to Perry around Eleanora makes Will's stomach churn. Turning to his meal and pushing the eggs around, he says, "Fine, you stay here."

"If a Molinaro jumps out of a bush and asks where I am, tell them you wore me out with all the hot sex we've been having."

Will almost flips him the bird. "Okay. Just remember, be discreet. We can't have suspicious behavior getting back to the Molinaros."

"Got it, Starshine. No problem." Patrick gets up, leaving his towel behind, and wanders naked back to the table, investigating the chocolate sauce and strawberries. His cock dangles thick and enticing right in front of Will's face.

Will leaps up and grabs his coat. "I'll be back before long, okay? Don't go anywhere without me."

Patrick waves him away, thrusting a strawberry into the chocolate and then licking it off in a way that makes Will groan.

Will's shaking all over as he firmly shuts the door on Patrick's tempting body.

HEALING ISN'T A big town. It's twenty blocks built around an old church and an even older saloon from pioneer days. These are Healing's only historical monuments, and Will passes them as he walks to the Good Works office to get his car from the lot. His nose tingles in the crisp November morning air, and he tries to imagine how Healing will look from Patrick's perspective.

Everything else in the town proper is mostly modern. A few of the very oldest neighborhoods, all within a hop, skip, and a jump of Old Healing—small square of local shops and restaurants—sport houses from the turn of the century. But for the most part everything built prior to the nineteen forties has been demolished and replaced.

It's a shame, really.

The size of the town has been an issue with the expansion of the hospital. There isn't a lot of entertainment for the families of doctors, nurses, or patients. It's a problem Good Works is tackling soon: how to revitalize Healing without overstepping. Here on the edge of the Cheyenne River Indian Reservation, the 'rez', there are only so many ways to expand the town itself, so building things like golf courses or malls is out of the question. But there are ways to improve the life of Healing's citizens and visitors without expanding the borders, and creating job opportunities for people living on the rez would be an extra bonus if his plans work out.

The streets are mostly empty this early in the morning, though there are a few cars on the road and a flurry of people outside Brown Gargle for coffee. Will trudges ahead, spying the Good Works building. It's a new stone and brick one-story full of office space built on the site of a former strip mall. In Will's opinion, the building is a nice addition to the town: classic, sturdy. And the location can't be beat. It's close to the hospital, Old Healing, and the Tallgrass. And it isn't far from the Methodist church where AA meetings are held twice daily in the basement.

Like a lot of small towns, Healing has its fair share of alcoholics and other addicts.

Will has dedicated employees, but it's not yet eight in the morning, so the parking lot of Good Works is empty and Will's BMW is right where he left it. Snug in his coat and heated car, he drives the short distance to Eleanora's house.

When Eleanora Molinaro arrived in Healing thirty years ago, the house she chose reflected the new life she intended to live. In the old money neighborhood of Langershire, she purchased a two-story

Sears Alhambra built in the twenties and massively renovated and enlarged it. It's one of the oldest houses remaining in Healing.

As Will parks the car, he considers his grandmother's home. It's as classically beautiful as she is herself. To the right, set off behind the large, currently hibernating rose garden, is a guest cottage with a full kitchen, its own back entrance, and separate drive. It's a perfect location for him to hide away with his strange new husband.

He wipes his sweaty hands on his jeans, cold air stinging his nostrils as he heads to the front door. His heart pounds. The ground sways beneath his feet. He presses the bell and within moments, Reba, his grandmother's "woman" (what that means, he's never quite sure), opens the door, still in her robe, and yawning. The gray in her dark hair glints in the morning sun, and her walnut eyes blink sleepily until she recognizes him.

"William! Come in, come in. Your grandmother'll be so pleased to see you. She thought you were traveling this week in Nevada."

"I'm sorry to wake you."

"No, we're up. Having coffee and breakfast. Come along." She takes his coat and hangs it in the entryway closet.

Reba's been part of Will's life for as long as he can remember. When he was little, she fed him crispy strips of bacon and told him Lakota stories her grandfather taught her. While Reba lives in his grandmother's home, Will's never understood the nature of their relationship. They sleep in the same bed at times, but his mother says that's just loneliness. Will's not sure of that at all, yet Eleanora is more apt to treat Reba as a servant than a friend or a lover.

It is what it is. Will decided that years ago, and he thinks it again as he follows Reba's slender back down the spotless hallway to the sunny breakfast room.

"William, darling!" Eleanora exclaims. Her blond hair with gray streaks is curled into an elegant bob, and her makeup is freshly applied. She sits at the table wearing a cream pantsuit, and Will suddenly wants to ask if Reba dresses her, but that's absurd.

"Hello, Nonna."

"Kisses."

Will crosses the sunny room, the scent of coffee and warm bread in his nose. He bends down to receive his kiss on the cheek. As he straightens, Eleanora grabs him by the collar and glares into his eyes.

"Out with it. What've you done? I recognize that look. It's your I-have-a-confession expression."

Reba snatches up her coffee and plate of jellied toast and leaves the room as quickly as if she'd been dismissed.

As soon as the door is shut behind her, Will admits, "Yeah, Nonna. I messed up."

She sighs and pats his cheek. "Sit down. Tell me everything. I'll see what I can do."

Eleanora's not impressed with his screw-up, to say the least. By the time she's done lecturing him and very successfully guilt tripping him over the danger of binge drinking with diabetes, haranguing him about his irresponsible and reckless behavior, and most embarrassingly, insisting on the importance of safe sex at all times, Will feels about three inches tall.

With an air of taking pity on him, she draws the lecture to a close. "Now the important question, darling," Eleanora says, pouring herself some more coffee from an ornate pot. "Is he handsome, this Dr. McCloud?"

"*Nonna.*"

Eleanora chuckles. "Well, I can see from your face that he is. I look forward to meeting the man who inspired my grandson to such heights of foolishness." There's a hint of threat underlying her warm words. "In the meantime, I'll make a few calls, see what I can discover."

"Can I ask you for another favor?"

"You're being quite brave, darling, after your ridiculous shenanigans. But you know your Nonna can't say no to you, don't you? What do you need?"

"It would raise alarm bells if the Molinaros found out I'm not exactly head over heels for my new husband. We need somewhere to stay until we can get this situation resolved. Obviously, we can't stay at Mom's or Grandma Betty's. It'd be suspicious for newlyweds to not want a place where they can be alone. The Tallgrass is doable, and the expense isn't a problem, but it's very public. I was hoping we could move into your guest cottage. Temporarily, of course."

Getting Patrick out of the Tallgrass and to a more private location seems key to continuing the charade long enough to manage the divorce. Will's not sure how many more situations like the one with Perry he can endure. Not to mention, the idea of being crammed into a hotel suite day in and day out with Patrick makes him feel a little faint. He wonders briefly if he can still keep the Molinaro's trust money if he murders Patrick. He's pretty sure there's no Molinaro stipulation against *that*. Murder's always been a viable Molinaro alternative to accepting the consequences of any situation that's gone wrong.

"I wish I was able to say yes, but I'm afraid I'm having the place renovated. It's completely gutted inside at the moment. If you're still married this spring, though, you're welcome to move in."

"Oh," Will says, crestfallen. "I guess we'll just stick with the Tallgrass for now. With any luck this will all be over in a few weeks, right?"

"I'll do my best, darling. But we both know the Molinaro family." She chuckles. "Oh, what a shock I had when I married into that bunch! They're impetuous but thorough. When they want something, they'll do anything to get it, and the consequences of trying to circumvent their family codes, or doing anything to violate their precious 'honor'? Well, it can end badly. It might even be dangerous."

"I know." Will presses his lips together. "I don't want you getting mixed up in anything that could get anyone hurt, Nonna. So, please, if it looks like it's verging on that kind of thing, just let it go. I'll figure out another way."

"And what way would that be, Will? Offing Dr. McCloud? Please. You don't have it in you to do something like that. For which I thank God, by the way. You are nothing like Tony, blood be damned." Eleanora sips her coffee. "No, it might take some time, but I'll give this my undivided attention."

"Thank you, Nonna." Will kisses her cheek. "And please don't say anything to Mom until I get a chance to talk to her. She needs to hear it from me."

"Spoil my fun." Eleanora pouts. "Well, all right, but you'd better tell her soon, because news spreads like wildfire in this town. That is, I suppose, the point of you telling the hotel employees all about it. Word will get back to the Molinaros that you're happily bedding down in the honeymoon suite. Good thinking. But you'll have to be careful who you let in on the truth of this secret."

"Mom can be trusted."

"Of course she can. And your uncle too. But not the children. They're too young for secrets this heavy."

"I agree."

"And, well, I'm also thinking of…well, darling, what about Ryan?"

Will bites his lower lip and shakes his head, keeping his eyes on the floor. "It won't be a problem."

"I know the boy broke up with you. What a stupid young man. I can't begin to know your problems, but really? Darling, he's an idiot."

"Nonna…"

"Will, I know you care for him, but you can't possibly be honest with him. It's too big a risk, especially when his loyalty isn't guaranteed."

"Ryan still cares about me," Will says, but there's a whole lot of doubt on that point swirling inside. "He wouldn't do anything to jeopardize—"

"Darling, don't fool yourself." Eleanora sniffs. She's never liked

Ryan much. "No, William, this is something you can't trust him with. You'll have to make him believe, like everyone else, that this is a love match."

"Come on, like that's even possible. He knows me too well."

"You'll just have to be very, very convincing, won't you? I don't think I need to remind you what's at stake here. You've got to act your butt off, do you hear me?"

Will nods. He slumps in his chair, trying to make himself small; make himself stronger by taking up less room.

Eleanora comes around the table and Will hugs her close, smelling her perfumed hair and clinging hard.

"There, there, darling. This is quite the bungle, but we'll make it through. In the meantime, you take care of yourself. No more drinking, do you understand? Or do you need some help in that regard? A stay in rehab might do you some good?"

Will pulls away and shakes his head. She searches his eyes. "Good. I know you can cope with this, William. It's going to take some time. This is a delicate situation and I can't rush into it making demands. The Molinaros don't like demands."

"A month?"

"Maybe more."

"*More* than a month?"

"Hush. Some messes take longer to clean up than others. Just have heart and be patient. Can you do that?"

"Yes." But he's not so sure about Patrick.

Chapter Six

W ILL NEEDS SOME liquid bravery before confessing everything to his mom, and since he's absolutely back on the wagon, that's going to have to come in the form of caffeine. Lots and lots of caffeine.

He parks back at Good Works and heads for the only coffee shop in town. Brown Gargle is relatively new but built to resemble a Wild West saloon. It's all wood on the outside, with a front porch to drink iced coffee on in the summer. It even has fake batwings painted onto the weatherproof glass doors. It's thirty-six degrees and overcast, snowflakes spiraling slowly down as he walks. It's not cold enough yet for them to stick, but before long snow will start to accumulate. In January, they'll have some real depth for sure, but with flurries this early, the chances of a white Christmas have gone up.

Will sighs. The Christmas decorations around town depress him even more. It's as though the wreaths, bows, and tall Christmas tree in the middle of Old Healing are mocking him with their brightness. He's already got Ryan's present. He's had it for months, and now he's not sure he can even give it to him—or if Ryan will even want it.

As he enters Brown Gargle, Christmas cheer pours into his ears in the form of "Joy to the World" performed by a chorus of small children. His eyes sting and his throat goes tight.

"The usual?" Jax asks. He's Will's favorite barista, what with his sexy way of leaning against the counter, his black hair buzzed neatly, and his dark eyes always sparkling with warmth. He comes in from the reservation for the work. And Will's always thought it's too bad the guy is straight.

"I'm not sure. Give me a minute."

"No problem." He wipes down the counter and starts to organize the shelf of tiny personal, multi-colored teapots. Jax looks over at him. "You okay, man?"

"Yeah. Why?"

"Your hands are shaking. And people are talking about you."

Will shoves his hands in his coat pockets. "What've you heard?"

"I don't listen to gossip. I just hear names. Yours has come up a lot this morning."

Will's heart pounds and he tries to pull himself together. "Yeah, well…"

Jax smiles. "Just take care, okay? You're a good guy. We like you around here."

"Got it. Thanks." Will clears his throat, blushing a little, and looks over the menu hanging over the wooden bar-cum-coffee-counter.

Normally, he orders the Buckaroo size of the Medium Roast Brown Gargle, which is Wild West speak for coffee. It's small but energizing. If he's overtired, he gets the Bangtail size: medium and super-charging. Today? Today he's going to order a Bronco Buster of the Dark Roast because if his heart explodes from caffeine overload at least he'll be out of his misery.

He places his suicidal request and while Jax pours his drink, he lingers over all the Christmas-themed pastries. Snowmen gingerbread cookies appear especially enticing. But he hasn't worked out in days now, not really. Sex doesn't count. He shouldn't eat one no matter how good they look. He forces his gaze away from the luring treats. He needs to collect Patrick and get over to his mother's house before the gossip does. But he's not ready to face the music.

Turning to see if his favorite table in the front corner is open, Will sucks in a breath, gut-punched. The room tilts and he grabs the edge of the counter, his head swimming and bile rising in his throat.

It's Ryan and Hartley.

They're sitting close together on a bench not even six feet away. Ryan's dark, closely shorn head is bent down so that Hartley, smaller and more compact than Ryan by far, is speaking directly into his ear. Hartley Kills Enemy's shoulder-length black hair is braided and his broad, handsome face is as smooth and calm as ever, even as Ryan cracks up over whatever story Hartley is telling. Ryan's blue eyes sparkle and his mouth spreads wide with a happy smile Will hasn't seen in a very long time.

Will swiftly turns back to Jax and pays for his coffee.

It's Ryan's joyful laughter, and Hartley's voice layering on top of it that stills him and roots him in place.

"And John La Beau still didn't get the joke," Hartley's saying. "You're *wašicun*—not Lakota. No insult intended. But even you get it."

Ryan sounds so damn happy as he teases, "I don't know, Hartley. Are you sure you're not calling me something dirty?"

Hartley answers with his usual seriousness. "Some people believe that *wašicun* means 'he who steals the fat.' But that's not right. It's word-play on *wašin icu*. Literally 'takes the fat.' The meaning of *wašicun*—is it an insult or is it neutral—is in the tone and timing." Hartley's typically impassive expression turns incredibly tender. "I'd never call you something dirty, Ryan. Not unless you wanted me to."

Will snorts and rolls his eyes. This relationship is already doomed. Ryan hates dirty talk.

Ryan glances at Hartley sideways, his lip curling into an embarrassed half smile. "Maybe someday if I feel safe enough. Is that okay?"

Will goes cold all over.

"Of course. I want you to feel good when you're with me, like you did last night. I never want you to feel embarrassed or humiliated by what we do together; who we are for each other."

"I do trust you, Hartley."

"Well, I'm glad you trust someone," Will spits out before he's even decided to speak.

"Uh, Will." Ryan shifts guiltily away from Hartley, who lounges back and spreads his legs out casually. There's not even a hint of shame on his face. Ryan, though, looks like he just got caught with his hand down his pants in public. "You're back early. I thought you were supposed to be in Vegas for the rest of the week?"

"There was a change of plans." Will sets his jaw, glaring. "I see your plans changed too." His heart throbs painfully in his chest.

Ryan takes hold of Hartley's hand. "I know this is awkward, and I'm sorry if this hurts you. We never wanted that."

Will's shoulders tense and he crosses his arms over his chest. He uses his thumb to twist the ring on his finger. "Oh yeah?"

"Of course. I'll always care about you, Will. We had a lot of years together and those can't be erased. But…" He swallows and looks to Hartley. "We both haven't been happy together for a long time. You have to admit that."

"Do I?"

"Please, Will. We just want to finally do what's best for everyone."

Hartley nods.

"I've got news too. I met someone in Vegas."

"You met someone?" Ryan sounds like Will's not speaking English.

"Yep."

"As in you met a man?" Hartley asks quietly.

"Yes." Will can't even feel his lips but he yammers on. "I'm in love with him. And he's in love with me too."

"Will," Ryan says, pity swimming in his eyes.

"We got married." He waggles his left hand in front of them. He sounds insane. He suspects he looks it, based on the way Ryan and Hartley are staring at him.

Ryan's face goes pale and his eyebrows crawl together. "You what?"

"You heard me." Will can't breathe. He spins on his heel and walks out of the coffee shop. The fresh, cool air slaps his face and he gasps it in like a floundering fish. He hasn't gone fifteen steps before Ryan grabs his arm and pulls him around. Hartley lingers in the background, radiating concern as the end of his dark braid flaps in the breeze.

"Will, tell me you're not serious." Ryan's grip is tight on his arm.

"I am. Deadly serious. We met the other night and, well, one thing led to another." The smile on his lips is a tight, painful mask.

"You married a man you met in Las Vegas? After what? One day?"

The fact that Ryan's expression slides somewhere between worry and disgust just eggs him on. Will shrugs. "What can I say? He's incredible and we both just knew it was right. You know how it is."

"No. I don't *know*." Ryan's grip tightens enough to hurt and Will jerks his arm free. "Will, two days ago, you were going on about how *we* were right for each other. And now you're *married*?"

Will lifts his brows slightly in Hartley's direction. "Funny how things change, isn't it?"

Ryan gapes at him.

Hartley steps forward gingerly, saying in his quiet, calm way, "Congratulations, Will. What's his name?"

"Dr. Patrick McCloud." Will lifts his chin. "He's a neurosurgeon."

"Will?" Ryan sounds like he's speaking to a wild animal or a very stupid child. "Have you been *drinking*?"

Will snarls, turning away.

But Ryan grabs his arm again, holding him fast. "Does your mother know about this? She doesn't, does she? She would have said something when I dropped off your stuff from the apartment."

Will's laugh hurts. "So, you've already packed up my things and moved me out? In a hurry much?"

Ryan's eyes fly wide like Will's gone even crazier. "Me? I'm not the one who married some stranger on a drunken fling in Vegas!"

Will flashes cold and hot. He's shaking all over. He wants to deny it, wants to say that Ryan's accusation is entirely untrue, but people are standing around outside the coffee shop listening. He remembers Eleanora telling him to act his butt off, and he hears Patrick's voice in his head snarking about Molinaros lurking in bushes.

"I'll have you know," Will says, jabbing his finger in Ryan's chest. "That Patrick is the love of my life, and I am *ecstatic* to be married to him." He's vibrating with so much rage and hurt he doesn't even feel like he's lying.

Hartley raises one eyebrow and Ryan stares at him in shock. Will runs out of the square before Ryan or anyone else can stop and question him more.

PATRICK DOESN'T EAT the *entire* time Will's away. Even *his* stomach has a limit. Though, given how good some of the food is, he wishes it didn't. He flops back on the bed, stuffed to the gills.

His mind drifts to his other favorite thing: sex. His body tingles all over remembering how he and Will had clung to each other and explored pleasure for hours. He groans, remembering the humid breath between their bodies and the sticky, hot jizz pulsing out of their cocks. It'd been the delicious end-all and be-all of his world for long, glorious hours.

Analysis of his memories proves one thing beyond dispute: the night with Will had been the most intense interpersonal experience of his entire life. But that information is relatively useless now. Will's not interested in a repeat performance, and given how complicated everything has become, Patrick's sure getting in any deeper is a bad idea anyway.

So today, Patrick's going to be smart. He's going to google up everything he can find about Will Patterson. Amusingly, the first hit for Will's name isn't related to Good Works, but instead an online tabloid/slam book called *The Hurting Times*. It sounds like a porn movie and he finds it reads a lot like one too.

Quick perusal of its pages reveals that it's a gossip site, pure and simple. But, from what Patrick can tell, based on a cross-examination with the more reputable papers, *The Healing Times* and *West of Rez*, almost everything in *The Hurting Times* is pretty damn accurate. The site details not only truly newsworthy events such as shootings, rapes, attempted murders, and drug busts, but also features not-so-blind items about who's sleeping with who, and a scintillating message board that gets down to the nitty-gritty filth of Healing's citizens. The town is a Jerry Springer episode on drugs. And Will's name is all over the backlog.

The first mention of Will in *The Hurting Times* is a birth announcement from the archived remains of the original Yahoo listserv. A week later there's a follow-up blurb: *Baby Molinaro has a name! Sources close to Tony and Kimberly Molinaro say the boy will be called Guglielmo 'William' Michael Molinaro.*

Guglielmo. Will's real name is *Guglielmo*. Patrick already knew that of course, but seeing his full name in print like this…well, it makes him feel strange inside, like he's looking at baby photos. It's gross, or maybe cute in a way. His gut twists up but he focuses on the next trove of information on Will.

Tony and Kimberly Molinaro's divorce scandal! One Vanessa Miller of Minneapolis gave birth to a baby girl, Ellen Elizabeth Molinaro, last week. Sources say Kimberly filed for divorce the next day.

Holy drama, Batman!

Patrick clicks on the message board thread detailing Kimberly's string of short marriages, including one to a Roger Flemings. Apparently, despite being heavily pregnant with Roger's child, Tony and Kimberly were caught by police *in flagrante* on the hood of his car behind the movie theater.

"Dirty, dirty. Guess Will comes by it naturally," Patrick murmurs to himself.

Connor was born a month after that, and, according to the gossip, had red hair like Roger Fleming. Rumors that he might have been Tony's son are extinguished with that small detail. Four weeks after Connor's birth, Roger drowns in the YMCA swimming pool in the middle of the night, leaving many questions behind. First, Roger had no keys to the facility, no known way to get in, and most suspiciously, Roger possessed a terrible fear of water: the man couldn't swim.

The gossip pages don't hesitate to point the finger at the Molinaros. The same family that sent Patrick and Will a bouquet in congratulations for their marriage. *Okay, so maybe Will's not entirely crazy to be paranoid about that.* Not that Patrick's gonna let him know. The marriage being discovered as a fraud by the Molinaro family is still one very accessible escape hatch.

Patrick sighs and clicks on one last thread. It's full of gossip about yet another marriage for Kimberly, this time to a Monty Edison, and it also ends in the man's death. Luckily less mysteriously: a heart attack while on a camping trip with some pals in the Badlands.

Patrick rubs his eyes. So, okay. Will's had a chaotic life. After reading *The Hurting Times* gossip there's no doubt about that. Patrick can relate. His own childhood wasn't sweet or wholesome either. But for Will this entire marriage-in-Vegas thing should be nothing more than the comedic icing on top of the shit cake. Instead, it's going to cost Will everything. Whatever 'everything' is, which is a good question, and Patrick decides to look into that too.

After only thirty minutes of research, he leans back and sighs. Will's foundation does good work, just as its name implies. It's dumbfounding to consider the full impact Will's money has on the world. He pushes at the edges of Will's foundation a bit more, and finds that it just grows more impressive. Just what the hell is Will trying to prove with all of this do-gooding anyway?

Rolling his eyes, Patrick closes the laptop. He slaps his palms against his thighs and stands up to stretch. *So trapped. So, so trapped.* Beads of sweat start on this forehead, and he takes a long breath. *No. Not trapped.* He can still get a divorce and walk away.

Sure he can. If he wants to be the reason for the collapse of the Entirely-Too-Good-To-Be-Real Empire. Dammit.

He pockets his hotel room key and heads for the door. He's getting out of this room because at least he still has *that* option open to him.

IT'S COLD AS a witch's tit, and Patrick shivers in his business shirt and light jacket. When he left Atlanta, he packed for autumn in Nevada, not for this trip to hell, which has officially frozen over. He wanders around something called Old Healing, which takes him all of about ten minutes. There's a pharmacy and a bookstore, both with elaborate Christmas displays in their windows, followed by a shop displaying wedding gowns with holiday-themed bridesmaid dresses and accoutrements. Based on all the Patterson/Molinaro marriages and divorces alone, Patrick's betting weddings are a big business in this town.

The next store he passes is a sports utility place, with red and green canoes, camping gear, and Gore-Tex jackets on display in the window. Patrick heads into the warmth of the store and locates a shopping cart immediately, steering it to the winter coats and gloves. With the help of Google and his phone, he pulls up a suitable list of brands and requirements for cold-weather gear. He chooses a maroon-colored matching set of coat and gloves, and then he heads over to the boots department. There's a dark grey pair with lug soles and good insulation.

He grabs a box with his size and sits down on the floor to try them on. No salespeople appear to help him out, a fact he's glad for. He prefers to make his own choices without being talked at. The boots are suitable and lightweight enough to ship back to Atlanta, or wherever he ends up when this is all over. In the meantime, his toes won't fall off. The weather forecast on his phone is calling for lows near zero, possibly dipping below in the next few weeks. He takes the boots back off and shoves them haphazardly into the box, dropping it into the cart with all the rest.

Next he chooses some good wicking socks in gray and black. He grabs a dark maroon fleece and a navy hoodie, along with some sweat pants for lounging in the hotel room. His eye catches a pile of colorful rolled up yoga mats and he makes a detour to grab a couple of those too.

He takes the cart over to the register. "Charge it to Will Patterson's account."

The floppy-haired boy behind the counter stares at him. "Uh, who are you?"

"Dr. McCloud…er, Patterson." He sighs, presses his fingers to the bridge of his nose, and says, "Listen, does Will have an account here or not?"

"He does."

"Great. Charge it. I'm his husband."

"Oh!" He flips his hair. "I heard he got married. My girlfriend told me."

"Your girlfriend? How would your girlfriend—? Never mind. I can guess." The town's electricity is probably powered by gossip. "Just bag up this stuff and I'll be on my merry way."

The boy does as he's asked and Patrick wonders how bright the kid is. Could anyone walk in here claiming to be some townie's new spouse and walk out loaded down with charged goods? The kid hasn't required any kind of proof. He hasn't even called Will to check on Patrick's story. Maybe this town is full of feeble-minded, gossipy, sex addicts.

"Here you go, Dr. McCloud-er-Patterson," the boy says. "Congratulations! I hope you and Will are super happy together. I mean, I don't like guys myself, but I'm really glad your type can get married now. My dad said it's only fair."

Patrick starts to say something cutting but can't be bothered. He takes the bag containing the yoga mats, pulls on the new coat and gloves, and heads out of the shop.

"Come back soon!"

Patrick rounds the corner and he's back where he started next to the pharmacy and a tall, tinseled Christmas tree. Bored with shopping and ready for some caffeine, Patrick heads into a place named Brown Gargle and peruses the pastry case. There are gingerbread men, women, and snow-people, and brightly colored iced cookies in the shape of elves, Santa, and Mrs. Claus. He's amused by the sight of an entire nativity cookie set—Joseph, Mary, Wise Men, and Shepherds, and a tiny Baby Jesus. They all look good, but they're not exactly what he's looking for.

Then he spots it. A lone, fat doughnut, jam dripping from its side. His stomach gurgles and saliva floods his mouth. He begins to place his order, but to his horror it's snatched from the case, put on a plate and handed to a tiny blond woman.

Patrick splutters. "Hey, that's my doughnut." The barista doesn't seem inclined to agree, taking money from the woman and grinning as she deposits an extra folded dollar into the tip jar.

He slams his hand down on top of the glass display case. "I was just about to order that. *She* just walked in and hasn't said a word."

The barista raises an eyebrow, then pointedly looks down at Patrick's hands splayed on the glass. "Hands off, please. It's fragile."

Patrick yanks his hands away and bites out, "Well? That's my doughnut."

"She's a regular. This is her usual."

"But I was here first." It doesn't matter that he had doughnut holes that morning; it's a matter of winning now.

The woman's red sweater stretches over her ample chest as she puffs it up. "There are other doughnuts," she says, shifting her blond ponytail to the side and staring up at him like he's grown an asshole where his mouth should be. "Glazed, chocolate, sprinkles. Why don't you just pick another one?"

"Why don't *you* just pick another one?"

"Because I like the jam." She lifts her brows and stares at him with wide, innocent blue eyes, belying the sass in her tone. She cocks a hip, little black pencil skirt hugging her curves, and one shiny black dress shoe tapping ominously on the clean, brown tile floor. Luckily, Patrick isn't impressed by pretty women. Being gay is sometimes a tactical advantage.

"Well, so do I."

"Ladies before gentlemen."

Patrick snorts. "Lady, I've been accused of being a lot of things but never a gentleman."

She puts her hands on her hips and tilts her pointed chin up. "Oh my God, what is wrong with you? Just let me have the doughnut!"

"No!"

A sudden wailing cry pierces the air and the woman turns to bend down to the stroller Patrick hadn't noticed before. She picks up a baby and cuddles it close. "Hey, hey, baby," she murmurs. "It's okay, you're okay."

Patrick turns back to the barista while she's distracted. "I'll take that doughnut now."

"Hey!" The woman punches him on the shoulder, surprisingly strong, especially for someone holding a baby in her other arm.

Patrick sighs. He hates to admit defeat, but the baby is staring at him, stopped mid-wail as if waiting to see what Patrick is going to do. "Fine. Split it?"

The woman cocks her head at him, evaluating him narrowly, and then she smiles. "Sure. Why not? It's a much more civil solution than fighting about it, isn't it?"

"I guess."

"If you'd led with that suggestion, then maybe—"

Patrick interrupts her to order an extra glazed doughnut and a latte, refusing to call it by its ridiculous menu name: the Calamalatte Jane.

Patrick takes the plate of doughnuts over to a table, splits the jam one and holds half out to the woman who has followed him. She puts the baby back into its stroller, and Patrick waits to hear howls again, but nothing comes. A quick glance shows that the child's somehow fallen asleep.

Patrick waits. The woman takes the doughnut but doesn't leave. In fact, she sits down, apparently deciding that since they are splitting the doughnut, they're also splitting a table. She takes a bite, the jam leaving a dollop on her pink lower lip. She licks it off.

"What are you doing?" he asks.

"My name's Jenny. And this little guy is Dylan," she gestures to the baby.

Patrick grunts.

"And?" She motions at him, rolling her hand in a circle.

"What?"

"Aren't you going to introduce yourself?"

Patrick wonders for a moment what she would say if he declined the invitation to socialize. "Dr. McCloud," he says tersely, returning to his doughnuts, hoping she'll take the cue and move along to another table, or, even better, leave the shop altogether.

She polishes off her half of the doughnut and sighs contentedly.

The barista brings over Patrick's latte. It's beautifully made with a Wild West pistol design in the foam. He tastes it and moans. He supposes the baristas in Healing must have nothing better to do than perfect the best-tasting lattes in the world.

As the barista turns to go, Jenny touches his arm, ordering a coffee and another doughnut with sprinkles. Then she settles in at the table, putting away her purse and diaper bag and covering the baby with a blanket.

Patrick raises one eyebrow. "By all means," he says sarcastically. "Feel free to join me."

Jenny smiles warmly. "Thank you. I will. So," she says, leaning forward. "Healing's a tiny little place. Everyone knows everyone else. And you're a stranger around here." She grins, white and toothy. "What brings you to town?"

Patrick sighs, tapping his fingers rhythmically against the table. He's not quite sure how to answer that question or what Will wants him to say. "I'm a neurosurgeon."

"Oh! So you're here for the neurology unit at the hospital!"

"I've heard good things about it."

"You have?" Her eyes shine at that news. "We're all hoping that the expansion of Healing Regional is going to be great for us. For the whole region, really."

Patrick nods and shoves a bite of the glazed doughnut in his mouth, hoping she'll go away if he doesn't engage her further in conversation.

"We're all excited to meet the doctors and nurses they're hiring to staff it. Someone told me there'll be a lot more travel nurses who've worked contracts all over the country, sometimes the world! Can you imagine the stories they must have to share? It'll be so enriching to our community to have some new blood."

Patrick isn't much for discussing other people's life experiences. Unless it's filthy, dirty gossip, and then he's all in. But prideful tales of other people's self-actualizing hike up the Alps? Pass. Give him a remote control and an episode of *Alaska: The Last Frontier* instead. Now that's some life experience he can enjoy from the comfort of his sofa—no social interaction needed.

"Anyway, are you here for the head of department position?" Jenny asks, obviously still excited by his 'new blood'-ness despite his surly demeanor. "I know they've been looking for someone."

Be discreet. He hears Will's voice in his head. "I'm not sure what my plans are just yet. It depends on a few things."

"Oh." Jenny's face falls. "That's a shame. I can put in a good word for you. Don Knife, the chief of staff, is an old friend of mine."

"Don *Knife*?"

"Sure. Good traditional Lakota surname." She grins. "We have some pretty great ones around here. Kills Enemy is a favorite of mine. And Jax back there behind the counter has a fun last name too." She nods toward the barista preparing a tray to bring over her coffee and doughnut. "He's Jax Taken Alive."

"Taken Alive, huh? I can relate."

She laughs. "But, seriously, I'll take you on over to the hospital after we finish here and give you a personal introduction to Don."

"Why?"

She shrugs. Jax arrives with her coffee and she says, "Put it on my tab, hon." He winks at her before walking away.

"It's not like I've been very nice to you." Patrick takes another sip of his latte. It really is too delicious to be true. He breathes in the warmth of its steam.

"That's okay. You're not from around here. Everyone knows that people from other places are assholes." She laughs and shoves his shoulder again. "Right? Don't you think outsiders are always assholes back wherever you're from?"

"Maybe."

"Where *are* you from?"

"Atlanta." By way of Alabama, Kentucky, and Connecticut, but she doesn't need the details. "As for meeting Dr. Knife—" Patrick can't hold back a snort. "Well, I should probably let my husband do the honors."

She cocks her head. "Wait, what did you say your first name was?"

"I didn't." She looks unimpressed, and he sighs. "Patrick."

"Oh my God!" Jenny nearly shouts, drawing the attention of the patrons lined up at the counter. "You're Will Patterson's new husband! I thought you might be when we met over at the counter!" She grips his arm and shakes him, causing him to spill a little of his precious latte onto his navy button-up shirt. "I've heard all about you!"

Of course she has. News of his marriage to Will is probably burning up *The Hurting Times* server by now.

She points at his half of the jam doughnut. "Are you going to eat that or not?"

He thrusts the jam doughnut into his mouth, mind spinning, trying to figure out what he's supposed to say now. He should probably get up and go, but maybe that would be suspicious. He glances toward a man tucked in a corner ostensibly reading a paper. He has a dark complexion and is wearing a business suit and glancing at him from around his paper occasionally. Is Patrick paranoid to think it might be a Molinaro spy? Probably. But it's better to be safe than dead in a YMCA pool.

"What have you heard?" he asks Jenny.

"Not a lot. My niece Beth told me all about how you and Will checked into the Tallgrass last night. You're just like she described."

"And how's that?"

"Delightfully jerky." She smacks his arm and laughs. "How do you think? Handsome. Inappropriate. Grouchy. Pretty much exactly how you are!"

Patrick nods. If she'd said anything else, he'd have to hate her. But as it is, she's honest at least. Honesty is a quality Patrick likes. Give him a bitter pill if the situation demands it, but don't tell him it's chocolate.

"So, how did you meet Will?"

"How did *you* meet Will?"

She cackles. "I babysat his little butt when he was just a kid. Well, that's not entirely accurate. I mainly took care of Caitlin and Olivia. Will was pretty self-sufficient by that time, and I'd outgrown babysitting before Connor came along and Will was plenty old enough to watch the kids himself."

"So you didn't change his diapers?"

"Nah. He's only six years younger than me." She gazes off. "I think he was ten when I first came over to the house to watch the girls." She meets his eye again. "But it's Healing. Everyone knows everyone just like their own brother or sister. It's downright incestuous at times." She squeezes his forearm. "Come on, tell me things. Was it love at first sight? Give me all the juicy details!"

Patrick's certain no matter what he says now Will won't be happy. So he just goes all in. "I met him in a bar."

"Was he drinking?" Her concern is palpable.

"Not really," Patrick fibs. "The lights in the bar weren't so great. It was hard to see in there, but I thought he was the most handsome man I'd seen in a long time." That's still the truth even in broad daylight. His gut flutters and twists again.

"And?"

"I seduced him."

Jenny lets out a little happy sound.

"Don't tell Will I said that. He's embarrassed by how easily he fell for me."

"Will can be impulsive," Jenny says, and she doesn't sound entirely approving. "But this is *really* impulsive even for him."

"Well, don't be too hard on him." Patrick puffs out his chest. "I can be quite persuasive."

She giggles. "Right. It was your glorious grouchy charm that won him over."

Patrick shrugs. "Whatever it was, he was into me too."

"Uh-huh." Jenny smirks.

"And the sex was, without a doubt, hands down the best I've ever had." He has to admit if Will gives it up again soon, this entire detour to frozen middle America won't seem like such a waste. "I came like dynamite every time."

She smiles with a fevered giddiness. "I understand completely.

Sex like that can make anyone act impulsively."

Patrick knows most people don't talk about these things like this. They don't candidly break into a discussion of orgasms and screwing on the first date, but he doesn't care. He's always sucked at appropriate chitchat and prefers to get to the gritty truth of things. Besides, Patrick likes Jenny. She's not running screaming away from him at any rate. And she's not slapping his face or scolding him. She's holding her own.

She checks to make sure Dylan is still sleeping. "Did he…feel the same way?"

"He was putty in my hands when I was done with him."

"I knew he needed someone more passionate than Ryan. That's his ex." She looks a little embarrassed to have brought him up.

"I know."

"Ryan's always been such a cold fish." She sighs. "I shouldn't talk about him like that. But they never clicked, despite being together so long. I'm glad Will came to his senses, no matter what inspired it."

"You don't think he's made a mistake marrying someone he's just met?"

"Maybe. It's all pretty fast, isn't it? But sometimes things just happen. That's how it was with Dylan's dad. We slept together on the first date and I just *knew*. I would have married him immediately, right there in his bed still shaking from how good we were together. It was perfect. We were perfect."

Ding, ding, ding. Jenny wins at the real, honest, and dirty award. She's his favorite kind of person.

"That's how Will felt," Patrick says, oddly wishing it was true.

She goes all dreamy for a moment, but then she clears her throat and frowns. "Hopefully you and Will last longer than me and Tom. He's been long gone since the day I found out I was pregnant. Packed his bags that night and skipped town. I haven't heard from him since." She shrugs. "But that's just how life is, right?"

"Not really, no."

"Excuse me?"

"Life had nothing to do with it. He was a dick. End of story."

She seems to take a few seconds to decide if she's going to be offended. "True." She flips her ponytail over her shoulder and leans down to touch Dylan's sleeping face. "Well, I got a beautiful boy out of what I had with him. I guess that's better than nothing."

"I don't really do 'looking at the bright side.' I prefer bald truth."

"Thank you. I appreciate that, actually. Being positive all the time gets tiring. Sometimes being a single mom just sucks."

"That's more like it. It sucks and you sometimes hate it."

She smiles and glances around to make sure no one is listening. "Sometimes I do hate it. It's true. But I never hate *Dylan*."

He nods at the kid. "He's cute at least. It'd be even harder if he was ugly."

Jenny laughs again. "Yeah, I guess it would be."

"That's as positive as I get."

She sips her coffee and they're silent for a few seconds. "So, go on. What happened next? You know, after you seduced Will?" She props her chin on her hands and stares at him avidly.

Yes, it's clear that the people in this town live on gossip as much as on air and food. "Well, after I came my brains out six times—"

"Six!"

"Yeah. After that, I had to take a break from screwing him for a few hours. It was long enough to realize he's a pretty awesome guy." Another truth, but not one Patrick's very happy about.

"So you married him."

"I married him."

He's fudging the timeline and the details, but what she doesn't know won't hurt her. It's better if the story is more believable than the insanity that actually went down. He doesn't want to embarrass Will by admitting they were both drunk. And he doesn't want to embarrass himself by admitting he married Will before they even had sex. Everyone knows you should test drive before buying. His idiocy doesn't need to be part of the town's gossip.

"To be crass—"

"Oh, yes, be crass."

"It was love at first fuck."

"Patrick?"

"Yes?"

Jenny smiles and squeezes his hand, which he should hate, but somehow doesn't. "You and I are gonna be good friends."

Terrific. Just what he needs.

Chapter Seven

PATRICK'S ALONE AND on his third latte when Will runs into Brown Gargle, screeching to a halt by the table.

"Yes, dear?"

"You're an awful person." Will scowls.

"I get that a lot."

Arms akimbo, Will's the picture of domestic irritation. *Aw, my angry little wife.* Well, big wife. Will is quite a bit taller than him after all. "I thought you were going to wait at the hotel."

Patrick shrugs. He never promised anything. "I got bored. And hungry. Thought I'd take a walk." He licks the end of his finger to dab up the last crumbs of a gingerbread snowman he's only just polished off. He pops his finger in his mouth. Will grimaces.

Collapsing into the chair only recently vacated by Jenny, Will stares at him. "What did you do exactly? Who did you talk to? What did you say?"

"Well, first I spread evil rumors about you at the hotel, telling everyone I saw in the lobby that you're a snorer and a rude sleep-groper." That's not true, but Will looks suitably annoyed. Patrick pats his shopping bags by his feet. "Then I stopped by the sporting goods place to buy a few things to survive your hellish weather."

"Hey, at least it's not North Dakota. It's two degrees colder up there."

"Oh, two whole degrees."

"Believe me. It makes all the difference."

"Then I stopped in here, lured by the promise of coffee, and ended up raising some hell."

Jax, wiping down a table next to theirs, snorts and shakes his head before heading back to the counter to take another order from the dark guy who's been hanging out with his newspaper.

"What did you do?"

"Got in a fight with your former babysitter Jenny."

"Jenny Burger?"

"Her last name's Burger? Don't tell me that's a traditional Lakota name too."

"She's German. I think. I don't know. Her ancestors have been here longer than mine." Will rubs his forehead like he's getting a headache. "So you met Jenny?"

"We fought over a doughnut, finally agreed to split it, and had a little talk."

"No! She's a huge gossip!"

"So? I only said good things about you."

"Like what?"

"Like you know exactly what to do with your asshole to make a guy blow his load in seconds."

Will gasps.

"Take a joke, Will. Of course I didn't say that! I just told her we were happy and in love. The way we planned."

"I can't believe you!"

"Why? Don't you want her to tell the whole town that our sexual chemistry sets the world on fire and that I love you like breathing? Isn't that…" He glances toward Jax and whispers, "What we want?"

Will shifts in his chair uncomfortably. "Yeah, I guess so."

Patrick shrugs. "By the way, Jax makes a good latte."

Will glances toward the tall, warm man behind the counter and gives a nod. Jax nods back.

"I had a nice time with Jenny, thanks for asking."

"You could have left me a note. I've been looking all over for you." There's residual panic to his tone and Patrick realizes that Will thought he might've skipped town.

"Never fear. I'll always be just a phone call away, *honey*." He waves his phone at Will.

Will grits his teeth. "I don't have your cell phone number, *darling*."

"Oh, yes, we skipped the exchange of numbers and went straight to bed, didn't we?"

Will attempts a smile but just ends up grimacing instead.

Patrick tosses him the phone. "Text yourself, my sweet little puddin'-pop."

Will does and Patrick enjoys another sip of latte. "So? How'd things go with your granny?"

"Let's talk about it later." Will glances toward the customer Jax is making a drink for and frowns.

"We can keep our voices down."

Will shakes his head. "No. I don't think so." He whispers, "I don't know him. He's a stranger. He looks Molinaro to me."

Patrick's eyes feel like they might bug out of his head. "Great. Are you kidding me?"

Will examines the man closely.

"I have a wonderful idea. Let's go home and make love," Patrick says loudly for the benefit of the man going back to his table with a foamy latte. If they're really being spied on, let the man send *that* report home to Will's creepy mafia family. "I miss your tight butt on my huge dick, babe."

Will gapes and flails. "Shh! What are you—" His cheeks turn fiery red and he hisses, "Stop humiliating me!"

"I'm being a loving husband!"

Will shakes his head, eyes wide. "You're being gross! Can you at least please try to act, I don't know, charming? Please?"

Patrick shrugs. "Charm's for people with no substance to back it up."

Will huffs and crosses his arms over his chest. Patrick notices again how well formed his biceps are. "Oh, funny. I thought it was for people who wanted other people to like them."

"Exactly. And that's not on my agenda. I don't need people to like me, so long as they respect me. And so long as they respect that *I'm in love with you*," he says loudly, aiming his voice to the man in the corner.

"They'd respect you more if they liked you."

"Show me statistics to prove that." Patrick slurps his last sip of coffee. "New topic: I should probably go buy some actual clothes to wear. I grabbed a few things at the sporting goods place, but not nearly enough to get by. And you're paying, by the way."

Will sighs and rubs a hand over his face. "Yeah, okay. Let me just get a Buckaroo to go and I'll take you somewhere. Just please don't talk to anyone, okay? Keep your mouth closed." He walks wearily to the counter.

Patrick doesn't want to embarrass Will. But he's nervous and out of his routine. He's never been good with the social skills at the best of times. If he'd been born five or six years later than he was, he'd probably have been diagnosed with Autism Spectrum Disorder. As it is, he's always been inappropriate and weird and he knows he does life wrong. But why can't Will be more like Jenny? Jenny doesn't seem to care.

He taps his fingers against his leg and stares at the back of Will's blond head. Jenny isn't married to him. She can laugh and walk away and no one will judge her for what Patrick says or does. Hot shame prickles his neck, something he hasn't felt in a long time. He wishes, for Will, he could be different.

But then he shakes it off.

For God's sake, he's Patrick McCloud, neurosurgeon. He cuts into people's brains and saves lives. He's a superhero, a savant, a saint, a genius. If Will can't handle his social ineptitude, that's his problem. Patrick's the best damn catch in the ocean and if Will's not proud of himself for reeling Patrick McCloud in, even for pretend, that's his loss.

He doesn't need Will's approval.

Will leans his elbows on the counter, bending forward a little so that his pants stretch tightly across his ass. Patrick's dick thickens in response.

"Traitor," he mutters.

AFTER SHOPPING AT a local men's boutique, Will isn't sure if he's happy Patrick's so easy to please, or appalled that Patrick buys two pairs of black jeans, two navy shirts, and two maroon shirts, all of them basically the same, and calls it a day. For Will, shopping has always been a bit more of an ordeal. He spends hours looking for the right fit, the right material, the right color.

Dress to impress, Nonna always says, and so Will does.

Back at the Tallgrass, Patrick dumps his shopping bags on the bed and immediately grabs the room service menu. Will can't even believe what he's seeing, given that, in between the store where they bought shirts and the store where they bought pants, Patrick had stopped by the Talking Hog food truck. He'd moaned around his bites of burger in a way that'd made Will blush with memories.

Will looks at the clock. He's missed the two o'clock AA meeting. There's another at eight. He doesn't know if he's got the energy to make it. He should call Owen at least. He'll be worried.

He sends a text instead: *Back in town. At Tallgrass for now. I'm sober and I'll stay that way. See you tomorrow.*

Owen's reply is typical: *Remember: The program works if you work it. I'm always here for you.*

As Will tucks his phone away, he hears Patrick order a salad with grilled chicken.

"What dressing do you like?" Patrick asks.

"Who? Me?"

"You, my diabetic hubby, need to eat."

"Oh." Warmth bubbles inside. It's nice that Patrick remembers his disease even when he's so distressed he's basically forgotten it himself. "Okay, uh. Oil and vinegar is fine."

Patrick wrinkles his nose but orders accordingly and asks for a fruit bowl for himself before hanging up. "Are you always so forgetful about eating? Or is it just situational stress messing you up? Because you need to take better care of yourself. I don't want you ending up in the hospital."

"Thanks, Dr. Bossy. Do you actually care?"

"No, not really," Patrick says cheerfully. Then he sighs, squeezes the bridge of his nose, and it obviously costs him a little to add, "Yes. I do, actually. I could say I'm a doctor and it's my job to care, and that would be true. It's also true that I care specifically about *you*. It's probably all the orgasms you gave me. Coming so hard while looking at your face screwed up my head."

Will doesn't understand how Patrick can almost be so sweet and then turn around to ruin it immediately.

Room service arrives. While Patrick signs for it, Will does his calculations, lifts his shirt, and injects himself on the opposite side of his abdomen from his last shot. He deals with the needle and tosses his insulin pen back in the bag.

Patrick must be tired too, because while they eat he doesn't press Will for more information about his meeting with Eleanora. He just pops grapes and strawberries into his mouth and watches Will swallow like it's somehow fascinating. When they're both done, Will puts the tray out into the hallway to be collected.

Now that every other excuse is gone, Will intends to go see his mom before more of the day gets away from him. He really does. But he's completely wrung out. He collapses on the sofa, letting his head fall back. He'll just close his eyes for a second. Maybe he'll wake up to find this has all been a terrible dream.

Patrick, though, is ready to talk. He sits beside Will and rubs his hands together in anticipation. "What did Granny say? Can she free me from the shackles of our loveless union?"

Will puts his head in his hands. "It's not going to be as easy as I hoped initially. It might take some time."

"We knew that. How much time? A week? Two?"

"Maybe a month?"

"What?" Patrick's voice is loud.

"Maybe more than a month? Possibly up to a year?"

Patrick's eyes grow dark with anger. "Don't tell me the all-powerful Eleanora Molinaro you were going on about so enthusiastically when you were convincing me of this half-baked scheme can't make a little inadvertent marriage disappear."

"Could you hold it down?" Will whispers. "Or do you want someone to hear?"

"Oooh, right, the Molinaro spies. Might have the place bugged. Guess I shouldn't yell then? *I'm not your toy, Will. I want a divorce and I want one now,*" Patrick hollers.

Will glares, raising his own voice. "Don't be so dramatic, baby!" He stares Patrick down, daring him to say something else. "You know I love you more than life!"

Patrick stares daggers at him. "Who do you think you're fooling, Will? The bellhops? The maids?" He wipes a hand across his face and stands. "You know, no. I can't believe I've let your paranoia and insanity drag me across the country into this hornet's nest of absurdity and—"

He rants on, but Will's not paying attention anymore, because Patrick's tossing his new clothes onto the bed and getting out his suitcase.

"Wait." Will gets up and puts his hands on Patrick's arms. "Wait, don't."

Patrick throws a shirt into the bag and sighs. "What do you want from me? I gave your plan a chance, but there is no way in hell I'm going to hang around this town for a *year*. Not when I could be at the

Mayo Clinic or Cedars-Sinai or Vandy. Not when I can be honing my skills and expanding my practice. I am *not* small-town material, Will. I'm the big-time. I have absolutely no desire to play your loving spouse indefinitely and if your grandmother can't get us out of this mess? Well, I sure as hell can."

"Look. I know you can. I just need you—no, no, stop that. You're not going anywhere." Will pushes Patrick, trying to move him away from the bags.

Patrick lurches toward him, gripping his forearms and shoving him back with surprising strength. "I've been *pushed around* enough in my life, Will. Now, if you'll excuse me. I'm going to take care of this my way."

Will breathes in hard. Terror and attraction jolts through him at once. He swallows and backs away from Patrick, his hands shaking and his throat dry.

Patrick picks up his suitcase and heads for the door, and as he opens it, Will tries to block him.

"Really? It's come to this? Holding me against my will?"

Will pushes the barely open door shut with a hard slam. "I don't know what you're talking about, Patrick. This is just our first lover's spat. That's all. The first of many to come in our long, wonderfully happy marriage."

Patrick stares at him like he's kind of impressed by this level of insanity. "Good God, you're drinking your own Kool-Aid."

"Yeah, well, it's a very, very expensive drink."

"You think you're so clever don't you?"

Will shrugs. "I think I don't know what else to do."

Patrick studies him for a moment and then eases his suitcase down to the floor. Will's not sure what makes Patrick change his mind about walking out, but he steps away and throws his suitcase back on the chair by the bed. He stands with one hand jiggling by his leg and stares at Will.

Will takes a deep breath. "It won't take a year. I promise. A month? A few months, tops?"

"And I should believe you because?"

"Because I don't want to be married to you any more than you want to be married to me."

"Right. Because of your boyfriend. *Ryan.* The noble asshole who dumps you over the phone while you're in a bar, knowing full well you're an alcoholic, alone in a city with no support system—"

"Just leave Ryan out of this." It's a reflexive defense. "You don't know him at all."

"Somehow I feel like I know him better than you do, Will." Patrick rolls his eyes, waves his hands dismissively, and says, "Never mind. Forget I brought it up. A month. Maybe a whole year of this, you, this *town.*" Patrick shudders. He sits at the table, opens his briefcase and pulls out his laptop. He snaps it open. "Excuse me while I look at pictures of cancer-stricken kids."

"What?"

"To inspire me to stay the course of this stupid plan."

Will's still standing by the door, half blocking it. Deep down he expects Patrick to make another run at it. Patrick clicks away at the keyboard, and then turns his laptop around for Will to see. There's a full-screen photo of a bald, sick little girl in a hospital bed.

Patrick makes a fake crying face complete with fake sniffles. "So brave. She's such a hero," he says with a put-on quaver.

Will stares at him, incredulity rearing up inside him.

The moments tick by and Patrick pulls up a second photo, this time of an infant attached to wires. "Boo hoo. Sick baby."

Will blinks wildly at him.

Patrick rolls his eyes and then clicks around some more on the computer but doesn't show Will what he's looking at. As the minutes tick by, Will's muscles unclench one by one. God, he's so exhausted. So damn tired.

He sinks onto the sofa and listens to the tapping of Patrick's fingers on the keyboard, wondering if Patrick's going to try to escape again. He snorts softly at the thought. Escape. Like he's a prisoner.

But he is. They both are.

Slowly, he shifts down until he's mostly supine, a pillow under his head, and the room sways gently with his exhaustion.

He just wants to be back at the apartment he shares with Ryan—correction, *shared* with Ryan. He wants to curl up on their couch with his head on Ryan's shoulder and their fingers intertwined. Who cares that they've haven't cuddled like that in a very long time? Ryan is everything that Will's ever known, and the best he could ever hope to get, and now…?

Will squeezes his eyes shut because he's *not* going to cry about this again. He remembers Ryan and Hartley together in the coffee shop, hearing Ryan's words and *knowing* that he's been played for an even bigger fool. And Hartley. Seeing Hartley's hands on Ryan's body, his tender, satisfied expression, and listening to the crap he's feeding Ryan like some puppy he's going to nurse back to health?

Will grits his teeth.

A moment later the sofa dips and Will looks up. Patrick's kneeling on the floor next to him, elbows on the edge of the sofa, and eyebrows drawn together in something that might be worry.

"Look, how can I put this so you'll understand? You've been more stressed out than usual the last few days, which can mess with how you metabolize food, and I don't want to have to deal with your corpse, okay? I face off with death every day in my job, and I don't want it invading the confines of my fake happy marriage." Despite his words, Patrick sounds surprisingly gentle.

"It's not that. If I thought I needed insulin or food, I'd be the first to admit it."

"Oh, really? Because there was this guy on the airplane with me yesterday moping about how he didn't know if anything was 'worth it' anymore."

Will flushes at Patrick mocking his moment of weakness. "You don't have to worry."

"Who said anything about worry? You could keel over anytime and I'd be a free man. It's the mess of it that gets to me. And the Molinaros. If they're this whack about you being happy in your marriage, I don't want to know what they'd do to the husband that let you die on his watch and, I suppose, since there was no pre-nup, inherited your vast fortune. Then again, just think of all the gamma knives I could buy with all your pretty money."

Will stares at Patrick.

"Oh." Patrick lifts a brow. "You're only just now thinking of that? You should be thanking your lucky stars I'm a respectable man. After all, I'm a doctor. I own scalpels and have access to poisons. I wield power over life and death."

Will's nearly completely sure Patrick's screwing with him, but a fine sweat breaks on his forehead. Patrick cracks a smile. "Your face, Will. Don't ever play poker. You'll lose."

Will swallows. "You play? Poker?"

"Nope. Prefer chess. You?"

"Both. I'm pretty good, actually. At chess. Not poker."

"Yeah, I believe that. Okay, so out with it. You're keeping something back from me. If it's about your visit with Granny, I have a right to know."

Will sits up and runs a hand through his hair. He pats the sofa next to him and Patrick moves up into the spot. "It's not that. I ran into Ryan."

"It's a small town. Bound to happen."

Will exhales noisily. "He was with Hartley."

Patrick nods.

"God, Ryan's such a dick."

"Yup."

"You don't know him."

"I'm just agreeing with my husband."

Will laughs bitterly. "Yeah. Okay." He rubs a hand in his hair. "I guess when Ryan told me he needed space, he just meant space from me. They were practically fused together."

"I'm glad they weren't literally fused together. That can be messy."

Will snorts. "Well, from what I overheard, they may have been literally fused last night. Though Ryan doesn't like to…" He pauses, not sure if it's okay to reveal this information about his ex. "He doesn't enjoy penetration. Either way."

"To each his own."

"Right. It doesn't matter. But they're together and have been intimate in some way. I heard enough to know that. And it had been ages since Ryan even held my hand."

"Ouch. It's like the hits just keep on coming, don't they? Makes you wonder what you did to deserve it."

"Are you saying I *deserve* to be unhappy, Patrick?" Will asks, a weird mix of emotions rocking through him. It's not like he doesn't think it's true. It just hurts to hear someone besides Ryan actually have the nerve to say it.

Patrick shifts a little and doesn't meet his eye for a moment. "I'm an asshole, Will. You haven't taken anything I've said seriously for our entire two days of marriage, and *now* you're going to start?"

Will can tell Patrick wishes he could take it back. He doesn't know how he knows, but he does. Something about the way Patrick holds his shoulders and rubs his hand over his nose.

"I'm *saying* I don't like being held hostage," Patrick mutters.

But they aren't even talking about that at all. He thinks this is Patrick's form of an apology, stunted as it is. "So, what? You're saying you said that because you're *grumpy*? Or because you're just plain mean?"

"Take your pick, Will. I don't do heart to hearts."

"Could've fooled me. Ever since we woke up together, all you've done is talk about your *feelings*. How you don't *like* this situation, or me, or this hotel, or the town, and how you're *hungry*, and tired, and angry. You're just a big ball of seething emotions. And all you do is talk about them. You know what you need, don't you?"

"A divorce."

"No. A chill pill." Patrick looks at him like he's an idiot. Will doesn't care. "A chill pill, or a *nap*. Little Paddy's tired and being a jerk again. Time for his nappy-wappy."

"Little Paddy? Nappy-wappy? That's the best you could come up with?"

"Maybe I need a nap too. Sorry if I don't have my best material."

Patrick makes a face but doesn't say anything for a few minutes. He gets up and grabs two water bottles. Will's just reclining on the sofa again when Patrick forces him back up by acting like he's going to sit on Will's head. Will sighs as Patrick kicks his feet up on the table across from the sofa. Their shoulders brush together, and he hates the tingle that shoots through him.

"So, Ryan's banging this Hartley kid." Patrick hands Will one of the bottles, indicating with his head that he should drink it. "Why? Is he hot? It can't be that. *You're* hot. And you've got money too. Does this Hartley have money?"

"No. He lives out on the rez. His family's not quite at poverty level, but they're not well-to-do by far." The water is cool and calming going down.

"Okay, so it's not an ambition thing. You said this guy is younger than Ryan, right? And you're younger than Ryan too?"

"Yeah, but not by much."

"Maybe it's a power thing for him. Ego."

"Really? You want to play therapist now?"

"I'm bored." Patrick shrugs.

"There's a TV and a computer."

"Everything on the TV is mind-numbing and, as far as the internet goes, frankly, I'm all porned out."

Will wrinkles his nose. "Gross."

"So, go on. What happened?"

"Well…" Ah, hell. He might as well tell him. Like it or not, they're in this thing together. "I uh, did something kind of stupid."

"Well, you're on a roll for stupid. Hate to break the streak." Patrick takes a drink of his water, his long throat bobbing with each swallow.

Will ignores how that makes his heart skip and goes on. "I told them about you." His stomach churns like someone poured battery acid into it and then stuffed a toilet plunger down his throat. "I said I was in love with you, that you're my husband, and that we're very happy together."

Patrick frowned. "And? Why is that stupid? I thought that was the plan."

"It was! But when I saw them together like that, I—I don't know. I just lost my temper. I told them that you're *crazy* in love with me, that you're the *love of my life*, and that I'm *ecstatic* to be married to you. I sounded insane."

There's a flash of something soft in Patrick's eyes, but it's gone a moment later. "That's probably a good thing."

"Excuse me? We're back to you insulting me now?"

"No. What you told him. About us being in love. It's a good thing."

"Well, I don't know about that, because I don't think he believed me. I mean, he clearly thought I was drunk or high or plain crazy." Will pulls his hair with both hands. "I mean, God! Could I mess this up any more?"

"Sure you could. Probably without even trying."

"You know what? Never mind. I don't want to be your entertainment." He picks up the sofa cushion. "Get off my bed. I'm going to take a nap."

Patrick stands up, stretches, and lets his arms drop to his side. "Well, like I said, it's probably all good. It fits our plan perfectly."

Will avoids looking at him. He hits the cushion a few times and settles onto his side, closing his eyes, determined to sleep for a few hours before he really, truly has to face his mom.

Patrick keeps talking. "Stop fretting, puddin'-pop. Once this mess is cleared up, you'll win your man back. Not that you should want him, but to each their own."

Will remains quiet.

"Happy with that plan?"

"Yeah," Will says dryly. "I'm ecstatic."

"Good." Bed sheets rustle. "Because I've heard unhappy jailers are the worst, and you're bad enough as it is."

THERE'S A CELL phone ringing out of control. Will jerks up on the sofa, rubbing his aching neck, when something hard hits him in the shoulder.

"Yours," Patrick says, his voice crusted with sleep. "Make it stop."

Will yawns, rubbing the sleep from his eyes. He glances at the clock on the microwave by the mini-bar. It's almost five in the afternoon. *Crap.* He checks the caller ID on his phone and cringes. He isn't surprised. Someone's told her by now. *And,* even if they haven't, it's been almost three days since he last called her, which is kind of a record. Still, he doesn't want to answer. It goes to voicemail, only to start ringing again moments later.

"Make it stop," Patrick growls from the bed.

Will shoots him a look, but Patrick's got his head buried under a pillow. He looks awfully cozy in that big bed. His long, sinewy back is on display, jolting memories of those muscles playing under Will's hands as Patrick had thrust into him only two nights before.

The phone goes to voicemail. Immediately, it rings again. With a deep breath, he swipes the screen.

"Hey, Mom."

"William Patterson, what have you done?"

Will & Patrick

EPISODE TWO

Meet the Family

BY

Leta Blake & Alice Griffiths

About This Book

Follow Will & Patrick as they cope with the fallout from their Vegas wedding in this second instalment of the romantic-comedy serial, Wake Up Married, *by best-selling author Leta Blake and newcomer Alice Griffiths!*

Meeting the family is challenging for every new couple. But for Will and Patrick, the awkward family moments only grow more hilarious—and painful—when they must hide the truth of their predicament from the people they care about most.

Throw in the sexual tension flaring between them, uncomfortable run ins with Will's all-too-recent ex-boyfriend, an overprotective mobster father, and a mafia spy tailing them around Healing, South Dakota, and you've got a recipe for madcap laughs and surprisingly heart-warming feels.

Episode 2 of 6 in the Wake Up Married *serial.*

EPISODE TWO

Chapter Eight

MEETING THE IN-LAWS is something Patrick *never* thought he'd have to do. He'd rather eat yak brains or visit Russia in winter or set himself on fire. Okay, maybe not set himself on fire. But he'd be down with Russian winters or yak brains for sure if it got him out of this.

As Will talks far too loudly to his mother on the phone, Patrick has a sinking sensation that his blissful nap is going to be cut short.

"Uh, what have you heard?" Will asks, scratching behind his ear nervously. "Mom, Mom, calm down. I'm okay." There's a long pause. "Yes. But it's not what you think! Well, it is what you think. I mean, I'm safe. I'm okay. It's nothing like that."

Patrick buries his head under the pillow. Worried mothers are exhausting.

"Ryan? Of course he'd go tattling to you." Another pause. "Mom, my numbers are fine. I'm testing. I'm good. Yes, yes, really. Mom, I can't talk about the details of this over the phone."

Patrick groans. "This is not *The Godfather*," he reminds Will, who shoots him a glare.

"Mom, remember those rules Owen explained to us when I came into the Molinaro inheritance? You know, about the money I used to start Good Works? Well, let's just say that it's a good thing my marriage to Patrick meets *every single one of them* because I got a big congratulatory bouquet from the Molinaro family the next morning."

Rolling onto his back, Patrick sighs. Okay, it was a little bit like *The Godfather.* He hopes Healing's equine population will not be losing their heads.

"Listen, can we talk about this later?" Will asks. "Yeah, okay." He hangs up and squares his shoulders. "Get up. You have to come meet my family."

They ride to Will's mother's house in silence. The seats are heated and the car is toasty warm. Christmas carols play quietly through the speakers. Patrick wonders if he's going to have PTSD from all this trauma. He'll forever have flashbacks to being trapped in this South Dakotan hell every time he hears sleigh bells.

The BMW is a smooth ride, but Patrick can't help but pick at it. "A 6-Series Sedan? Really, Will? Are you *trying* to look less like a trust fund brat? If so, it's not working."

Will says nothing.

Patrick shrugs. "I prefer the 650i, but to each his own."

"I've got two younger sisters and a little brother, okay? Some-times I help out by driving them places. Despite what you may think, my life isn't all fun and games."

Patrick holds his hands up in mock surrender. Will's obviously on edge, and Patrick can't blame him. There's probably nothing quite like the sweaty, nervous feeling of bringing home a stranger you had a lot of filthy sex with and introducing him to your mother as your brand-new husband.

"I could've stayed at the hotel you know."

"No, you couldn't. It would've been suspicious. The Molinaros would wonder why I wasn't proud to show you off." Will's voice is strained.

"What's not to be proud of? I'm brilliant, handsome, amazing in bed, and you're desperately in love with me. So chin up, buckaroo. You got this."

Will snorts. "I wish you were in love with me."

"Excuse me?" His heart seems to stutter in his chest.

"No." Will waves his words off with one hand before gripping the steering wheel again. "I just mean I always imagined this totally differently. I thought if I got married, it'd be to Ryan, or at least to a guy who is as crazy about me as I am about him. Not…not *this*."

Patrick shrugs, thinking that Ryan was never going to fit that bill. "Yeah. Sucks for you."

"I kinda think it sucks for you too, Patrick."

"Not being in love with you? Nah. It's working out great for me so far. It'll make this eventual divorce go a hell of lot easier from what I understand."

"You know what I meant." Will doesn't even crack a smile.

Patrick opens the glove compartment, looks inside, and shuts it with a huff.

"What?"

"There's just an owner's manual in there."

"So. What were you hoping for?" Patrick's stomach rumbles and Will rolls his eyes. "No, let me guess. A tiny delicatessen that serves hot sandwiches and french fries."

Patrick lets the edge of a smile peek through. "A bag of fruit snacks, skittles, life savers, or hell a frosting tube wouldn't be out of the question. Especially with your diabetes."

"I've got an emergency kit in here." Will pats the console between the front seats.

"It's got a glucagon shot?"

"Of course."

"Well, you should keep protein bars in here. Or peanut butter packets. And water. Do you have water? You should have water."

"In the trunk. God, you're bossy."

"I'm also hungry."

"You're a bottomless pit, and I refuse to enable you much longer."

Patrick shrugs. "Like I said, food comforts me. Don't disparage my coping mechanism. You could use some better ones yourself."

Will sends him a sly look. "What, drinking gallons of alcohol to deal with life's upsets doesn't impress you much?"

"No."

"Ah, come on, Dr. McCloud. It didn't seem to bother you the other night. And then there's this little, itty-bitty thing called hypocrisy. It's just screaming there in plain sight. After all, you were drunk too."

Patrick looks over at Will, the setting sun shining on his profile, and admires the wicked twist of his mouth.

"I'm not an alcoholic. You are. Besides, think we both know things are different now than they were two nights ago."

Will hiccups a bitter laugh. "Yeah, we're screwed."

"I'll drink to that."

They pull up a short suburban driveway to a newly built, dark gray clapboard and stone two-story house that's decorated with a red-ribboned wreath on each window and door. There are Christmas lights in the bushes, though they aren't turned on at the moment, and giant Santa and Rudolph inflatables wobbling in the front yard. The house isn't as big as Patrick's expecting, but it's not small either. As they park next to the garage, he says, "So, what do you want me to do?"

"I guess asking you to keep quiet is probably too much."

Patrick shrugs. He doesn't consider himself a particularly chatty person, but things do seem to just come out of his mouth.

"Look, be yourself, okay? I'll take the heat." Will sighs. "Just, please, Patrick, try to keep in mind that this is my mom? You might not care about her opinion at all, but I do. And this is humiliating enough."

Patrick nods. He gets that. He does. There are a couple of people in the world he doesn't want to know a damn thing about this mafia-enforced marriage to Will. People he hates the idea of letting down. And he's being honest when he says he's not into humiliation for fun.

And God help him, he's starting to like Will. Or maybe he's liked him the whole time. Regardless, he doesn't want to shame him. Will's got plenty of shame to deal with on his own.

As they walk up the stone path to the front porch, a truck roars up the road, screeches into the drive, and shudders to a halt next to Will's car. The flustered driver climbs from the cab. Patrick recognizes Kevin Patterson from the pictures *in The Hurting Times* archives.

He's tall, broad, and strong, and his winter coat doesn't obscure his athletic frame. He's maybe ten years older than Patrick's thirty-five, and he's wearing blue jeans and brown boots. It's easy to see he's related to Will. He's good-looking in similar ways: blond hair shining in the sinking rays of the setting autumn sun, illuminating his handsome face. His gray-green eyes flash angrily as he approaches them with hands clenched into fists at his sides.

Patrick comes to the sudden uncomfortable conclusion that he'd happily allow Will's sad, gay uncle to bang him. For hours. And hours. Like whoa. If the situation was entirely different, of course. And if Kevin stops glaring at him like he has plans to murder Patrick immediately, no questions asked, and dump his body deep out on the reservation.

Patrick shifts closer to Will, hoping for some protection if Kevin's fists come flying.

Will shoves his hand into his pockets as his cheeks flush red.

"What the hell is going on, Will?" Kevin asks as the front door of the house slams open.

"William Patterson! Get your butt inside this house right now, young man." Will's mommy's sharp voice carries in the air and everyone jumps to obey her at once.

The house smells like gingerbread and cinnamon. Patrick's stomach gurgles. Will darts a glare his direction as Will's mother leads them through the well-appointed hallway. In the center, near the long staircase, stands a tall, real fir Christmas tree, strewn with color-coordinated balls and blinking, colored lights, and topped with a

Santa-hat wearing horse.

Will's mom is a stunning blond beauty with wide green eyes set into a face that's either aged well or has already enjoyed a surgeon's knife. Like Kevin, she's fit for forty-five. Her long legs are encased in tight blue jeans and she wears a blue silk blouse that shows off her cleavage nicely.

Yes, Patrick decides, Will comes by his looks entirely naturally. Kimberly Patterson is a babe. Or is it Kimberly Molinaro? Will's mommy has had more marriages and divorces than Patrick's had microwave dinners.

The living room she leads them into is spacious, with wide windows and a throw rug that's so plush Patrick would be happy to take a nap on it. The sofa and chairs all match, and there's a table in the corner piled with art supplies and crafts for children. Games and dolls, stuffed animals, and the odd shoe are sorted into bins next to the table. They spill over onto the otherwise immaculate floor.

Patrick turns his attention to Kimberly, who's dragging Will by the arm to stand in front of the brick fireplace. The kids' stockings hang vibrantly behind him. Patrick takes his place at Will's side. As Will's fake husband, it's where he belongs.

Kimberly crosses her arms over her chest and glares at them both. "So this is *Patrick*, is it?" She looks Patrick up and down like he's a murderer.

Patrick gets it. No one initially likes to meet the strange man who shoved his dick up their baby boy's butt until he yelled for Jesus and jizzed buckets. But the hateful glare is still a bit much.

"Dr. McCloud to you," Patrick says.

Will elbows him hard, and Patrick rubs his arm.

"Ignore that. He's—" Will starts, but Kevin interrupts.

"What the *hell* is happening, Will?"

"He's just hungry," Will finishes lamely. He runs a hand through his hair. "Let's all calm down, okay? If you'll both have a seat and take some deep breaths—"

"Don't talk to me about deep breaths, William!" Kimberly cries.

"Mom, calm down. I'm going to tell you everything."

"Damn right you're going to tell us everything." Kevin paces in front of them before whirling to point at Patrick. "Who is this man?"

No one's moving anywhere near the sofa. No one's offering snacks. No one's suggesting refreshments of any sort. They're just standing there glaring at each other. Patrick sighs. He'd hoped for meet-the-son-in-law hors d'oeuvres at the very least. He's heard that's a thing some people do. Somewhere not in Healing, South Dakota apparently.

Kevin speaks first. "There was a stallion delivered to the farm this morning. A top-quality thoroughbred, with a note stating it was a wedding gift for *you*, Will." His jaw tightens. "A gift from Tony and the entire Molinaro family."

"A stallion?" Will turns until he's backlit from the last splash of sunlight, glowing like an angel, despite his mouth hanging open. "What kind of wedding gift is that?"

"He could have at least sent two. One for each of us," Patrick agrees. "Stingy."

Kimberly and Kevin shoot him filthy looks. Patrick shrugs. If they'd just put out some food, he'd be happy to keep his mouth filled. It seems like maybe Will's whole family is stingy.

"Will, this—whatever this is—has gone too far," Kimberly says. "If Tony knows—"

"If Tony knows what?" Kevin interjects. "Is someone going to tell me what the ever-loving heck is going on?"

Patrick presses his lips in a straight line but he can't help himself. It's just too good. "Surprise! I'm married to your nephew!"

The rage in Kevin's eyes when he turns to Patrick makes him suddenly remember that this man more than likely has a shotgun in his truck and knows how to use it.

"Patrick," Will warns.

"Did you just say, you're married to my…?" Kevin asks. "Will, who the hell is this man?"

Will sighs, rubbing a hand over his face like he can scrub the whole problem away. He turns to Patrick. "Mom, Uncle Kevin, this is Patrick McCloud."

"*Doctor* Patrick McCloud," Patrick corrects.

Will rolls his eyes.

Kevin extends his hand automatically at the introduction and Patrick shakes, but Kevin's eyes are still appraising, like he's deciding if he is going to take Patrick apart limb by limb. Or maybe pull him in for a hug. Patrick's not entirely convinced Will's uncle is a bright man.

Kimberly puts her hands on her hips and glowers. "So you're the one who took advantage of my son."

"Mom! It's not like that."

"I still don't understand?" Kevin says.

"Will married this man, Kevin!" Kimberly crosses her arms over her chest in a good imitation of Will when he's angry. "This…this…*doctor.*"

Patrick's never heard the word sound so insulting before.

"If you ask *me*, I'm a damn good catch," Patrick notes.

"No one's asking you, *Dr. McCloud*," Kimberly spits out. She turns back to Kevin. "They met in Las Vegas!" She shakes her head, pacing back and forth in front of the sofa.

"Where in Las Vegas?" Kevin asks.

"At a hotel bar," Patrick adds helpfully. "I *wasn't* working as a waitress, though." He sings the words, "That much is true."

Will shoots Patrick a disbelieving look, his eyebrows sky high.

Patrick can't believe it. No one even cracks a smile. "Come on, you all know that song, right? Who doesn't know that song?"

Will draws a finger across his throat, shaking his head.

"Fine. Whatever. It was a cocktail bar anyway. In the song." Patrick's tried to lighten the mood. If everyone wants to be pissed off, he'll just let them. "I guess what they say about in-laws is true."

Kimberly and Kevin stare at him like he's a talking pile of shit someone's dragged into the living room and they don't know how to get rid of it.

Will motions toward the couch. "How about we all sit down? This explanation could take a while."

And indeed it does.

"So, you see why we can't just get a divorce, right? I can't risk losing Good Works. There's no way I'm letting that money go back to the Molinaros when it can be used to help so many people."

Patrick's amused at the way Will phrases it like it's all up to him. *Will's* not letting the money go back to the Molinaros, as if Patrick doesn't even have a say. Despite Patrick's reputation, he's not heartless, and he'll stick this thing out for a week or two, a month at most. But in the end, he's not going to give up his career for Will's hero number.

Kimberly is next to him on the sofa, with Will on her other side. She smells like a mixture of cut grass and a lush rose perfume. Kevin alternates between sitting in the brown leather armchair and pacing on the rug across from them. He's sexy despite his apparent lack of brains, and occasionally Patrick gets a waft of his horse and hay scent. He can't say it's bad. Now if only there was some food sitting out on the wide, wood coffee table, things would be almost tolerable. At least the couch is comfortable.

"No, of course you can't, baby," Kimberly says. "But you also can't stay married to this…man. How do you know he's not just trying to worm some money out of this situation? Or worse?"

"Or worse?" Patrick asks. "I'm a *neurosurgeon*. I don't need any-one's money."

Kimberly ignores him. "Not to mention, he's so much *older* than you."

"Hey!" Patrick's mostly kept quiet after the song joke fell flat, having too much fun watching Will squirm while summing up their night of debauchery. (He doesn't ever think he'll forget Kimberly's face when Will said, "We—uh—consummated the marriage," and Patrick had jumped in with, "A lot!")

But he's had just about enough of Kimberly Patterson looking at him like he's the scum of the earth. And now she's playing the age card? "I'm not *that* much older than him."

Though he's not actually sure just how old Will is. Old enough for them to be legally married, that's for sure. He's guessing twenty-four? Twenty-five? Okay, so basically ten years younger. It's not like it's cradle robbing. All that much.

"*Mom.*" Will follows his mother's lead by ignoring him entirely. "Patrick's being really good about this. He could have insisted on getting a divorce immediately, but he's very kindly agreed to give me and Nonna some time to try and work our way around this problem. We should be really grateful."

Huh. So his bride's finally hopped on board the gratitude bus. It's about time.

Kimberly eyes Patrick critically. "Well, yes. I suppose we do owe him that much. But I don't know what sort of man, let alone *doctor*, would let you drink so much and take advantage of a vulnerable—"

"Mom, Mom, stop!" Will takes hold of her hands. "Patrick had nothing to do with that. I'm an adult and it was my decision to drink, and believe me, I feel really, really ashamed about that."

"Oh, honey." Kimberly squeezes Will's hands before letting them go and reaching up to touch his cheek.

"And he didn't take advantage of me either," Will says, catching Patrick's eye. "I—I wanted it to happen."

Patrick stares at Will for a long moment, his lips curling up at the edges in a slight smile. "We both wanted it to happen."

Will takes a deep breath and faces his mom again. "I'm the one to blame here, not Patrick. And I *will* get this mess sorted out. Nonna's already making calls."

"How long do you think it will take?" Kevin asks.

"Not long, hopefully," Will answers.

"Will, there's something else you should consider. The stallion Tony sent came with a note." Kevin stops pacing and thrusts a small envelope toward Will. It's made of a thick paper and has an already broken, old-fashioned wax seal on it.

Will takes the envelope and pulls out a small, vanilla-colored sheet of paper. Patrick wants to roll his eyes over the melodrama of it all. But then Will clears his throat, grows pale, and passes the note to Patrick.

The script is masculine but elaborate.

Congratulations, my dearest Guglielmo. I hope your marriage is long and prosperous, and that you love your new husband with the same fierce devotion that I have always felt for your mother. (Even if she never felt the same devotion for me.)

The stallion is sent as a symbol of masculine strength and beauty, much like your handsome doctor. As much as I failed you when I left you behind with your mother, I intend to support you now. Your happiness means the world to me, son. No other thing in life could mean as much. So long as your new husband takes good care of you, he has my blessing.

<u>However</u>, if he does not care for you as you deserve, well…let's just say that a surgeon is not much good without his hands.

Enjoy the honeymoon suite at the Tallgrass, son. I've heard the Jacuzzi tub is sumptuous. Use it well.

Your father,
Tony Molinaro

It's the single creepiest thing Patrick has ever seen. And he's a doctor, so he's seen some freaky shit. Patrick isn't sure what's more disconcerting, though, the not-so vague threat to his hands, or Daddy sanctioning sexy hot tub times between his son and new husband. The combination of both has Patrick itching to call the whole thing quits and get his hands far, far away from Will and his whole family.

Kimberly takes the note from Patrick, reads it over and gasps a little indignantly, but not with nearly as much horror as Patrick thinks she should. When she hands it back, Patrick reads the note again. His chest is tight. His heart races. The doors and windows out of this ridiculous situation are being systematically blocked, one by one.

He must look as panicked as he feels, because Will says, "Patrick, it's not as bad as you think."

"Oh? How bad do you think it is? Are you a situational diagnostician? Are we at red alert? Threat Level: Hand Loss?"

"Patrick," Will soothes like he's trying to calm a child. Patrick doesn't like it. "You're the one who's been reminding me this isn't *The Godfather*."

"Sorry. My bad. Clearly this situation has been written by the idiot who dreamed up part three, because this…this is ludicrous. Did your father just threaten my *hands*, or am I having a very bad flashback to an LSD trip I've never been on?"

"Tony's a little overprotective," Will says. "But this note is good, actually."

"Good? This note is good?"

"Will, you know your father's a criminal." Kevin shakes his head. "If he's involved in this, we need to go to the police."

"Finally, someone who actually talks sense," Patrick says. Though he's conflicted about agreeing with Kevin after pegging him as pretty simple.

"No!" Will exclaims. "Mom, you agree with me, don't you? If Tony sent this note—and the seal has the Molinaro imprint, so I believe that he did—then he currently believes we're happily married. That's good, right? Good for Good Works and good for—"

"My hands," Patrick finishes, waggling the appendages in question. "Okay, I give you that, but what happens when we finagle this divorce? Will your father be coming to chop my fingers off one by one for breaking your heart? No. No, thank you. I'd rather speak to the police about these threats now."

It suddenly occurs to Patrick that the likelihood of the force in Healing being competent is slim to none. And given that Tony Molinaro is running around gifting horses (complete with heads, at least) and sending creepy notes instead of already residing behind bars shows that Tony is very good at being bad.

"I'd never let that happen." Reassurance lights Will's eyes. "Your fingers are far too skilled to let any harm come to them." He suddenly blushes and coughs. "As a surgeon. I mean. Of course. I'm assuming. So you've said."

Patrick lifts his brows.

"God, kill me now," Will says so softly that Patrick's not sure Kimberly and Kevin hear him.

"So, you're just going to walk around married to him." Kimberly stands next to Kevin, gesturing at Patrick like he's an inanimate object.

"Yes," Will says. "Until Nonna can find a way out of this."

Patrick lifts his hands. "Hold up."

Will, Kimberly, and Kevin all look like they're indulging him by letting him speak.

"If your happiness means the world to your father, wouldn't *he* be willing to help you out? It sounds like he's made his share of poor decisions, like, I don't know, marrying your mom here." Patrick's gratified that Kimberly makes a noise of offense. "Sounds like he's the kind of man who can understand that a stupid choice made in the heat of the moment can lead to a big, sloppy mess, or, say…to *you* being born. This can't be all that different."

"Patrick, are you saying it was a mistake that I was ever born?" Will sounds resigned in a way, and not nearly appalled enough for Patrick's liking.

"I'm saying maybe your father, creepy though he is, can get us the hell out of this mess a lot faster than Granny."

"No!" Kevin and Kimberly say at once.

"You can't trust Tony," Kevin insists. "The only person Tony cares about is himself."

Patrick holds up the letter and reads aloud, "*Your happiness means the world to me, son. No other thing in life could mean as much.* Sounds like he cares a lot about Will."

Will says seriously, "I promise that contacting Tony is the *last* thing we want to do. It isn't safe. Not for you. Not even for me."

Patrick nods slowly. Will's face is so honest that Patrick can only believe him.

Will claps his hands against his thighs. "Well, now we wait to see what Nonna can turn up. And in the meantime, Patrick and I will pretend to be happily married. No one else can know the truth. Not Caitlin, or Olivia, or Connor." Will swallows. "And as hard as this is for me, it's really important, Mom, okay? Ryan can't know either."

"Will, honey, what's he going to think?" Kimberly asks.

"What he already thinks. An approximation of the truth. That I got drunk and married a stranger in Vegas."

Patrick feels marginally insulted, though he doesn't know why.

"No matter what I do or say, that's what Ryan will believe. And even though Patrick and I will have to act like we're in love, I don't think Ryan will ever fall for it. Even if he thinks he knows the truth, it's just too risky to actually tell him." He glances at Patrick and then motions to the note still clutched in Patrick's hand. "Especially now. I can't have Patrick getting hurt when he's doing such a huge favor for me. For all of us."

"This threat from Tony," Kevin says. "How serious do you think he is?"

Will shrugs. "I think so long as Tony believes I'm happy, there's nothing to worry about."

"Are you insane?" Patrick asks. "Oh, wait, you *are* insane. All of you are."

Will sighs. "Fine. Do you have a better idea, Patrick? If you do, let's hear it."

Patrick's mouth opens and closes as he looks up at the ceiling. If he walks away now, Will loses Good Works, cancer kids lose funding, LGBT youths commit suicide, Healing loses its new hospital, and Patrick could lose his hands. "Don't think I'm not clear on how your father's threat works in your favor," he mutters.

Will is deadly serious. "Patrick, I never wanted this to happen. Any of it. I'm sorry you're stuck in the middle."

Patrick rubs at his nose and leans forward to rest his elbows on his knees. "Fine. Now what?"

"The same plan as before. We'll pretend that we're in love, and we'll figure this out. I promise."

Kimberly says, "I'll set up a guest room for Patrick to stay in."

"No, Mom. That would be suspicious. What newlywed couple is going to want to live with their mother? We need to act like…" Will clears his throat. "We're just going to stick with the Tallgrass. It's what the hotel is for, after all: mid-to-long-term living for doctors."

"Baby, are you sure? I feel like you'd be safer here at home." Kimberly looks only at Will. Patrick knows she's referring to *him* as the potential threat at hand, and not the Molinaro family. He rolls his eyes.

"It's okay, Mom. The Tallgrass is great. Perfect, really."

"Who's going to make sure you're testing and taking care of yourself?"

"I can take care of myself, Mom."

"The hell you can! Look at what's already happened without Ryan around to take care of you!"

"Mom, stop. I am a grown man and I will deal with my illness just fine."

Kimberly turns to Patrick, eyes blazing. "If anything happens to him, I will hold you entirely responsible."

"Mom, back off. Patrick and I are going to go now, but first I need to grab some stuff. I only have the bag I packed for Vegas and I'm out of clean clothes already."

"Fine. Go on up to your old room. Ryan dropped off your things from the apartment."

Will smiles sadly.

"We need to talk about what happened with Ryan too, Will," Kimberly says, a hint of disapproval and blame leaking into her voice.

Patrick's really not sure how that's any of her business, but Will doesn't seem to agree.

"I know." Will blows out a long breath. "Just—just not today, okay?" He stands and asks Patrick, "Come help?"

Patrick's eager to get away from Kimberly's narrowed eyes and pursed lips, so he follows Will. As he goes, Kevin stares at him like he might use that shotgun after all.

Upstairs, Patrick wanders around Will's childhood bedroom. He takes his time checking it out while Will goes through some boxes and bags sitting in a neat pile by the bed. Will's picking out shirts, pants, jeans, and pajamas, adding them to the suitcase he pulls out of the otherwise empty closet. It's dark outside now, and Patrick admires the reflection of Will's ass in the window as Will bends over.

There are some trophies on a shelf from high school chess team competitions: regional champions once, state champions twice. On the table beside the bed, there's a posed photo of Will and some tall, thickly muscled guy with dark hair and blue eyes. Their arms are around each other and they're smiling.

Patrick can only assume the guy's Ryan. He starts to make a snide comment about the hours Mr. Asshole must put into his workouts to have ripped arms like that, but Will picks up the last box, curses under his breath, and dumps all of its contents on his bed. He runs his hands through his hair, staring at the jumble of T-shirts, boxer shorts, DVDs, and deodorant.

"Great. It's not here. Hartley's probably sleeping in it now."

"Problem?"

"No."

Patrick watches a little breathlessly as Will pulls a green T-shirt out of the pile on the bed, sets it aside, and then stuffs all the other junk back into the box. Will's flushed face and tense body, almost quivering with rage, reminds Patrick of a pent-up thoroughbred. He needs to be exercised and put through his paces to work off that anger. And Patrick knows exactly how hard and long to ride Will to wear him out and leave him sated.

Patrick hisses between his teeth. Maybe he should have quickly rubbed one out after his nap.

"What?"

"Nothing. Just hungry."

"I'll feed you soon, okay? You're a lot more expensive than a puppy." Then almost to himself, he whispers, "I should have gotten a puppy. Why didn't I just get a puppy?"

Determined not to pop full-on wood, Patrick turns his attention back to examining Will's room. There's a pin board over the desk. It's got a single photo of Will back in what Patrick guesses is his high school days tacked to the upper left side. In it, Will's a lot heavier, with dark circles under his eyes and pudgy cheeks. He's wearing a short-sleeved plaid shirt with a front pocket and a pair of loose-fitting jeans that make him look even more overweight. Patrick tilts his head, considering the picture.

"Nice pocket protector."

Will glances up from the clothing he's sorting. "I'm really *not* in the mood right now."

"Oh lighten up, Will."

"I don't need you picking on me."

"Who said I was picking on you? I was a nerd too. Massive science geek."

Will considers him. "I bet you not only wore a pocket protector but had a favorite protractor too."

"Starrett 509 series," Patrick admits.

Will's lips tug up in a half smile at that. "I preferred the General Tools 318."

"Nice."

Will tosses some white boxers into a second suitcase. "Was high school bad for you too?"

"Yeah." Patrick taps his fingers against his thigh.

"Because of the gay thing?"

"Because of that, yeah, and because of my dad." A swell of jittery memories floods him. His dad's beery breath. His glossy eyes. Patrick hates thinking about that time. He's invested a lot of effort in simply *not*. He turns back to the picture of Will.

"Were you bullied?" Will asks.

"At home? Yes. At school? Ha, *no*." Patrick's a little surprised by how forcefully it comes out. "Not at school."

"You were bullied at home?"

Patrick takes down the old photo. "Why do you keep this up on the board?"

"You're not answering my question."

"I know."

Will gazes at him a long moment. "Ryan says I need a reminder of how I used to be so I don't ever let myself become that guy again. He kept another one on the bathroom mirror at our apartment."

Patrick blinks at Will, trying to process what he's just heard. "That doesn't sound like a standard AA motivational technique."

Will shrugs. "Some people use it. Ryan keeps a picture of himself in his sock drawer. A frat brother took it of him passed out in his own vomit. It's to remind him how far he can fall."

"Why does he get to keep his in the sock drawer and yours are out where everyone can see them?"

Will shrugs again. "I need a more regular reminder I guess. It's to help motivate me to work out too. I work out almost every day." He takes the photo from Patrick's hands and tosses it on top of the clothes in the suitcase he's packing. "I should take this, I guess."

Patrick plucks it out again. Will tries to grab it back and there's a small scuffle until Patrick shoves the picture down his pants. "If you want to grope my junk to get it back, feel free."

Will's eyes fly wide. "Why?"

"I don't want it in our hotel room. I don't want it anywhere near you. It's trash."

"That's my history. That's who I was; who I used to be."

"And if that's a fond memory for you, I'd say bring it along. But it's bullshit that you need to shame yourself into being a good man. You *are* a good man. Chubby or not."

Patrick hears his own words and feels a little itchy. What is it about Will Patterson that brings out the inspirational speeches in him? "I'd have screwed you," he adds, just to make it less awkward.

Will shakes his head and turns away from him. "Fine. Whatever." He tosses some deodorant and a bottle of hair goop into the suitcase. He goes still after a moment, and then looks up at Patrick, his eyes uncertain. "Do you mean that? Really?"

"What?"

"What you just said." Will sounds vaguely annoyed, but also hopeful.

"I'd have banged teen-angel Will so hard he wouldn't have walked straight for a week."

Will's cheeks flush. "I meant about me being a good man."

Patrick shrugs. "Yeah. Probably. What do I know?"

Will looks down, and Patrick feels sick as the light of hope goes out in his eyes. "Of course I mean it, dumbass. You're a freaking angel of light to cancer-stricken kids and LGBTQ youth and abused animals. You're so good it's kinda gross." Patrick's fingers are twitching against his leg hard. "I like it. I like *you*. Okay?"

Will's smile is shy. "That's all Good Works. Not me."

"It's enough you." Patrick turns to the ensuite bathroom. "It's all your idea, isn't it? To use the money this way? Now, if you'll excuse me. I'm going to get this itchy picture of your cherubic baby face out of my pants."

The bathroom is small but clean, and Patrick fishes the picture of chubby, nerdy Will out of his underwear. It's wrinkled and torn at one edge. Patrick thinks about finishing the job and ripping Will's photographic version of a hair shirt into pieces. But something about the warm brown eyes staring up at him prevents him from doing that. He carefully folds the picture in half and puts it in his wallet. He doesn't let himself think too hard about why.

When he exits the bathroom, Will's still on a trip down memory lane. "Did you have a boyfriend in high school? Were you out?"

Patrick scoffs. Even if he hadn't been a string bean of kid, a late bloomer of the worst sort, he wouldn't have had time for a boyfriend. Not between his studies and his father's endless demands.

Memories flood in: nights spent at dingy bars he had no business at, playing requested songs for money. His dad drinking Patrick's earnings right out of the glass fishbowl put on the back of the old uprights for tips. Cleaning beery vomit from the rug, the sofa, and once from the keys of the piano in the living room. He remembers middle C never functioned after that, sticking down whenever struck.

Stuck. Forever.

No, his life in high school had been about so much more urgent things than boys.

Will repeats, "Well, were you? Out?"

"No."

"Why not?"

Patrick isn't going into that. Not here, not now. "You know how it was. Why risk it?"

Will snorts. "Yeah, well, back in high school? The guy I wanted? Wanted cheerleaders. Unless we were both drunk and his dick was in my mouth. Then I was good enough for him."

Patrick sits on the edge of Will's bed, watching as Will tries to close the very full suitcase. "I'm guessing that didn't work out for you."

"You can say that again." Will almost looks like he's going to laugh or smile, but then his face falls. "Seems like it's the story of my life. I make bad choices. Fall for the wrong guy. Things don't work out for me."

Patrick looks down at his watch. "Oh, I'm sorry, but you missed the pity party. Come back on Thursday. We'll be hosting another one then."

Will rolls his eyes. They're silent a few minutes, but as Will's collecting some stuff from his bathroom, he calls out, "So, a science nerd, huh? Big geek? No friends?"

"Pretty much," Patrick calls back.

"Not even one friend?"

"Nope. I was focused on getting the hell out of there and into med school. That was all that mattered to me."

Entering the room again with a new toothbrush in one hand and three bottles of what looks like even more hair gunk in the other, Will says, "That's pretty sad. But your parents must have been proud of you."

"Like I told you, Mom was long dead." Patrick keeps his eyes trained on the bottles of gunk in Will's hands so he can miss the expected expression of pity. "As for my dad, proud isn't really a word I'd use in relation to him."

"Patrick," Will murmurs. "I'm sorry. About your parents."

"Don't be. Nothing you can do about it." Patrick shrugs and stands. He pats his wallet in his back pocket and thinks about the nerdy, younger Will inside it. "It was a long time ago. Now let's go get dinner." *And stop with all the damn feelings.*

Chapter Nine

Patrick's vocal when he's hungry. Will's figured that much out already.

"And would it have been too much to offer a little refreshment after—"

"We'll go to Jimmy's. It's a diner," Will says, cutting off Patrick's rant about the lack of manners amongst the upper crust of Healing: namely Will's mother and uncle. "It's on the way."

Will thinks the meeting with his mom and Uncle Kevin went about as well as can be expected. It'd been humiliating, sure, but in the end they'd been supportive (kind of), which is more than enough. Now, if only Nonna can pull the right Molinaro string sooner rather than later, he can put this behind him and start to rectify his life.

Jimmy's is a traditional American diner on the outskirts of Old Healing. Red awnings cover the doorway and walkway. The large front windows feature lightly flaking window art in a fifties style: freckle-faced kids, business-suited fathers, and lipsticked mothers grinning widely as they eat burgers and milkshakes.

Patrick sniffs the air and groans deeply. "Grease. My favorite." There isn't even a hint of sarcasm.

Will's relieved. He wants to get him fed, head back to the Tallgrass, and hopefully hit the hotel gym before bed. He needs to burn off some of this horrible stress before the hotel bar starts to look more tempting than he can handle.

As they approach the door to Jimmy's, Patrick grins. "What's the best thing on the menu?"

"The onion rings are great. So are the mac 'n' joes."

Patrick wrinkles his nose. "What's a mac 'n' joe?"

"It's like a sloppy joe with bonus macaroni and cheese. If you've never had one, you're in for a treat."

Patrick squeaks, his normally deep voice going all high-pitched with anticipation. "Hurry up then! I can't wait." Patrick throws the door open hard enough that the wreath swings precariously, his eyes shining like a kid on Christmas morning. "My stomach is going to eat itself."

Patrick's kind of cute when he gets all excited about food like this. Maybe if his annoying complaints always pay off with Patrick glowing in anticipation, Will can learn to see them as a kind of foreplay. Uh, if foreplay leads to silence, not sex.

"In, in," Patrick says. "Go on."

Will winks at him, but stops short just inside Jimmy's doorway. Colored Christmas lights blink all around the door closing behind them, blocking off their exit. "Hard Candy Christmas" is playing and Will thinks it's horribly apt. His feet won't budge. He shakes his head. "We have to leave."

"What? No!" Patrick's thin body coils to spring past Will and dart deeper into the diner before Will can drag him out. "Why the hell would we leave?"

"It's Ryan." Will nods toward a table. "With Hartley."

"Oooooh." Gossipy delight drags the single syllable out to four or five. "Is it really?" Patrick's eyes rake over Ryan and Hartley slowly. "Ah. So, Hartley is the sexy twink with the ponytail and your asshole ex is the dumb-but-hunky one."

Patrick thinks Hartley's sexy? God, even his fake husband can't be loyal to him in the face of Hartley's pouty lips and black eyes. Unreal.

There's nowhere to hide. Jimmy's isn't that big and it's currently pretty empty of patrons. Mrs. Wilder and her young twins, Erik and Eiven, sit in the booth nearest to the front window eating burgers.

Andy, the proprietor, is putting together a salad behind the very open and exposed counter, but that's it. No cover.

"Awkward. Oh well," Patrick says, undeterred.

Will's stomach churns. If they can make it unnoticed across the room, they can have one of the four red booths along the wall, but the rest of the room is chrome and vinyl, retro tables and chairs. That's where Ryan and Hartley sit, out in the open, blocking the path to the booth Will's always preferred in the back corner.

"Let's just go," Will hisses, grabbing Patrick's arm, but it's too late. Ryan spots them and, after a fast whisper with Hartley, waves them over.

"Oh look. Someone wants to make nice." Patrick's eyes gleam.

"Oh God," Will mumbles under his breath as he lifts his hand in limp acknowledgement. He swallows thickly. "Remember to act like you love me, all right?"

"How could I forget?" Patrick plasters a creepy fake smile on his face.

"Stop." Will swats his chest with the back of his hand. "You look demented."

"Just trying to look in love," Patrick says through clenched teeth.

"Yeah, well, you're doing it wrong."

They're at Ryan and Hartley's table now, and Will pastes on the most gloriously happy, joyful fake smile he can summon. He wraps his arm around Patrick's slim waist. "Hey, Ryan. Hartley."

"Will," Ryan greets them, sitting forward a little and dislodging Hartley's arm from around his shoulders. "Aren't you going to introduce us?"

Hartley takes a sip of his coffee and eyes Patrick over the rim of the mug. Will resists the urge to reach over and slap his face. "Of course." Will twines his fingers with Patrick's. "Ryan Whitehead, Hartley Kills Enemy, this is Dr. Patrick McCloud. My husband."

Ryan doesn't stand, but holds out his hand, and Patrick pries his fingers loose from Will's desperate grasp to shake it. Patrick shakes

Hartley's hand as well.

Ryan says, "I've read a lot about you, Dr. McCloud."

"You have?" Will asks.

"Of course, I googled him after I found out about your marriage." Ryan frowns. "I was worried about you."

Hartley adds, "No matter what's happened between us, we still care about you, Will."

Will wonders why *he* hasn't googled Patrick yet. He supposes he's probably the only one who hasn't. Eleanora will have done more than a simple web search on Patrick by now. Ryan's clearly done his homework. And if Will knows his mother, she's probably bringing in a private investigator to dig up any dirt, and then calling Eleanora to find out what she's willing to share of her research. But Will? Will hasn't thought of looking into Patrick's background even once. He doesn't know if that makes him stupid or just really damn distracted.

Ryan's eyes dart back and forth between Will and Patrick's left hands, and Will realizes he's looking at their matching rings. *Huh.* Will touches the gold with this thumb, feeling the smooth, warm weight of it, and it occurs to him that at no point, not even before the full impact of their situation had hit them, not even during the initial panic of discovering they were married, had either of them considered taking the rings off.

Ryan's talking again. "From what I saw online, you're an accomplished man, Dr. McCloud. One article described you as a world-class neurosurgeon with his star on the rise—"

"Oh, my star's high in the sky already, thanks," Patrick says. "Brightest one you'll ever see."

Ryan cocks his head, asking genuinely, "So what do you want with Will, I wonder?"

It shouldn't hurt, but it does. Still, Ryan's just looking out for him. He's not really implying that Will's not *good enough* for Patrick. Is he?

"I mean, let's be honest here." Ryan leans forward with a sad, concerned smile on his face. "You were drinking weren't you? Both of you." His worry cracks into irritation, and he mutters, "Drunk and drunker, getting married in a hotel in Vegas."

Hartley grunts a warning and puts his hand on Ryan's back, rubbing gently. "Ryan, don't say anything you're going to regret."

"Why would I regret the truth?" Ryan doesn't look away from Patrick's eyes. "They were both drunk. Do you know how I know? Because Will can't stay sober."

Hartley grips Ryan's shoulder and shakes him gently. "Ryan, just stop. You're being an asshole. It's not a good look on you."

Ryan glances toward Hartley, but he can't seem to help himself. "You don't know him like I do."

"Will, don't listen to Ryan. He's being a dick." Hartley drops his hand from Ryan's back and Ryan shoots him a betrayed glance.

Stomach acid lodges in Will's throat. He's half afraid it's going to come up and he's going to puke all over Ryan and Hartley's shared basket of fries. He tries to get his feet to move, but all he can do is stare helplessly into Ryan's blue eyes and sweat.

Suddenly, Patrick wraps his arm around Will's shoulder, tugging him against his body possessively. "I'm sorry, but were you there, Mr. Whitehead? Somehow I don't remember seeing you at our wedding. Let me assure you, it was *beautiful*—" Patrick waggles his fingers at Ryan. "Lots of shiny confetti falling down, romantic Christmas lights, and flowers everywhere. It was perfect." He cocks his head. "Nor do I recall you being along for the three blissful, painfully erotic, and highly orgasmic nights of our honeymoon so far."

"*Patrick.*" Tears burn in Will's eyes.

"So, I ask again, Mr. Whitehead, what do you think you *know* about our marriage?"

"Nothing," Ryan whispers, pale and shaking a little. "But I know Will. I know he wouldn't have married you sober. And I know he doesn't love you." He swallows and lifts his chin. "And you don't love him. You don't even *know* him." A familiar darkness fills his eyes, and Will sucks in a breath, looking around to see if Mrs. Wilder or Andy is listening. "And if you did? Heh. Well, we won't even go there."

Patrick's arm tightens on Will's shoulders.

"Hey, now." Hartley's eyes flash and he shifts away from Ryan.

"I'm being honest."

"No, you're being cruel. What is it about Will that brings this out in you?" Hartley asks, shaking his head. "You'd never say these things to anyone else."

Will's throat convulses, and he really might vomit on their table.

"Jealousy is never a pretty thing, but it's extra ugly on you," Patrick says. His voice sounds dangerous, like truck wheels spinning in gravel. "Makes your face all—" He waves his hand in Ryan's direction. "Be careful or it might get stuck that way."

Ryan addresses Will. "Listen, we both know what's going on here. I broke up with you. You got drunk. And you married this…this *doctor*—"

Patrick snorts. "What is it with this town? That is *not* an insult."

"You married this guy to get back at me. But Will, this is sick! It's dangerous! You need help!" He puts his hand on Hartley's chair, not seeming to notice Hartley's pissed expression. "And this ploy to hurt me isn't going to work. I'm happy with Hartley."

But Hartley doesn't seem that happy with Ryan at the moment. He stands and throws money from his wallet down on the table.

"Hartley, wait." Ryan grabs hold of his arm, releasing him sheepishly when Hartley lifts a brow. "Don't go." Ryan's head swivels between Hartley, who's buttoning up his thick coat, and Will.

"We hate to cut this short, but Will and I are starving. We had quite an energetic night last night." Patrick tries to steer Will past the table, but Ryan reaches out and grabs his arm.

He spits, "Will, seriously? How can you let him touch you? You don't even *know* him."

"We're married, Ryan," Will says, and it feels like his tongue is numb. He can barely form the words. "I love him. Of course we're sleeping together." He jumps when Patrick pats his ass.

"Don't know how you gave him up, Mr. Whitehead, but I'm grateful you did. Now, if you'll excuse us, we're going to have some dinner. I'm sick of looking at you."

Hartley mutters, "Me too."

"Hartley! Please, wait a second." Ryan grabs hold of his arm again.

Hartley's jaw tightens. "I'm going to get my dad for our meeting." He meets Will's eyes and says with a measured urgency, "We'd like to see you there, Will."

Will shakes his head.

Hartley glances at Patrick before speaking to Will. "And if it turns out you do need help, I know I'm probably the last person you'd ask, but I'd be willing."

"Come on, honey," Patrick says. "A booth in the back is waiting for us."

Will's feet are still glued to the floor, but Patrick tugs him away. Will's stomach aches as Ryan pulls on his coat too, his mouth moving quickly, saying God knows what to Hartley, who tilts his head and listens skeptically.

"Forget them." Patrick grabs him close.

"What are you—"

Patrick's mouth is soft and skilled. Will's head spins and his knees give as he clings to Patrick's shoulders, kissing him back. Heat roars through him. Patrick cups Will's head with his hand, teasing his mouth open.

When Patrick pulls away, he smiles softly, pecking Will's lips one more time before sliding into the booth. Will drops like a rock into the seat opposite and sits in stunned silence while Patrick takes off his coat and starts scanning the laminated menu.

"You said onion rings are good?" Patrick glances up at Will. "What?"

"You—you kissed me." Will resists the urge to bring his fingers up to touch his still wet lips.

Patrick shrugs. "Keeping up appearances."

"Oh."

Patrick goes back to reading the menu.

Will's grateful his back is to Ryan and Hartley. Taking off his coat and settling deeper into the booth, he rubs his face. His insides hurt, sharp and stinging. He wants to go home and cry in his bed. But he can't. Because he doesn't have a home, or a bed. Because he's married to Patrick. And he has to go back to the Tallgrass and act happy and in love. And sleep on the sofa.

A solo piano version of "What Child is This" tinkles over the speakers. He hears Hartley's low voice, calm and reasonable, followed by Ryan's soft pleas. Will shakes his head, staring at the menu he's had memorized since he was ten. He can't believe Ryan's with Hartley at all. Ryan had sworn up and down they were only friends.

"I'm having the burger," Patrick says. "And fries. And the mac 'n' joe. Does it come with a pickle? I'm in the mood for a pickle."

Will stares at Patrick's mouth. That'd been some kiss. He'd enjoyed it. A lot. Not just for petty revenge, either. It'd been a visceral reminder that Ryan never made him feel—physically or emotionally—the way Patrick had during their one night together.

Not ever—not even once.

Shame beats at him until he feels like one big bruise.

PATRICK HAS ALREADY heard all about the life and times of Ryan Whitehead back when Will spilled his guts in the bar in Vegas. Having now met the jackass in person, his initial impression of the guy as an emotionally abusive dickweed has only been reinforced.

Patrick pinches the bridge of his nose between two fingers as he flips over the diner's laminated menu. He hates getting involved in other people's business. His childhood was nothing *but* dealing with another person's business—taking care of his father and cleaning up his drunken messes. He's always vowed to never get mired in someone else's damage again. But look at him now: balls deep in Will's.

He can tell himself he kissed Will just to piss off Ryan or keep their cover for any lurking Molinaros. But the truth is, Will's broken expression as they'd walked away from Ryan had tugged at the part of Patrick that wants to fix things; the part that makes Patrick a doctor. And Patrick did the only thing he could think of. He'd tried to kiss it better.

And then there was the fact of Will's *mouth*.

Patrick's only human. Much as he's loath to admit it. And Will's mouth is a thing of soft, valentine-shaped beauty. It tastes like sex, it's hot like summertime, and it's responsive like piano keys springing up beneath his fingers. It's fair to say Will's mouth makes Patrick's knees go soft and his heartbeat in double time. It could be a registered weapon. And should be, if it's going to lead Patrick into messes like this.

Patrick stares at Jimmy's menu but all he sees are memories of Vegas: Will kneeling between Patrick's legs, hungrily sucking cock. Will, naked and gorgeous, riding Patrick with his head thrown back. Will flushing. Will crying out. Will *coming*.

Patrick's dick pushes against his pants and he grits his teeth, glaring at the laminated menu. Burger, fries, onion rings, mac 'n' joe. A pickle. He needs a pickle. God, does he need a long, thick pickle. Hell, he's so hard he might need to dart into the Jimmy's bathroom to rub one out. He scowls at Will. A man who's put him in such a terrible situation and trapped him in a frozen wasteland in the middle of South Dakota should not be able to do this to him with just his pretty *mouth*.

Patrick shoves aside the menu. "What are you getting?"

Will doesn't answer.

Patrick spies Ryan and Hartley holding hands again as they head toward the door. He doesn't see a happy outcome for that couple, but saying so isn't something he plans to do. Patrick's sure Ryan's got some damage in his past that makes him need to hurt Will, but he's not interested enough to want to know what that is or why, and he never allows even the worst childhood abuse as an excuse. Not for himself. Not for anyone else. As far as Patrick's concerned, Will's lucky to be away from that jackass.

The bell over the door rings as Ryan and Hartley leave. The sound seems to rouse Will out of the shock he's been sitting in for the past few minutes.

"Your boyfriend's an ass," Patrick says casually.

Will blinks, shaking his head a little. "Please, just. Don't."

Patrick shrugs. Fine. If Will wants to mope after a jerk like Ryan, let him.

Their waiter, a forty-something guy with a weird, super-high blond 'fro, walks toward their table. He's smiling cheerfully and wearing Christmas colors head to toe: green jeans, a red shirt with reindeer waltzing with snowmen, and a white apron. There's something about him, though, that makes Patrick squirm in his seat.

"Happy Holidays!"

"You too, Andy," Will murmurs.

"Little Saint Nick" spills through the speakers and Andy's hips move to the beat.

Patrick swallows with a click. A nauseous crash of memories rolls over him.

Mr. Roland. Thirty-five, fuzzy blond hair, and always reeking of pot. The neighbor who liked young guys—who liked *him.* Patrick had only been fifteen when Mr. Roland approached with his wad of fifty dollar bills, asking Patrick if he was sure he didn't want to suck him off in exchange for one of them. "*And I'll pay for more when you're ready,*" Mr. Roland had whispered in the gloom of the hallway, his eyes red-rimmed and glassy.

Will catches his eye, and Patrick clenches his eyes shut hard, shoving the memories back into their box. He wishes he could bury them, or burn them. He wishes he could forget.

"What can I getcha?"

When Patrick opens his eyes, Andy is looking at him, clearly expecting an introduction. But Will says nothing and Patrick doesn't offer one either. He can barely stand to look at this man who reminds him of someone Patrick hopes is long dead.

Will orders first, and Patrick changes his mind about the hamburger when he hears what Will's getting. They both order breakfast for dinner, and Patrick gets the mac 'n' joe too, and a pickle.

Andy whistles. "Mighty big appetite!" He heads back behind the counter to hang up their order for the cooks behind the window.

"Pretty big queer scene for a two-bit town in the middle of nowhere," Patrick says, dragging his eyes away from the counter and its decoration of tiny, phosphorescent Christmas trees. He's determined not to look Andy's way again.

"Huh?" Will's face scrunches up adorably. "What are you talking about?"

Patrick nods toward the counter. "Between him, you, Hartley, and Ryan, and your uncle? There're quite a few gays in the village, wouldn't you say?"

"Andy's not gay."

Patrick glances over at the man again. He's taller than Mr. Roland and thicker too. He's got a rounder face and a fat nose. Maybe there isn't such a resemblance after all. "He's not?"

"No."

"Could've fooled me. Could've fooled a lot of people."

"He's married."

"To a woman?"

"Yes, asshole."

"Is she an idiot?" Patrick's determined to find some fault with

Andy for triggering memories of Mr. Roland with his stupid blond 'fro.

"No? She's an attorney."

"Huh. Why is she dating a waiter? Aren't there any better fish in the sea?"

Will rolls his eyes. "Andy's not a waiter. He's the owner."

"I thought it was Jimmy's?"

Will growls, and Patrick has an instant flashback to Will making that same noise in Vegas. After Patrick had spent several minutes eating Will's ass but refused to put his fingers in, Will had growled, frustrated and horny, *"Finger me, Patrick. Please!"*

Patrick blinks away the memory.

"It is called Jimmy's because it's always been called Jimmy's. For…forever. But Andy Sicko owns it. He bought it from the original Jimmy's son back in the nineties."

"Sicko? Andy Sicko?" *What is with the last names in this town?*

Will nods.

Patrick thinks that, along with resembling Mr. Roland, Andy's name is probably a portent of evil. "What's his sign?"

"Whose? Andy's?"

"Yeah."

"How would I know?" Will wrinkles up his nose. "You can't believe in that stuff. You're a doctor."

Patrick narrows his eyes. Astrology is something Patrick resents sorta-believing in. It's bullshit and unscientific in every single way, and yet he's never met a Sagittarius he likes. Not a single one. And the fact that both his father and Mr. Roland were Sagittarians doesn't make him biased. Much. "Do you know his birthday?"

"June? Yeah, June I think."

Patrick relaxes a little. "Oh. Okay then."

"Anyway, Andy bought this place for more than it was worth after Jimmy's death because his son needed cash to pay for the funeral and estate taxes but was too proud to take donations. Andy's a good guy."

Of course he is. What's with all the do-gooders in this town any-way? Patrick supposes it might make sense in the way that the world often seeks balance, right before it tumbles out of control into chaos and entropy.

Said suspicious do-gooder, the apparently *not*-gay Andy, reappears with their dinner. While Will does his diabetic testing/injection thing, Patrick digs in, moaning in pleasure as he takes his first bite of bacon and eggs. Food can make anything better. Even horrible memories of Mr. Roland. He takes another bite and moans again.

Will gives him a strange look but says nothing, tucking his test kit into his murse and digging into his own food.

After a few minutes of eating in silence as *God Rest Ye Merry Gen-tlemen* pipes in cheerfully from the speakers in the ceiling, Will says, "By the way, I'll take you to Healing Regional tomorrow. I promised you a tour and an introduction to the chief of staff."

Will smiles, and goes shy for a moment. It's not a bad look on him, and the fact that there aren't many bad looks on Will is something Patrick finds very frustrating.

"I hope you like what we've built. We want it to be one of the best neurology units in the country. We've got two neurologists on staff and we were looking for at least three neurosurgeons to come on board. There are two teams of surgical nurses already lined up and they've agreed to start as soon as we have a surgeon. You could be the answer to our prayers."

"Probably not. But don't worry. I'm sure your unit will be just peachy keen with or without me."

They finish their meal, and Andy shows up with the tab. Patrick looks pointedly at Will.

"I paid last time. And the time before that. And every time since we met," Will complains.

"You're loaded. Why should I have to buy my own dinner? Cough it up." Patrick notices that Andy looks appalled.

"Will, is this jerk giving you trouble?"

"This jerk is my husband." Will pushes two twenties into the black leather envelope. "Andy Sicko, Patrick McCloud."

"It's Dr. McCloud, actually. But nice to meet ya, Sicko."

"It's *Andy*, actually," Andy says, looking Patrick up and down. His obvious concern for Will is nothing like Mr. Roland's lecherous gaze, and Patrick feels marginally better about the man. "Will, is this a joke?"

"No, but it's a long story," Will replies.

Patrick shrugs. "Actually, it's not. Met in Vegas. Love at first sight. Married within hours. Happily ever after. The end."

Andy blinks and sputters.

Will smiles weakly. "Yeah, guess it's not such a long story after all."

"But you and Ryan?" Andy frowns and Patrick is happy to realize he really, truly looks almost nothing like Mr. Roland. That's good, because the food is amazing and he hates to think he couldn't come back to enjoy it again. Andy shakes his head, still confused. "I don't understand."

"I doubt that's a new feeling for you," Patrick mutters.

"It's okay. Everything's fine, Andy. I promise." Will stands up quickly and grabs his things, along with Patrick's wrist. "Come on, *honey*, let's go."

Patrick wipes his mouth, throws his napkin on the table, and shrugs on his coat. "Sure thing, *puddin'-pop*."

Andy sputters more, staring at them both.

"Later, Sicko," Patrick calls as Will tugs him out of the diner. "Great mac 'n' joe, by the way."

Chapter Ten

THE MAID SERVICE has visited the room. The wet towels Patrick left on the bed are gone, fresh linens have been added, and there are two Christmas tree-shaped chocolate mints on the pillows. Patrick unwraps and pops them both into his mouth as he flops back onto the mattress.

"Eventful day. We should hit the hay."

"Eat and sleep, eat and sleep. You're not going to fit into this room for long," Will says, dropping his bags on the floor next to the sofa.

"And whose fault is that? I don't normally have time for food, much less naps, but out of the loving kindness of my giant heart—"

"I know, I know. You're awesome. I've heard all about it."

Patrick watches appreciatively as Will bends over to pull some things out of his bag. He remembers the hot, tight clench of Will's asshole, and Will's enthusiasm as he'd gripped Patrick's hips and held him inside.

Will pulls his shirt over his head, revealing the muscles of his broad back. There's a long line down the right side of it, a scratch mark that Patrick must have put there when they were fucking. And when Will turns around, Patrick sees the red hickey underneath his collar bone, right above the soft thatch of chest hair he'd tugged while pounding cries of pleasure out of Will in Vegas.

Patrick presses the heel of his palm against his hard cock and shifts it to a new position, hoping Will won't notice.

Will grabs a loose T-shirt, hiding his skin. He steps out of his pants and into a pair of sweat shorts. "I'm going to head downstairs to the gym. It's open twenty-four-seven and I need to burn off some of this negative energy."

"What am I supposed to do in the meantime?"

"I thought you were going to hit the hay?"

"I changed my mind."

Will rolls his eyes. "You're a big boy, Patrick. Surely you can amuse yourself for an hour?" He looks pointedly at Patrick's flagging erection. "I'm sure there's plenty of porn on the internet just waiting for you to find it." Will gets some fruit snacks and water from the snack bar, snatches ups his murse, and walks out the door. He sticks his head back in and calls, "I'll be back soon, honey! Love you!"

Patrick scowls, but after only a few seconds, he moves to the desk and powers on his laptop. He pulls up his favorite porn sites, but can't really find what he's looking for. "Twink, twink, daddy, hunk, twunk." He sighs and clicks to the next page on the site.

It's sadly lacking in men of Will's height and build. There are literally none with golden chest hair and sweet, innocent faces. He tries covering one guy's head with his hand and just focusing on his strong, pliant body being slammed by a long, thick dick, but his cock isn't fooled. It's horrifying that he can't just jerk off and be done with it.

Maybe it's because he's getting older and he shot his load so many times in Vegas his body still hasn't recovered. He's fairly sure, though, if Will came back all sweaty from his workout, flopped down on the bed, and spread himself open, he'd be up to the task at hand.

He sighs, closes the porn site window and types in the URL for *The Hurting Times*. He may as well see what's being said about him and Will today. After a few clicks, he shakes his head in annoyance. The gossip isn't as flattering as he'd imagined. The descriptions of him vary widely, some calling him a handsome, sexy catch, and others describing him as a kinda-freckled almost-ginger with absolutely no redeeming qualities. He half suspects that the user BobFrApple is actually Ryan and he's just jealous.

Most of the gossips talking about them on *The Hurting Times* speculate that Will fell off the wagon again and married Patrick while drunk out of his mind. It irritates him that they're right. They also suggest that Patrick's in it for the money and that Will obviously didn't have a pre-nup in place.

"That's why he brought him back home," someone going by ElvisCat writes. *"He'll have to give him half of everything if they divorce."*

"Do these people have any idea how much money a neurosurgeon makes? I don't *need* his money."

Another person speculates that Patrick's got some nefarious plan regarding Healing Regional but doesn't offer any details about just what that might be. Others swoon over the romance of "love at first sight" and a Vegas wedding.

"Drunk or not," a user called Dolla$ writes, *"there's nothing quite as juicy eloping with a stranger. So exciting!"* BobFrApple speculates that Patrick's dick is small. *"He's scrawny all over. No meat on his bones. He can't have anything between his legs."*

"Oh yeah, Ryan? I'm packing, okay? Like a mother-truckin' hammer of the gods down there."

He gives up on the gossip pretty quickly, because it's surprisingly boring reading all the nonsense people are making up in lieu of hard facts. He moves over to the sofa and flicks the television on. There's nothing to watch except infomercials and weepy Lifetime movies. He flicks it back off.

Patrick's not used to having to amuse himself or fill time. He hasn't had more than a day off since medical school. He works; it's what he does, and who he is.

Once again he takes a minute to ponder the absurdity of his life. How has he allowed himself to be talked into this situation by a pretty piece of ass? He should be calling Johns Hopkins or Cedars-Sinai, not sitting around playing hotel-husband in Podunk, South Dakota.

Patrick drums his fingers against his leg, his foot tapping staccato against the leg of the coffee table. He considers checking in with Phil and Dinah in Mobile to see how the niblets are doing, and if anyone's in need of anything money can buy. But if it's late on Mountain Time, then it's even later on Central. He sifts through the snacks in the room, but nothing looks appealing. He's still full from Sicko's or Jimmy's or wherever. He could go down for a cup of coffee they keep brewed in the lobby, but he's not a big fan of the brand the Tallgrass serves. And it's pretty late for caffeine. He stares at the walls. He looks at the ceiling.

"Screw this."

WILL'S FOCUS IS on the blinking red light saying he's got another forty-five seconds on the steepest incline. The slap of his feet and whir of the machine has become a hypnotic rhythm. His legs burn. It's amazing how quickly he gets out of shape if he doesn't work out every single day. It feels like he took a month off.

"Hot."

Will jerks and almost stumbles on the treadmill. Patrick's leaning in the doorway to the fitness room, dressed in running shorts and a T-shirt. "Oh my God!" Will's hand goes to his chest and he barely gets his feet righted to prevent a tumble.

"Sorry. Didn't mean to scare you."

"What are you doing here?" Will asks, finding his stride again. "It's almost midnight."

"Same as you. Burning off the bad juju." He strides over to the long bar that runs along a mirror at one side of the room and starts to stretch.

Will stares at Patrick's pert, tight ass as he bends over and presses his nose to his knees. Patrick's flexible. Really flexible. Will knows exactly how bendy Patrick can be. A strangled gurgle escapes.

Patrick turns his head. "You okay?"

"Yeah, just…" He coughs. "I'm out of shape. That's all."

Patrick straightens and kicks his leg up onto the bar, doing another stretch that gives Will a view of his ass. "The hell you are. I've never met a man with more stamina. You nearly wore me out the other night and you were still begging for more." He switches sides and Will's blood rushes south.

In the fluorescent glow of the hotel gym at midnight, with Patrick's ass on display, the idea of sex with him again doesn't seem nearly as shameful as it does in the broad light of day. Arousal tugs in Will's gut and, in his buzzing exhaustion as he runs, the pleasant burn in his muscles warms him. He wants to give in to it.

But he can't.

"Do you work out a lot?" he asks, hoping to shake his thoughts free.

"Yoga, mainly. Some jogging. I run the steps at my apartment for cardio. Since I live on the fifteenth floor, that's an ass-burner."

"Sounds good."

"What do you do?"

"Weights, running, and sometimes I swim. But mainly it's weights."

Patrick waggles his eyebrows. "Gotta keep up the physique."

"I was fat. You saw. I don't want to be fat ever again."

Patrick blows a raspberry. "You were cute. I've already told you: I'd have screwed you no questions asked."

Will rolls his eyes.

"You're supposed to work out for health, not appearance."

"You're a gay man. Get real."

Patrick laughs. "Okay, fine. I admired your build before hitting on you in the bar. And there's a certain allure to a man who's bigger and stronger than me. Especially when he's begging me to fuck him."

Will's dick aches and hardens. "Do you have to do that?"

"What?"

"Bring everything back to sex?"

Patrick crosses over to the pull-up bar on the wall opposite the mirror. "Sex is fun. It's a great way to let off steam. It releases endorphins and, even better, oxytocin. Ever heard of that?"

"Maybe." Will realizes that he's been on the easy stretch of his run for most of the conversation when the machine makes a whirring noise and the incline elevates again. He digs deep for strength and keeps running.

"It's a hormone released during breastfeeding and sex—and some other social activities like hugging." Patrick wrinkles his nose like hugging is exceptionally gross. "Oxytocin is happy juice. It's the cornerstone of civilization, bonding people together, making them more likely to reproduce and pair-bond, which, in turn, makes them less likely to murder one another."

Sweat rolls down Will's back and his half chub isn't going away.

"Here's the thing: sex is what civilization is built on. Sure, maybe some people don't dig it. Asexuals, people in the gray area in between, whatever. That's fine. To each his own. But I speak on authority when I say that *you* love sex and you're good at it. It's a waste of time and pleasure to be ashamed of that."

Will shudders as arousal pulses in his groin and he almost loses step.

Patrick jumps up to grip the pull-up bar, and Will watches him bob his chin against the metal rod ten times before dropping to the floor. Patrick's strong. He's lithe and smaller than Will, but he's got muscles that bunch up when he flexes his arms, and wiry legs that draw Will's gaze when he walks. Will remembers what it's like to touch Patrick and feel his strength. He lets out a long breath.

Will's dick doesn't seem to understand how important it is they *not* fall under the sway of Patrick's physical appeal and persuasively lenient views on sex. It doesn't understand the *risk*. No, Will's cock stays stubbornly full and jolts with each slap of his feet on the treadmill.

Patrick dusts his hands together before twisting from right to left, and then left to right.

"It's not that I'm ashamed," Will says, breathlessly. He's panting now as he battles the treadmill's incline. "I just think there are better things we can discuss. Like getting to know each other."

"I already told you the important things about me and my past. Piano. Neurosurgeon. No besties to party with. No living family. Likes sex. The end."

Will's head tilts. "Piano? You never mentioned anything about piano, actually. Do you play?"

There's part of Will that wishes he could leap off the treadmill, shove Patrick against the wall, and—

Stop. It can't happen. It can never happen.

They aren't really married and casual sex is wrong. Didn't he learn all the painful consequences of not being loyal to one man from watching Roy die? Didn't he see first-hand what comes of sleeping around and having casual sex with strangers? He's just lucky they used condoms in Vegas.

Patrick stares at the wall. "I did. But I haven't in years."

Will's almost forgotten the question, distracted by the lustful heartbeat in his shorts, thudding and rising again. He wipes his face with one of the small white towels the hotel provides and tries to get it together. Piano. Patrick's talking about the piano. "But the piano was important to you? In the past?" Will pushes the down arrow to decrease the incline and speed.

"I guess." He jumps up for the bar again, and Will's asshole squeezes and releases as he hungrily eyes the sinewy strength in his biceps and forearms. Patrick pulls himself up ten more times before dropping to the ground again. "I loved the piano once, but you can grow to hate anything if free will is taken out of the equation." His breath is a little short.

"Your dad forced you to practice, huh?" Will says, laughing. "My little brother Connor takes lessons and he hates my mom for making him practice." *Connor, yes, think about Connor. He's a boner-killer for sure.* Relief washes over him as his arousal retreats. He's got this. He can make it out of this sweaty, pheromone-filled room without compromising his values again. He can jerk off in the shower before bed and everything will be okay.

Patrick rubs his hand over his nose and then shrugs. "Yeah. Too much practice. That's what killed it for me."

Will keeps running, watching Patrick closely. He wishes he could go back and not say anything at all about practice. He wishes he hadn't been so distracted by horniness. Certainty settles in his stomach that he's missed an opportunity to get Patrick to open up, to find out something real about his childhood. Something about the darkness he senses there.

"Were you a good pianist?"

"I was great."

Will chuckles. "Of course you were. The great Dr. McCloud is amazing at everything he tries."

"I suck at people. But I can't say I really *try* not to suck at people." He grins. "So, yeah, I'm awesome at everything I attempt."

"Did you play in competitions? How does that work?"

"No. I played in bars."

Will cocks his head. "How old were you?"

"Pretty young. My father chaperoned." He leans against the rack of weights by the bench press. "I'd come home from school, do my chores, study, and then around ten my dad would take me out. I played until one or two in the morning for tips. It paid the rent. It put food on the table."

"Is that legal?"

"No one cared."

"Did you need to do that? I mean, could your father not find work?"

Patrick shudders slightly and doesn't meet Will's eye. "Gerry was a drunk. Jobs didn't work out for him. Before my mom died he was a music teacher at the high school. After she died—" He scoffs. "Well, let's just say he was a music teacher just for me. Gerry never held a job again. We barely got by on the tips I earned."

Will's erection is one hundred percent under control now. He's not sure what to say so he keeps his mouth shut. He's back on a flatter incline. He doesn't remember the machine moving down or him pushing the buttons to make the run easier.

"You asked earlier about practice." Patrick's voice is tight and his hand is jiggling up a storm at his side. "It's probably not what you think. People in bars don't want to hear Chopin or Beethoven. They don't give a crap about any of that. Even though that's what I loved to play. Gerry drilled me on radio music. He wanted me to be able to play any request at any time. I was trained to memorize a song on first listen and play it back. It wasn't fun. It wasn't even the kind of music I enjoyed most. So, yeah, I got burned out on 'practice.'"

"Is that why you quit?"

Patrick stares at him and his fingers go still against his thigh. "No. I quit because of what he..." He shakes his head hard once.

"Did he abuse you?" Will asks. He hopes it sounds gentle even though he's panting hard now. He wants to stop running and focus solely on Patrick, but he's afraid Patrick will clam up if he does.

Patrick doesn't answer directly. "I never even stood a chance at being a normal kid."

Will leans forward, a tug of horrible fascination pulling him in. He knows what it's like to not be able to really be a kid, to be too old for your age, but there's something more here, something terribly fragile that he can sense under the surface. He wants to reach in, touch it.

"What'd he make you do?"

Patrick looks everywhere but at Will and finally hisses between his teeth, "All that mattered to him was whether or not I brought in enough cash to buy his next bottle."

Hot shame floods Will. "I'm—I'm sorry."

Patrick frowns, annoyance in his sharp gaze. "Why?"

"Because I'm an alcoholic, and I feel like—it's just—hearing that your father hurt you when he drank makes me feel—" Will doesn't know how to explain.

"Well, don't. You aren't him." Patrick rolls his shoulders like he's shaking the whole conversation off. "You couldn't ever be him."

"I could."

"No, believe me, you couldn't."

Will's heading back into another incline and he can't do it. He slows the treadmill. His head pounds and he should test and eat the fruit snacks he brought soon. He's pushed himself hard. There's a sharp edge to Patrick now, and Will's certain that if he asks more questions, Patrick's just going to get rude and maybe loud. But there's more to what Patrick's saying and Will wants to know. He decides to go for something less threatening than what he really wants to ask.

"Do you miss it?" He asks, walking out the cool-down period on the machine. "Playing, I mean?"

Patrick looks at his hands, wriggling his fingers like he's seriously considering the question. "I'm a surgeon. I love what I do. The piano's in my past, and as far as I'm concerned, it can stay that way." He stares at his fingers a few moments longer and drops them to his side. "Get off the treadmill. You're hogging it. If we're going to stay here for months you might want to drop a few dollars on getting another one for this gym, because I'm not so good at sharing."

Will wipes his face and ends his cool down early. He heads over to sit on the bench press and, feeling Patrick's eyes on him as he tests and eats his fruit snacks, a sloppy, hot warmth opens in his chest. If Will can get past the cactus act, he might be able to be friends with Patrick after all.

Chapter Eleven

THE NEXT MORNING, they have a quick breakfast at Jimmy's. Thankfully neither Ryan nor Hartley is there. Sicko is, though. And he gives Patrick the evil eye from the moment they walk in.

"You don't think he'll spit in my food, do you?"

Will glances up from his phone. "Who?"

"Sicky over there."

"Sicky? You mean Andy. His last name's Sicko, and, no, he's a great guy. I told you already."

"He doesn't seem to like me much."

"Maybe because he can sense you're the kind of jerk to call him Sicky."

"I haven't called him that to his face. Yet."

"Right, you just called him Sicko last time like it's an insult and not a perfectly good Austrian name."

"He's Austrian?"

"Yes. Or his great-great grandfather was. I don't really know, Patrick. Does it matter?" Will sighs and goes back to his phone. "I'm trying to go through my work emails."

"Austrian. That explains a lot, actually." Austrians capitulated to Hitler, didn't they? Didn't even put up a fight. He decides maybe he can hate Andy Sicko for racist reasons instead of personal-trigger ones. It feels safer for some reason.

A dark man in a long, black overcoat steps in the door and looks around the joint. His eyes linger on Patrick and Will.

"Be right with you," Sicko calls out and then does a double take.

"Have a seat anywhere!"

Patrick kicks Will under the table.

"Ow!" Will looks up from thumbing at his phone obliviously.

"Do you know that guy? Sicky looked surprised to see him."

Will's brows furrow. "Wasn't he in the coffee shop yesterday?"

Either that or he's the guy's slightly tanner twin. "Yeah. I think so."

Will purses his lips and his eyes dart away when the guy looks toward them. Patrick doesn't, though. He stares into the man's dark, dead eyes and feels his insides shrivel.

"He's one of Tony's isn't he?" Patrick whispers. "One of his enforcers."

"Maybe." Will doesn't look that concerned.

"What's the dealio? I thought you gave a damn about whether or not they think we're happy."

"We *are* happy, honey." Will puts his hand on Patrick's forearm where it rests on the table. "We are so happy." He smiles in a fake, warm way. "But, baby, I have to do some work right now, all right? I still have Good Works to run."

Patrick swallows and looks over at the man who's chosen a table angled with a perfect view of Patrick and Will. "I think I get it, puddin'-pop."

"Good." Will gives him a real warm smile and goes back to his phone. "Just chill out, okay? Everything's going to be fine."

Right. Fine. They're just being tailed by a mafia hit man, but it's all going to be fine.

Will makes a phone call to someone named Owen while Patrick sits and listens. Will agrees that he needs to go to "a meeting." but his mouth twists in a way that makes Patrick think he won't. He admires the sprout of chest hair sticking above Will's top buttons, and takes a moment to appreciate the creamy-colored skin of Will's neck. There's a dark little mole on the side that he's eager to lick again, but knows it won't be anytime soon. Probably never.

Sicko delivers water and orange juice with a smile for Will and a glare for Patrick. He's wearing another monstrosity of a shirt: a long-sleeved faux-Hawaiian one this time with naked women wearing Santa hats on surfboards. Patrick's pretty sure it's sexist.

Sipping the orange juice slowly, Patrick waits for Will to conclude his work. He misses everything about working, even the abominable paperwork associated with his old job. He's a little surprised news hasn't gotten around of his availability and preliminary offers aren't already showing up in his inbox.

Of course, it's barely been three days. He should technically be arriving back from the conference just this afternoon. He wonders what his surgical team is going to think of the news. He wonders who that talentless hack Schaeffer is going to hire to replace him. He wonders if anyone aside from his patients will really care. He hopes Dinah and Phil don't hear the news before he's got a new placement to brag about. He doesn't want them to worry.

"Gotta take a leak," Patrick announces as Will ends his call.

Will nods and is back at his email again. Patrick gives him a perfunctory kiss on the cheek with a glance toward the man in the dark coat. He'd heard the guy order up a plate of meat: bacon, sausage links, and sausage patties. Patrick thinks such a carnivorous man wouldn't think twice about taking off Patrick's fingers. He might even eat them. With maple syrup or ketchup.

Grimacing, he heads toward the restroom and relieves himself in a surprisingly clean toilet.

On his way back, he's ambushed by Andy right next to the table where the dark man plays a game of Bejeweled on his phone. Andy holds a couple of takeout boxes and wears a grave expression.

"Listen to me, buddy." Andy gets all up in Patrick's space. "Will and Buttercup might think you're great, but you can't fool me. I have very good intuition and there's just something about you that's not right."

The dark man looks up from his phone and Patrick's heart horse-kicks against his ribs. "Buttercup?" He focuses on the most incomprehensible part of the moron's little speech.

Sicko narrows his eyes. "Don't act like you don't know who I'm talking about."

"I have no clue, Sicky."

"It's *Sicko*. I mean, Andy. Now think harder."

Patrick sneers. "*Buttercup*—the Power Puff Girl?"

"What's a Power Puff Girl?"

"Hell if I know what you're talking about! Are you mentally ill?"

"Buttercup is Jenny," Andy says, like it's obvious.

Patrick pinches the bridge of his nose. "Jenny? Jenny who?"

"Jenny Burger, you asshole."

Right. The woman with the baby he'd talked to the day before. He wonders what *her* sign is. "Buttercup, huh? Okay, I can see that. Is she a Sagittarius?"

"No, she's a Libra." Andy's face wrinkles in confusion.

Trust him to make friendly-ish with a Libran woman who looks like sunshine and is on a nick-names basis with this naked-girls-on-surfboards-wearing weirdo. Patrick looks over at Will, sitting in a spill of morning sunlight. Trust him to *marry* someone like that too. It's always the shiny ones that bring a man down in the end. He needs to do something about his very obvious type. Like change it. To frowning, dark, and Capricorn.

He glances toward the probably Molinaro man at the table to his right and catches his closely observing eye. He reflexively offers him a grin and the man's lip curls up hostilely in return. Patrick's blood rushes in his ears.

"I'm warning you," Andy says. "If you're not all you claim to be—if you're taking advantage of Will—you'll have to answer to me." Andy narrows his eyes like he thinks he's actually scary, and Patrick's tempted to tell him that next to Molinaro spies, like the one sitting *right there*, he's really not all that.

But Patrick just jerks his arm away with an annoyed grunt. "I love

Will with all my heart and soul. Got it? If you have a problem with that, we can take this out back and hug it out with our fists, but only if you insist on being a jackass."

Andy stares at him. "Really? You truly love him?"

Patrick swallows and looks over to where Will scowls at his phone. "You've met him, right? What's not to love?"

Andy presses his lips together and his eyes go soft. "Oh my God, you really love him!" He throws one arm around Patrick and squeezes him, the takeout boxes wobbling in his other hand.

Patrick grunts and holds himself as stiffly as possible. "What the hell are you doing?"

"Hugging the hell out of you. Will's a good kid. He deserves this."

Patrick feels like he's going to puke with Andy's hair rubbing against his cheek. Bad memories of Mr. Roland's 'fro rubbing against his skin rush up, and he shoves Andy back. "Stop touching me!"

Andy wipes at his eye. "Sure. Of course. I'm a hugger that's all."

Patrick shudders like bugs are crawling over him. The dark man rises, relieves Andy of the takeout boxes, and stuffs cash into Andy's hand without a word. He puts on his coat and sweeps out of the diner.

Patrick turns on his heel and heads back to the bathroom. He washes his hands and scrubs his cheek. Then he splashes cold water on his face and neck. When he can breathe again, he takes some deep, centering breaths, and heads back to the booth.

"You okay?" Will asks.

"I'm fine." He motions toward Andy. "Apparently he knows Jenny."

"Yeah. He's her cousin."

"Is everyone in this town related?"

Will shrugs. "Or they've known each other so long, they might as well be." He frowns. "That was part of what attracted me to Ryan, I think. I met him in college, you know. He's from Minneapolis, but he moved here to be with me."

Patrick doesn't want to talk about Ryan. He thinks of Buttercup. "Whatever. Do you have any nicknames?"

Will face crinkles in confusion. "Why?"

Patrick rolls his eyes. "I'm, I don't know, making conversation."

"You're very bad at it. Stop."

Patrick takes a swig of coffee and starts to hum under his breath. If Will doesn't want to play, Patrick won't make him. It's not like he doesn't have plenty of things to think about. Like, oh, how he has no career, how memories from his past keep getting by his normal defenses, and how every frown of Will's might be interpreted by Molinaro spies as the perfect reason to chop off his fingers. He's got tons of entertaining things to think about.

He must look agitated, because Will relents. "Okay, sorry. I've got my mind on my work." He smiles at Patrick. "Let's talk. So, what was the topic? Nicknames, right?"

"Yep."

"Well, my name is already a nickname. Guglielmo is my given name, and William is the English version of that. So, Will and William are my nicknames."

Andy finally drops by with their breakfast and takes a moment to congratulate them. "Today's meal is on the house. Okay?"

"You don't need to—" Will starts.

"I know! But I am just so happy for you!" He sings along to a jazzed-up cover of "Happy Xmas (War Is Over)". As he twirls off, his hands whirl above his head and he shakes his hips to the sleigh bell beat of the carol.

Patrick watches him go. "Are you sure he's not gay?"

"Well, he's odd. I'll admit that. But, nope, not gay." Will does his usual pre-food testing/injection bit, and then turns back to Patrick. "Anyway, what about you? Got any nicknames?"

"Snake," Patrick says, his lips curving slightly, enjoying Will's eye roll.

"As in 'meaner than a'?"

"No. As in 'long as a.'" He pops a piece of sausage into his mouth.

Will snorts. "Yeah, you wish."

Patrick smirks. His father had called him Snake, actually, for the way Patrick learned songs by basically swallowing them whole, but Will doesn't need to know that. He realizes for the first time in years he doesn't *do* that with music anymore. He doesn't hear a song and immediately know how to reproduce it with piano keys. Hasn't in years. It's like that last fight with his father turned the music off in him. He wonders if he sat down at a piano now whether his fingers would remember how to play.

"Quid pro quo." Patrick takes a bite of buttered toast and lets it melt on his tongue.

Will pauses in eating to smile at him again. Patrick's stomach flutters and his breath is shallow. *That smile, though.*

"Okay, Dr. Lecter. What's the question?"

"Which of your many stepfathers did you hate the most?"

Will blows a lungful of air out. "Okay, how did you know there were more than the two I mentioned? Was it Jenny?"

"Gossips gonna gossip," Patrick hedges.

Will shrugs in concession and casts his gaze up as he thinks. "Well, that's a tough one. I liked Grant, but what he did to Summer Solstice…" Will grimaces. "It was awful. He was my mom's favorite stallion."

"Did he give or receive?" Patrick asks. The gossip in *The Hurting Times* called the Sorensen horse incident 'perverse.' Patrick's no fool. He knows what that means.

"Huh?"

"Did he screw the horse or have the horse screw him?"

Will's nose wrinkles up. "What the hell is wrong with you?"

"Wrong with me? I'm not the one—"

Will holds his hands up, stopping Patrick's justification. "He whipped her. To get back at my mom for cheating on him. With my dad."

Patrick goes cold. "Someone should shoot the asshole."

Will doesn't agree or disagree, instead going back to Patrick's original question. "I liked Roger okay, but he couldn't put up with Mom and Tony's regular hookups." Will's lips curl up in a half-amused sneer. "Mom just can't stay away from Tony. And Tony can't stay away from my mom. They're like catnip to each other." He shudders. "I don't get it. Their inability to commit to one person has messed up our lives. Me, Caitlin, Olivia, and Connor. None of us will ever know what it's like to grow up in a normal family."

"Good thing those don't exist, then."

"They do. I have friends who grew up in normal, loving families where no one was Mafioso or arrested for screwing their ex-husband in an alley."

Patrick bites his lip to keep from laughing. "Sounds boring. Who doesn't want to grow up with a parent that just can't stop making mistakes?"

Will shakes his head. "You of all people don't believe that." His tone reminds Patrick of their conversation in the hotel gym the night before and the confessions he'd made. What is it about Will? *His mouth, his eyes. His earnest damn face.*

"I *know* you don't believe that," Will repeats.

"No. I don't."

"I guess if I had to pick a favorite stepfather it would have been Roger. He always treated Olivia and Caitlin like they were his own. I hated Monty, though. He was a dick." His face darkens and he murmurs, "Good riddance."

Patrick makes note to check the gossip about Monty on *The Hurting Times* so he doesn't have to ask Will why. "What about any half-siblings on your dad's side?"

"There are two, Ellen and Isabelle, but I've never met them." Will frowns. "That's two questions. I get to ask one now."

Patrick swallows coffee and shrugs. "Hit me."

"What do you dream about?"

Patrick goes hot and he blinks wildly at Will. "You're asking about my dreams?"

"Yeah. Everyone has them, don't they?"

Patrick does, yes, and the last few nights they've been all about fucking Will. Dreams of Will's hot, tight ass gripping Patrick's cock. Dreams of Will's heels digging into Patrick's thrusting hips.

He doesn't think Will wants to know about those dreams.

"Like, do you want to be head of department? Or are you dreaming of a chief of staff position one day? What's your ultimate career goal?"

Patrick eats his toast and stalls, trying to ban sex images from his mind. He stuffs most of an egg into his mouth and chews. "Not chief. I don't like people. The chief has to deal with staff." He grimaces and shrugs. "Not for me. Head of department sounds good on the surface, but the more I think about it, the more I'd rather just have a clinic of my own. I'd build my own place, and hire someone who likes people to run it, and just do what I'm good at: surgery."

"Hands-off doctoring."

"I guess my dream job is cutting into brains. Lots and lots of brains."

"Cool if gruesome dream you've got there." Will stretches, yawns widely, and rubs the tense muscles in his neck.

"So, Guglielmo, tell me. Has anyone ever called you Elmo?" Patrick asks.

"Nope."

"It fits you."

"Nope."

Patrick laughs. "Admittedly, Snake fits me better. Since I'm 'long as a.'"

Will smiles softly and takes the last bite of his breakfast. "Again, nope. Aw, don't pout. Learn to cope with disappointment."

"You had no complaints the other night. In fact, I remember you commenting on my massive size."

"Girth is more important to me, and you're plenty thick." His face turns scarlet.

Patrick's ego is mollified and a few quiet minutes pass before Will checks the time on his cell phone, swallows the last of his coffee, and leaves some cash on the table.

Patrick hurries to stuff in another bite before grabbing his coat.

"Let's go," Will says. "The neurology unit is amazing. I'm sure you'll be impressed."

Patrick is doubtful, but even if the place is a dump, it'll be good to be in a hospital again.

Will puts his hand on the small of Patrick's back and guides him out the door, and Patrick leans back into the touch. Will doesn't pull away until they're on the sidewalk and a chill goes up Patrick's spine at the loss.

Once at Healing Regional, Will introduces Patrick to a woman with liquid-dark eyes and short, brown, fussy hair, wearing a long skirt over generous hips. Patrick's sure he's going to be expected to remember her name, but damned if he has a clue. She and Will lead Patrick on a tour of the facilities with an almost frightening level of enthusiasm.

True, the hospital's bigger than Patrick expected, and surprisingly well equipped considering it's in the middle of nowhere, but the new neurology department is nothing to write home about. Not if they truly want it to be a world-class facility.

"We're so proud of how far we've come in the last year alone," the woman says and pats Will's arm. "That's all due to Good Works, of course, and the vision Will, Don, and the town planners have for revitalizing Healing."

"Revitalizing, huh?" Patrick asks. "Did it ever have a heartbeat? The town's always been dead on arrival. Admit it."

"Shira, you'll have to forgive Patrick," Will says. "He's…" He waves his hand, like he's trying to think of an appropriate word. "Unique." Will turns back to the woman-whose-name-is-apparently-Shira. "Is Don almost out of his meeting?"

"He should be soon. How about I take you and Dr. McCloud to the boardroom?"

Patrick follows through the clean, white halls of the hospital, loving the sounds of beeping machinery, echoing voices, and the hush-squeak of nurses' shoes as they scamper by. It's the sound of home. The only thing better is how it smells: antiseptic and harsh. Perfection.

Shira abandons them in the boardroom, and Will turns to him, grinning. "Isn't it amazing?" Before Patrick can answer in the contrary, Will talks over his attempt. "I know it's probably not as nice as your old digs in Atlanta, but you have to admit it has potential, and with you on board, you can guide us towards making this place truly special. Good Works can fund additional improvements to your specifications if you're willing to commit to us. You can start practicing here immediately and bring in some of those clients from that long waiting list of yours. We're ready to handle them. We've got the lodging, the support in place, and now we've got you."

Patrick's flummoxed for a moment, but the temptation of getting back into an OR, any OR, is huge. "Not so fast, puddin'-pop. You realize that my list of demands will be long. And expensive. And time consuming. I don't plan to commit to anything. I won't be here long enough to—"

"I know." Will flashes a grin again, his eyes shining with hope. "But even if you decide not to stay here and practice for good, we'd still have an incredible facility by following your lead. We'd be better able to attract someone else of your caliber, right?"

"There's no one else of my caliber."

"Then maybe you'd want to stay after all. You know, since no one else could possibly deserve to work in a facility updated to your specifications."

Patrick's brain is spinning between a wide-open sense of possibility and a fear of utter imprisonment when an old, balding man in a lab coat comes in. He looks like an archetypal grandfather like Patrick's seen in movies and TV shows—the one who sweeps into a scene with a bag of candy and a lot of wisdom to impart. The kind of grandfather Patrick never had.

"Well, hello," the man says, turning his twinkling eyes on them both. "Will, what are you doing back in Healing already? I thought you were in Las Vegas until tomorrow?"

Patrick wonders how this man has escaped being caught up in the Healing gossip mill.

"Don, hi." Will nervously runs a hand through his hair. "You're right. I was supposed to be out there a little longer. But, uh, I had a change of plans."

"Oh? What's that?"

Will grins and puts his hand on Patrick's shoulder. "This kind of change. Dr. Don Knife, this is Dr. Patrick McCloud. We met at the conference in Vegas. Dr. McCloud is a neurosurgeon from Atlanta." He turns to Patrick and says somewhat pointedly, "Dr. Knife is the chief of staff here."

"I've heard of Dr. McCloud, Will." Dr. Knife takes Patrick's proffered hand. He's got a firm, confident grip that Patrick thinks bodes well for his competency.

"You have?" Will blinks in clear surprise.

"Of course, He was one of my top picks in the dossier I gave you."

"Oh," Will says, looking away guiltily. "Right."

Patrick remembers the dossier now. It'd been sitting on the bar in front of Will and Patrick had opened the folder, flicked through the particulars of a dozen or so other neurosurgeons, and summarily dismissed them all before flinging the folder into the trash behind the bar.

Dr. Knife appraises Patrick and apparently likes what he sees.

"I'm glad you've chosen to give our hospital an opportunity to woo you. I couldn't have hoped for a better outcome when I sent Will to Vegas. I have to admit, I wasn't anticipating you'd say yes to any proposal. I know Atlanta has quite the facility."

Will slides his hands into the pockets of his dress pants and rocks back and forth on his toes. "Shira and I were just showing Patrick around the hospital and the new neurology department."

"Wonderful, isn't it?" Dr. Knife says proudly.

"Close, but no cigar." Patrick gestures toward the door to the boardroom, vaguely indicating the direction they came from. "It's good, but not great. You can hardly call this a state-of-the-art facility when you don't even have your own dedicated neurosurgery laboratory."

"Patrick—" Will grits out between his teeth, brown eyes going flinty.

Dr. Knife holds up a hand. "It's quite all right, Will." He studies Patrick carefully. "We had an excellent neurosurgeon consult with us on the plans for this facility, Dr. McCloud."

"Oh yeah?" Patrick asks. "Who?"

"Dr. Phillip Prentice from Mercy in Chicago."

He snorts. "You're not serious?"

"Dr. Prentice is a fine surgeon," Dr. Knife replies. "He was on the short list of candidates to head up our facility due to his invaluable input into the design."

"I know Prentice. He uses a craniotome like a chainsaw. You should have come to me to begin with. You've wasted a lot of money and time. Since I'm stuck here in Healing for the foreseeable future, though, I'll be happy to help you correct the problem."

Dr. Knife's mouth narrows and he ignores Patrick's comments, turning to Will. "I feel like I'm missing out on something. Exactly why has Dr. McCloud come to Healing Regional today?"

Patrick stands a little closer to Will and tries to look love-struck, but suspects he looks ghoulish instead, given Will's elbow in his ribs.

Will nervously clears his throat. "Um, actually, Don…Patrick and I are, well we're…this might seem a little sudden, and I'm sure you'll be surprised, but you know how things are when you're out of town, and stuff just happens, things get clearer sometimes and you just—"

"Oh for pity's sake," Patrick cuts him off. "Will and I are married."

"You're married?" Dr. Knife glances back and forth between them. "To each other?"

"What can I say, it was love at first sight. Right, honey?" Patrick gives him a squeeze.

Will shoots Patrick a murderous look. "Yes, love at first sight."

Dr. Knife crosses his arms over his chest and gazes at them intently. Finally, he laughs and shakes his head, a kind of joyous surrender to absurdity enveloping his expression and stance. "Well, how about that? You've always been full of surprises, Will. Just like your mom and dad. The apple doesn't fall far from the tree."

Will stiffens, but accepts the congratulatory handshake and shoulder clap Dr. Knife offers him. He chuckles like Will is a brash young boy he just can't help but admire the gall of, and looks Patrick up and down. "Love at first sight, huh?"

Patrick nods. "I saw him across the room, and I just knew he was the one for me."

"Sometimes that's the way it happens," Dr. Knife agrees warmly. "So, Dr. McCloud, our facility doesn't appear to have impressed you. How would you suggest improving it?"

Patrick takes only a brief second to consider and then plows on ahead. "Well, doctor, the stereotaxis system could be updated. And you really need another lab in there. Two even."

"Please call me Don." Dr. Knife motions toward the conference room table. "Let's sit down. I'd like to hear your thoughts and ideas."

"Thank you, Don. And you can continue to call me Dr. McCloud."

Will groans but Don just laughs. "Got one with a sense of humor, huh?" He winks at Will. "Spouses that laugh together stay together."

"Laugh it up, honey," Patrick says, pulling out a seat for Will at the table before sitting beside him. "Don here gets my jokes. Don't you, Don?"

"Of course." He sits across from them and pulls out a notepad and pen from his lab coat pockets.

It doesn't take Don long to cut to the chase. "I'm assuming you'll be staying here in Healing, for a while at least. As soon as you're ready to start here at Healing Regional, I can arrange privileges for you."

Patrick shrugs. What else is he going to do with his time? Take up whittling? "I accept the proposal."

"Wouldn't you like to confirm a few things first? Salary? Benefits?"

"Get me back in the OR and you can pay me in peanuts for all I care."

"Luckily, I plan to pay you a great deal more than that," Don laughs. "Does this sound acceptable to you, Will?"

"Of course."

Dr. Knife claps his hands together. "Well then, we'll continue to negotiate on the rest of your proposed improvements. I'm happily surprised at how well your trip worked out, Will. For us both."

Will smiles weakly.

Dr. Knife stands. "I have another meeting in twenty minutes and I need to look over a few patient charts. Dr. McCloud, we'll talk again soon about the unit and your future here, all right?"

"Sounds great!" Patrick says with a big fake smile.

Don chuckles and walks off. "Love at first sight," he mutters to himself. "Helluva thing."

Will exhales hard and long, his cheeks glowing an attractive pink. "Oh my God. I can't believe he bought that."

Patrick can't either, but at this point there are so many things he can't believe about his life he thinks it's best to move on to something he does understand.

"So." He claps his hands together in a mockery of Don. "Your neuro department sucks."

"I should just take your word for that?" Will's mouth draws down in a frown and his eyes narrow dangerously.

That's more like it. A riled up Will is a sexy Will.

"Puddin'-pop, I'm at the top of my field. Do you——"

"I know you're at the top of your field, Patrick," Will snarls. "You've only told me a dozen times. Don't you have anything else to be proud of in your life?"

Patrick lifts one eyebrow. Interesting. Seems his husband has claws. "Saving people's lives like a freaking *superhero* with a scalpel is pretty much at the top of my list, frankly."

Will sighs and casts his eyes down, his shoulders slumping. Patrick wants to sling his arm around him and kiss his cheek. Maybe tickle his stomach to make him laugh. He doesn't know how to do that. Or why the hell he wants to.

Will grabs his murse and tests his blood. Patrick watches silently. "Well?"

"It's a little low." Will puts away his supplies before popping a few glucose tablets. Finally, Will looks up, eyes dark and determined. "Hey, maybe at the end of this mess, you'll have the best facility in the country at your command. You could change not just the playing field but the whole damn game. Doesn't that appeal to your massive ego, Patrick? Just a little bit?"

"You know it does."

Will sidles close and whispers in Patrick's ear. "I thought so."

The wet tingle of his breath makes Patrick shudder. He swallows thickly as his husband saunters out of the boardroom. "Damn tease," he mutters and hurries to follow.

Chapter Twelve

THAT AFTERNOON IN his office at Good Works, Will sees Owen again for the first time in only a few days, but it feels like it's been a lifetime. He's grateful that the first thing Owen does is wrap him in a big hug and tell him everything's going to be all right. Will kind of wishes his mom or his Uncle Kevin had done just this. Or his Nonna. Anyone really.

"I messed up big time," Will murmurs.

"We all mess up, Will. It's how you deal with the fallout that matters." Owen hugs him closer and pats his back before releasing him. His gray eyes search Will's face. "Now talk to me. Are you safe?"

"What do you mean? The Molinaros aren't going to murder me or anything."

"No, not from them."

"Oh, you mean from Patrick?"

"Yes."

Will hiccups a laugh and sits back down at his desk, letting Owen fall into the seat across from him. Owen straightens his tie and crosses his legs. He admires that Owen always dresses in a suit. Will doesn't go quite so far, usually opting for dress pants and a button-up shirt instead.

"I'm safe. He's harmless." He remembers Patrick's inability to keep his mouth from shooting off rude remarks. "Well, physically harmless. He might do or say something to further ruin my reputation, but I guess I've done a good enough job at that all on my own.

What's really left of it anyway?"

"Plenty. You have Good Works to think about."

"I know." Will runs his hand through his hair.

"What happened out there, Will? Who is this man?"

Will bites his lower lip, a weird surge of emotion pushing into his throat, making it hard to talk. He's not going to cry. It's just so much. It's so hard to sum it all up. "I met Patrick when I was drinking." He splays his hands on his desk and meets Owen's eyes. "That's where it starts. And it ends where I married him. At the time, it didn't seem like a bad idea." It'd seemed like a marvelous, sexy, wildly perfect idea.

"Is he that charming?"

Will laughs so long and hard that tears come to his eyes. Owen stays still across from him, until Will finally calms enough to answer. "No, he's not charming. He's an asshole. Except when he's not."

"Oh, so exactly your type of man."

Will covers his face with his hands, half-crying now as he laughs again. "Holy crap, Owen. What have I done?"

"Is he unkind to you?"

"No, he's not a jerk like that. He's sweet sometimes, really." Will thinks of Patrick's soft touch on his asshole when he'd checked to make sure Will wasn't injured. His neck prickles with heat. "He's egotistical and loudmouthed, but he doesn't want to hurt anyone. Not even me. And *I* got him into this mess."

Owen cleans his glasses with his tie. "So where is he now?"

"Patrick's at the hotel making some calls. He's got a long patient waiting list and he needs his former assistant in Atlanta to make the calls for him. He's not exactly a people person. I think Don probably has someone on staff already who can help him going forward."

"And you? How are you holding up?"

"I want to go back in time and make different choices." Will taps his pen against the legal pad on his desk. "But I can't, so that's resistance talking and we all know pain lives in the resistance."

Owen nods.

"So I'm trying to be a big boy and move forward. This is my life and dealing with it minute by minute is the best way to function. Patrick's not a bad person and, seriously, it could've been so much worse." Will smiles and tries to sounds as confident as he wants Owen to think he is. "In a way, I'm grateful. If Patrick had been another man, there's no telling where I'd be. As it is, he's on board to make the best of this situation for the time being. It's lucky, really."

"And perhaps another man couldn't have tempted you to pledge yourself in marriage to begin with. Maybe there's something bigger here?"

"Owen, logical arguments are your strong suit. You're bordering on New Age superstition now."

"Let go and let God," he says seriously. "I'm proud of you for not trying to run from this situation. You're exercising real bravery."

"I'm doing what has to be done for Good Works."

"What about for you? I'd like to see you at tonight's meeting."

Will shakes his head. "Ryan, or Hartley and his dad, or all three of them might be there and I'm not in the mood to deal with that."

"Don't let your animosity and jealousy undermine your sobriety."

Will barely keeps from rolling his eyes. "I'm not going to drink, Owen. I know you're being a good sponsor and you're trying to keep me on the right path, but believe me—seeing Ryan and Hartley and having to deal with them in a meeting setting is a lot more likely to send me running for the Tallgrass's bar than not going to a meeting at all. Besides, I need to keep track of Patrick until he's settled in and less likely to bolt."

"Ryan and Hartley can't be at every meeting, Will. It would do you good."

"I don't agree." He grits his teeth. Everything in him rebels against going to a meeting right now, and it's not because he's dying to guzzle a bottle of gin. It's because AA is something he started attending with Ryan back in college, and everything from the Serenity

Prayer to the church basement where he's gone to meetings for the last few years remind him of what he's lost; of *who* he's lost. "And I honestly don't even want a drink right now. I just want to get to work." He slaps his hand on the pile of paperwork he has to sign for multiple Good Works grants to proceed.

Owen frowns but he doesn't argue with him. "I figured you might say something like that. So I brought you this." Owen holds out a silver coin.

Will takes it from his fingers. *To Thine Own Self Be True. 24 Hours.* "Thanks, but I should go to a meeting to get one of these."

"Take it, Will."

"I don't—"

"Just take it. You know where I'll be if you need me."

Will swallows, guilt making his stomach hurt. He doesn't want Owen to think he's going to slip again. He knows Owen loves him like a son. "It's okay. I promise. I'm going to be okay."

Owen stands up and nods solemnly. "I'm always here for you. Night or day. And I'd like to meet Patrick sometime." His eyes take on a bit of a sparkle. "I'm guessing he must be quite the looker."

Will flushes. "He's…well, I guess he's…"

"Tall, built and dark like Ryan?"

Will shakes his head. Ryan is taller even than Will. He's dark, tan, and thick with muscle from lifting weights at the gym. He's strong but bulky. Ryan takes up so much space that Will feels invisible beside him.

Patrick is all pale skin with a few freckles, light auburn hair, and sinewy muscles that seem to barely hold back all of his energy. They're nothing alike. "Patrick's pretty much the physical opposite of Ryan."

"Interesting." Owen smiles back at him. "You're strong, Will. You can do this."

"Thank you. I'll do my best."

The door closes on Owen's back and Will lets out a long breath.

He studies the coin in his hand. He's held dozens like it over the years. He slides open one of the file drawers of his desk and pulls a small mason jar from the back. It rattles with white chips, silver chips, several gold, a few red and yellow, but no green chips. Green had been his goal until this last slip. He'd been close to achieving it too. Nine months sober.

Now that's out the window with all the rest.

"I can call all those patients tonight." Hunter, Patrick's former assistant in Atlanta, whispers down the line. The afternoon sun shines through the open hotel room windows, and Patrick reclines on the sofa. It's not very comfortable. He hates the idea that Will is sleeping on it.

"Great. Have them contact Shira at Healing Regional. I can't remember her last name. Surely there can't be more than one."

"All right. Will do. I've got to go before someone notices what I'm doing for you. And Patrick?"

"Yes?"

"I hope you're okay. You're a total dickhead, but you deserved better than Schaeffer gave you."

The line disconnects before Patrick can reply, but it reminds him that there's another phone call he should probably make. He sits up and taps his phone against the coffee table, trying to decide just how much he wants to tell Dinah. In the end, he puts the call through without a plan. Winging it. Like an idiot.

"Dinah?" He's barely able to hear her greeting over the swell of children's voices around her. It sounds like she's in the car, probably on her Bluetooth.

"Pat! Oh my goodness, it's so good to hear from you. It's been so long! How are you, sweetheart?"

Has it really been a long time? Patrick's not sure. He remembers calling Dinah when he was still back in Atlanta with Hunter looming over him, eyebrows drawn low and his arms crossed over his chest. *"You said you'd fire me if I let you forget her birthday one more time. So I'm standing right here until you make the call."*

Patrick clears his throat and is about to issue a vague apology when a tough, young voice cuts over the connection. "Give me the frickin' bag of Cheetos, dude, or I'll kick your ass!"

Dinah sighs. "Eric, baby, we don't threaten each other over Cheetos. Get back in your seat and put on your seatbelt or I'll have to pull this van over, and no one wants that."

"She's gonna lecture us," another young voice pipes up. "And take the Cheetos away. So shut up and share, okay?"

"Eat it, Scarface."

Jane screeches, "My name isn't Scarface! Just stop! Eric! Ugh!"

"Pat, as you can hear, it's the same as ever around here. I really do want to talk with you, but I'm taking these two peanuts home from hockey and they're all riled up. Can we talk later?"

"Of course. I just wanted to check in, see if there was anything the kids need. Money, or clothes, or whatever. Video games."

"We're fine, sweetheart. You send us more than enough every month. You just be happy, okay? Don't you worry about me and the kids."

Patrick pinches the bridge of his nose between his fingers and feels the sting of tears. Who else in this world has ever prized his happiness? Only Dinah. And Phil too, he supposes. Though he suspects Phil prizes Dinah's happiness the most and just wants Patrick to keep on doing whatever helps make Dinah smile like the sun rises in her eyes. But Phil's a good man. Dinah and the kids are lucky to have him.

"Well, holy cah-rap," Dinah growls into the phone. "We have a hostage situation with the Cheetos, Pat. I'm going to have to pull over and deal with this."

Patrick huffs a laugh. "Poor idiots."

"Oh, they bring it on themselves."

"I know. Listen, things are…" Weird? Busy? "In a state of flux right now. I might be out of pocket, but if you need me just text."

"Everything okay, Pat?"

Jane says, "She's pulling over, Eric. Way to go!"

Patrick sighs. "Deal with the kids, Dinah. Everything's fine. I'll talk with you soon."

"Sure thing, sweetheart. I love you."

Patrick hangs up before he says anything stupid back to her. His heart hurts a little thinking of her nut-brown hair and gray eyes. Maybe he loves her. Maybe he doesn't. He just knows she's the kindest, most generous person he's ever known.

Shaking off uncomfortable feelings, Patrick grabs the room key and heads out.

The town bustles with Christmas shoppers, and Patrick remembers his few Christmases with Dinah as he passes by friendly faced people with gift-wrapped presents poking out of bags. He takes in the ribboned wreaths hanging from the lampposts and the swirling snowflakes that don't seem to be accumulating yet.

It's not even Thanksgiving, and yet the sounds and sights of Christmastime are all around. It stirs up mostly bad memories, and even-more-painful good ones too. He's relieved when he gets to Brown Gargle, eager to put them all to rest.

He's just taking a soothing sip of his coffee, comfortable at a back corner table, when someone sits down across from him.

"Well, good day, *Buttercup*." Patrick nods at the stroller. "I see you brought the drool machine with you." Slobber hangs from Dylan's mouth all down his bib.

"I see *you've* had a run in with Andy." Jenny yawns as she hangs her purse off the back of her chair and settles in.

"Yeah, I don't think Sicko likes me."

"You don't say!" She leans across the round, wooden table with wide, amused eyes. "I wonder why that is, Patrick?"

"I'm just being my usual charming self. I don't know what his problem is."

"Uh-huh. I'm thinking *that's* the problem."

Patrick lets his lips turn up in a bit of a smile. A jazz version of "Santa Claus is Coming to Town" begins playing, and Dylan garbles a bubbly noise, drool sliding between his lips. "Teething, huh?"

"You know it. He's so uncomfortable. This is the quietest he's been in close to twelve hours. I'm exhausted. I guess it's good that I work from home or else I don't know how I'd cope. Cat naps. They're lifesavers."

"Yep. Every surgeon knows that." He reaches to pick up Dylan out of the stroller. "May I?"

Jenny slurps the coffee Jax has delivered to the table. "Oh God. I guess so. Don't jostle him too much. I will kill you if you make him start crying again."

Dylan grins as Patrick picks him up, waving his arms around. "You won't cry will you, buddy?"

Dylan speaks gibberish and grabs for Patrick's open collar, bobbing his head forward and darkening Patrick's maroon shirt with slobber.

"Strong, aren't you? Gorgeous smile. Yes, I see, you've got a few teeth poking through, huh? Handsome. And your mom's eyes too." Patrick tsks and turns his attention to Jenny as he snuggles Dylan in his arms. "He's gonna be handsome. Gay men of the world look out."

Jenny laughs. "And the women?"

"Whatever team he ends up on, he won't be striking out." Patrick lets Dylan gnaw on his shirtsleeve. "He doesn't have a fever, which is good. If he gets one, then break out the Baby Tylenol for that. And let me give you a tip from a man who graduated Yale Med School at the top of his class: those teething tablets are for chumps. Just give him a frozen kiddie toothbrush and he'll be fine. Won't ya, kiddo?" He bounces Dylan. "You can sanitize it in your dishwasher and then throw it back in the freezer. S'all good."

"Top of the class at Yale, huh? Who is this guy? I'd like to meet him." She bats her lashes teasingly. "I've always wanted to marry a doctor."

Patrick rolls his eyes. He indicates his wedding ring and she feigns surprise that he's referring to himself. "Gay and taken."

"They always are." She takes a deep drink of her coffee and leans back with a sigh. "So? Where's Will?"

Patrick makes a face. "I don't know. Somewhere being all…" Sexy, sweet, and sporting all that chest hair like it's no big deal at all. Annoying. "Being all Will-like probably."

"N'aww, you're so cute. If anyone doubts you adore him, they just need to a look at your face right now."

It's like the entire world sees only what they want to see. "Yeah, well, what can I say? Will just does it for me."

Jenny props her chin on her hand. "He makes you go all squirmy." She clucks her teeth and her blue eyes shine like they're illuminated by some bright, romantic sun. "You've got it for him so bad."

"I am not *squirming*." Patrick shifts in his seat.

"Don't be embarrassed. It's cute."

"So you work from home?" He doesn't really care, but it's a better topic of conversation than his feelings for Will.

"Medical transcription. I can set my own hours and that helps for taking care of Dylan. I get lonely, though. I'm an extrovert, so I have to get out and see people or I'll lose my will to live."

"I guess it's good someone likes people. I sure don't."

She narrows her eyes. "Oh, come on. You like people. You save their lives."

Patrick shrugs. "I don't enjoy their company while I'm doing it." That isn't altogether true. He's had many enjoyable conversations with patients while he's poking around in their brains.

"You like babies!" She hurls it like an accusation.

"Well, this one isn't too awful." He smiles down at Dylan, who blows a bubble at him. "Others, though." He shudders. "They're pooping, screaming vehicles of misery and horror. But this guy's all right."

Jenny shakes her head like she doesn't believe him. Before she can say anything else, her phone makes a long beeping sound. She bites her lip, looking anxiously at whatever message comes through.

"You okay?"

"It's the hospital." Her voice sounds like all the sunshine has been drained from it.

"That's not reassuring. Tests or something?" He puts Dylan back into the stroller and hands him the teething ring attached to the tray with a string.

She slips her phone into her purse and straightens her shoulders, putting on a false cheer that Patrick finds offensive after her previous honest ease. "You need to be *reassured* about me, do you, Dr. McCloud? Are we *friends* now?"

Patrick sneers a little, hoping it does the trick, but Jenny just glints and glimmers at him more genuinely until he groans. "I don't really do friends." Unless he counts Dinah and Phil, but they aren't *friends*, and they aren't family; they're…Dinah and Phil.

"I kind of figured. Something tells me you didn't do relationships before you did Will either."

Patrick shrugs. "The clue bus hurt when it hit?"

"You mean the big shiny one with 'Patrick's a Jerk' painted in pink on the side?"

"And yet you're still sitting here!"

"I fall for jerks. It's what I do. The call from the hospital was about Dylan's uncle. Well, Tom's uncle, really. Dylan's great-uncle. Details." She waves her hand distractedly before leaning forward to breathe in the steam from her coffee.

"Okay? So it's bad news?"

"You could say that. Radar needs a new kidney."

"Radar?" Patrick counts himself as incredibly awesome that he doesn't snort at that name.

"Yes, Radar." She gives him a challenging look. "As in *M.A.S.H.*, and yes, I know. It's a nickname. It doesn't matter. He's only forty-six and needs a kidney, okay?" Jenny's voice breaks a little. "And I—I don't know what to do about that. I mean, I know what they want me to do, but…"

Patrick frowns. "What do they want you to do?"

"Donate." Her eyes glisten.

"You're a match?"

"Yes. Who would have thought it was possible?" Jenny wipes at her eyes with a napkin.

"Well, it's a small town. The chances of inbreeding around here are pretty high."

She shoots him a disgusted look. "Stop. This is serious."

"I'm being serious. Genetically the likelihood…nevermind. Just go on." He reaches out and takes her hand. It's small and trembles against his own steady fingers.

"No, I'm sorry. It's just, God—I don't know what to do. Life is so unfair. Radar has two kids under the age of ten. They need their dad." She sniffles. "And Tom's gone. I have no idea where to find him. So Dylan just has me. I'm his only parent. I can't just go around giving pieces of myself away. Even to good people with families of their own." She pulls her hand away and rubs her face. "I'm an awful person. I was praying I wasn't a match. I mean why should I be?"

"Inbreeding."

"This is a big decision. I mean, there's risk involved, and Dylan's just a baby—"

"You're getting all splotchy." Patrick wrinkles his nose. "Your eyes are swelling."

"This is how you cheer people up?"

"No, this is how I tell people to get over themselves. You have a chance to save a life and you're sitting in this coffee shop whining to me about how life is unfair? About how it's full of risk? Hell, yeah, it's unfair. Hell, yeah, life is risky. Every day I go to work and I fight death. I take massive risks on behalf of my patients, because that's the only way to save them. And that's the way life works. Suck up your tears, call the hospital back, and make plans for someone to help with Dylan while you're recovering."

"But…" Her eyes go wide. "Dylan's so young. He won't understand what's happening. He'll be scared with me in the hospital. He won't know where I've gone or when I'll be back—"

"He won't remember anything about it when he's older. Take a deep breath and let it go." Jenny does take a long deep breath and lets it out slowly. Patrick smiles at her before leaning forward to whisper, "Now build a bridge and get over yourself. You know what you should do."

Jenny glares. "You are so rude."

"At least you can't call me self-centered."

Jenny stands, shoves her blond hair behind her ears, and grabs her purse. "We're leaving." She grabs the stroller and pauses. "Maybe Andy's right about you. You're an ass."

"That's what I've been telling you."

Jenny careens out of Brown Gargle and Patrick watches her go. He sighs and shrugs. So much for making friends.

"STARVING," PATRICK MOANS pitifully, and Will rolls his eyes.

"You just ate a snack not even an hour ago."

"And?"

Will sighs and motions toward the hotel room phone. "Order me the chicken, some grilled red bell peppers, rice, and a side of applesauce." He opens his suitcase and rummages around for a pair of sweatpants and a T-shirt. After changing in the bathroom, he comes out to see Patrick hanging up the phone.

Will throws himself down onto the sofa and closes his eyes.

"Shove over." Patrick nudges him and sits down. "Want to play?"

Will opens his eyes to see what Patrick's talking about. He's holding a chess set. It'd been sitting on Will's desk back at his mom's, so he'd grabbed it at the last second, tossing it into a bag. Patrick must have fished it out.

Will shrugs. "Why not?"

Patrick's smile glints and Will's stomach flips over. "Great. I'll set it up."

An hour later, room service has come and gone, they've both eaten, and Will's beaten the snot out of Patrick in eight straight games of chess. Patrick's obviously simultaneously annoyed and grudgingly impressed.

"I guess being on a high school chess team has long-term advantages?" Patrick asks.

"What it lacked in hot guys, it made up for in teaching me a mean chess game. So yeah, I guess it did." Will grins cockily. "Competitive, aren't you?" He's amused by the way Patrick fairly twitches at being outdone at anything.

"I like to win. I like to be the best. There's nothing wrong with aiming for the top, so long as you always get there."

"Well, if we keep playing chess, you should get used to losing, because you, good sir, suck at it."

He glares. "I'm just hungry."

Will flicks a meaningful glance to the crumbs left on Patrick's plate, which had only just recently boasted a hamburger, fries, pickle, and a side of slaw. Apparently, Patrick had paid extra for one of the bellhops to run over to Jimmy's to pick it up because the hotel burgers "aren't good enough for pig slop,"

"Dessert. I need something sweet and cold." Patrick looks at Will thoughtfully. "Yes, I think I definitely need a little something to cool me down."

Will knows that look. It's the look of a man who wants to eat

Will alive. The look Patrick wore in Vegas. He shivers.

Patrick's voice is a low purr. "Want to join me?" He stands and stretches, revealing the fuzzy strip of his happy trail beneath an untucked button-down maroon shirt. The trail disappears under his pants, which are held up by a slim black belt with a shiny, small buckle. Heat rises up Will's neck.

"Join you where?"

"Downstairs."

"Where downstairs?"

"Not the gym!" Patrick declares, rubbing his shoulder. "I'm still sore."

"Not the bar, though?"

Patrick wrinkles his nose and shakes his head. "Of course not. I have no desire to get us both drunk and married all over again. Don't get me wrong, it's been quite the adventure, but not one I'd like to repeat." He strides over to the door and jerks it open. "You coming?"

Will follows him to the stairs at the end of the hall and down to the lobby. The sound of clinking glass and silverware on plates drifts out of the Meadowlands, the hotel's restaurant, along with some savory scents and lots of laughter. The lobby is dotted with guests standing in groups of two or three, chatting, some of them leaving the Meadowlands restaurant in the lobby, and others just milling about. Most Will recognizes as travel nursing staff and doctors for the hospital.

But one of the strangers, Will doesn't know. It's the man from the coffee shop and Jimmy's. He's leaning with a casual, observational air as he relaxes on the lobby couch with a newspaper. The hair on the nape of Will's neck raises up. A Molinaro spy. In the hotel. Where else would he be staying? It's the best establishment in Healing and Molinaros do like the best.

The man meets Will's gaze and lifts his chin in acknowledgment before going back to his paper.

Maybe he's just a traveler, here on regular business. Maybe it's not a big deal at all that he keeps turning up in places where Will tends to be. It's a small town. There aren't a lot of options.

He doesn't want to scare Patrick, though, not when there seems a fifty-fifty chance that it'll inspire him to want to flee Healing rather than stay.

"Come on, puddin'-pop," Patrick calls over his shoulder as he strides past the reception desk, nodding at Beth. "Dessert is so close I can almost taste it."

The small twenty-four-seven snack shop around the corner from the restaurant is open, though no one is manning the register. This time of night, guests pay for their purchases at reception. It's an honor system, but apparently there hasn't been much loss of inventory. Will's gratified that the nurses and doctors staying in the hotel are honest people.

Patrick goes directly to the freezer at the back of the store. He throws it open and gestures Will over to gaze inside. "Frozen Snickers bars," he says, like he's showing him a work of art. "I tossed them in here this morning. They're better this way. Snappier."

"If I correct my dose for it, I could have one too."

"My thoughts exactly." Patrick smiles and pulls out two bars.

They pay at reception. Beth's too distracted by whoever she's texting to ask any questions about their honeymoon, thank God. On the way back to the elevators, Will greets a few folks and then finds himself slowing to a stop by the baby grand piano in the lobby.

Patrick's hips roll sexily as he makes his way to the elevators. Will almost decides to let it go, but he can't help his curiosity. The words burst out. "Hey, do you really never play?"

Patrick turns back to him and his eyes slide over to the piano. He shrugs. "I'm sure I probably could." The *probably* seems to hang between them. "If I wanted to." And Patrick's eyes glint with the unanticipated challenge.

Will sits down on the bench. "I can play a little." He puts his fingers on the keys and plunks out a halting "This Old Man", mangling it in a few places. "Bet you can't beat that, genius," he says, laughing at Patrick's grimace over his mistakes.

Patrick rolls his eyes but strides over to the piano, pushing Will aside and handing him the two frozen Snickers bars. "That was unbearable. Let me show you how it's done."

Patrick's long, thin fingers light on the keys and after only a moment's hesitation a jazzy, bluesy version of "This Old Man" comes tumbling out of the baby grand. Patrick's foot works the pedals and his arm brushes against Will's chest as he shifts keys and adds flourishes. It's fun, and almost funny, to hear the old nursery song played so richly.

"I knew I could do it," Patrick gloats.

Other guests start to gather, but as soon as Patrick notices them, it's over. He pulls away as if burned. The scattered applause clearly unnerves him even more. He rubs his hands together and clears his throat, before standing up to say stiffly, "And that's all you're getting out of me tonight, Guglielmo."

Patrick's lashes flutter, and his cheeks are pale beneath the navy pools of his eyes. Will wants to pull him closer to tuck him against his side and shield him from the curious eyes of the guests. The thought freezes him, and they stare at each other, exposed.

"Show's over," Will says finally, smiling at the people around them.

The atmosphere grows thick and awkward. The other guests walk away, whispering and glancing back. Will clears his throat. "That was great. Amazing."

Patrick's eyes flash, and he is rigid with hurt betrayal as he snatches the candy from Will's grasp. "We're done here."

"Wait." He grabs Patrick's wrist.

Patrick trembles and his expression shatters, utterly defenseless. Will wants to do *something* about that, but he forces himself to let go of Patrick's arm.

"I can't," Patrick says, like that means something. "I won't."

Will doesn't know what to say, so he stays where he is, letting Patrick take the stairs up to the room without him. He wants to apologize for baiting Patrick into playing, but he doesn't know how.

WILL LEAVES PATRICK at the Tallgrass, sleeping soundly. He heads out into the early morning seeking some solitude and coffee before he goes into Good Works for the day.

He'd tossed and turned all night, unable to sleep.

He doesn't know if it's because the sofa is so uncomfortable, or if it's the memory of Patrick's face after he'd played for Will that had kept him up. He's never seen an expression that vulnerable on anyone else in his life. Not even on Ryan when he'd confessed all of his drinking triggers.

No one has ever looked so fragile to Will as Patrick had last night. It'd been an intimate, horrible, and all-too-fleeting moment. Will wants to know what it's about, but he can't ask. He's afraid to hurt Patrick even more if he does.

But his brain won't let it go. Walking down the street after leaving Brown Gargle with a Buckaroo-sized coffee, he's almost as tired as he was after the first night they spent together, though certain parts of him are decidedly less sore. Other parts, though, are sore as hell.

Will rubs the back of his neck and rejects a half-dozen ideas about how he can sneak a mattress or rollaway bed into their hotel room without it looking suspicious.

It's early morning yet, and all the stores are closed. The streets are pretty much deserted too, and Will wanders around Old Healing until he stops across from the apartment that, until a few days ago, he'd been sharing with Ryan. The building isn't very attractive. It's basically a brown three-story square with too-small windows, but it'd been his home. Almost.

He gazes up at the window that is their—no, *Ryan's*—bedroom. It surprises him to realize that with all of his obsessing over Patrick and the piano this morning, he hasn't thought of Ryan at all until now.

He fiddles with the brown cardboard sleeve of his to-go cup.

It wasn't that long ago that he and Ryan were almost happy. Just a few short months, really, before Hartley showed up at the Al-Anon meetings Ryan had helped to organize out on the rez. He's been attending Al-Anon meetings on his own and AA meetings with his father ever since. Will should be happy for the guy that his father is doing so well, but he can't help but resent Hartley. His presence forced a wedge between him and Ryan from the start. A wedge Ryan didn't fight. And now Ryan's with Hartley, touching Hartley, and *sleeping* with Hartley. Will can only guess that some part of Ryan's wanted this from the start.

Humiliation opens up in him like a room, big enough that he could move in and furnish it if he wanted. He scrubs a hand across his face. When he looks up, Ryan's there testing the lock of the apartment building's front door before adjusting his scarf.

"Ryan, hey," he says tentatively.

"Will, uh, what's up?" Ryan's arms dangle loosely at his sides, and his expression is sleepy, soft, and curious. He looks like the boy Will fell in love with.

"Just walking to work. You?"

Ryan yawns. "I've got counseling sessions today out on the rez."

"Gonna see Hartley?"

"Not sure why that's your business."

"It's not."

Ryan scratches at his artful stubble before approaching Will carefully, like he's afraid Will might contaminate him with ebola or, worse, *regrets*. "I'm worried about you. Look, we might not be together, but I still care about what happens to you."

"If you still care about me, then what's going on with you and

Hartley?"

Ryan tenses. He seems to have a hard time spitting out the words. "Please leave him out of it."

"Why? I've been watching him go after you for months, and all the while you've been saying, 'It's nothing, Will'; 'You're exaggerating, Will'; 'It's not like that, Will.' So tell me what it *is* like, Ryan. I'd really like to know."

Ryan squirms. "The thing with Hartley just kind of happened, okay? I don't expect you to get how hard this choice has been for me, but it hasn't been easy." He looks at Will with deep, black pupils nearly overwhelming his blue irises. "Besides, you sure moved on quickly enough."

Will presses his lips together and his stomach churns. "Well, Patrick and I just sort of happened too."

Ryan's face twists up and his jaw clenches. Will can tell he's biting back something mean. He knows Ryan too well.

"But I still care about you too, Ryan." If he's ever going to be able to make this right, he has to lay the groundwork for it now. He needs Ryan to understand that he's still in his heart.

"No, you don't."

"Ryan, you were my everything."

"'Everything' isn't worth very much to you then." Ryan sighs and struggles for words. "Okay, here's the thing: I can believe you'd sleep with him when you were drunk. You always want sex when you've been drinking. But I still can't believe you *married* him."

Will says nothing. He doesn't know what to say. He considers lying, declaring his love for Patrick, but he's too tired and too sad. Instead he just stands there and lets Ryan stare pityingly at him. He deserves it.

Ryan crosses his arms over his chest. "I think you owe me an apology."

"For what?"

"Your new husband was a jerk to me and Hartley the other day."

"Well, you weren't saying very nice things about me at the time, Ryan. Can you blame him?"

"Can you blame *me* for being disgusted by even seeing him with you?"

"And what about me seeing you with Hartley?"

Ryan looks away. "Why do you have to make everything about you?"

"Because you make me feel like I'm the problem."

Ryan sighs again. "Maybe you are the problem, Will. Maybe if you were different we wouldn't have ended up here, like this."

Will stomach rebels, and he rubs a hand across his forehead, trying to keep his feelings from bursting out in a vomity mess. He's on the verge of tears as it is. Patrick and his stupid, long, pretty fingers that the Molinaro family have explicitly targeted come to mind, and he tries to keep himself under control.

"You're right. I'm sorry. I wanted to change for you. I tried."

Ryan sneers, clearly validated but still angry. "Are you really sleeping with him?"

Will lifts his eyebrows. "Aren't you sleeping with Hartley?"

"It's different. It's not like what you wanted me to do with you."

"How?"

Ryan's lips tremble. "He doesn't need the things you need, Will. He just wants to make me feel good."

Will stares at him, shame owning him inside and out.

"Never mind. It's none of your business. I shouldn't have said anything. Telling you makes it feel dirty."

Will swallows back puke. "What would you say to someone in counseling if they were in our situation?"

"I can't be my own counselor, Will. That's rule number one."

"But you counsel other people in similar situations all the time. I can't believe *this* is how you'd suggest they'd handle it."

Owen always says Ryan is a completely different person around Will—that he changes into a stranger, nothing like the understanding, warm man he is when he's working on the rez or with a sponsee.

If Will could just fix himself then Ryan would be that warm with him too.

"The people I counsel aren't in situations like *this*. No, I'd say our situation is pretty unique." Ryan looks thoughtful. "But I guess I'd tell them to speak their truth to each other and move on."

Cliché, but getting somewhere. "And what's your truth, Ryan?"

He stares at Will for a long moment. "I ended things because I can't imagine a future with you where I didn't end up with a drink in my hand. Not when you're so selfish and deeply messed up. The things you want sexually are disgusting." His jaw hardens. "You'll never stay sober. You'll never have the strength for it. I know you better than you know yourself, and you're hopeless. I wasn't going to let you take me down with you."

Ryan walks away, leaving Will to stand with his cooling cup of coffee and his gut churning with shame.

Chapter Thirteen

"WELCOME BACK," DON says, gripping Patrick's hand. "It's an honor and privilege having you on staff, no matter how you left things in Atlanta." He holds up his hand to stop Patrick from speaking. "Yes, I talked to your former chief. But I don't share his concerns about you. I take it as a sign of good faith that you've chosen to stay here in Healing for Will's sake. This town and his family mean a lot to him."

Patrick doesn't know what to say to that, so he slaps his hands together. "Point me to your OR and get me a brain, and we'll call this whole thing a win."

Don chuckles. "I understand your impatience to get back to work. I admire a doctor as dedicated as you."

"Brains just do it for me." He remembers saying something similar about Will.

"Unfortunately, we don't have any cases that require your specialty at the moment, Dr. McCloud. I'm sure you're in the process of transferring your patient list, but in the meantime we're fresh out of brain traumas."

"That's okay. I'm sure you've got some other patients that need to be looked in on. I'm happy to use some of my less rarified doctoring skills. Just set me up so I can get started. Anything is better than hanging out another day in the hotel watching *Cupcake Wars* on Netflix."

A few hours later, Patrick's all set. He flips to the first chart and heads toward Room 312: Sarah Rogers, incomplete late-term spontaneous abortion.

Damn, that'll be a bitch. There's bound to be weeping involved.

"Patrick?" Jenny stands outside an exam room. "What are you doing here?"

He slows to a stop, scratching his nose. "Funny thing. Got a job."

Jenny sniffles and wipes at her eyes.

He stands there awkwardly. "So, I'll just—" He motions with his hand and starts to walk around her.

"Don't feel bad about what you said. I'm not crying about how mean you were to me or anything."

Patrick groans, pinches the bridge of his nose, and turns around again. "Are you okay? Did you decide to do it?"

Jenny crosses her arms and nods before wiping at her eyes again. "It's the right thing to do. But the problem is now he won't take it. He says he can't burden me like that when I'm not family. Dammit, I just want to shake him and scream, 'Take my kidney, you asshole!' God! You know?" She takes a deep breath, pulling it together. "I think his wife is going to talk some sense into him, though."

"Good." Patrick moves to walk past.

She grabs his arm. "Patrick? You were so right. I was being selfish and stupid. If it was me needing a kidney and someone who could help me was going to say no because they were too cowardly to step up? Endangering my ability to stay around for Dylan? I'd be so disappointed. So thank you."

"Eh, don't get all—ew. It was nothing. I insult people all the time. It's what I do."

Jenny smiles and steps closer. "I've got your number, Patrick McCloud, and I think Will does too. You're a good man. Deny it all you want, but we both know who you are."

"I'd never deny I'm a good man. I'm a stupendous man. Have you met me?"

She smiles and her eyes twinkle a little. "Don't hide behind your pompous jerk act, okay?"

"You're making me feel dirty."

Jenny grins. "Coffee later? When you're done here?"

"Are you going to bring the brat?"

"Of course."

"Then it's definitely a date." Patrick nods and turns back to his chart. "Until then, I've got a hangnail to attend to."

He nods toward Sarah Rogers' room, where he knows he'll be facing a lot more than that.

Miscarriages are messy and traumatic in the best of circumstances, and a later-term one is even worse. Add incomplete on top of that, and it's pretty much an emotional nightmare. This is why Patrick ran like hell from obstetrics.

Patrick spends just less than eight minutes with Sarah Rogers, letting her know what to expect from the upcoming D&C and explaining that the nurses will be in to help her shortly. It's more than he normally spends with a non-OR patient and he feels proud. He even manages not to insult her husband, and to give her shoulder a friendly squeeze. That's something a resident he respected in med school had told him once: if a woman loses a baby, she deserves a comforting touch.

"Dr. McCloud!"

Patrick turns on his heel, hoping that he can avoid Will's mother by going the other way.

"Dr. McCloud, don't act like you didn't hear me."

Patrick groans, throws his head back, and slowly turns to face Kimberly. She's dressed in tight blue jeans and a silk, cleavage-exposing shirt. She looks like she's about to attend some hot-and-heavy rodeo or a super-sexy rancher's party, but she was dressed the same way the last time Patrick saw her too, so he guesses this is just how she always looks.

"Dr. McCloud, you and I need to have a little talk."

"Excuse me?"

Kimberly crosses her arms over her chest and peers up at him with nearly comedic determination. "I don't trust your intentions toward my son."

"Okay." Patrick turns to go.

Kimberly grabs his arm. "I won't let you use him."

Patrick gapes at her a moment. "You're a little too late with the mama bear act. I married him already. Back off."

"I don't think you're being honest."

Patrick chuckles. "You don't say?"

"And I don't like what I know of you so far."

"And just what do you know of me that has you so appalled? Is it my stellar reputation as an amazing neurosurgeon, or the loving commitment I share with your son?" Patrick strokes his chin. "Hmm. One of these things is not like the other."

Kimberly sidles close to him. Clearly Will learned his lack of physical boundaries from his mother. "How could Don just let you work here like this? Does he know anything about you?"

Why, yes. My reputation precedes me.

"I guess your son's good word is enough for old Donny. Now if you'll let me get back to my work, I'll make sure I'm extra super nice to the next whining hypochondriac I'm scheduled to see."

"Is this how you talk to everyone? You should be ashamed of yourself."

"Patients to traumatize, nurses to make weep, all in a good day's work, Ms. Patterson—or is it Mrs. Edison? Or Mrs. Fleming? Or Mrs. Molinaro? I'm sorry. I'm confused."

"Patterson," Kimberly says through her teeth.

"Well, adios, Ms. Patterson. I'm just gonna go be ashamed of myself over there." He waves toward the nurses' station, where he's going to pick up his next patient file, and where the nurses don't look too pleased to see him coming. Just the way he likes it. "If that's all right by you, of course, Mrs. Mol—Ed—Flem—Patterson."

"No it is most certainly *not* all right by me!"

"Oh, can it. I'm working, can't you see that? I don't have time for a tête-à-tête with my husband's mommy right now."

Kimberly gasps and Patrick waves at her, a little ta-ta over his shoulder, and turns to the nurse. "Hand it over."

She shoves another chart at him, and he flips it open. Will's mother stalks away and he wonders for only a moment if he should have been a little nicer.

"WILL, BABY, ARE you okay?" his mother asks over the phone.

Will rubs a hand over the back of his aching neck. "Sure. I guess. I mean, why?"

The Good Works paperwork is almost wrapped up, and he thinks he'll look through one more grant application and answer the last three emails in his inbox before heading back to the Tallgrass.

"I ran into Dr. McCloud at the hospital and he was quite unpleasant to me."

Will can't help but laugh through his sigh. "I'm sorry, Mom. He's kind of a jerk sometimes. But I swear, he has a good heart."

"Was he rude when you met him?"

Will remembers Patrick sitting next to him at the bar and needling him about the very loud breakup he'd just had with Ryan over the phone.

"Yeah. He was." For some bizarre reason, a fond smile spreads over his face.

"And you found that funny? Compelling? Attractive?" Kimberly asks, her outrage clear.

"Yes. No. I don't know. He's his own person. I can't help but admire that."

His mother huffs. "I'm sorry, Will. I just don't understand. He doesn't seem like your type. Ryan's a loving man. He's always been beyond kind to me. He was there for us both when things were tough with your drinking. And we can't ever forget everything he's done for you! He's helped keep you sober. He's helped keep you *safe*. And Dr. McCloud is…I don't even know what Dr. McCloud is."

"That's my point, Mom. You don't *know* him. Give him a chance." Will fiddles with a pen on his desk, thinking about Patrick's expression by the hotel piano, the vulnerability that had tugged at Will's seams. "He thaws out over time. I promise. And then you'll see the truly decent man he is on the inside."

"With any luck giving him a chance won't be necessary." Kimberly makes a prim sound that is completely at odds with all that Will knows about her past. "Have you heard from your grandmother? Has she been able to make any headway at all on getting this mistake taken care of?"

Will shushes her, paranoia hitting him again. Surely his office phones aren't tapped, but with the Molinaros, he can't be too careful. "Mom, I know there are some things you don't understand, but I'm very happy with Patrick, remember? And no, Nonna has nothing new to report on that project she's working on. There's some red tape, and some people in high places making things difficult, but she promises she'll find a way."

"If anyone can do it, it's your Nonna. You're right to put your confidence in her, Will. Just don't get too comfortable."

Will snorts. "What do you mean?"

"I know you, and I'm worried. That's all. I don't trust him. Are you sure you're safe?"

"Mom, I'm safe as houses."

"If you're sure."

"I am."

"Sure, sure, *sure?*"

"Mom."

A few minutes later, Will hangs up the phone feeling drained. His mother's dramatics always wear him out. He knows it's just that she cares about him, but he's dealing with enough right now without her questioning his decisions. It frustrates him (even though *that* makes him feel guilty too) that he's the one who always ends up reassuring *her.*

He hurries through the last few things he's planned to do and stops by Jimmy's on the way to the Tallgrass for takeout. He orders two gyros and two mac 'n' joes. He's not sure what Patrick might want, but he knows Patrick will eat all of whatever he brings.

"Are you in some kind of trouble?" Andy asks him, leaning over the counter.

Will takes the two bags Andy hands him. "What do you mean?"

"You and that so-called husband of yours. There was a man around here yesterday and earlier today, a stranger. He's been around a lot lately."

"Yeah?"

"He's been asking weird questions about you two."

"What kind of weird questions?"

"How do I know you, and what do I know about Dr. McCloud? Stuff like that. I asked him why he wanted to know, and what he was doing in Healing, and he said 'Family business,' I kid you not. Made me think about, you know…" Andy looks around, leans forward, and whispers, "Your dad."

Sweat breaks out on Will's neck and he glances behind him like the Molinaro spy is going to be standing there waiting with a gun, a sneer, and the declaration that the money in the trust funding Good Works is forfeit.

"What's going on? Does this guy want to hurt you? Is it blackmail? How can I help?"

"Um, it's okay, Andy. Thanks for the concern, but everything's just fine."

"It's about the marriage and how it's a fake, right?"

Will blinks at him. "What?"

Andy shrugs. "I'll play along. I decided the other day, so long as you're not sporting a shiner or looking scared out of your mind, I'll pretend to believe he loves you and that you love him. But you were with Ryan way too long for me to fall for—"

"Andy, I do love him." Will's heart is beating a mile a minute.

He rolls his eyes. "Right. Of course. I'm so stupid to doubt you."

"Andy—"

"Shh. I understand now. It all makes sense. Mafia stuff, am I right?"

Will shakes his head. "I don't know what you're talking about."

"If you're in too deep, just call me, okay?" Will's bemused by the way Andy looks around again like he's making sure no one's listening even though the restaurant is empty. Then he leans forward again. "I've got connections. In the FBI. I've got your back, Will. If you need anything at all. Even if it's help getting out of this so-called marriage situation. You're my bro." He slaps his chest with two fingers, some kind of gangsta sign. "Plus, I know jiu jitsu."

"O-kay. I'll keep that in mind. Thank you." Will holds up the bags as a kind of goodbye, and heads out the door with his heart beating hard. He peels his eyes for the dark man in the black coat as he walks back to the Tallgrass. Then he remembers that the man is *staying* at the Tallgrass, so what's the point?

He takes a break from paranoid vigilance to wonder if Andy's skepticism about his marriage to Patrick is anything to be worried about. So far, he seems to be the only person in town, aside from Ryan, Owen, and Will's family, who's expressed any suspicion about his marriage to Patrick. Nearly everyone else has been surprisingly happy for him and offered hearty congratulations.

After a few minutes of thinking it over, Will shrugs it off. Andy's an oddball. He spent most of last year in a skirt to protest cultural restrictions on male clothing. People don't consider him entirely credible. Will's got enough to worry about if there really is a Molinaro spy in town asking questions about him and Patrick.

It isn't until he's riding in the elevator to their hotel room that it hits him. Andy hadn't believed him capable of marrying Patrick and had asked if Will needed *help* out of the situation. Hartley had done the same. But Ryan? Hadn't. Ryan hadn't offered to help at all.

Will has to put the bags down for a moment, a wave of dizziness rolling over him. It's been a while since he ate. As the elevator dings and the doors slide open, he pops three lifesavers from his pocket into his mouth to get his sugar up before he passes out.

Keying open the door, he tries to fake some cheer. "Honey, I'm home! And I brought dinner!" He stops and grips the bags more firmly as his cock rushes with a sudden influx of blood.

"Just put it over there." Patrick's ass is in the air, his hands flat on the floor, and he's wearing nothing but his black boxer-brief underwear. "I'll eat it when I'm done."

Will stares as Patrick swivels, his body moving fluidly and his legs flexing in strong, limber movements.

"What are you doing?"

"This is downward dog. And this—" Patrick moves down with careful, slow strength. "Is plank position." The muscles in his arms, back, and thighs are like bundles of wires, and Will's mouth goes dry, remembering clearly how they felt under his hands.

"Looks hard."

Patrick doesn't answer. Will turns to put the food on the table, because if he keeps watching, something else is going to be hard too. He focuses on testing his blood to make sure the lifesavers are doing what they're supposed to do.

He clears his throat, glancing over his shoulder at the flexing muscles in Patrick's back. "When we met, I wouldn't have pegged you as a yoga kind of guy."

Patrick grunts. He's in a position now that Will can't even imagine twisting himself into.

"I mean, you don't seem like an '*om*' type."

"Yoga, and meditation for that matter, are legitimate, effective, and scientifically proven means to an end: physical health and reduction of mental stress. In other words, it helps keep me sane." Patrick moves into an upright position, sweeps his arms over his head, and brings them back to a prayerful place at his chest. "Sanity is something you could stand to try. And none of that spiritual mumbo jumbo has anything to do with it."

"So says the guy who believes in astrology."

"Sure, be a Libra about it."

Will feels heat in his cheeks. "The yoga doesn't seem to hurt as far as keeping the rest of you in shape either."

Patrick's lips turn up into a smirk.

Will clears his throat, turning to the bags of food. He keeps his back to Patrick as he unpacks the takeout packages onto the small dining table. "So, do you want the gyros or the mac 'n' joes, because I can go either way."

Patrick's breath is tingly in Will's ear and his body heat warm along Will's back. "I go both ways too. It's your call." He reaches around and plucks up one of the Styrofoam boxes without looking inside.

Will swallows and gestures at the box still on the table. "This will be fine."

He doesn't know for sure which it is, but it *will* be fine, so long as his dick stops acting like a traitor and his mind stops supplying him with images of Patrick bent over, taking Will's fingers into his tight, hot—God!

He shakes himself.

"Mmm, gyros," Patrick murmurs from his perch on the bed. "So good."

Will's eyes flutter closed as he sits at the table and spreads a napkin over his crotch. No matter how good Patrick looks almost naked, they aren't doing that again. It would be wrong. Because Will loves Ryan.

Who are you trying to convince?

He sighs, tests again, calculates his insulin dose, sticks himself, and begins to eat. Mac 'n' joe is always tasty. Though at the moment it seems hard to choke down.

Chapter Fourteen

A WEEK PASSES, and Will finds, like with most bad things that have happened to him, he can't sustain the same level of agony and outrage he felt at the onset. Seeing Ryan and Hartley together still hurts like hell, but he focuses on Good Works, looks for Christmas presents for his friends and family, and works out in the hotel gym.

The rest of his time is spent brainstorming with Patrick on the improvements to the neurology unit. Surprisingly, he finds some regular glimmers of joy and fun in the progress they're making together, and he begins to take quite a lot of confidence and pride in their work.

For his part, Patrick seems to do the same. After a few more phone calls to his old assistant to arrange for the contents of his rented apartment in Atlanta to be boxed up and stored, Patrick's old life seems wrapped up entirely. He devotes himself to getting his surgical team up and running and making appointments with patients from his waiting list. But as far as Will can tell, Patrick's main focus is on spending more of Good Works' money. He wants new equipment, even better labs, and higher salaries for the nurses on his team.

"Can't bring in first class brain injuries to a sub-par unit" is Patrick's explanation. *"Every day Healing Regional isn't up to handling some of my potential patients is another day a person dies because I'm not the man operating on his head. Just hand me a blank check."* Will's nearly content to do just that.

As the days pass, Will's not sure when it happens, but he starts to look forward to his evenings with Patrick at the Tallgrass.

"Come on, it's not so bad," he says when Patrick spits out the sushi Will picked up at the grocery store after Patrick whined about missing his favorite Japanese restaurant in Atlanta.

"If by 'not so bad' you mean 'only a little rancid,' then sure."

They're sitting at the hotel room table. Will reaches out to fork a piece from Patrick's plate. He pops it in his mouth, grins widely to call Patrick's bluff, and then promptly gags. His mouthful ends up next to Patrick's on the napkin.

"Oh God, that's disgusting."

"The offerings of Healing," Patrick says, holding the napkin up toward the ceiling, and closing his eyes as though in prayer. He then takes the napkin and the remaining sushi to the bathroom. Will laughs as he hears the sound of the toilet flushing.

"The porcelain god was happy to accept the sacrifice." Patrick picks up the phone. "Yeah, room service? Send the usual for me and a slice of pecan pie for Will." He glances up. "You're still craving it, right?"

Warmth blooms in Will's chest. "Yeah, but I'd need to adjust my insulin dose for it." He takes another bite of his veggie-hummus wrap. Patrick confirms the pecan pie order and hangs up the phone.

"Your BG numbers have been good the last few days," Patrick says as he sits across from him, nodding.

"How do you know?" It's not like he tells Patrick his numbers usually.

"You have tells."

"I do?"

Patrick nods. "You get irritable and you rub your hands over your face a lot when you're going low. And when you're high, the skin around your mouth goes whiter than normal. Makes you look like you're wearing lipstick."

"Oh. Huh." He looks down at his hands and studies his nails. No one's ever noticed these things before. *He* didn't even know about them. Why hasn't anyone else ever cared enough to watch for these kinds of tells, if only to prevent a hypoglycemic episode?

Will has had a really great streak of results the last few days. Ideal management, really. He wonders if it's because Patrick keeps a close tab on Will's food intake and, eating so much himself, reminds Will to eat small amounts often. Before, Will sometimes forgot to eat until he was shaking and swoony.

Patrick looks up and smiles. Will's heart stutters at the sharp whiteness of teeth against soft lips. "You know what I miss about Atlanta?"

"Sushi?"

Patrick's smile glints again. "Besides sushi."

"Cuban food."

"Besides Cuban food."

"Soul food."

"No, dammit, I miss brains!"

Will laughs.

"My fingers are just itching for a stereotactic laser and some squiggly brain tissue to use it on."

"You want me to round one up for you? Put my Molinaro genes to good use? Shove some people off high things? Hit people in the head with vases full of flowers like on *Magnum P.I.*?"

"I can't believe how much you love those reruns. You just like his mustache."

Will gasps. "You can't deny that Tom Selleck was a hot mofo."

"I admit I like a hairy chest, but a hairy upper-lip not so much."

Will's fingers rise self-consciously to the open top buttons of his shirt, touching the curly, blond tuft of chest hair there. He remembers Patrick rubbing his face in it as they'd fucked in Vegas. He flushes but returns determinedly to the topic of procuring a brain for Patrick. "Do you want me to run someone over with my car?"

"Sure. Who would you hit? No, let me guess. Hartley the hottie."

Will feels his smile lose some joy, but gain in vindictive pleasure.

"I think he deserves the shove-off-high-places treatment instead."

Patrick considers this and nods. "Yes, it's a plan. I'll even shave more hair than necessary when I fix him, just to make him suffer a little extra."

"You'd do that for me?" Will grins.

"You betcha. Just call me the most generous guy you know."

"Well, that's not too far off the mark. You're incredibly giving."

Patrick's expression changes—a hint of heat—and then it's gone. Will clears his throat. He hadn't intended it to sound so suggestive. He'd just meant to reference everything Patrick's done for him since this whole mess began, and instead he's now thinking about how generous Patrick is in bed, and how well endowed, and he's getting hard, which just sucks.

It's times like this when Will wishes they could get divorced already. But the moment passes, and Patrick greets the room service guy with his usual enthusiasm for the food, if not for the person delivering it.

"Here. Five dollars extra for no chitchat. Just hand over the goods and leave me to this gorgeous hunk of beef." Patrick shuts the door in Perry's face. He eschews the table for the sofa and, balancing his plate on his thighs, flips on the television. "Sit where I can see you eat. Even though you adjusted for it, there's a lot of sugar in pecan pie. Don't want you spiking."

After sticking himself yet again, Will moves to sit next to him on the sofa, and Patrick shifts so he can both look at the screen and still easily check Will over.

"Thanks," Will murmurs. The first bite is heavenly. The sugary middle melts all over his mouth and he sighs blissfully.

Patrick's eyes are on his mouth and he sounds a little breathless. "I'm not paying for it. It's your credit card on the room bill."

"No. Thank you for caring enough to keep an eye on me."

Patrick's smile is gentle and his eyes warm. "I've already told you, I don't want those Molinaros seeking revenge on me if you die on my watch." But somehow it sounds like he's saying, *I like you way too much to let you get hurt.*

Will's insides go all squirmy, like a thousand caterpillars are turning into butterflies in there.

Patrick's eyes drag from Will's mouth to the TV. "Oh, look. *Family Feud.* The idiots they round up for this show are astounding."

And the spell's broken.

Will eats his pie in silence missing the butterflies and studiously ignoring what that might mean.

PATRICK SITS IN the comfortable leather chair across from Will's desk at Good Works, looking through the latest threads on *The Hurting Times* app on his phone and listening to Will's fingers tap as he answers a final email of the day.

"You're avoiding your friends, huh?" Patrick asks. "Don't you think that probably looks suspicious?"

"What are you talking about?" Will's still typing.

"*The Hurting Times* forums are all abuzz with how you're holed up in the Tallgrass with me, blowing off calls and texts from, and I quote, 'lifelong pals.'"

Will turns away from his computer screen and stares at Patrick. "You follow *The Hurting Times?*"

"Of course." He waves his phone at Will. "It has more actual content than the so-called paper around here. It's an amazing, endless vat of gossip stew."

"About people you don't know."

"I know some of them. There are pages and pages about your mother, for instance."

Will puts his hand up. "I don't want to know."

"So you're claiming you've never looked? Not even to see what they say about you? Or Ryan?" Patrick looks at Will coyly. "Or

Hartley?"

Will's cheeks turn red and his mouth moves without words. Of course he's looked—Patrick can tell.

"Fine. I looked up what they had to say about Hartley before I left town and…" He sneers and shakes his head. "It was all good."

"Yep, they think he's a steady hand for your Ryan."

"Ha! They always thought Ryan was a steady hand for *me*," Will snarks bitterly.

"I guess even a steady hand needs a steady hand."

Will turns back to his email, but his fingers don't move on the keyboard. "Don't look at the threads about you. You won't like what they say."

"*Au contraire mon frère*. I love what they say about me. I'm apparently Satan himself according to 'anonymous sources at the hospital,' aka the nursing staff. Let's see, someone I highly suspect of being Ryan says I'm a douche who lacks moral fortitude, and then there are the people who claim they've heard good things from Andy and Jenny. They say their word and your marriage to me is proof enough that I'm actually a good person."

"Please just stop." Will rubs a hand over his face and leans back in his chair. "You're being such a dick right now."

Patrick glances at a clock. "When did you have lunch?"

"Earlier. At lunchtime. When do you think I had it?"

"Huh. Test yourself. Then eat this." He tosses Will a bite-size Snickers bar. "Well, after you eat one of your hard candies from the drawer. That'll hold you until our dinner with your Granny and her lover." He grins. "At least she is according to *The Hurting Times*."

"Reba is—" Will breaks off, tests himself and rolls his eyes. Then he opens his desk drawer, and brings out a jar of white coins dotted with a few red, followed by a big bag of individually wrapped lifesavers. He opens a yellow one and pops it in his mouth. He closes his eyes and leans back in his chair. It only takes a short time for the candy to work. "Fine, I have no idea who Reba really is to Nonna."

Patrick shrugs. "Does it matter?"

"Not to me."

"Your lack of curiosity is sad." Patrick stares at the jar of coins. It's half full. He knows what they are. "That's a lot of white chips. A lot of silver too."

Will slowly unwraps the small Snickers and pops it in his mouth, chewing silently for several seconds. "I've never made it to nine months," he says after he swallows.

Patrick shrugs. "My dad never made it a month. You've got him beat." He motions at the other colored coins in and amongst the white. "At least a few times anyway."

"I made it to six months a few times, and I was on my way to nine months." Will says this with strangely bitter fondness, like he's almost proud he's been denied it. "I had another three weeks to go. Before Vegas."

Patrick lets that sink in and then he stands up, grabs the jar, and opens it.

"What are you doing?"

He pulls out one white chip and holds it out to Will. "This is all you need. The rest of these are just reminders of failure and who the hell needs that?" He pours them into the trash next to Will's desk and throws the jar in too. "Start fresh. You've got a white chip and eleven days down. That's enough. Don't beat yourself up over things you did last year or the year before that or ever. Be done with every time but this time."

Will stares at him, mouth open. There's a speck of chocolate in the corner of his lips, and Patrick wants to lean down and lick it away. He shoves his phone in his pocket and grabs his coat, scarf, and gloves from the rack by Will's office door. "Let's go. I'm starving."

As he turns to leave Will's office, he sees an older, balding man standing in the doorway staring at him with an odd expression.

"Owen." Will pockets the white chip Patrick forced into his

hand. "This is Patrick." He stands up and motions between them. "Patrick, this is Good Works' attorney and my AA sponsor, Owen."

"Nice to meet you," Patrick says. "By the way, I did your job just now."

"My job?"

"The sponsor work." Patrick takes in Owen's soft face and wrinkled suit. He looks tired, but that's no excuse. "Let me guess, you're probably good with the acceptance and love stuff, right?" He wriggles his fingers at Owen like that's all hoodoo-voodoo. "But someone's got to make sure his sorry ass moves on from the past. I never want to see him holding on to more than one chip again."

Owen, obviously confused, just nods. "Everyone in AA has their own preferences about—"

"No. It reinforces hopelessness."

Owen looks nervously to where Will is still standing behind his desk. "Everything okay?"

"Yeah." Will's smiling and shaking his head, as though he's surprised at this truth. "Everything's fine."

Owen glances toward Patrick warily. "If you're sure?"

"Oh, for heaven's sake," Patrick mutters, pushing past Owen to leave the office. "I'm not the boogeyman sent to Healing to destroy Will's life while scaring nurses and small children."

"It's okay," Will says as he gathers his own coat and gloves. "He's hungry and he's right. That always makes him a bear. But I promise, everything's fine."

Owen grips Will's shoulder and looks meaningfully at him. Will shrugs and Patrick's done here. He walks down the short hall, past the blond receptionist whose name he hasn't bothered remembering, and out onto the sidewalk of Healing.

The cold air bites at his nose and he rubs it. As he starts off toward the Tallgrass without Will, he doesn't know why he's so angry that Owen's allowed Will to self-flagellate with those chips for so long. But he really, truly is.

"OF COURSE THE man is a spy, William. What else were you expecting?"

"Nonna—"

"Your father is very interested in your happiness." She rolls her eyes. "But that's not the important thing I wanted to talk to you about. Darling, everyone is going on about how you're in hiding with your new man." Eleanora's rings glint in the low light of the Meadowlands' chandeliers.

The fairly classy restaurant in the lobby of the Tallgrass is full of people, mostly locals it seems, though Patrick recognizes a few nurses and doctors from the hospital gathered in groups of their own, sharing a meal. He wonders if he'll ever be invited to join in. Knowing how beloved he's already made himself at the hospital, probably not. It's never bothered him before, so he's not sure why it would now. At least Don likes him.

"Apparently, Caitlin has told her pals at school that even *she* hasn't met Patrick yet. The entire teen set is whispering about it. From what I understand, they believe the S.E.X. is just so good you can't leave the room."

Patrick puffs up his chest.

Reba slides a rough-edged hand through her loose, dark hair and murmurs, "It's become a point of pride around town for those who can admit to having met Patrick."

"If they really want to make my incredible acquaintance," Patrick says. "I'm not that hard to find. I'm at the hospital, here with Will, or at Brown Gargle with Jenny."

Will glances his way, brow furrowed. "I didn't know that."

"What?"

"About Jenny."

Patrick reaches out and pats his hand. "It's okay, puddin'-pop. She's lovely but doesn't hold a candle to you. Not enough chest hair or a big enough dick."

Reba chokes on her wine, and Eleanora puts a hand on her shoulder until Reba waves her off.

Will's face is the color of the table cloth: radish red for Christmas. "Patrick, please."

Patrick doesn't apologize often, but Eleanora may end up being the key out of this fake-marriage prison. "Sorry, ladies. I forgot my manners."

Eleanora snorts in a delicate, ladylike way and lifts her glass. "To God's honest truth. Just the way I like it."

Will's reluctant to toast, but Patrick lifts his soda cheerfully and they all clink. He watches to make sure Will drinks and smiles at him when he does. Will rolls his eyes.

"Now," Eleanora says. "You've told Patrick about Thanksgiving, haven't you William?"

"I haven't even thought about it, Nonna. I'm sorry. I've been so busy."

Eleanora's eyes narrow with a hint of annoyance, but she slaps her hand gently against Will's cheek. "Of course you have, darling." She turns her attention to Patrick. "Every year, Betty hosts Thanksgiving and Christmas, but she's in Florida visiting her brother and tanning her round tush. So, for the first time in almost a decade," she spreads her hands dramatically, the rings catching light, "I will get to host the Thanksgiving feast at my house."

Reba leans in close enough that Patrick can smell her shampoo: rosemary and mint. "Betty's a dear woman and she does serve a wonderful meal, but Eleanora has missed playing hostess to the family."

Eleanora huffs gently. "I've never understood why they don't allow me to host. They use the excuse that I'm not actually blood family." She makes it sound like that qualification is utterly absurd. "Certainly, William is the only Patterson I'm related to, but that shouldn't matter at all. He's my favorite grandchild and, at this point,

I know Kimberly better than my own son. I am as much family as anyone else. I've earned that place, haven't I?"

"Of course, Nonna."

"Not that the Pattersons aren't annoying. Hypocritical, sanctimonious, and always getting into trouble. Except for Kevin. He's just boring and a bit of a tool, but—"

"Nonna!"

"He is, William! He's got a stick shoved up his ass so far that—"

"Nonna, I'm serious." Will glances around to see who's listening. "Please be respectful. He's my uncle."

Eleanora leans toward Patrick and whispers, "You'd think that after watching his lover die slowly he'd want to honor the man by living a little, but instead he simply wastes away in his own dull manner."

"He's still grieving," Reba says. "Some people don't get over the death of their loved ones so easily."

Eleanora gasps. "Are you implying that I took Max's death too well?"

"Of course not."

"Well, Max was an asshole, so I was well rid of him."

"Roy wasn't an asshole," Reba says softly. "He was a sweetheart."

"And a little slut."

"Nonna!" Will hisses.

"There's nothing wrong with promiscuity, William." She lifts her chin haughtily, as though she's being quite open-minded. "Unless you bring death home to roost."

"Now you sound like Mom."

"Oh." Eleanora shudders. "Well, then I take it back. Roy was obviously the picture of devotion and loyalty. The last thing I'd want to do is sound like Kimberly. She's far too hypocritical for her own good."

Will sighs. "I don't like it when you talk about the family like this."

"I like it," Patrick says, eating his green beans eagerly. "Eleanora, are you QueenBea on *The Hurting Times*?"

Eleanora blushes. "Oh, hush."

Reba shakes her head and rolls her eyes. "Will, I understand Connor's been sick with a double ear infection. How's he feeling?"

Will frowns. "I'm sure he's better or I would have heard about it by now."

"Olivia rode her bike over after school the other day." Reba's dark eyes search Will's. "She's worried about you. I think you need to introduce the kids to Patrick soon. I know it's only been a few weeks, but they're used to seeing you a lot more often, and apparently your mom has made it sound like Patrick doesn't like children, and that's why you don't bring him around."

"What?" Will's ears go red.

"I like kids. For the record," Patrick says, patting extra butter onto his dinner roll and taking a bite. "They're better than adults most of the time, anyway. And they'll probably love me, just so you know. Don't want you getting jealous or anything when they decide that I'm the best thing that ever happened in this family."

Eleanora smirks and clasps her hands together, her knuckles jutting up and pressing against the thin skin. "Yes, darling, you should let the children meet him, just to ease their minds."

"Soon," Will agrees.

"They'll meet him on Thursday regardless," Reba says. "Thanksgiving, remember?"

Will swallows visibly and pokes around at his chicken Caesar salad. "Right. Thanksgiving."

"Will there be pie?" Patrick asks.

"I've been working on the menu for a few weeks." Reba smiles at him. "What's your favorite? I'll make sure to have one just for you."

Patrick decides he loves Reba and that if she was younger he'd marry her and allow her to have his genius babies. "Pecan pie with chocolate chips."

Reba pats his hand. "Done."

"Eleanora, you've won yourself quite the woman." Patrick's feeling generous since he hasn't even tasted the pie yet. It might be terrible, but the thought of someone making pie just for him fills him with warmth. "I hope you compensate her well."

"She's never complained." Eleanora has her eyes on Reba's and a fond smile on her lips. "Not even once."

"Wish I could say the same about Patrick," Will mutters and then flushes again, rubbing his neck and wincing. "Not that you and Reba are like me and Patrick…because you're not married, and you're not—"

"Hush." Eleanora rolls her eyes at him. "You're ridiculous, darling. Now, where is that waitress? I think we should all have dessert. Don't you?"

Patrick grins. Eleanora might not be able to get them out of this marriage quite yet, but she's going to treat him to dessert and a full-on Thanksgiving dinner. Another week of being married to Will seems a fair trade for that.

Even if Patrick's starting to worry Will's neck is going to be permanently damaged from sleeping on the couch.

FINALLY, PATRICK GETS the page he's been waiting for a few days later, and Will is morbidly excited for him.

"A gunshot wound from an attempted suicide out on the rez. They're 'coptering it into Healing Regional for my expertise," Patrick says, shoving his arms in his coat and heading toward the hotel door. He smiles, sharp and beautiful. "Don't wait up for me, puddin'-pop."

Will paces restlessly by the window for a few minutes, a vicarious jolt of adrenaline coursing through him. But as the evening wears on, he calms down and works through some Good Works emails and grant applications. The hotel room is weirdly quiet without Patrick in it, so after a lonely dinner in the room, Will changes into running shorts and a T-shirt to hit the gym. He works out hard until his limbs feel like Jell-O.

The next morning, Will wakes up alone. He does all of his usual morning routine before heading over to Brown Gargle to pick up a jam doughnut and a Calamalatte Jane for Patrick.

Surely he's out of surgery by now.

In the corridor near the OR, he chats with a travel nurse named Heidi. "The patient's expected to pull through," she says. "But I can't say much more than that. As for the quality of her future life…well, that's up to God."

"It's a testament to Dr. McCloud's surgical skills that she's alive at all," Don says, approaching from the opposite side of the nurses' station. He leans against the counter and smiles warmly at Will. "One might imagine with his narcissism and raging ego that he's exaggerating his abilities, but amazingly, his own opinion of himself…" Don shakes his head. "Well, it doesn't even cover it."

Will grins and hugs Patrick when he exits the on-call room. "Hey, congratulations." Will squeezes tightly, feeling the length of Patrick's slim body against his own. "I'm proud of you."

Patrick hugs him back. He smells like antiseptic and Will is tempted to hunt for the scent of his skin beneath the harsh chemical. "I know to you it's impressive, but really it's just me doing what I do."

Will's heart pounds as he steps out of Patrick's embrace. His cheeks flush and he tries to cover for it. "As usual, you've got no modesty about being killer in the OR."

Patrick laughs. "Just what I need—another terrifying rumor about me." He grabs Will's hand and tugs him back against his body, taking hold of his chin and gazing up into his eyes. Will's knees go weak and he grabs Patrick's shoulders, clinging to stay upright against the wave of *want* when Patrick's mouth brushes his tenderly. His head swims as the kiss deepens, and when Patrick sucks on his lower lip, a whimper escapes Will.

Don clears his throat. "This is a hospital hallway, not your honeymoon suite." He sounds amused.

Will dizzily clings to Patrick's arm as their kiss breaks with a wet pop. He's not sure what had brought the display on, but as he stands dazed, wiping his lips on the back of his hand, Patrick's already talking to Don about his next surgery tomorrow. Apparently, there's a baby from the reservation hospital with hydrocephalus, and Patrick's going to demonstrate to one of the peds specialists a new technique for dealing with the problem.

Will can't even begin to understand the specifics and doesn't want to. He's still reliving the wet, hot press of Patrick's mouth. He startles when Don grips him on the shoulder. "Congratulations again, on not only such an obviously happy union, but on bringing this hospital real prestige in the form of your new husband. I believe they call that a *coup de main*."

"Ooh, fancy," Patrick says. "And here I thought you'd go with the more rustic 'two birds, one stone.'"

Don walks away as though Patrick's said nothing, and they stand together for a moment at loose ends in the hospital corridor. Finally, Patrick rubs a hand over his neck. "I'm beat. I'm heading back to the hotel. Coming?"

Will should go to Good Works now, but there's something appealing in the idea of calling it a day at nine in the morning and heading back home with his husband. Except that Patrick's not his real husband. The Tallgrass isn't his home. No matter how many kisses Patrick lays on him in public, or what everyone else has been willing to believe, Will can't fool himself. Patrick doesn't love him. And Will still loves Ryan.

"Come on," Patrick says. "You need some rest. You've been working hard lately."

"I can't. I'll meet you there for dinner, but I'll be a little late. I want to see my Nonna first."

"Sounds good. Tell the *grande dame* hi from me."

Will falls into step beside Patrick, heading toward the elevator to the main floor. They ride down alone and exit to a nearly empty corridor.

"You *were* great," Will says again. "That girl's going to live because of you."

"Don't jinx it. She's not out of the woods yet. Infection or any number of things could take her down before I could count to ten."

Will slides his hand into Patrick's, enjoying the loose twine of their fingers together. He swings their clasped hands lightly. "Yeah, I know. But I'm impressed."

Patrick pulls his hand free and wraps his arm around Will's shoulders. Their hips bump as they walk. He leans over and whispers, "Glad I can impress my husband. He's been a tough ass to crack lately."

Will bites the inside of his lip and then jumps when Patrick swiftly smacks his butt right in front of the nurses' station.

Patrick laughs and calls out as he walks away, "Meet you at home tonight, Will."

IT'S THE MIDDLE of the night, and Patrick can't sleep. His back is aching like a bitch from another nine-hour surgery, and his neck feels like it's on the verge of clenching up into a crick, which won't do at all since he's got another surgery in the morning.

He sits up in bed, listens to Will's soft snores from the sofa, and then flops back down.

It's no good. His hamstrings are too tight, and his lower back is arcing pain up to his shoulders and neck. With another glance at the sofa, he flips the side light on its lowest setting and gets out of bed.

He grabs his yoga mat and begins with a sun salutation. It's all going well until he's on his back, bringing his legs over his head for plow pose when his toes hit the coffee table, knocking over the chess set and sending pieces skittering all over the floor.

"Shut up!" Will grumps.

"Sorry."

"Patrick, I'm trying to sleep," Will says a little more calmly than his initial outburst, but he's clearly still irritated.

"Sorry. Back hurts." Patrick grunts. The stretch is difficult and doing its job. "Got surgery tomorrow. Yoga helps."

Will grumbles but doesn't say anything else. Patrick finishes his routine, but his neck is still killing him. He sighs, goes into the bathroom, and pops an ibuprofen.

He's getting ready to turn the light off and go back to bed when he decides he should shower first. He's sweaty and the hot water might help his neck relax. He pulls his shirt over his head just as Will comes into the bathroom.

"Gotta…" Will waves at the toilet.

Patrick starts the shower, turning it to hot, and begins to shuck his underwear.

"Wait." Will's finishing up pissing. "Let me—I'll just—"

He washes his hands and then comes around behind Patrick. His fingers are warm from the hot water when he digs them into Patrick's shoulders.

Patrick leans against the bathroom sink, moaning with pleasure. It's good. So very good. His skin tingles and his dick wakes up. Will pushes his thumbs in at the base of Patrick's skull, and then works the tension down his neck, through his shoulders, and into his arms.

"If you ever want to give up your career as a professional do-gooder, you'd make a killing as a masseur." Patrick moans again as Will presses firmly on the worst knot, using his slight height advantage to get good pressure on it.

"Just relax."

"God," Patrick moans, and Will shifts behind him.

The steam from the shower fogs the mirror until Patrick can't see

Will's face. He holds very still as his cock stiffens and aches. It's the middle of the night. Will still seems half asleep, but he's doing a great job on Patrick's body. Anything could happen. Patrick starts shaking in anticipation.

Will's heat radiates against his naked back, and the relatively humid air in the bathroom leaves a slick residue on his skin. The material of his boxer-briefs clings and he thinks Will's T-shirt must be damp too. The image makes him close his eyes, breathing through the lust coiling hard behind his taint, making him even harder.

Will pushes and pulls, rubs and works. His breathing comes in soft pants across the back of Patrick's neck. Patrick swallows, takes a step back, and feels Will's erection against his ass. Will's fingers pause and Patrick clenches his jaw. God, he wants to turn around and kiss him. But he does nothing and Will moves away, ending the massage. "Better?"

Patrick nods, and Will leaves. He looks at the fogged-up mirror and sees swirls in the condensation from where they both wiped it off to shave in the morning. He pulls off his underwear, taking his erection in hand and jerking off in the shower, imagining Will had crouched behind him and eaten his ass instead of hightailing it back to the safety of the couch.

Shaking slightly with the exertion to stay silent as he reaches orgasm, Patrick watches his come circle and flow down the drain. He rolls his neck and groans softly.

"Christ. I've *got* to get divorced. This marriage crap is killing me."

Will & Patrick

EPISODE THREE

Do the Holidays

BY

Leta Blake & Alice Griffiths

About This Book

Follow Will & Patrick as they do the holidays in this third installment of the romantic-comedy serial, Wake Up Married, *by best-selling author Leta Blake and newcomer Alice Griffiths!*

A couple's first holiday season is always a special time. Thanksgiving, Christmas, and New Year's Eve are magical when you're in love. Too bad Will and Patrick's marriage is a sham and they're only faking their affection for each other. Or are they?

Sparks fly in this episode of the *Wake Up Married* serial. Will the sexual tension between Will and Patrick finally explode into a needy night of passion? Or will they continue to deny their feelings?

Episode 3 of 6 in the Wake Up Married *serial.*

EPISODE THREE

Chapter Fifteen

"IT'S A GOOD day for a Thanksgiving feast, isn't it?" Kevin asks as he jumps down from his truck wearing jeans, cowboy boots, and bundled up against the weather in a thick, brand-new barn coat.

Patrick can certainly agree that it's an excellent day for feasting—not that there's ever a *bad* day—and puts on his best polite smile. It makes his cheeks feel plastic, but he's determined to do his part to convince the world that he's the happiest camper who ever pitched a tent. So to speak.

Yep, his marriage is *totally* real and being stuck in a one-horse town in South Dakota to avoid the ire of Will's mob family is peachy keen.

Well, to be fair there are actually a ton of horses in Healing.

"You're looking good," Kevin says to Will. He simply nods at Patrick like he's not worthy of further consideration.

Patrick shares the sentiment wholeheartedly, though his blood does rush faster at the sight of Kevin's nice front bulge in his jeans. If everything were different, he'd still let Will's cowboy uncle plow him for a night or three. He'll never share that information with his handsome, hunky bride, though.

Kevin squints at Will. "You going to come out and see that stallion soon?"

Patrick bites back a chortle that good ol' Uncle Kevin is actually talking about horses now. How the hell did Patrick end up in this farce? Oh, right. A night of drunken, mind-blowing sex with Will and a Vegas wedding. He still can't believe this is his life.

Will hugs his uncle and they slap shoulders manfully before Will pulls back, smiling. "You know I have no time for riding these days."

"Well, he's a prize. A real looker. He goes off hot, but not too hot. If you wanted to sell him, I could facilitate that, but he's a damn fine animal."

"It feels wrong to sell him without even seeing him."

Kevin squeezes Will's shoulder and shakes him a little. "That's my boy. Make sure you know what you're giving up. You might even decide to spend more time out on the farm."

"I doubt even the prettiest stallion is going to turn my head quite that much, Uncle Kevin."

"You used to love to ride. You and Roy would head out on Applesauce and Joyful—" Kevin clears his throat and looks up at the sky. "Those are good memories."

"Uncle Kevin's partner Roy taught me to ride," Will says to Patrick. "When I was just knee-high to a grasshopper." He puts his arm around Kevin and guides them toward the front door. "So, what are you calling our wedding gift?"

"He's yours. I didn't want to get too attached to a stable name. But I've been calling him Manny. He's registered as Be Your Own Man, so it seems to fit."

"Sounds good to me," Will says. "Manny it is."

Patrick thinks Eleanora's house could stand to be grander, more like the lady herself, but it's quite elegant inside and out, which is evident as soon as they enter the glamorously wallpapered entry hall. Reba greets them all enthusiastically and takes their coats. The scent of various pies and meats floats down the hallway and Patrick's stomach gurgles in anticipation.

Will looks at him out of the corner of his eye, laughing under his breath.

Pounding feet come charging down the hallway. A freckle-faced, redheaded, demon child around the age of six bounds into Will's arms and kisses him soundly. "Will! I've missed you!"

Will hugs him hard and props him on his hip. "I've missed you too, buddy. I'm sorry I've been so busy the last couple of weeks."

The kid lets go of Will's neck long enough to examine his eyes closely. Apparently satisfied with what he sees, he turns his focus to Patrick. "You have red hair too."

"Auburn," Patrick corrects, but nods. "It was redder than yours when I was your age, though."

"Connor, this is my husband Patrick."

"The one Mama doesn't like?"

Will's smile is a little frozen. "Yes. But Patrick's a nice guy. I think you'll like him too."

"But why didn't you marry Ryan?"

"Because I fell in love with Patrick." Will's voice is strained, but Connor doesn't seem to notice.

Patrick adds, "And I fell in love with your brother."

"So we had to get married, you see?" Will taps his brother's nose. "That's how love works."

Connor assesses Patrick slowly. "Do you like to play Legos?"

"For your information, I'm a master Lego builder."

It's like Patrick's said the magic words. Connor slides down from Will's arms and grabs hold of Patrick's hand. "Come on. Nonna has the best Legos. They used to be Will's but I get to play with them when I'm here."

Patrick waves off Will's protest that he doesn't have to play with the kids. Will starts to follow, but is corralled by his uncle, probably to discuss the horse some more. Patrick doesn't mind. He's not really interested in having to spend too much more time with the man, and he's hoping to avoid Will's mother for a while longer.

The room Connor drags him into is high ceilinged with a wide, but rather thin, Persian rug across the entire wood floor. There's a leather sofa and a rocking chair in the corner, but otherwise the only furniture is beanbags and large pillows.

"This is the playroom." Connor pulls Patrick toward the massive pile of Legos next to one of the beanbags. "We can make a mess in here."

Patrick notices a girl with dark blond hair curled with a book in another beanbag in the corner. This one is…what was her name? Ophelia? No, *Olivia*, he guesses, based on her age. He's pretty sure the other one is older. Caitlin, maybe? Will said something about her being a teen. She's probably off trying to be a grownup with the rest of the family.

Olivia doesn't greet him, so he ignores her too. He's discovered over the years of working with kids that sometimes the best way to gain their trust is to leave them alone for a little while. He plops down with Connor and starts putting Legos together.

Connor keeps his eyes on the Legos. "Mama says you and Will got married too fast."

"Your mama isn't one to talk."

Olivia laughs but Connor just looks confused.

For a while they build. Connor shows Patrick each of his creations and Patrick gives him thumbs up. Connor is enthusiastic about the fleet of space ships Patrick's designing and begins to contribute some of his own.

"Are you just after Will's money?" Olivia asks out of the blue.

"Nope," Patrick says, a flash of irritation shooting through him at whoever told her that. "I'm loaded already. I probably have as much money as Will does." That's not even close to accurate. The Molinaro patriarch left Will beaucoup cash, but given how very little Patrick cares about money, it may as well be. "So tell your mommy I'm not after Will's fortune."

"Caitlin said it, actually," Olivia replies. "Mom is pretending you guys are super happy together."

"Well, we are."

"Maybe. But my mom's mad Will married you. She likes Ryan.

He took care of Will."

"I take better care of Will." He knows this is certainly true. He takes damn good care of people.

"Ryan kept Will from making bad choices. He kept Will safe."

"Safe from what?"

"From AIDS," Olivia says.

Patrick goes cold all over. "What do you know about AIDS?"

"Roy died from it." Olivia's chin goes up. "I don't remember Roy, but Uncle Kevin loved him. And I know you get it from, *you know.*"

"Enlighten me."

"From *being with* a lot of people."

Patrick ignores the implication that if not for Ryan Will would have "been with" untold numbers of people and shakes his head. "No, you 'get it' from being with an infected person. And, technically, you contract a virus known as HIV, which develops into AIDS if not properly treated."

"AIDS kills you."

Connor eyes are dark and fearful. "Is Will gonna die?"

Patrick tousles Connor's red hair reassuringly. "No. Well, yes, Will is going to die one day. Everyone dies one day. But he's not going to die from AIDS."

Hopefully.

Nothing in life is a guarantee. He can't really promise this. But still. He turns his attention back to Olivia. "When your uncle's partner contracted the virus, death was a more common outcome. But medication has come a long way since then. Don't get me wrong, people still die from AIDS, sure, but there are good treatments for HIV now. I promise, even if your brother became infected he has all the money in the world for treatment."

Though the diabetes would complicate things.

He pats Connor's head again. "But Will doesn't have HIV or AIDS. And your brother will always make good choices to significantly reduce his chances of being exposed to it."

"He doesn't make good choices without Ryan," Olivia says, her eyes glinting. "He got married to you. Was that a good choice?"

Touché. "Ryan isn't the source of your brother's good sense, no matter what your overprotective mommy may think. Will can take care of himself."

Olivia's eyes are too-knowing. He returns her gaze steadily until she looks away. She shrugs. He sighs.

"But where *is* Ryan?" Connor asks again, his face crinkled in confusion.

Olivia answers, "He came by last week, remember, Connor? He said he'd come visit us again soon."

Connor's little shoulders sag with relief. Patrick feels a sinking in his gut. Is that jealousy? Over a child's fondness for his older brother's long-time boyfriend? *Get a grip, Patrick.*

More ships are added to his and Connor's Lego fleet.

"Do you know how to break a horse?" Olivia asks suddenly, like her judgement of his worth as a human is in the answer.

"No, because I don't want to break my skull."

She lets out a small imperious noise. "Are you afraid of horses?"

"Let's just say I keep my distance from giant animals with the power to crush me when they're angry."

Olivia rolls her eyes. "Then don't make them angry."

"Eventually, I make everyone angry."

"Horses aren't people."

"You're just chock full of wisdom, aren't you?"

"Yes." She tosses her dark blond hair and pins him with her brown eyes that are so like her older brother's. "Will's good with horses but he never rides anymore. You should get him to take you out to Uncle Kevin's. Maybe you'd find out you like horses more than you think."

"Doubt it. I'm twitchy. Horses don't like twitchy things."

"True. Maybe you'd hit it off with the barn cats. You could be twitchy together." She smiles winningly at him. "Don't tell me you don't like cats either."

"Cats are fine."

"Professor McMuffins just had kittens," Connor says.

"Uncle Kevin would give you and Will the runt, I bet," Olivia suggests.

"That's okay. I'll just keep Will instead. He's company enough for me." Though not the kind of company Patrick wishes for lately. He thinks a man should at least get laid for dealing with in-laws and snarky little siblings.

"Will's a dork," Olivia says, fondly.

"He is." Patrick nods. "So what kind of pie can I expect later?"

"Yes! Pies!" Connor exclaims. "Reba put the pies out on the counter! I counted ten!"

Olivia rests her book on her chest to count on her fingers. "Two pumpkin, two pecan, apple, pecan with chocolate chips—"

Patrick pumps his fist. "Yes!"

"And chocolate and two lemon meringue, and one shoofly."

"I'm going to have a piece of each," Patrick declares.

"Me too!" says Connor.

Olivia lips curve up into a naughty smile. "Really, Patrick? Do you think that's a good choice?"

And Patrick has to laugh.

ELEANORA SITS AT the head of the table and Kevin at the foot. Then it's Will, Patrick, Olivia, and Reba down one side, and Kimberly, Connor, Caitlin, and an empty seat that someone murmurs used to be Ryan's down the other. The table is long and fills the ornate dining room, leaving just enough room for everyone to sit comfortably. The press of bodies and hot food makes Patrick overly warm and a little sweaty, but he's too excited about the spread to care.

Patrick hasn't had a real Thanksgiving dinner since he lived with Dinah. The meal itself is amazing and so long as everyone is putting food into their mouths, Patrick feels very nearly happy. Before long, a heavy lethargy pulls at his body, even before he's done with his second plate of food. After dessert, he's so stuffed he feels nearly catatonic.

Patrick drowses a little between Will and Olivia, who, after their conversation in the playroom and a secret pie-eating competition between them (agreed upon through eye signals and winks), has warmed to him considerably. Maybe because he lets her win. When she and Connor are dismissed from the table to go back to the playroom, Patrick wishes he could join them, but Will, as though reading his mind, shakes his head.

"Finish your pie, okay?" Will murmurs.

Patrick does as he's asked, taking his time with his last piece. But all good things must come to an end. He's blissfully swallowing the final bite of shoofly pie when Kimberly addresses him.

"I'd appreciate it, Dr. McCloud, if you showed even a hint of interest in the conversation going on around you."

Patrick feels Will stiffen, and places his hand on Will's arm to keep him from talking. "If anyone says anything interesting, I'll be happy to listen. But, as it is, it's all just yap, yap, yap about nothing."

Caitlin, plump and blond with blue eyes like her mother, coughs into her napkin. Kevin harrumphs, and Reba presses her lips together to keep a smile in. To Patrick's left, Eleanora chortles into her wine glass.

Kimberly's ire turns on Will, though. "This is how he speaks to your mother? Will, I don't understand, I will *never* understand—"

"It's a good thing you don't have to, Mom. My marriage is my business."

Kimberly clenches her jaw. "Not when you bring him to a family dinner."

"He was invited, darling," Eleanora interjects.

"And not when you allow him to spend time with your younger brother and sisters. Just think what example you're setting."

"Oh yes, letting them see their older brother married to a brilliant, handsome, successful neurosurgeon is a rotten idea," Patrick says.

Caitlin cackles. Kevin huffs and folds his arms over his chest, but doesn't say a word.

"Your mouth is going to get you in real trouble sometime!" Kimberly shoves her blond hair behind her ear, her blue eyes sparkling angrily at him.

"And what was I supposed to do with him, Mom?" Will asks. "Leave him at the Tallgrass? That's not what happily married people do!" He shoots a significant look at his sister to remind his mother Caitlin doesn't know the truth.

She seems to cool her engines at that, but she still shoots Patrick a glare. "Caitlin, go keep an eye on your little brother and sister."

"I'm sixteen now. You said I could stay with the grownups this year."

"I've changed my mind."

Caitlin sits up straighter, her cleavage bobbling in her sweetheart-cut blouse. "Why?"

"Because someone should make sure Connor and Olivia aren't messing up Nonna's playroom."

"Then you go watch them. I'm staying here." She folds her arms over her creamy bosom and glares at her mother.

"Mom, you're ruining Thanksgiving," Will murmurs.

"Let's all settle down," Eleanora says, raising her hands to take command of the room. "Kimberly, this is the first time in eight years I've had the opportunity to host Thanksgiving with the family. Do you want me to think you're sabotaging it?"

Kimberly sighs and leans back in her seat. "No. It's fine. I apologize for making anyone uncomfortable." Though she glares at Patrick like it's his fault.

Patrick's phone buzzes in his pocket and he prays there's been a massive multiple-party Thanksgiving Day pileup so he can get the hell out of Dodge before things go further south.

But it's not the hospital. It's a text from Dinah.

"Excuse me," he says, rising from the table. "I need to take this."

Will nods tightly, his focus still on his mother.

Patrick catches Eleanora's curious eye as he steps through the doorway to the kitchen. It smells amazing in there and if his stomach could hold another bite, he'd pull a plate down from a cabinet and serve up more from the pots and dishes on the counter.

Three more texts have come through by the time he finds the quiet, private nook in the corner behind the kitchen fireplace. He ducks into it, leaning against the brick wall and taking a deep breath.

Pat, wishing you a beautiful Thanksgiving Day. I give thanks for you every day.

The next three texts are photos of the kids around the table: two with Phil and one with Dinah. They all look happy. He touches the screen, expanding one of the pictures to get a better look at Eric. Redheaded and still angry, he sees. He trusts Dinah to do all she can to help with that, but maybe he should send more money for extra counseling sessions. It can't hurt.

"Patrick?"

Will's voice makes him jump and he shoves his phone into his pocket.

"Everything okay?"

Patrick taps his hand against his pant leg and puts on a smile. "Sure. Great. Just…" He feels weird lying to Will, but he can't tell him about Dinah or the kids. He's never told anyone. "Something I needed to handle."

But he hasn't handled it, has he? Not that Dinah will be waiting for a reply. He's awful at getting back to her and that's something he resolves every year to be better at. And every year he fails completely.

"Patrick?" Will steps closer, his head tilted earnestly and wide brown eyes gazing down at him in worry.

"It's fine. Can we get out of here?"

Will swallows and looks over his shoulder, then whispers, "I know my mom was being—"

"A real bitch."

"Overprotective, but she's scared for me. She's always credited Ryan with keeping me safe."

"I know, I heard all about it."

Will cocks his head. "You did?"

"Kids say the darnedest things. Apparently, all that's kept you from death by gay plague is Ryan's steady hand."

Will's cheeks flush. "It's been hard for my mom and Kevin to accept the risks associated with me being gay. They're afraid I might end up like Roy."

Patrick grips Will's shirtsleeves and tugs him deeper into the alcove. "That's absurd. She's more likely than you are to catch HIV, what with her multiple sexual partners and inability to keep her pants on whenever your daddy comes to town!"

"Patrick, I know—"

"But you've been with two people in your life! Me and that dick-weed! And you've always been safe. Even drunk out of your mind, we were safe."

Will's cheeks stain darker.

"What?"

"Once, Ryan didn't—"

"He *what?*"

"Just once. A long time ago. I've been tested since and I'm fine." Will's eyes tighten around the edges. "He thought maybe it was the condom."

"Maybe what was the condom?"

Will's shoulders sag as he wipes a hand over his face. "I can't talk about this here. It's too personal."

"Why do you let her believe he's some kind of saint?"

Will's eyes close. "Because I needed her to support me, to support us—"

"You mean, you and Ryan."

"Yes. And she doesn't trust me!" His eyes pop open again. "For good reason. I was reckless in high school and in college before I met him. Not sexually—well, not that she knows about, anyway. She never found out about the guy I used to blow in high school. But I was reckless with my illness. With drinking."

Patrick swallows back words, reaching up to brush Will's soft hair back from his forehead and then trailing his fingers down the side of Will's face. "Trust by proxy is as good as no trust at all."

Will tucks his lower lip into his mouth. Patrick remembers the soft fleshy feel of it. He slides his hand up Will's arm to his shoulder, the hair at the nape of Will's neck brushing against his fingertips. Will's gaze falls to Patrick's lips. His pupils dilate and his breath hitches softly. An electric tension vibrates between them. Patrick rises up on tiptoe, the space between their bodies vanishes, and their lips nearly touch—

"Oh, don't let me stop you, boys." Eleanora's coy voice cuts in. "But just so you know, William, your mother and uncle are leaving with the kids. Something about needing fresh air."

Will jerks away, his neck and face red. "Thanks, Nonna. We'll just go say goodbye."

"Actually, I'll pass," Patrick says, stalking out of the corner and over to a plate of brownies on the sideboard near the oven. He stuffs one in his mouth. "Think I'll just stay out of their hair."

Will doesn't seem inclined to argue. "It's not your fault everything went bad here today, okay?"

"Whatever."

Eleanor gives Patrick a sly smile as she follows Will out of the kitchen. He pulls his phone out of his pocket again, and with chocolate smudged thumbs he types:

Thanks for the photos of the kids. I'm grateful for you too. Happy Thanksgiving.

Chapter Sixteen

CHRISTMAS IS A week away and, for Patrick, life is looking up.

Ever since Thanksgiving, his new assistant, Stan, has filled his schedule with patients pilfered from Atlanta. Between patient consultations, reviews of files and tests, and actual surgeries, he's in his happy place. He even compliments nurses just to see them smile.

In additional joyful news, neither Will nor Patrick has seen any sign of the Molinaro spy in three whole days. Patrick's feeling pretty good about that. A few well-placed questions to Beth at the front desk confirms the gentleman has indeed checked out of the Tallgrass, and a call placed to Eleanora settles that the Meddling Molinaro Marriage Enforcers seem content, for now, that Will's in a safe and relatively happy marriage.

On the flip side of all that positivity, it's the weekend and Don has forced him to take it off, even calling him at the Tallgrass to say his appointments for the day have been cleared from the hospital schedule.

"But my patients are—"

"Fine with waiting until Monday, Dr. McCloud. It's a stipulation of employment here: every physician on staff must take off at least one weekend per month, and preferably at least one day per week as well."

"That's against OSHA regulations."

"Good try, but I happen to know that's not true." Don clucks down the line. "Don't forget that you have a young husband to please. Take it from me, late nights and medical emergencies can be hell on a brand new marriage."

And so Patrick has no choice but to hang up the phone, flop back on the sofa, and watch Will pace and check over his Christmas list in advance of heading out shopping.

"You're really not going in?" Will asks, his amber-brown eyes lighting up.

"Don says he'll fire me if I step one foot over the threshold."

Will grins. "Then you can come shopping with me. It'll be fun, Patrick. You won't be stuck here in the hotel at least."

"I won't be in a brain," he says morosely, staring up at the plaster ceiling. He doesn't add, *"And I won't be in you either."*

It's become more and more difficult to deal with his sexual needs lately. He tries to jerk off twice a day, just to let off steam. Usually he manages it. He also tries to make himself think of anyone but Will while he's doing it. Usually he doesn't manage that at all. In the end, when he's blowing his load, eyes rolled back and hand flying over his cock, it's always Will. Every single time.

Will snaps his fingers in Patrick's face to get his attention. Patrick bats his hand away, but the little jerk uses his hip to push Patrick into the back of the sofa, making room to sit next to him. "Oh no. It's so sad. No brains for Patrick today. Let's all cry about it."

"Boo-hoo." Patrick throws his arm over his face dramatically.

Will crowds him on the couch even more. Patrick feels every millimeter where Will's hip presses against his own. "C'mon, Patrick. Don't you need to make a list too?"

"For what?"

"For Christmas?"

Patrick shrugs.

"You're telling me there's not a single person you like enough to give a Christmas present?"

He's actually already ordered gifts for Dinah, Phil, and the kids. Scooters and a bike and lots of clothing items. He's arranged for violin lessons for Jane and a sewing machine for Eric. He's paying for sewing lessons to go with it, and he's sprung for new swing set for the backyard. Then there's the weeklong trip to Disney World he's saving to give as a surprise. He's arranged it for the kids' spring break.

Yeah, he's spent a lot of money so far on the people he'd like to give Christmas gifts.

"Just come out with me," Will wheedles, bouncing up and down on the cushion, forcing Patrick to open his eyes again. Will grins down at him.

"Fine. I'll go."

He can either hang out here and jerk off in privacy thinking about Will's soft chest hair, his thick meaty cock, and annoyingly charming smile, or he can walk around in the freezing cold of winter in South Dakota with the man himself. It says something, though Patrick's not sure just what, that actually being with Will is more appealing than an orgasm while thinking about him.

Will pulls him up and gets their coats together. "It's going to be fun. You'll see!"

Patrick follows out the door and regrets only that Will's coat hangs down so far it covers up his juicy, perfect butt.

They hit Brown Gargle first, and Patrick gets his usual, along with an iced gingerbread snowman. Will orders a Buckaroo of black coffee and stares enviously at Patrick's cookie until Patrick offers up half. Watching Will work out his insulin dose, stick himself, and then happily lick the icing off the cookie makes Patrick's heart beat so fast he distracts himself by writing Jenny a little note on a napkin and giving it to Jax behind the counter. "For my wife."

Jax laughs and tucks it in his pocket. "I'll give it to her when she comes in later."

Will watches the exchange with a hint of wondering confusion, but he doesn't ask. He just sips his coffee and follows Patrick back outside. On the gray, cold streets of Old Healing, Patrick eats the rest of his cookie, offering the final bite to Will, who takes it with a sweet, almost puppy-ish smile on his face.

"Where to?" Patrick asks, aching to brush the crumb out of the corner of Will's mouth, and he's disappointed when Will licks it away.

"Let's stop by Tate's first."

"The sporting goods place?"

Will heads off in that direction and Patrick hurries to follow. "Yeah, I need to get Olivia's present and there are probably things there that Connor will like too. And maybe Uncle Kevin."

"Well, if it's for Olivia..." Patrick takes the lead, pulling Will along behind him.

Of all Will's siblings, Patrick likes Olivia the best. After spending two afternoons with Will while he babysat them because Kimberly was stuck at the tack shop working, he thinks he has some idea of what makes each of them tick.

Caitlin is a typical teen girl: into fashion, boys, and gossiping with her friends by text. Patrick likes her, though, because she doesn't suffer Kimberly's idiocy without some pushback of her own, and anyone who can make steam come out of Kimberly's ears is awesome in Patrick's book. And Caitlin? Well, Caitlin's a champ at it.

Connor's an earnest little cutie who has stolen a piece of Patrick's heart, no doubt. They could build Lego space ship fleets forever and never grow sick of each other's company. So, the competition for favorite sibling is pretty steep.

But Olivia's a bookworm and a tomboy. She goes out riding on Will's new stallion and stomps around Kimberly's poshly decorated house in badass boots she ordered from a military supply store online. She calls Patrick out on his bullshit, and she told Will she wanted a tent for Christmas so she and her favorite farm dog, a beast called Rupert, could camp on Kevin's farm together this summer.

Patrick thinks he likes her best because she owns her life in a way none of Kimberly's other kids do. Not even Will. Especially not Will.

Patrick glances over at him, admiring the way his cheeks and ears turn pink in the frigid air. He looks too delicious. It's not fair that

Patrick doesn't get to eat him.

Inside Tate's, it doesn't take long for Patrick to get bored listening to the floppy-haired boy detailing all the latest advances in tent construction and pointing out which tents he thinks Will should consider first. For his part, Will listens avidly, and since the decision is entirely up to him, Patrick wanders off even deeper into the store.

In the back near the canoes, there's a wide, rounded entrance to another store. Patrick hadn't noticed it at all during his first visit to Tate's, but at the time he'd been fixated on getting what he needed to survive the South Dakotan cold. Now he looks closer and sees the arrow sign on the wall. *This way to Tate's Music!*

He glances over a few aisles where Will is studying some aspect of the tent the floppy-haired boy is pointing out. Patrick raises his hand, but Will is studying the tent closely, and so Patrick shrugs, rolls his eyes, and steps on through to the other side of the building.

The room is large and airy. The windows face south, getting good sun. There doesn't seem to be anyone there, customer or employee, but then he spots a tall, fair woman in a glassed-in office near the back. She's on the phone. When she sees him, she waves at the horn and indicates she'll be with him soon.

Patrick explores the room slowly. Near the back, where he's come through, the displays show used instruments for rent: guitars, trumpets, clarinets, keyboards, pianos, and even a harpsichord. Next to that, there's a section with rows and rows of sheet music for sale. And in the opposite corner, near the front of the store, there's a walled-off area around an upright piano, obviously used for lessons.

His breath comes in slow and tight as he circles the older, used uprights for sale or rent, and heads toward the very front of the store near the windows. He's drawn by the shiny, black baby grand glimmering in the sunlight. He should leave now before he reaches it. He should turn around and walk away. If he learned anything from the little show for Will in the Tallgrass lobby it's that he still can't do this. He still can't let himself feel all the things he's shoved down so deep and hard.

But he doesn't leave.

Instead, he sits on the bench and stares at the keyboard. Black and white, each key a place he can go if he wants. And he feels *music* open up inside him. It's laced in anticipation, fear, and possibility. Like the moments before he makes the first cut into a patient's skull. Music grows until it fills him.

His fingers know what to do. It's his heart that doesn't think it can handle this.

He closes his eyes. He places his hands.

It all comes pouring out: his life and love and horror and pain. *That* night, especially, roars through him and out his fingertips. The night he can't live with and can never forgive.

He yanks his hands back from the keyboard. His heart climbs into his throat and gags him. Sweating, he knocks over the bench in his hurry to stand, and he doesn't stay to right it. Scurrying through the hole back to the sporting goods store, he's like a rat outrunning a flood. Seeking safety and high ground.

When he's back beside the baseballs and footballs, he grips the metal racks of colored jerseys rioting around him and presses the back of his hand to his mouth to keep from throwing up.

It's fine. I'm fine. We're fine.

The words of comfort spin in his mind, and he thinks of Dinah's soft hands. Patrick straightens up, tugs on the bottom of his jacket and shirt, and nods. He's fine. It's all fine. He can shove the feelings down again and never have to feel them, because it was a long time ago now, and it's over.

Patrick shakes his shoulders out and turns his back on the door in the wall. He focuses on his breath the way Dinah taught him when they first met. He forces himself completely into the present by looking closely at everything around him, not allowing his mind to think of anything else.

He moves through the store, jittering his hand against his pant leg, until he stops and pauses by the front register, forcing himself to look at each magnet and keychain closely. It's all nature-lover bullcrap, but one keychain catches his eyes. It carries the Caduceus, the Greek symbol for medicine.

He picks it up and holds it in his palm. Glancing over his shoulder at Will, who's talking to the floppy-haired boy *still*, Patrick puts the keychain back on the hook before pulling up Amazon on his phone. He quickly finds exactly what he's looking for, taps purchase, and feels his panic release at having accomplished something. "That's another present down," he murmurs to himself.

At that same moment, Will finally chooses a tent and heads toward the front.

"I'll put it on your account, Will," Floppy says. "And have it gift wrapped for you to pick up tomorrow. It's gonna be a hit, I know it!"

"Thanks, Scott," Will says, hands in pockets, and a sweet smile on his face. "Ready?" He turns to Patrick. "Was that you playing piano over in the music store earlier?"

"Nope."

Will narrows his gaze. "Okay, if you say so." His fingers slide over Patrick's hand and for a moment Patrick thinks he's going to twine their fingers together again like he had in the hallway of the hospital just before Thanksgiving, but then he pulls back and scratches behind his ear self-consciously. "I've still got a few more presents to buy, but we could probably both use a snack break first, huh? How about Jimmy's?"

Patrick wishes Will hadn't let go. He can feel where Will's fingers had been like an electric trail across his hand. "Sounds good."

"Share the pickle with me?"

"Of course."

Will walks out of the store ahead of him and Patrick follows. The cold air slaps him in the face, a welcome shock.

"Ah, the acrid smell of insulin in the morning." Patrick's voice is still gravelly from sleep as he turns on the shower and pulls down his black boxer-briefs revealing his tight ass.

Will looks quickly away and back to the syringe he's filling by the bathroom sink. "I can never get the last dose to eject from the insulin pens. I always have to pull it out with a needle."

"After living with you, I have an entire list of ways they can improve insulin pen injectors."

"I should have my lawyer queue up an appointment for you with the pharmaceutical company."

"You do that, puddin'-pop, and I'll be there with a PowerPoint presentation. It'll consist of four words over and over. 'Do your damn job.' If pushed, I might throw in a 'Don't make me do it for you' as a closing argument."

Will pinches a bit of fat from his abdomen and sticks himself quickly. He's done this for years, but he never stops hating it. Especially syringes. They're somehow worse than the insulin pens. "I'll ask Owen to make that happen."

Patrick snorts from behind the curtain. Will glances over and heat floods his gut as he notices the shadow outline of Patrick's morning wood. "Oh, um, let me just—" He hustles to deal with the used needle and ends up dropping the syringe in the sink. The scent of insulin grows stronger. "Why does it smell like Band-Aids?" Will muses as he finally gets rid of the used needle and cleans up the syringe, tossing the now-empty insulin pen.

"It's the preservative. Meta-cresol," Patrick says. "Mmm, so clinical. So sexy."

"And you're so weird."

"Nothing like the smell of a hospital to get my motor running."

Will glances back at Patrick's shadow behind the shower curtain. He's still got a half chub flopping around as he washes his hair. Will clears his throat.

"Have you considered an insulin pump?" Patrick asks.

Will tries to drag his mind from Patrick's erection. "I don't want one."

"Because?"

"I don't like the idea of having something attached to me. All the time. Something I have to rely on to do its job."

"You trust insulin pens have the right dosage, that the dial works, that they're—"

"I know, Patrick. But I have the right to my own preferences when it comes to my medical treatment."

"Fair enough. So what's the deal with your daddy?" Patrick asks sans segue.

"What are you talking about?" Will packs up his testing kit and uses a black marker he keeps in his murse to make a dot on the back of his left hand. He can't forget to drop by the pharmacy and pick up his replacement insulin pens.

"Papa Molinaro. What's the deal with him and the holidays? He wasn't around for Thanksgiving. Will he be dropping down the chimney on Christmas Eve with a bag full of presents for you and a nice hard dick for your mommy? Or what?"

Will rolls his eyes. "Thanks for that image."

"You're welcome."

"He spends Christmas with his daughters. Or at least he used to. I don't keep in touch with him."

"Ah, the half siblings you've never met. So, no Christmas phone call from Papa?"

"No." Will feels the familiar hot, impatient squirm of nastiness in his gut. Conversations about his father usually bring it on.

"No Christmas card stuffed with cash?"

"No card, no text, no Skype, no email."

"Huh."

"What?"

"He's obsessed enough with you to have you followed by mobster spies but he can't pick up a phone. At best, that's inefficient."

"At worst?"

"At worst, Starshine, you have a deeply dysfunctional father/son relationship."

"Wow. You really are a genius."

Patrick barks a laugh and then begins to hum the new Madonna song he's been singing off and on for the last two days.

"That's still stuck in your head, huh?"

"Mmm-hmm."

"Better than 'We Three Kings' mixed with 'Scarborough Fair,'" Will mutters. Finished with his morning insulin rituals, he starts the water in the sink to begin his shaving routine. "Tony doesn't do anything he doesn't want to do, and being a reliable member of our family was never something he was good at."

"When did you last see him?"

"It's been three years. It can be ten more for all I care." Will pumps shaving cream into his hand and smears it on his face. "He sweeps in on a whim, wreaks havoc on our lives, and sweeps out again."

Patrick is quiet behind the curtain and Will glances over to see that he's rinsing out his hair.

"There's no pattern, unless you count my mom getting serious with anyone. As soon as my dad gets wind of her being happy with someone else, he has to come to town and wreck it."

"With his dick."

Will sighs. "Everything's about sex for you, isn't it?"

"Nope. A lot of things. But not everything." He turns off the water and throws back the curtain. Will averts his eyes quickly, but his hands are already shaking enough that he's not sure he should be trusted to shave himself. Patrick goes on. "But it's all about sex between your parents. *The Hurting Times* churns with scintillating tales of your mom inappropriately hopping on your dad's pole."

"Like you know anything about 'inappropriate'."

Patrick laughs. "Like I know about that time they banged in the bathroom at some old lady's funeral. *The Hurting Times* forum had pages dedicated to that one."

Will's ears grow hot.

"And, hey, for the record, even I know a funeral home toilet is a bad place for sex. Public bathrooms are tourist destinations for germs." He shudders and slings a towel around his hips, thankfully covering his dangling dick. "It's not sanitary."

"You are such a jerk."

"So you tell me." Patrick grabs a hairbrush and runs it through his wet hair. The dark auburn looks almost brown and glistens brightly in the overhead bathroom lights. "There's evidence of a genetic component to addiction." Patrick's eyes go foggy as he muses, "But is it addiction or abuse? Both probably."

"What are you talking about?"

"You, mainly. But I'm also talking about them. If *The Hurting Times* gossip about the two of them is even half true, they are their own kind of addicts. Addicted to each other. Addicted to sex. Addicted to falling in love. Especially your mother. But it's possible your father uses the intense sexual connection between them as abuse."

"I…" Will's fingers clutch at the razor and he drags it against his skin carefully. "I didn't think you believed in psychology mumbo-jumbo."

"I don't believe in spiritual mumbo-jumbo. And, yes, psychology is a lot of bull-honky, but as a neurosurgeon, I can't deny that thoughts and experiences have physical effects on brain tissue. Dubious and whoo-hoo as most psychological theories seem compared with hard science. What's your dad's sign?"

"Really?"

Patrick shrugs and sidles up next to Will at the sink, examining his own face in the mirror.

Will sighs. "Early November. So, what's that? Scorpio?"

"Ah. And your mother's a Scorpio too."

"How do you know? *The Hurting Times* again?"

"I know because I've met her."

Patrick's arm slides against his as he reaches for the can of shaving cream. Will moves slightly to the side but Patrick just scoots closer. Will can smell soap on his skin and shampoo in his hair. He wonders what those curls would feel like slick and wet under his fingers.

Patrick rubs on shaving cream and reaches for his razor. His naked chest slides against Will's bicep.

Will tries to concentrate on shaving, but Patrick's reflection in the mirror is distracting. His normally pale skin is flushed from the shower and his nipples are pink and peaked. Will clears his throat and scrapes his razor over his face again.

"Addiction," Patrick muses on. "You didn't stumble into that on your own. You drink…and your parents screw. That's how these genes play out. And with both of them being Scorpios…"

Patrick's arm rubs against him, and Will clicks his tongue against his teeth. Between this *touching* and Patrick's speculation about his parents' sex life, Will can't tell if he's going to pop an inconvenient boner or if his balls are going to shrivel up into his body.

"Two Scorpios can burn down a barn from the heat of their mutual orgasms."

Ball-shriveling wins out. "Okay, well, this conversation has covered everything I never wanted to think about. I'm going to be late to work."

Patrick studies Will in the mirror.

Will wipes his face clean of cream, decides not to care that he's got one stripe of shiny skin on an otherwise stubbly face, and, grabbing his murse, leaves the sink to Patrick.

He dresses quickly. He really is going to be late. Not that anyone at Good Works would say anything to him.

"Do you have surgery scheduled?" Will calls out as he slides his wallet into his back pocket and hitches his bag on his shoulder.

"No."

"Meet you here tonight?"

"Will there be more Capheus?"

"Yes. And more Lito."

"It's a TV date with the hubby, then," Patrick says, stepping out into the room with his sharp grin in place.

The hubby.

"First person home calls room service," Patrick adds. "Order stuff we both like. We can share."

"Deal."

"Oh, and Will? For the record, you'd still be hot even if you wore an insulin pump."

"Thanks. But I'll stick with the pens."

Walking out of the pharmacy twenty minutes later with his new insulin pens, Will wonders what kind of sex Libras and Aries are supposed to have. *You already know the answer to that. Hot enough to burn down a barn.*

"God, just stop."

He rubs a hand over his hair and decides to focus on the day ahead. He'll take it one step at a time. Just like AA has taught him.

WILL IS ALMOST ready to wrap up his work for the day when Owen steps into his office. He strives to keep a smile on his face. He's supposed to meet Patrick back at the hotel in twenty minutes. They've upgraded their earlier plans to include working out together in the hotel gym after they finish their binge watch of *Sense8*. He's been looking forward to it all day.

"Don't look so excited to see me." Owen laughs, dropping into the chair and crossing his ankle over his knee. His eyes are tired and his bald head shines as if he's rubbed his hands over it a lot through the day.

"Of course I'm happy to see you. Are you all right?"

Owen nods and smiles at Will kindly. "You haven't been to a meeting in a month now."

Will swallows. He knows where this conversation is going. "Owen, I don't think the program is—"

"The program works if you work it," he parrots, holding out a silver chip and spilling the party line.

"I don't want the chip, Owen. I haven't earned it by AA principles."

"Maybe not. But I know you haven't been drinking. I know you've been sober since your return from Vegas."

"Yeah. But that's not what you get a chip for. You get a chip for going to meetings. It's not for sitting around not drinking."

"Have you been sitting around? Or have you been working a different kind of program?"

Will doesn't want to play verbal games right now. He wants to go watch *Sense8* with Patrick. "What are you getting at, Owen?"

"Just take it. Take it." He nods at the chip in his hand.

Will doesn't want to, actually. He isn't sure what Owen wants from him in exchange. "I'm not going back to meetings, Owen."

"I know."

"Then why?"

"Because you're doing better than you ever did attending them."

Will cocks his head. "I thought you believed in AA as the end all and be all of recovery. That's why you're a sponsor. Why you're my sponsor."

"It's the end all and be all of *my* recovery. As for why I'm your sponsor, well, there's more to that story and you know it. You needed a new one and your grandmother knew I'd been successful at making the program work for me. Eleanora asked me to sponsor you and I did." He smiles. "I have." He runs a hand over his bald head again. "But I've learned a lot over the years of attending AA meetings."

"I'm sure you have."

"Both by being sponsored myself and by sponsoring you, and also by watching people in the program. Seeing who comes and who goes, and who comes back. One thing I've learned is that some people grow harder in their sobriety. Dogmatic. It has to be done this one way or you'll fail and die drunk and alone in a gutter." His gray eyes glimmer at Will. "You know those types of people. We both do."

"I dated one."

"Yes, you did. But I've come to see there's an alternate route. Instead of becoming dogmatic, I've mellowed, grown more flexible." He smiles. "The way I see it, everyone walks their own path."

"They do their own steps."

"In a way. But I've seen some people thrive better outside the AA dynamic. I'm not supposed to say that. We both know that's not an AA-approved comment, but it's true. And, surprised as I am to say it, the path you stumbled on seems to be working for you."

"I think it's called hitting rock bottom, Owen."

"Yes. You certainly did that." Owen smiles. A silence infuses the room and Will thinks maybe he can dismiss Owen now and get home to Patrick.

But then Owen speaks again. "Have I ever told you how I met my wife?"

Apparently, Owen's in the mood to impart wisdom. *Sense8* and Patrick will have to wait. "Rhonda?"

Owen places the chip in the middle of Will's desk and then leans back in his chair, sighing. "She was my secretary. When we met, I was married to another woman."

"Oh."

"Yes. I know how you feel about infidelity, but hear me out." Owen looked over Will's shoulder into the past. "I started an affair with her at the height of my alcoholism. Lost my wife, my kids, my car, my house, my job." He laughs and looks down at his shoes.

"Lost my girlfriend."

"Yeah?"

"And when I finally got sober, I realized losing Rhonda was when I kissed concrete. If Rhonda had stayed with me, I'm not sure I'd have hit for a long time."

"So you think Ryan leaving me was my rock bottom?"

"No, I think marrying a stranger was your rock bottom."

Will rubs a hand over his face.

"But I also think maybe your situation with Ryan is more like my situation with my first wife, Tandy. She and I were like oil and water. Drinking came easy around her."

"Owen…" Will shakes his head. He can't hear this. He doesn't know what he feels for Ryan anymore. Things get more and more confusing every day. But he knows he doesn't want Owen making Ryan into the bad guy. "I know you never liked him."

"I like him just fine. And you? Well, you love him. I know that. I loved Tandy too. It doesn't mean we were right for each other."

"Thank you," Will says, standing. He puts the silver chip in his pocket. "For bringing the chip. Maybe I'll make it to six months this time."

Owen stands and gives Will his hand. "Just think about what I've said."

"I will."

"My money's on you." Owen walks around the desk and pulls him into a hug. "My money's always on you, son. Now get out of here. Get home to your husband."

Chapter Seventeen

CHRISTMAS DAY WITH the Pattersons goes pretty much as expected. The entire family's gathered at the farm, a medium-sized horse ranch on the edge of the reservation. Patrick's heard enough to know this is where Will spent a lot of his childhood, riding, mucking out stalls, and being an almost-farm-kid. Patrick's curious about the place almost despite himself.

The land is dotted with white fences and horses run over the hard ground. It's the kind of place Patrick's read about in books and, as a kid, sometimes imagined running away to when things with his father were at their worst. It makes him feel a little dizzy in its "this is where love grows" way.

Snow started the day before, and it's piling up fast. White and beautiful. Patrick's a little bit amazed by it. Seeing it blanketed over meadows and trees mesmerizes him and he's silent for most of the length of the half-mile driveway up from the main road to the house. Even though he spent his higher educational years in the Northeast, deep inside he's still the little Southern boy who never got his fill of snow.

As they draw closer to the white clapboard farmhouse, there's an intimidating number of unfamiliar cars parked in a line down the driveway. Will stops behind the last one and before he turns off the motor there's already a truck pulling up behind them.

"How many cousins did you say you have?"

Will winks at him. "I've got zero first cousins on this side of the family. These are all second and third cousins. And there are a lot."

"Great."

Will puts his hand on the back of Patrick's neck and rubs gently. A sizzle of heat and wishful thinking burns into Patrick where he touches. "Are you ready?" Will asks, his voice soft and reassuring.

"With all the practicing I've been doing, I'd better be."

For most of the last week, Will's been randomly zinging him with things like, "I'm my Great-Aunt Polly, and you're you. I shake your hand and say, 'Oh, dear me, you're a lovely boy!'"

Apparently the right response to that is not, "Lady, I'm a neurosurgeon, not a boy." Who knew? Well, now Patrick does.

As they walk over the powdery snow to the house, the chimney is puffing smoke and the whinny of horses echo from the barn. Patrick's nervous as hell. Like this is the real thing. Like these people are his actual husband's family and he's got to impress them.

Christ, he's drinking the Kool-Aid too.

"You're going to be great." Will presses his hand into the small of Patrick's back before slinging the same arm around his shoulder and shaking him a little. "You'll see. Don't look so scared."

"I'm not scared, I'm…" He can't think of any other plausible thing he might possibly be. He's at a loss for words. This is terrifying and a very bad sign. Who knows what might pop out of his mouth to fill the silence?

Will kisses his cheek and Patrick's skin tickles where his lips touch. Why can't they just go back to the hotel and make this day end in an orgasm? Because that's what Patrick wants. Not some fake family time, not to pretend they're in love, not to have people judging him and finding him lacking. No, he wants to be alone with Will naked and without pretense. Like they had been in Vegas.

Will kisses his cheek again, a little softer this time. His eyes catch Patrick's and his lips shift into a sweet smile. Patrick swallows hard. "I promise it'll be all right."

The lingering tingle distracts him as they enter the house and take off their coats to a flurry of Christmas greetings. He can't stop thinking about the kisses or feeling the echo of them in his skin.

At least meeting Grandma Betty is shockingly easy. She's a roly-poly woman with warm green eyes and dark brown hair. Not ugly, but she isn't remarkable looking either. How she birthed the blond wonders that are Kimberly and Kevin, Patrick's not sure. Nor is he sure how a woman with a heart obviously the size of the state itself raised such suspicious and sad creatures. Within moments of his introduction, Grandma Betty sweeps him into a hug and kisses his cheek. Stunned, Patrick just lets her. When she pulls back, she squeezes his face until his lips fish-pucker and says, "You are *welcome* in this family, young man."

Well, then. He'll take it. It's better than someone accusing him of being a nasty, awful neurosurgeon again. *Pfft.*

It's only moments, though, before Patrick's hopelessly lost and confused again. There's no way he can keep all of Will's extended relatives straight. There are simply too many of them.

He smiles wanly at an attorney with a wide nose and a face like a hammer. He nods along to the yammering of a woman with a butch-dyke haircut and cat-eye glasses. There's a kid with a runny nose who Patrick avoids like the plague. He chats mindlessly with a brunette woman who has a black purse with mints in it; he knows because she asks everyone who talks to her if they'd like one. The farmhouse is big, but it's not big enough, and the common rooms are so crowded he feels trapped. His temples throb.

When he's released from the mint lady's company, he's relieved to be immediately taken aside by Will, Eleanora, and Reba. But then Will's pulled away by Connor and a small cousin, and Eleanora sends Reba off for another plate of hors d'oeuvres. Patrick can feel Eleanora measuring him as he sips his coffee and watches Will help Connor and the tiny cousin put ornaments on the tree.

"So, Dr. McCloud. Am I sensing a sea change in you? Is there a similar one in my grandson?"

Patrick shrugs casually, a small prick of sweat starting at the back of his neck as he taps his hand against his leg. "No change here. I'm the same man I've always been."

Eleanora smirks and takes a sip of her wine. "I see. All right then, if that's how we're going to play it."

Patrick shoots her an irritated glance. "Play what? I don't play games."

"If you say so, darling. Just don't blame me later when the divorce is final."

"Is there hope the divorce might come through soon?" His pulse pumps muddy and dark as his stomach drops to his toes.

"Hope?" She laughs. "No. I'm afraid not."

Patrick's sharp intake of breath clears the darkness away. "But you are working on it?"

"I am. Though maybe I shouldn't bother. What say you?"

"I say you certainly should bother."

She laughs delightedly again.

"Mrs. Molinaro, are you drunk?"

"Of course. Of *course*." She rolls her eyes. "No, I'm not drunk. I'm just not sure you really want what you say you want. You realize my grandson *is* quite the catch, and you could do worse than to be loved by someone like him."

Patrick's heart kicks his chest and he remembers the tingle on his cheek after Will kissed it. "Excuse me? Who said anything about love?"

He realizes he's nearly shouted when half the room looks his way. Will starts toward him, leaving Connor and the little cousin behind.

Patrick whispers, "The last thing on earth I'd want is to further involve myself with your grandson. We've made the best of it and that's as far as it goes."

"I think you actually believe that." Eleanora looks up at the ceiling. "Heaven forfend. You're an idiot too. And I had such high hopes when we first met. Oh well, here he comes. Look innocent now, darling."

She kisses Will's cheek as he draws near. "I'm going to go find Reba and refill my glass. Your husband is *charming*, as always."

Will watches her walk off and then turns to Patrick. "What was that about?"

"Nothing. Your grandmother is crazy."

Will smiles softly, leans against the wall, and looks over at his family and then Patrick with affection. "Yeah. I know."

Patrick shakes his head. The whole Molinaro-Patterson family is insane. Will too, for that matter.

The food, though—the food is *magnificent*.

In the kitchen, things are busy, but there's more room to breathe. He huddles up against a small built-in desk against the front wall and watches the women bustle around making things that smell delicious. Grandma Betty's put on quite the spread. Patrick's mouth waters just looking at it, but every time he dares to reach out to try to grab a bite of something, Betty swats his hand away.

"Dinner isn't served yet, young man," she says to him sternly, but then she grins and sneaks him a cookie.

All in all, Patrick thinks both Will's grandmothers like him. Eleanora, for all her weird innuendo, is always pleased to see him, and he thinks that's kind of cool given the fact that she knows he's not really Will's true love. Grandma Betty, oblivious as she is to the truth, seems to have accepted him solely on the basis that if Will loves him, she will too.

Patrick finds something heart-achingly wonderful about that. He's never known a woman so trusting. He hates to think that probably makes her stupid, especially since he likes her so much already.

Even though Betty's busy rushing around the kitchen, she seems pleased that he's practically salivating with every dish she pulls out of the oven or prepares on the countertop. Patrick stands off to the side and admires the pies—the many, multiple *pies*—until Betty finally cuts him a piece of pumpkin. Patrick hopes he can keep his mouth so full of food all day long he won't have the chance to say something offensive to her. He wants her to stay ignorant of what a terrible man her grandson is married to. He wants her to smile at him in her warm way forever.

After a long afternoon of pretending he's crazy in love with Will while avoiding actually talking to anyone in the family, Patrick ends up in the kids' messy playroom in the back of the house, building Legos again with Connor and some of the cousins.

"There you are." Will leans against the door jamb, watching as Patrick puts the final touches on what he's dubbed the Tower of Doom. "I missed you."

Patrick smiles at him. "You found me."

"Come out to the barn with me." He shoves his hands in his pockets and smiles softly. "I want to show you something."

"Gonna show him Manny?" Connor asks.

"Maybe." Will winks at his brother.

Patrick's heart flops at the slight innuendo in Will's voice. He knows it means nothing, but he finds himself leaving the kids behind without question and following Will to get their coats before heading out into the freezing cold.

"Is this some kind of surprise?" he asks as Will opens the door to the barn. The scent of hay, dirt, manure, and animal heat spills warmly into the frigid air.

"Come in and see." Will pulls the door closed behind them.

In the gloom, the barn dust motes swirl and fall. The sound of horses stomping and nickering reaches him, and Will drags him closer to the stalls.

Will's fingers are warm on his wrist. "Were you having fun with Connor?"

"Sure. I told him and the other kids a story called The Deadly Brain Worms. They liked it."

"Oh?" Will brings him to a halt in front of a stall with a gigantic, black horse in it. Patrick keeps back. "Is it a good one?"

"The best. It's about a boy who gets infected with brain worms. They eat his skull hollow from the inside out. It's gruesome and avoidable. All he needed to do is drink milk and eat his veggies. Vegetables and milk are anathema to brain worms."

"Great. They'll all have nightmares on Christmas."

"They're kids," Patrick says, taking in the fuzzy scent of hay. It's almost enough to make his nose itch, but not quite. "They loved it."

Will pats the snout of the mammoth animal in front of them and then reaches for a carrot from the bucket on the wall. "Well, when my mom sends Connor to stay with us at the Tallgrass because you're the one who gave him nightmares, you'll think differently."

"Ah, more stellar parenting from Ms. Patterson."

Will feeds Manny the carrot and Patrick glimpses the horse's huge, white teeth. "My mother isn't perfect, but she loves us."

Patrick shrugs and gingerly reaches out to touch Manny's nose too. It's velvety and soft, but when the horse's lips curl up to reveal those teeth again, he snatches his hand back. "All that back and forth between her and your father? All the men who come and go? All the guilt and fear she's stuffed into you about being gay? If that's what they call maternal love, I'm glad I missed out on it."

Will sighs softly and turns to face Patrick. The shimmering dust motes and backlighting from the sunset through a window make him appear almost angelic. "Come on, you don't mean that."

"Yeah, I guess I don't." Patrick thinks of Dinah and what a wonderful mother she is—the kind of mom he'd always hoped his own would have been if she'd lived. "I wanted my mom any way I could've had her growing up."

Will sidles closer. Patrick can feel the heat of him, all bundled in his warm coat. "It's okay to want what you never had, you know. It'd be weird if you didn't."

A long moment passes and the puff of their breath curls in the air around them. Their eyes meet. Will licks his lips and Patrick's gaze lingers on their shine.

Manny snorts. Wet, cool air hits them both, making Will laugh and Patrick jerk a step back.

"Oh, hey," Patrick says after Will feeds Manny another treat. The silence between them seems to fill with meaning until Patrick has to break it apart. "This is for you." He reaches into his coat pocket and pulls out a small, square package. He tosses it to Will.

"You got me something?"

Patrick shrugs. "Merry Christmas."

Will looks down at the gift in his hands and then slants a glance at Patrick from beneath golden lashes. Patrick's heart trips over itself and the rest of him seems to tumble down after it. "Patrick, this is so nice of you."

"It's no big deal."

"I left yours under the tree in the house."

Patrick frowns. "Well, open it already."

"It's just…" He rubs his fingers over the paper. "Did you wrap it yourself?"

"Yes. And I should warn you that you might not like it."

Will's eyes glow. "I like that you wanted to give me something."

Patrick feels a little lightheaded and he wants to grab Will and kiss him. Instead, he snatches the gift back from Will's hands and rips off the red and white wrapping paper. "Here." He shoves the bare box back at him. "Open it."

Will laughs. "Okay. Gee, have some patience." He pops back the lid and laughs softly. "Really? This is what you got me?"

Patrick lifts the big, clunky, and absolutely unmistakable medical alert bracelet from the box. "Damn straight. It's for your own protection. If you're ever in Vegas, drunk out of your mind, and about to marry some schmuck of a doctor, at least he'll know what he's getting into."

Will chuckles and his neck flushes along with his cheeks. His voice is soft and sweet when he says, "You're such a dick."

Patrick's blood thrums hard enough his skin shivers. Trying to focus, he fastens the bracelet onto Will's wrist, pushing back the fancy one to make room for it. "And if you happen to go into shock somewhere people don't know you, there'll be no confusion or delay in getting you the right help." He taps the gold, fancy design of the old one. "This is just a trip to Deathland waiting to happen."

Will swallows and looks at Patrick with such a soft expression that it makes Patrick's insides ache. "You really care about me."

Patrick's gut twists hard and he can barely breathe.

"Don't you, Patrick?"

He can't do this. He wrinkles his nose. "Did that horse take a dump? It stinks like bullshit in here."

Will rolls his eyes and shoves the now empty box into his coat pocket. "You can be a jerk if you want, but I've got your number. You care about me."

Patrick's knees shake, and he pushes his heels into the ground to steady himself. "I'm a doctor. I care about people's health."

Will leans closer and sing-songs in his ear, "You care about me, you do, you really do."

A shiver runs through Patrick and his cock stirs. He is so close to grabbing Will's shoulders and kissing him for every reason that isn't about appearances. He scratches his nose and looks away. "Fine. If thinking that makes you happy, then go right ahead."

Will laughs. "See? You care about what makes me happy."

Patrick rolls his eyes and turns back to examining the horse they came out to see. Manny is striking, dark, and tall. Patrick will never, ever ride him.

"Now I feel like a jerk. I didn't get anything this special for you."

Patrick shrugs. "Well, if that isn't grounds for divorce, I don't know what is." He flicks a smile Will's way. "Get this marriage dissolved, puddin'-pop, and we'll call it even Steven."

Will slings his arm around Patrick's neck and drags him in for a hug. The warm scent of Will's skin fills him up, and he fights the urge to burrow in, to get closer. He wants to kiss the pulse beating in

Will's neck. He wants to thread his fingers into Will's hair. He wants it so badly but knows Will doesn't want it at all.

He shoves back and dusts Will's touch off his coat sleeves and chest. "Stop being ridiculous. It's just a medic alert bracelet."

"Right," Will whispers. "No big deal."

"Won't your grandmother be serving dinner soon?"

Will stuffs his hands in his pockets, a small furrow appearing between his brows. "Sure you don't wanna feed Manny a treat first? He'll be your best friend?"

Patrick reluctantly takes a carrot from the bucket of treats and smiles a little as Manny's soft lips tickle his palm. It's kinda sweet and he has a moment of seeing himself from a distance. Atlanta is a long way from this quiet intimacy in Will's family's barn.

As they make their way back to the house, the winter sunset lights up Will's hair, and the cold turns his lips ruddy and his nose and cheeks pink. Patrick's unmanned by the rushing feeling in every atom of his being. It's so big and yet he can't name it.

Will looks at him, dark eyes glowing, and smiles. "Race ya!"

Something bright bursts inside, painful and perfect. He races after Will, determined to win.

THE REST OF the late afternoon is tolerable. Presents are exchanged between the family and Patrick is the recipient of a surprising number of them. He's given sweaters, lots and lots of sweaters, in all kinds of colors he will never wear. He smiles and thanks everyone for thinking of him. He's vaguely touched by the fact that they did. He's a stranger after all.

Will gives him two navy blue button-up shirts and a new wallet. He's oddly disappointed but smiles at Will and thanks him anyway. Will flushes and leans in to whisper, "I'm sorry. I'll do better next year." And then he colors like he realizes that hopefully there won't be a next year.

Betty's dinner is good and there are too many witnesses for it to all go to hell like it did at Thanksgiving. As he downs the last bite of his final piece of pie, Patrick counts the day as a win.

At least, until Ryan arrives to drop off gifts for the kids. Then everything halfway good about the day is flung into the fieriest of fiery pits and burnt to a black crisp.

Ryan enters the room to a round of greetings from the extended family. Of course he's all sweetness and smiles in front of the Pattersons, giving Betty a kiss on the cheek, laughing with the kids, and even getting a smile out of Caitlin, who's been sullen all day for some teenagery reason.

And then Ryan's gaze lands on Will. The way Will flinches back, it might as well have been a blow. Instantly, Ryan goes prickly and tense, as though it's somehow Will's fault that Ryan should find him here, at his own family's Christmas Day celebration.

Patrick clenches his jaw and watches closely. Ryan turns from Will without a word of greeting, hugs Kimberly, and musses up Connor's hair. "It's just not Christmas without you guys. I've missed you."

"Well, at least he came alone." Eleanora appears suddenly at Patrick's elbow. She gives him a look that makes it very clear where Ryan Whitehead stands in her estimation.

"A true gift," Patrick agrees.

Eleanora snorts and then declares loudly to one and all that she and Reba really must be leaving.

On her way to gather her coat with Reba in tow, Patrick sees her whisper in Will's ear. Will attempts a smile for his grandmother, but then walks out of the living room toward the hallway leading to bedrooms. Patrick should follow him, but he really doesn't want to deal with Will's lovesick misery over Ryan. He sighs, rubs a hand over his eyes, and follows Will anyway.

He finds him in a guest room, standing in the dark by the window looking out at the shimmering snow with his arms crossed and his face lined and pale.

Patrick hovers in the doorway. "I'm going outside to get some air."

Will says nothing; he doesn't even turn his head.

"Okay. Well, I'll be outside."

Patrick feels a strange tug to stay with Will, but he ignores it. He heads past the small mass of traitorous Ryan worshippers in the kitchen and out the back door to the covered porch. Wrapping his coat tightly around himself, he settles in a rocking chair by a large pile of wood. There's a wood stove that heats the area and he's warm enough despite the cold air drifting through the screens. Out in the early winter darkness, the stars are filling up the sky.

He checks his phone to find that Dinah's sent more pictures of Christmas morning. There are enough smiles and dropped jaws to satisfy him. He lingers over the one of Eric and the sewing machine and one of Jane with her surprise roller blades. He texts back a simple: *Merry Christmas* before sliding his phone into his pocket.

Full from dinner, he drifts in a comfortable haze until he hears the crunch of footsteps coming around the side of the house. The automatic lights at the corners of the farmhouse light up the yard and Will appears in their glow, looks around, and seems to settle on the barn. He's only gone a few feet when Ryan comes around the same corner with his arms full of gifts. Those must be from the family to him, Patrick realizes. Ryan stops halfway to the driveway and stares at Will.

"Ryan," Will says, finally. "Leaving without even saying good-bye?"

He didn't say hello.

Ryan snorts. "Yeah. Well, you didn't make me feel very welcome here." He starts walking again, away from Will.

Patrick's stomach twists when Will goes after him.

"Ryan, please, don't do this. Don't end things this way."

This sounds familiar to Patrick, and he remembers Will saying those exact words on the phone in the bar in Vegas.

"How do you want it to end, Will? With a hug and a kiss and a 'maybe someday'? Because even without Hartley in the equation, you are everything I don't need in a partner."

"Ryan…" Will swallows.

His lips curl into a sneer. "Do you need me to spell it out?"

"No."

"You remember what you asked me to do to you before you left? How you wanted me to…" Ryan trails off and shakes his head. "The things you want sexually are sick."

"It was just a question, just a thought…"

"You knew how I feel about anal sex period, and you asked anyway."

"Just once. I just asked once."

"You've asked before. I even did it for you a couple of times." Ryan shudders.

"Okay. I'm sorry." Will's voice is trembling and Patrick wants to hurt Ryan for making Will sound like that. "I still don't think wanting to make love once or twice a year is too much, Ryan. I need affection."

"Sex isn't affection."

"I know. But you don't even hold me, or hug me, or hold my hand. You don't want to touch me at all!"

"Just stop," Ryan says. His face is dark and his eyebrows low. Patrick's gut clenches and he's almost ready to go out there to protect Will. He doesn't trust Ryan not to throw a punch. "It's over. You're a disgusting, perverted drunk, and until you see yourself the way I do and make lasting changes, top to bottom, inside and out, you'll always end up with a drink in your hand, and you'll die alone. Unloved. Unwanted."

"That's not true." But Will's voice trembles, and he doesn't sound certain at all. Patrick's blood boils.

"It's true, Will, and I'm better off without you."

"Oh yeah? You say that but you always come back." Will seems to puff up with some small measure of confidence, and Patrick realizes the instant Ryan came on the scene everything bright and strong about Will had leaked out like a balloon. "Why don't you admit why you're really here, Ryan?" Will asks, pointing his finger. "It's not because of the presents, or the kids. It's because you miss me."

"I don't miss you, Will." Ryan sounds pitying. "And I'm willing to bet you don't really miss me either."

Will looks like he might cry or grab Ryan or spit on him.

"Look, I came out here today because your mother said she and the kids had gifts for me. She asked me to come, and I agreed. But don't be fooled by the affection I have for your family. It doesn't change anything. I won't be coming back here again." Ryan brushes past Will and heads to his car. It's only then that Patrick sees Hartley's shadow in the front seat waiting.

Will turns away from them as his face crumples, and he brings the back of his hand to his mouth.

After Ryan and Hartley's car makes its way down the drive, Patrick walks into the snow-covered yard, the stars dulled by the house's yellow floodlights. When Will sees him, his cheeks burn even brighter, and it's not from the cold.

"You heard all that?" There's a tremble in his dimpled chin. Patrick wants it to go away.

Patrick nods. "Don't believe anything he said. He's a liar and he's not worth it."

"You don't understand."

"No. I don't."

"He doesn't want me anymore."

"You should be so lucky."

Will shakes his head and looks down at his shoes. "I thought we were going to spend the rest of our lives together."

Patrick throws up his hands. "You'd want to spend even a single minute more of your life with him? You call what he makes you feel *love*?" Patrick's blood rushes with rage. Will deserves so much better. Anyone does.

But especially Will.

Will opens his mouth to reply but Patrick cuts him off by slashing his hand through the air between them. "Your deep-seated masochism is ridiculous and offensive, and I don't want to hear another word about him!"

Will's chin wobbles and he stares at Patrick with burning eyes that are wet with tears. His mouth sets into a hard, stubborn line.

The side door bangs shut and Kevin calls out, "Everything okay out here, Will?"

Will doesn't look away from Patrick when he answers. "Yeah, everything's fine, Uncle Kevin. Patrick and I are heading home. Tell everyone Merry Christmas. I'll talk to Mom later."

Kevin starts to protest, but Will turns his back and heads toward the car.

Patrick thinks he should go back inside, thank Betty for the food, and say goodbye to the family and gather up their presents. That's what a person with decent manners does. But he's pissed off, and Will's pissed off, and neither of them is acting much like a decent person right now.

So Patrick follows Will to the car and rides to the Tallgrass in silence.

Chapter Eighteen

W ILL INJECTS HIS nighttime dose of insulin and leaves a note on the bed while Patrick is showering.

Going out for a run. Might hit the gym after. Don't wait up.

Patrick's got surgery in the morning and given the stony silence they'd driven home in, Will doesn't think Patrick wants his company anyway. The ride down in the elevator takes too long and is far too short at the same time. Is he really going to do this? He knows the answer.

The Tallgrass bar is busy, crawling with travel nurses and doctors who aren't going back home, wherever that is, for Christmas, but don't currently have a shift to work either. Will manages to avoid their eyes and finds an empty seat at the bar. The atmosphere is small and cozy, with nooks for tables and soft chairs. The lights are low and the Christmas decorations hung about glisten and glint invitingly. It's a room that calls for intimacy.

Too bad Will has no one to share any of that particular aspect of humanity with. Screw it. He'll share it with himself.

"What's your poison?" the barkeep asks. Will recognizes her as being from the reservation but doesn't actually know her name. He sends up a prayer of thanks that she won't know to stop him. It's a sign.

"Vodka shot. Make that two. And a Heineken, draft."

The girl lifts her brows. "Got sorrows to drown, huh? Or just planning to party tonight?"

"It's Christmas."

She grins. "That'll do it. Set up a tab or charge it to a room?"

"Charge it." He gives his room number.

When she pours the shots, she says, "Name's Ella, by the way."

"Will."

"I'll be back with that beer, Will." She shoots him a grin and he nods tightly at her.

He stares at the two clear shot glasses, filled to the brim with vodka. It'll burn going down, but within seconds that burn will turn into a loose, warm, everything's-better-now feeling in his body that'll travel up to soothe his mind. It's like a lover how alcohol holds him and rocks him in its familiar arms.

Not that he's ever had a lover who did that for him. And why would he? What's he ever done to earn that kind of devotion from a human being? He's lucky that alcohol will even have him.

"Oh, you already ordered one for me. Thanks, puddin'-pop."

Will jerks as Patrick's voice slithers up his spine. Patrick reaches around Will to steal one of the shot glasses. Hot, violent heat roars through him—shame, humiliation, and rage at being caught all at once. "What the fuck are you doing here?" he hisses, trying to grab the shot glass back. But Patrick downs it quickly with a gasp and a squint.

"Getting drunk with you, apparently," he whispers hoarsely, his eyes flooding from the burn of the liquor. "Damn, that's...*damn*." He plops down on the seat next to Will and nods toward the remaining shot. "Now you."

"You think I won't?"

Patrick shrugs. "I think you wouldn't be here if you weren't going to do it, so let's do it together. See where this bad choice leads. It'll be an adventure." He bangs his hand on the bar. "Barkeep!" he shouts, rough and attention grabbing. Will can practically hear heads swiveling in the room. "Two more rounds of shots for me and my husband."

"Patrick..."

"Yes?" Patrick rests his elbow on the bar and props his chin on his fist. His blue eyes are fringed in reddish-brown lashes that glimmer like the Christmas bulbs around them. "Don't tell me you're already having doubts about our next big adventure."

"You're supposed to be in bed."

"And you're supposed to be out for a run. Looks like we both had more exciting ideas for how to spend the night." Patrick nods at Ella as she pours four more shots and delivers Will's beer. "Oh, shots and beer, huh? Are we going clubbing? Does Healing even have a club?"

"You have surgery tomorrow."

"Surgery schmurgery! I'll reschedule it." Patrick waves his hand and downs another shot. He slaps the bar and his mouth screws tight as he swallows. "Bracing! I could get used to this." He takes his second, and then grabs one of Will's shots and downs it too.

"Stop."

Patrick pushes out his bottom lip, pouting. "Why? Don't I deserve to go in on the fun? What'd I ever do to you to be denied passage on your self-destructive ride into the mouth of hell?"

Patrick's speech is already slurring a little.

"You're going to have an awful hangover tomorrow. You're putting lives at risk."

"So are you."

"I'm—"

"Here to get wasted and maybe marry Dr. Johansson back there in the corner—the hot one with the moustache; I know how you like face fur—and take this marriage fiasco one step further by falling into unwitting bigamy. And then what'll you do? I fully intend to witness that. If only for the hot part where you and Dr. Johansson screw." Patrick wobbles on his stool and his brows furrow. "Now why don't I like that idea? I should like that idea!" He presses his lips together and shakes his head. "You've broken me, Will Patterson. I don't work right anymore."

"Patrick, just go back upstairs and go to bed, okay?"

"Nope."

"Why?"

"I already told you why. Maybe you can tell me why we're on this adventure?"

"You were there today. Ryan—"

"Oh! Let's make a drinking game out of it. Every time you say 'Ryan' we take a shot." He nods toward Will's two remaining shot glasses. "You gonna? Or can I?"

Will sighs. "You're an asshole."

"Such sweet nothings. Makes me feel so…" Patrick's hands rise to his heart and he shakes his head meaningfully. "So understood. You get me, Will. You really get me."

"Damn it, Patrick."

"What?"

"I came down here to get drunk and now I have to take care of you instead."

"So I can have this then?" He takes a shot and pours the last one into Will's beer, and then with a sweep of his hand, knocks the beer over. "Oops! Barkeep! Clean up in aisle asshole!"

Will wants to throttle him. He wants to be angry at him for coming down here and putting a stop to his celebration of pain and self-loathing. But he also wants to kiss him and cup a hand to his throat to feel his pulse beat. He wants to thank him for not giving some self-righteous lecture and then kick him for making it utterly impossible for Will to get drunk tonight.

Most of all he wants to hug him until he crushes all the snarky bullshit out of him. Until they both orgasm and pulse with come. Patrick makes him feel all kinds of things. Most of them complicated and all of them at once. It strikes him hard that some of those things are impossible now, but none of them is actually *bad*.

Ella is wiping the mess up and eyeing them both. "I'll get a replacement."

"Nah, he's had enough," Patrick says, standing up and gripping Will's shoulder for balance. "Wow, the floor in this room is lopsided. You should fix that."

Will closes his eyes and shakes his head. "Thanks, Ella." He peels a few bills out of his wallet for a generous tip. "Let's go back upstairs."

Patrick leads the way to the lobby and Will leaves the intimate heart of the bar with a mix of relief and regret. As they pass the baby grand, Patrick slows and stops, taking hold of Will's hand and bringing him around to the bench. The lobby is empty save for Mike Livermont at the reception desk, eating from a giant tin of popcorn and reading on his Kindle.

"Sit with me." Patrick urges Will down next to him on the piano bench and lays his long, elegant fingers on the keys. "Ryan makes you feel worthless." He plays a minor chord. "I know what that's like. How it feels."

"Let's not talk about Ryan." Their shoulders brush together.

Patrick plays another chord. "My dad was a lot like him. He talked a great game and when he turned on the charm people believed him."

Will holds very still.

"My dad had a great smile." Patrick's own smile glints at that, and Will feels sick to his stomach, because it's the first time Patrick sounds almost fond talking about his father. "He also had a way of knowing just want to say to make a person feel like nothing, like you weren't worth the shit on his shoes."

Another chord, this time shifting down the keyboard to a solemn, bass sound that makes Will's heart quiver.

"My dad never loved me."

He pulls his hands away from the piano keys and looks Will in the face. "And Ryan never loved you either. Maybe he thought he did. Or maybe hurting you feels so good to him he mistook it for love, but he doesn't and didn't love you."

"You don't know about us."

"Stop lying to yourself, Will. I can't always be here to drink your shots for you."

Patrick stands, looks over his shoulder to see if Will is following, and walks surprisingly straight for how wobbly he'd been in the bar. Will lets him lead the way, his heart heavy and his feet like lead. Going back to the bar isn't an option, but neither is forgetting all the years he had with Ryan. If he lets that go? What does he have?

A fake marriage and a suitcase full of shame. And Good Works. He can't forget that. It's all that really matters. He's ruined everything else.

PATRICK GOES STRAIGHT to the bathroom, pushes two fingers down his throat, and vomits up the alcohol he's consumed. Will stares at him from the bathroom doorway, eyes wide with guilt. After brushing his teeth, Patrick changes into sweatpants and a T-shirt and flops onto the bed. He's dizzy with alcohol and exhausted. The burst of anger he felt watching Will with Ryan has long ago faded into a bone deep weariness. The situation down in the bar has only wiped him out more.

He's got surgery tomorrow. He should get some rest.

But he can't let down his guard. Instead, he watches Will out of the corner of his eye, wondering if he'll head back down to the bar after Patrick falls asleep. How does he have the misfortune to be so deeply involved with a man who has more crazy in his life than a spinster has cats? How has he let him get so far under his skin?

Will sits on the sofa in his dress shirt and pants with his head in his hands. His back is straight and taut with tension, and he keeps rubbing one side of his neck. Patrick's heart wrenches with guilt about that. He's offered to switch out, but Will's always blown him off, saying Patrick needs to be sharp for surgery. Selfishly, Patrick's let that be his excuse for keeping the bed.

Wobbly and drunk, everything's so clear now: he can't let Will punish himself any longer. He climbs out of bed and stands behind the sofa. "Here, let me help you with your neck."

Will looks over his shoulder. "You don't need to."

"I know. You've helped with my back. Tit for tat, right?" Patrick presses down on Will's shoulders, the cotton of his shirt getting in the way of a good grip. "Take your shirt off. It'll be easier."

Will leans forward, dislodging Patrick's hands. "It's okay. I feel like…Patrick, can we talk about what you said at the piano?"

"No, we can't. I'm trying to help you."

Will says softly, "So you get to say what you want, but I don't get to reply?"

"Sounds about right."

"Whatever happened with your dad, it wasn't your fault."

"I know."

"Do you really?"

Patrick sighs and wishes he wasn't so drunk. He'll probably regret telling Will anything about his father. But right now he doesn't really care, except that he's done talking about it. It was years ago, and so long as he doesn't play the piano, he's fine with it. Usually.

"You were just a kid."

"I know, dammit. Stop talking about it now. Just let me rub your neck, okay? That's all I want from you."

Will stares at him, mouth open.

Fine. If he's going to be stubborn.

Patrick presses his fingers to his eyes. "Look, I've been thinking. Why don't you take the bed tonight. I'll sleep on the couch."

"No, I can't do that. It's really uncomfortable and you need your rest. Especially now."

Patrick snorts. "One night of drunkenly deep slumber won't end the world. I'm a doctor. I'm used to sleeping in uncomfortable chairs." He tosses up his hands. "Hell, I'm used to not sleeping at all.

I was awake for fifty-nine hours straight once when I was an intern. So, if you want to make me stop regretting my telling you anything about my past, stop talking about it and take the bed. Your neck is bothering you."

Will hesitates. "The bed *is* big enough for both of us, and it's not like anything's going to happen."

"No," Patrick agrees, his blood stirring. Memories of the last time he'd been drunk surging randily to the surface. "Nothing's going to happen."

"Okay. So we'll share." Will stands and starts on the buttons of his shirt.

Patrick's dick is so not on board with this 'nothing happening' plan. "Yeah, we'll share."

Once they've both changed into pajamas and brushed their teeth, Patrick waits for Will to finish in the bathroom. He flops back against the pillows, staring up at the ceiling, hoping that his arousal diminishes soon. Why doesn't he say something? Why doesn't he point out how ridiculous it is to be acting like virgins in a romance novel when they've been together in every way that counts already? He had those shots. He can claim inebriation.

But when Will walks toward the bed with a shy, uncertain expression, Patrick just jerks back the covers on the empty side. "Get in. I'm not going to touch you, you ninny."

After a moment's hesitation, Will climbs in and they settle with their backs to each other.

"Thanks for telling me about your dad, Patrick," Will whispers. "It means a lot to me that you trust me."

"It better not end up on *The Hurting Times*."

Will snorts and presses his back into Patrick's. "You're safe with me."

"And you're safe with me. So stop worrying about it and go to sleep."

Despite his curt order to Will, it takes Patrick a long time to drift off. He spends a woozy hour acutely aware of Will's body beside him, the rustle of the sheets when Will moves, and the soft sound of Will's breathing.

In the morning, Patrick wakes with his head pillowed on Will's chest and his mouth cottoned by liquor, just like their first morning together. But this time, instead of being nestled against Will's furry pecs, his face is resting against the soft cotton of Will's old T-shirt. Will's arms hold him close, strong and warm. Patrick doesn't want to move.

Then Will wakes up and jumps away, dumping Patrick unceremoniously on his back. "Uh, I'm going to take a shower." Will flees to the bathroom.

Patrick calls the hospital and postpones his morning surgery. His head aches and throbs, and he's drinking seltzer water and downing an aspirin when Will exits the steamy bathroom in a towel. He dresses in silence and Patrick doesn't break it.

Eventually, after Patrick's own shower, Will comes into the bathroom while he's shaving and leans against the sink.

"I need to thank you."

"Yep." Patrick scrapes a line of shaving cream away and washes it off in the half-full sink. "You do."

"I'm grateful for you intervening last night. If you hadn't, I'd…well, I'd have failed again."

Patrick shrugs. "Maybe. Or maybe you'd have thought better of it on your own."

"You know I wouldn't have. Not at that point." He closes his eyes and seems to be remembering sitting at the bar. "I'd have thrown my sobriety away."

Patrick carefully shaves his chin. "And for what?"

"Nothing. It accomplishes nothing. Just a momentary blotting out of my—"

"Your?"

"Feelings."

"Your self-loathing," Patrick corrects. "I'm not a big believer in therapy. Talking things out always seems like such a waste of time. But has anyone ever told you that you're worth a helluva lot more than you give yourself credit for?"

"Good Works—"

"I'm not talking about money. I'm talking about you. Will Patterson." He's irritated now and his hand slips enough that he nicks his jawline. Hissing, he grabs a towel and presses it to his face. "Chubby teen angel Will, and buff grown-ass Will, and all the other Wills. Stop throwing him away." Patrick frowns and drops the towel to the floor. He finishes shaving as Will watches with a flush in his cheeks and a thoughtful look in his eye.

"Did you order breakfast?" Patrick asks when there's a knock at the door.

"Yeah, I'll get it." Will heads out into the room and Patrick finishes up. He pulls on clean boxer-briefs and sits at the table to eat whatever Will has ordered him. Eggs and hash browns. No doughnut holes, but he'll stop by Brown Gargle on his way to the hospital.

"I know you can't drink all my shots for me," Will says after his testing/insulin ritual and starting in on his own eggs.

"Nope."

"Thanks for taking the ones you did."

"Am I supposed to say 'anytime' now? Because I'd prefer there isn't a next time, to be honest."

Will's lips tweak up at the corners. "I'd prefer that too."

They eat quietly for a few minutes until Will asks, "How did you know I was in the bar?"

Patrick rolls his eyes and nods toward the sofa. "Usually when people go for a run, they put on their running shoes. Yours were still under the couch. Genius, really, puddin'-pop. You're not a very good liar."

Will laughs. "Well, next time I'll be sure to take the shoes to the bar with me then."

"I thought we agreed no next time." Patrick's stomach churns at the idea of Will sitting in that bar without him, hates thinking of what might happen. Diabetes and alcohol can be a deadly mix. He doesn't want to imagine that for Will.

"Right. No next time." Will nods. "And thanks for letting me sleep in the bed. My neck feels a lot better this morning."

Patrick smiles. "You're paying for the room. Fair is fair. How'd you sleep?"

Will blushes and looks down at his eggs, pushing them around on his plate. "It's a really comfortable mattress."

"Yeah, and the pillows are soft and fat."

They talk about the merits of the bedding for the rest of the meal before heading out to work. Neither of them mention the cuddling.

Chapter Nineteen

TWO DAYS LATER, Will stands up from his desk at Good Works, stretches, and decides a walk and some coffee will do him good. He's spent far too long staring at spreadsheets and they stopped making sense hours ago. He waves to Hillary, the receptionist, and hits the sidewalk out front, dwelling again on what he's come to think of as 'the bed thing.'

There's nothing *wrong* with sharing a bed with Patrick. He knows this, and yet he can't stop wondering if he should have stayed on the couch. Things felt a lot more clear-cut then. *Now, though.* Will sighs as he walks toward Brown Gargle. *It feels different.*

They haven't talked any further about the night at the hotel bar and everything that came after. In the past, if Ryan found out Will was tempted to drink… Well, first, he'd never have come looking for him. Second, once Will stumbled home begging for forgiveness, Ryan would lecture him for hours—days—and suggest he move back in with Kimberly and the kids for a while.

It's so different from how Patrick handled it. It amazes Will that someone who doesn't even love him would barge in, take control in his own stubborn way, and steer Will out of the bar and back to safety. And when it was over, he hadn't lectured or shunned him. No, he'd drawn Will in more intimately. Confessed about his father's lack of love, and then invited Will to share the bed. Patrick had held him physically close in their sleep, and he'd never made Will feel ashamed about that, either.

The *cuddling.* That's another thing they don't talk about. When it comes time to sleep at night, Patrick just pointedly pulls back the covers on the opposite side of the bed and *looks* at Will until he crawls in. And no matter how many times Will tells himself he'll stay on his own side, they wake up tangled together. And it had never been like that with Ryan.

Ryan needs his space to sleep. He usually got up in the night and moved to their very large sofa because Will was too hot, too heavy, too smothering. But with Patrick, it's natural. They're like pieces that fit. Will slots right into Patrick's arms at night, effortlessly and without fuss.

It's because we're both lonely.

Will touches his new, clunky medic alert bracelet. Patrick wants everyone to think he's the kind of man who needs no one and nothing, but Will knows better.

He's so lonely. He doesn't want anyone to know.

And since they're both lonely, what harm does it do if they sleep together and find themselves in each other's arms? They aren't betraying anyone, and they both understand where they stand. It's comfort. It's human.

It's real.

In and amongst the pretense of their lives, this quiet thing that happens in the night is *real.*

After passing his old high school teacher on the street and exchanging pleasant greetings, Will turns the corner and spots his destination ahead.

He's pleasantly surprised to find Patrick inside Brown Gargle sharing a table with Jenny Burger. He knows they meet almost every day, but he's never actually seen them together until now. Patrick slumps comfortably in his chair, wearing dark pants and one of the blue shirts Will got him for Christmas. The color looks good on him, and just as Will had guessed, brings out his eyes.

Waiting for Jax to get his order, Will watches in astonishment as Patrick picks up baby Dylan from his stroller, tickles him under his chin and kisses his cheek. Dylan coos in delight and Patrick pretends that he's going to gobble up Dylan's hand.

Will's heart does a funny thing. *Holy moly. What was that?*

"Will!" Jenny waves him over. Her hair is swept up in a ponytail and she wears a soft red sweater and dark blue jeans.

Taking the coffee from Jax's outstretched hand, Will wipes what he feels is probably an incredibly stupid look off his face. Sweat prickles the nape of his neck as he conjures up what he hopes is a regular smile, not an oh-my-God-I'm-having-*weird-feelings* smile.

"Hey, Jenny!" Will says, bending down to kiss her cheek. "How've you been?"

"Great." She twinkles happily at him. "Just chatting with your hunky husband here."

Patrick winks at Jenny and she giggles.

Will grabs a chair from the next table to sit down next to Patrick. "Um, hi." Will feels like a stranger barging into a party uninvited, though not unwelcome. Jenny and Patrick clearly have their comfort together, and he feels a stirring in his gut when he thinks about that. Is it envy? Jealousy?

Maybe Patrick's not so lonely after all?

Patrick bounces Dylan on his knee and the baby drools on his pant leg. Kissing Dylan's fat cheek again, he says, "Jenny, clean up after your drool machine."

She rolls her eyes. "Your husband is such a princess." She grabs a napkin from the table to wipe Patrick's leg and Dylan's wet mouth.

Will nods his head rapidly like an idiot. He doesn't know what to say. He doesn't understand the feelings tingling in his veins and rushing in his ears. Until now, he hasn't known feelings can even *do* that.

"Have my doughnut," Jenny says, shoving it at him. "I don't need the calories. I was supposed to lose a few pounds before I put on my usual ten over the holidays. Oops."

"You might not need the calories, but he doesn't need the sugar,"

Patrick says.

Jenny rolls her eyes. "Oh, don't tell me you're one of those husbands."

"The kind who doesn't want his spouse going into shock and keeling over dead? Yeah, I'm awful."

She flushes and slides the doughnut back away from Will. "I forgot. Sorry."

"No problem." Will taps his foot. "Usually, I could have a doughnut, but Patrick's right. My sugar has been all over the place today. Had trouble with my new insulin pen this morning. I'm not sure the dose was right and I didn't bring my kit with me. I just planned on getting coffee."

Patrick frowns at that and then kisses the top of Dylan's head.

Will tries to make some space inside his body for all the feelings cropping up. First 'the bed thing' and now 'the baby thing.' He squirms and hopes he doesn't start laughing for no reason. He very well might and that will be embarrassing.

"But you tested okay before lunch?" Patrick asks.

"Yeah. I'm fine. Don't worry about me."

"I'll worry about you if I want." Patrick leans over to kiss Will's cheek and that makes everything worse. Will flushes like he's going up in flames. Hell, he thinks his inner *thighs* are sweating.

Dylan squawks and Patrick lifts him up and chucks his nose.

Oh my God, stop.

Patrick smiles at Will. "So why are you here? Didja miss me or something?"

Will doesn't think he can flush any harder, but the seductively challenging look in Patrick's eyes manages to do it. "A little."

Jenny clasps her hands together. "N'aaaaw! You two are so adorable!"

"Oh please." Patrick turns his attention back to the kid. "I'm sexy, brilliant and talented. But I am not adorable." He scrunches his face and sticks out his tongue in a way that Jenny seems to find pretty adorable if her grin is any indication.

"You can't fool me," she says, and he snorts.

"So, what conversation did I interrupt?" Will asks.

Jenny sighs. "We were just discussing my upcoming hospital stay."

"What?" Will looks between them. "Are you okay, Jenny? I didn't know anything about this."

Jenny waves his concern away like a fly. "It's somehow avoided ye olde gossip mill, but that can't last. Not since I told Andy about it yesterday."

"And what did Sicko say?" Patrick asks. "Let me guess: You can't do it, Buttercup! It's too risky!"

Jenny rolls her eyes right back at him. "You're such a jerk. Do you have to refer to him by his last name? But, yes, that's exactly what *Andy* said. And I told him that if it was me, I certainly hope someone would take the risk!"

"You're talking over my head now," Will says. "What's going on?"

She flicks a glance at Patrick. "I'm going to give Radar a kidney. Well, if he'll take it, that is. He's being incredibly stubborn for a man who has everything to lose."

"Yeah, as in his life. But I'm sure you'll wear him down. Won't she, Sport?" Patrick says to Dylan. "Your mommy's got no boundaries. Oh no! Oh no, she doesn't!"

Dylan gurgles happily and slaps a spit-covered hand against Patrick's chin. Jenny smiles at them both.

Will's stomach flips over and he forces himself to focus. "You want Radar Blackburn to take one of your kidneys?"

"Well, I don't *want* him to, obviously. I'm terrified! But it's the right thing to do."

Patrick nods.

It's clear that Patrick and Jenny know each other pretty well, and Will feels suddenly like he's been missing out. Has Patrick told Jenny things he hasn't told Will? Things about his past and his family? Does she know why he can't play piano anymore?

"You really didn't tell him?" Jenny asks Patrick and for a moment Will wonders if he's asked his questions out loud.

Patrick shrugs.

"Oh my God, I feel like your dirty secret on the side!" She laughs. "You don't tell your husband about our conversations?"

"I don't spread around other people's business. Besides, we're still in the honeymoon phase. Will and I don't do a whole lotta talking, if you catch my drift." Patrick waggles his eyebrows.

"*Patrick.*" Another hot wave rises up in Will. "I don't think Jenny wants to hear about that sort of thing."

"*Au contraire, mon chéri,*" Patrick drawls. "She got quite a kick out of hearing about the night we met."

Will's eyes widen.

"Patrick!" Jenny smacks his arm. "You're embarrassing him!" She turns to Will. "It's okay, sweetie. There's nothing to be ashamed of. It sounds like it was quite a night!"

"Oh my God," Will whispers.

Patrick snorts, and Jenny smacks him again.

"Hey!" Patrick protests. "Watch the arms! Surgeon, you know."

Jenny rolls her eyes and takes Dylan from Patrick, putting him back in his stroller. "I know, Dr. McCloud. You're the greatest brain surgeon in the whole wide world. I've heard it all before."

"Damn straight I am."

Will holds up a hand. "But wait, I'm still confused. You're giving a kidney to Radar? When is this happening?"

"Never if he has his way," Patrick says. "And if he doesn't decide to take her up on her very generous and painful offer—" Jenny reaches out to whap him again, but Patrick pulls away. "He might wait too long. Jenny, just tell him to crap or get off the pot."

"Yes, that'll convince him." Glancing down at her phone, her eyes widen. "Wow, I lost track of time. I have to get back home and type like the wind to finish before my deadline now." Jenny stands and grabs her coat from the back of her chair. "Will, congratulations." She kisses him on the cheek and squeezes his hands for a moment. "I can see why you married him."

"You can?"

Jenny chuckles. "Yeah, he's such a sweetheart."

"Lower your voice," Patrick says. "You'll ruin my reputation."

"I have to get back to work. You two be good to each other." She pushes Dylan's stroller and waves.

Once she's gone, Will turns to Patrick.

"What?" Patrick asks.

"I guess you and Jenny are what? Best friends?"

Patrick shrugs. "Sure. I like her; she's funny."

"Yeah, Jenny's great. It's just weird, seeing you so chummy with someone."

"Sorry. I didn't know that in addition to being imprisoned in this hellhole, I wasn't allowed make any friends."

"No, that's not what I mean. It's just…you seemed…" Will sighs. He's not sure he even knows. He wishes Patrick would share that comfort and connection with him. But that's wrong. He shouldn't want that at all. "Forget it. I'm going to head back to Good Works."

As Will stands, Patrick grabs his wrist. "Don't worry, puddin'-pop. You're my best friend, okay?"

Will's throat goes dry. "Yeah?"

"Of course. I'd never let Jenny share the bed. She'd be stuck on the couch forever."

Will can't talk about this. He'll come out of his skin if he talks about 'the bed thing' with Patrick.

Patrick releases his arm and scratches at his nose. "I'm going to finish this latte and head back to the hospital."

Will swallows. The sensation of Patrick's grip lingers. "Okay, well. See ya later. We can watch more *House of Cards* tonight if you want."

Patrick nods, and Will remembers they're supposed to be madly in love. He presses a fast kiss to Patrick's lips. He doesn't let it linger, but Patrick's eyelashes flutter, his mouth softens, and his voice is husky when he says, "Later, Will."

Knowing he'll humiliate himself if he doesn't escape, Will barely manages to walk and not run.

BACK AT THE Tallgrass that night, Will pulls a bunch of papers out of his messenger bag and spreads them across the table while Patrick calls room service. They're going to discuss some of the particulars for the improvements to the unit, but Will can't stop thinking about seeing Patrick and Dylan. Like King Kong holding Ann Darrow, it was beautiful and unexpected.

Patrick hangs up the phone and starts unbuttoning his shirt. "I'm gonna take a quick shower." He gestures over his shoulder as he goes into the bathroom. "The brochures for the gamma knives are in my medical bag. Take a look."

"Sure." Will forces his eyes away from the strip of pale skin that Patrick's fingers are revealing. He focuses on trying to find a pen at the bottom of his murse. A few seconds later, the shower starts and he abandons his search.

Reaching across the sofa for Patrick's bag, he finds various hospital administration files, a couple of pamphlets about neurosurgical equipment, and some new drug rep material. Nothing about the gamma knives Patrick's interested in acquiring.

He unzips a side pocket and reaches in, only to come out with a handful of color photographs. After glancing at the closed bathroom door, he shuffles through them.

Some are old, and some are fairly recent.

The first shows a brunette woman in a bathing suit, wearing a floppy hat. She's pointing off toward a brilliant sunset that spills light over her face and shoulders. Will glances toward the bathroom door, wondering if this woman is someone special to Patrick. She must be if he carries her picture around. It's too recent to be of Patrick's mother, but given the style of the bathing suit and the condition of the picture, he thinks it must be around ten years old. The edges are worn and it's faded a little over time.

He looks at the next photo. It's of a little brown-haired girl wearing a purple hat and a big smile. Will flicks through more pictures. They're all of the same family, as far as he can tell. The woman from the first photo is in a lot of the shots, but mostly it's pictures of six kids ranging in age from infancy to their early teens. There are photos of birthdays and Christmases, Halloween costumes, and one shot of the whole group, including the woman, holding a poster of a giant heart and the words: *WE LOVE YOU.*

Will frowns. *Who are these people? Why is Patrick carrying these pictures around?*

He looks at another, and then he comes across one that makes him stop short.

Patrick's in it, wearing a white T-shirt and kneeling on the ground next to the little girl. She's on what's obviously a new bike. She has a wide, gap-toothed grin, and Patrick's smiling too, a rare, sincere smile that makes Will's heart flutter.

The little girl looks so happy, one little hand clutching the handlebars and the other clinging to Patrick's fingers as she smiles for the camera. He doesn't know if it's the tilt of her chin, or the slant of her smile, but something about her makes him wonder if she's Patrick's child.

Will glances at the bathroom door; he can still hear the shower running and he flicks through the pictures again. These are family photos. Patrick's family.

But Patrick doesn't have a family.

He flips to the final photo and gasps to see that it's the picture of Will as a teenager from his pin board in his bedroom at his mother's house. Patrick's kept it with these other pictures of people he obviously cares about.

Will exhales slowly, returning to the one of the little girl on her bike, staring hard and trying to understand. Patrick had seemed so detached from the world in Las Vegas when Will asked him about his obligations. He'd made it seem like there wasn't anyone in his life that he needed to consider in his plans. He had his work and that was it.

But these pictures say different. They say Patrick has people in his life that he cares about a lot more than he lets on. But are they people he's left? Does he care but not care? Is he running away from the responsibility of them?

Will studies the girl's face again. Maybe he's imagining the resemblance. Maybe he's wrong.

He hears the sound of the water shutting off and hastily puts the pictures back inside Patrick's bag, digging around for the brochures about the gamma knife. He finally finds them stuffed inside another file, and pulls them out just as Patrick emerges from the bathroom wearing nothing but a pair of sweatpants slung low on his hips.

Will's heart thumps hard. The room sways as he watches Patrick rub a towel through his damp hair and sling it around his bare shoulders when he's done. There's so much about Patrick he doesn't know. He doesn't even know the most important things.

"What do you think?" Patrick asks, nodding at the brochures. His skin glistens damply, his nipples peaking in the cool air of the room. Will's eyes are drawn to the small trail of hair going down.

Head spinning, he says, "Looks good."

While Patrick throws on a T-shirt, Will clears his throat and sits at the table, trying to focus on the task at hand. He doesn't want to think about what those pictures mean. He doesn't want Patrick to be a man who cares but leaves anyway. And he can't afford to think of him as the man who looks good wet, watches out for Will's blood sugar, and kisses the cheeks of babies.

Patrick sits next to him, fresh-faced and smelling like soap. "Out with it."

"What?"

"What's got you looking like someone shoved a giant umbrella up your ass while making you watch a compilation of the saddest scenes from the greatest tearjerkers of all time?"

Will swallows and bounces his knee. He rubs a hand over his face and sighs when Patrick chucks up his chin, looking at his mouth and eyes carefully.

"Your blood sugar's fine. It's something else. What's the problem?"

Will laughs nervously and shakes his head.

"Did you slip today? Have a drink?"

"What? No! It's not that. I'm fine."

"Okay. Then tell me what's going on."

"I saw the pictures." Will's knee bounces harder. "In your bag."

It takes a moment, but red crawls up Patrick's neck and into his face. Will stares, fascinated. "Oh?"

"Yeah."

"Okay." Patrick taps his fingers on the table. "I guess I can't blame you for snooping when I gave you permission to look in my stuff."

"I didn't mean to snoop—"

"Whatever. You found them. It's fine." But he doesn't look like he means it. He taps wildly and his body jitters. "You're going to ask. There's no stopping you. Get it over with."

"Who are they?"

"Seriously? You can't pretend you didn't see them?"

Will throws up his hands. "That's what I was doing before you insisted I tell you what's going on."

Patrick's lips flatten out and he watches Will carefully for a few moments. "So who do you think they are? By the look on your face, I know you've got a theory."

Will rubs his damp palms against his pants. "I think at least one of them, maybe all of them, are…yours."

Patrick snorts. "I'm older than you, sure, but I'm not old enough to be the father of teenagers."

"Technically, you are."

"I'm also gay."

"There's that. But…"

"But what?"

"The little girl."

"Rebecca."

"She looks like you."

Patrick blows a raspberry in the air. "The hell she does. She's half-Iranian. I'm Scottish through and through."

"I don't see what that has to do with anything."

Patrick shakes his head firmly and picks up one of the gamma knife brochures. "She's not my daughter. I don't have any children."

"So that woman in the pictures isn't your wife…or ex-wife?"

Patrick's face twists in a way that can only be described as thoroughly disgusted. "Hell no. Dinah is my…she's…" He doesn't seem to know how to explain. He presses his fingers to the bridge of his nose and is silent for a long moment. When he finally meets Will's eyes again he speaks very quietly. "She was my foster mother. She and her husband Phil took me in after…" The brochure crumples in his hand. "After…the end."

Will's heart is in his throat. "It's okay. I think I understand now."

Patrick's eyes nail Will to his chair. "You don't understand at all."

"Then tell me."

A heartbeat of silence fills the room before Patrick speaks. "You know my father was an alcoholic and I earned our living by playing in bars at night under his supervision." Patrick flexes his fingers. "Over time, his drinking got worse. Then he started gambling. He lost more than he made. Unsurprisingly. He was an idiot. One night, it all came to a head." His voice is raspy and it gives Will the shivers. "I knew we were going to be evicted the next day if we didn't make rent. It was the third month in a row." He stares into space over Will's shoulder. "I did what I had to do."

"You played that night in the bars again?"

Patrick eyes snap back to meet Will's gaze, his face pale and his irises going dark as a storm cloud. "No."

"Then what?"

Patrick's gaze falls to the table and he shrugs. "I made a choice no teenager should be faced with. After—after everything happened…" He works his mouth like the words are stuck. "I went to Child Protection Services and reported my father. They placed me with Dinah a few days later."

Will knows he's missing something. "Do you feel guilty about that? About turning your dad in?"

"No."

Will's silent. Patrick's so perfectly still now. It chills him to the bone. "You don't have to tell me," he whispers. "It's enough that I know there's more. It's okay. I understand. It's gonna be okay." He touches Patrick's hand.

Patrick pulls his fingers away. "I've never told anyone… Not CPS. Not even Dinah."

Will swallows. He's tempted to push. He wants to know. But the idea of hurting Patrick by asking is more than he can stomach. He'd rather make it easy for Patrick to tell him, but he doesn't know how. "Dinah took good care of you, huh?"

Patrick nods, but his eyes are dark and his mind is clearly stuck in the past.

"Is she still in your life? Dinah, I mean? The picture with the little girl looks recent."

Patrick's comes back to the present, and relief spreads through Will like cool water. "Eight years ago. That's when that picture was taken. Rebecca's in college now. She gets straight As and has a boyfriend." Patrick's lips curve up. "She's Dinah's fifteenth foster child. The newest is a boy named Eric. He's her eighteenth. She's had him about five months and he's trouble." Patrick grins at that, the shadow still haunting him like a pall over his pleasure. "I haven't met him in person, but Dinah says he's a pill. Reminds her of me when I first came to her. I was her third foster child."

"And you keep the photos of the kids to stay close to them? Close to Dinah and—I'm sorry, what's her husband's name?"

"Phil. Yeah. And I—" He flushes again. Will is filled with the urge to kiss his cheeks and the red-hot rims of his ears. "I send them money. Gifts. I help out."

"Wow, that's really nice." *Nice? Amazing. Generous. Loving.*

Patrick can't seem to look at him. "I don't want people to know about it."

"I can keep a secret." Will sees that Patrick's trembling and he reaches out. "Hey, I'm sorry. It was rude of me to intrude on your past like this."

Patrick shakes his head, his eyes glued to the carpet. "That's what best friends are for, right?" His lips curl up into a small smirk. "Now you've got one up on Jenny, okay? Happy?"

"Will you look at me?"

Patrick's edgy and nervous, but he meets Will's eye and at least he's fidgeting again. "I'm looking."

"I promise to never use anything you say against you. All right?"

Patrick licks his lips. "Gonna slice our fingers open and make a blood oath on it?"

"If you want."

"Nah, that's okay. Let's just get back to work. You can tell me about your stupid ideas for saving money on the lab space and lowering the nurses' wages, and I'll tell you no." He runs a hand through his damp hair. "We can go back to arguing and all of this can just go away. Poof."

"Okay, if that's what you want."

Patrick smiles grimly. "We're done being touchy-feely, Will. Learn when to quit."

But when Will touches his hand again before opening the brochures, Patrick doesn't pull it away.

As Will pays the pizza guy the next night, Patrick notices he's wearing the new medic alert bracelet. It's really obvious what it is even from a distance, and seeing it on Will's wrist as he thrusts a twenty and a five into the delivery boy's hand shoots a strange, proprietary thrill up his spine.

This one's mine. I've claimed him. And he's wearing my talisman to keep him safe.

Will plops down on the couch, sliding the pizza box onto the coffee table before doing his usual testing/sticking thing. Then he rips open the box lid, grabbing a piece, and shoving it into his mouth like he's starving.

Patrick sits next to him, clicks the television on, and settles on *Jeopardy*. He loves the way Will's face grows ever more amazed as he out-answers the contestants. By the time Patrick turns to get a piece of pizza, Will's on his second slice.

"Hands off," Patrick says. "You're going to eat the whole thing."

"Sorry," Will mumbles. "Long day. Didn't get lunch. How 'bout you? Any good brain stuff today?"

Patrick ignores the question. "You're not supposed to skip meals. Don't make me call Owen about not taking good enough care of you. The man should earn his keep, at least."

Will shrugs, mouth still full as he answers, "He's a very good attorney."

"And an almost decent sponsor and a terrible friend."

"No, he's a good friend. It's not his job to make sure I eat."

"I can make it his job."

Will grins. "Patrick, I'll do better tomorrow. Tell me about your day."

Patrick sighs and lets it go. "A kid came into the ER with half his face blown off. It was cool."

Will makes a disgusted noise and drops his slice back into the box. "Thanks for that image. I'm *eating*."

Patrick grins and takes a big bite. "You asked."

"What happened to him?"

"Drinking while setting off fireworks with some friends out on the rez. He decided to use the rocket launcher as a hat. Amazing he's not dead, actually."

"Is he Lakota?" Will's eyebrows come down in concern.

"No."

"What's his name?"

"I can't tell you that. Confidentiality."

"Everyone will know by tomorrow."

"True. Okay, fine. Sean? Shane? Don't know, don't care."

Will looks even more worried. Patrick thinks Will needs stronger boundaries. He cares far too much about everyone except himself.

"Shane Hammond?"

"Yeah, that's him," Patrick says, taking another huge bite of pizza.

"Is he going to be all right?"

"I don't know. Probably not, to be honest. He might live, but be okay? Doubtful. There's considerable swelling of the brain and massive damage done. He's too fragile to scan, but I know what I'll find: large areas with no neural activity."

"But he's a really nice guy," Will says, pointing out the ridiculously obvious. "He just got married last fall. His wife is expecting a baby."

"Yeah. Sucks for him. Sucks for his wife even more."

"How can you act so cold, Patrick?"

"Who's acting?"

"I know you. I know you care about people."

"I thought you weren't going to use that information against me."

"I'm not talking about that. I'm talking about the fact that you're a doctor. I know you care about your patients."

Patrick shrugs impatiently. "I *am* a doctor. But I'm not powerful enough to go back in time and stop him from being a dumbass. I'm sorry if that disappoints you."

"I know. It's just…"

He sighs. "I've done all I can."

"What about that procedure you performed in Atlanta? The super-experimental one? Could that help him?"

Patrick lifts his eyebrows in surprise. "How do you know about that?"

Will looks away. "I read about it when I googled you." He frowns. "I didn't understand much. Just that it might help reignite neural activity in some damaged cells."

"I need staff and equipment I don't have here yet. Not to mention, his burns and other injuries are nearly as big of a priority right now. Infection is a real risk. If we can get the swelling under control and keep him from going septic on us, we can see about experimental treatments later," he says dismissively.

Will crosses his arms across his chest and stares at him so hard it feels like he's burning a hole into Patrick's skin.

"What?" Patrick asks, shifting uncomfortably.

"As soon as it's feasible to consider that procedure you will ask Don what can be done to summon the proper team and get the proper equipment to try it."

"I will?"

Will's eyes narrow and his arms clench even tighter. Patrick can't help but admire how that makes Will's shoulders look even broader and his biceps pop. Patrick clears his throat. "Okay, I will." He was going to do it anyway. This kind of risky, cutting edge procedure is right up his alley. But Will doesn't need to know that. It's more fun if he lets Will think he convinced him.

"Good." Will nods toward the television. "Unmute it. Stun me with your brilliance."

Patrick does as he's told.

He snorts, wondering when he became the kind of man who does *that*. It started in a bar in Vegas, and it's been snowballing ever since. If a divorce isn't procured soon, Patrick has no idea where he might end up.

And the thing is, he likes appeasing Will, making him smile, and easing his mind. Which reminds him of another thing that feels good.

He and Will have been sleeping in the same bed for five days now, and it's getting harder and harder to pretend that it's about comfort and nothing else. Every night they get into the bed and each lie on their own side, but by morning their bodies have gravitated together. If Patrick doesn't wake up with his head on Will's chest, it's because they're spooning instead. Mostly, it's Patrick pressed against Will's back, though this morning he woke up with Will behind him, his sizable morning erection pressed snugly against Patrick's ass. Will had slowly ground against him, moaning softly in his sleep.

And wasn't *that* awkward when Will finally woke up?

He wonders if Will's body knows something his conscious mind isn't willing to admit. Something about what they can mean to each other. Patrick's ears burn and his chest tingles with his quickly inhaled breath. But that's just too weird to contemplate, just like everything else about his marriage-cum-friendship with Will.

So he says, "What is an iPhone," before any of the idiots on the show, and focuses his attention on History for eight hundred.

Chapter Twenty

PATRICK TRIES TO get out of the New Year's Eve party at the Tallgrass. He really, really does. But he's thwarted at every turn.

First by Will: *"You have to come, Patrick! We're supposed to be newly-weds, why wouldn't we be ringing in the new year together?"*

Next by Don: *"Oh no, Dr. McCloud, you're not on call tonight. I insist you go out and celebrate with your husband."*

Finally by Jenny: *"Oh come on, Dr. Grumpypants. One night of mingling with the town's mere mortals won't kill you."*

So Patrick finds himself in the Tallgrass's decorated ballroom, hanging out by the buffet table while too many of Healing's citizens eat, drink, and make merry around him. Kimberly is there with a date. Will shakes his hand and calls him Mark. The younger kids are at home with a sitter, but Caitlin is there with Scott from Tate's Sporting Goods, and Kevin seems to be along to chaperone Caitlin.

Ryan and Hartley are there too. And though Ryan made it clear at Christmas, at least in Patrick's opinion, that he's moved on and isn't interested in Will anymore, he still shoots eye-daggers at Patrick and Will like they're doing something wrong by being at the party together.

Patrick ignores them both, but the pulse beating in the divot of Will's neck proves that it's getting to him. Patrick turns back to the buffet and adds more stuffed olives to his plate.

"Do you have any New Year's Eve traditions?" Will asks gamely, wiping his palms on his pants for the third time in just a few minutes. "Something you did with friends in Atlanta?"

Patrick just looks at him.

"What?"

"You're way too worried about that jerk."

Will blows out a long breath. "I know. And I know you don't want to talk about him."

"Do you?"

Will shrugs and shakes his head. "No. It's just that he was a big part of my life and—"

"*Bzzzzp*. Sorry. Heard all that before. New information or nothing."

Will rolls his eyes. They eat silently for a few minutes as Prince's "1999" plays as an echo of the past. "Ryan and I never once had a happy New Year's Eve."

"Imagine that. I'm so surprised I don't know what to do with myself. Pigs are flying. Hell is cold. You and Ryan had miserable New Years together. One of these is not like the others."

Will actually chuckles, and Patrick smiles. He reaches out and puts his arm around Will's shoulders, dragging them forehead to forehead. He can see the shimmer of Will's eyelashes.

"What are you doing?" Will asks in the humid space between their lips.

"Fooling Molinaro spies." *Being close to you.* "Pissing off your boyfriend."

"Hate to break it to you, but he's not my boyfriend."

"Are you available then?"

"No. I'm a married man."

Will's lips taste sweet with chocolate and their tongues brush together, a tingling whisper of promise. Will breaks the kiss, whispering, "My mother is watching."

"Let her see."

Will shakes his head, heat in his cheeks and a shy smile bitten between his teeth.

Glancing over, Patrick sees Ryan glaring at them from across the ballroom. Rolling his eyes, he's had enough. "Come on." He steps out onto the dance floor as a slow song begins, holding out his hand. "Let's dance."

"Really?" Will grins. "I thought you hate dancing?"

Patrick had mentioned that little factoid a few days earlier during one of his failed arguments to get out of attending this party at all. "I do. But I'm tired of seeing you mope after that jackass."

"Patrick," Will whispers, his eyes full of tender feeling. Patrick's heart thumps.

Will takes Patrick's outstretched hand and lets him pull him onto the dance floor. Swaying close, their bodies lined up perfectly, and with their hands clasped together against Patrick's chest, he's gotta admit, it's better than nice.

Some of Will's friends glide past them and smile. Will smiles back. Jenny is there, dancing with Andy and his wife. She's scheduled for surgery the second week in January and has declared this night her last big hoopla before she's out of commission for a while. Andy and his wife are making the night special for her: she's the belle of their little three-person ball.

Other people twirl around and past them, and sometimes he recognizes them, and sometimes he doesn't. But after a while, under the spell the balloons, the twinkle lights, and the slow music, he doesn't see anyone else at all. It's just him and Will with his brown eyes shining. Something beautiful and foreign claws right up Patrick's throat: a terrifying winged thing called hope.

"I got the spreadsheets showing your proposed wages for the nurses," Will says.

"And?"

"You're asking for a lot. Remind me, why do we have to offer so much more than the going rate anyway?"

Patrick smiles at the question, a measure of excitement rising in him. He knows how this works with Will. Discussing their joint work, making the hospital better—making it great. Arguing over it, the pink in Will's cheeks, the flash in his eyes, and the way Will's chest heaves when he's irritated. It's fun, and it's hot, and Patrick loves it.

"Well, aside from the fact that you have to lure them to this cursed place, it's because the nurses take care of the patients, not doctors. They're the ones who monitor and assess them, and attend to their every need. They let me know what they need from *me*, not the other way around. The floor nurses take care of every detail of every patient. They monitor what they eat, how much they piss, what meds they need. They deal with wound care, getting them to the bathroom. They check vitals, oversee the labs, sugars, pulse oximetry, Is and Os. They draw blood for countless tests, and deal with the family. They educate and answer questions so I don't have to. They cry when their patients die and they deal with asshole doctors like me. The truth is a patient sees me for the smallest portion of their stay at the hospital. The real heroes, the ones in the trenches, are the nurses. Not to mention—"

"Okay, okay. I get it. They deserve a bump up in pay. But why don't you want them to know you're going to bat for them?"

"It's easier when they hate me."

"How?"

"Because I'm no good at nurses. They have emotions all over me whenever I try. Especially the male nurses. They're the worst about it. Emotions. Everywhere." He shudders.

Will's eyes are shining, and suddenly he snorts and laughs. Patrick grins in return.

"You really are such an ass." But there's no malice in his voice and he squeezes Patrick's hand tenderly.

"If you say so." Patrick tugs Will off the dance floor.

When they reach the bar, Patrick orders a Coke and Will orders a club soda with a twist of lemon. He shoves his hands into his pockets, rocking slightly back and forth. When Will grins at Patrick, his eyes just *do* something to him. Patrick's dizzy, filled with a buoyant pleasure like he can fly.

Will licks his lips. They glisten in the low light.

Patrick could lean forward a few inches and they'd be kissing again. He suspects this time Will might not put such a fast stop to it.

"Sorry to interrupt." Ryan's sharp voice snaps them both out of the moment.

Will blinks dazedly and Patrick clears his throat.

"I'm sure you are." Patrick smiles but it feels more like baring his teeth.

Will slides his arm around Patrick's waist. "Ryan, Hartley, hi." He shudders lightly and then trots out a tremulous smile. "Having a good night?"

"We are," Ryan says. "How about you?"

Hartley shifts uncomfortably and shoots Ryan a dark look.

"Great!" Will says with false cheer. "We're having a great night too."

Ryan nods and Hartley looks past them with his lips pressed into a straight line.

There's nothing to say. They stand awkwardly looking at each other, or in Hartley's case, past each other. Patrick slips his arm over Will's shoulder and Ryan's eyes narrow, taking in their sideways hug.

"So, uh, do you have plans for the new year?" Will asks, directing his question to Hartley, who seems startled to be addressed.

"Yeah," Ryan answers for him. "Hartley's going to start school. We're moving back to Vermillion."

"Taking courses in counseling and Native studies," Hartley says, smiling at Will with apology in his eyes. "I'm looking forward to it."

"Oh." Will leans into Patrick's body a little, and he helps support Will's weight.

"Yeah." Ryan stares at them challengingly. "I'm excited too. I'm ready for a fresh start."

Will goes still but his voice doesn't waver. "Well, I'm glad for you." He smiles at Hartley and it's a good try even if it's brittle.

"Good luck at school. You'll do great. I know it."

"Thanks, Will. I appreciate that." Hartley pulls on Ryan's arm. "Now come on, let's go."

"I'm not done here."

"Yes, you are." Hartley glares at Ryan.

Will's face is pale. The bright glow that had been there only moments before when Patrick nearly kissed him is gone. Patrick grits his teeth together.

"No, I'm not."

"I think you are," Will finally says. His voice sounds like he's bleeding out on the floor. "Goodbye, Ryan."

Ryan stares at him and then nods. "So long, Will." He flings a glance toward Patrick. "Dr. McCloud."

Hartley nods apologetically again at Will who looks away, but Patrick says, "Good luck to you, kid. And I don't mean in school."

Hartley's eyes grow wide and his mouth flies open as he reaches to grab hold of Ryan's arm, and Patrick hears Will's gasp just before he feels the smashing pain of a fist against his temple.

Patrick crashes to the floor, his ass smarting and ears ringing. He touches his temple and looks at his fingers. No blood. His head swims.

Will kneels beside him, his eyes wide and hands gentle on Patrick's face. A small crowd gathers, and through wobbly vision, he sees Hartley shove Ryan towards the exit. Exclaiming strangers block his view.

Will hauls Patrick upright. "Oh my God, are you okay?"

"Didn't go unconscious. I'm fine."

Will throat bobs and he sounds breathless. "Should I call the police?"

"He's not worth it," Patrick mutters. "Just get me off this floor."

Will helps him up and wraps a steadying arm around his waist. Patrick sags against Will's side, his head throbbing. They face a wall of people and Patrick can hear Jenny's scared voice on the other side of the crowd.

"Move. Stop gawking," Patrick orders, anger coursing through him that he's become the sideshow event for the evening. The entire town will be talking about it for days. It'll be all over *The Hurting Times* how Dr. Asshole got punched and didn't even fight back. Will shoves him through the dispersing crowd, directing him toward the men's room.

The bathroom mirror shows a red knot rising on his temple, nothing to worry about, but his reflection isn't the nicest he's ever seen. He'll probably have a purple bruise by morning and look like he's been in a fight for a week or so after that, but otherwise he's okay.

Will hovers behind him holding a bag of ice someone must have pressed into his hand.

"I think he was going for my chin. He's got lousy aim."

Will snorts softly, but it's clear that he's still too worried to be amused.

Patrick takes the ice from Will and holds it to his head. "I've taken worse hits. Hartley redirected the punch and took a lot of the velocity out of it. Don't strain yourself fretting."

Will takes Patrick's chin in his hand and turns his head to look at his temple closely. "I don't know why he would do this." He flounders for words. "It doesn't matter. I can't believe he hit you. I'm so sorry, Patrick."

Patrick's gratified that Will's not making excuses for Ryan's bad behavior. But he's less pleased by the apology.

Turning away from Will and back to the mirror, he says, "Not everything is your fault, Will."

"I know."

"Did he ever hit *you?*" Patrick presses the bag of ice against his head again. He studies his eyes in the mirror. Both pupils are the same size. He's fine.

"What? No. Of course not. Ryan's not like that." Will stops, his face going pale as he stares at Patrick and the very clear evidence that Ryan *is* like that. "No, he never hit *me*."

"He's hit other people?"

Will swallows. "Once. Walker James, a guy at college I hung out with a lot while Ryan and I were on a break. He thought Walker and I were sleeping together. We weren't. After Ryan punched him, Walker called campus security. My mom had to get a lawyer for Ryan. It was a mess."

"Ah. I'm sensing a pattern." He turns from the mirror.

"I…" Will's finger on Patrick's chin is tender, and he searches Patrick's eyes. Patrick has no idea what he's looking for until Will says, "I'm really sorry."

"Yeah, well, I don't forgive you."

Will's eyes cloud with hurt.

"Because you didn't hit me. You didn't do anything wrong. Aren't you sick of letting him make you feel bad about yourself? Like there's something wrong with you? I sure as hell am, and I've only seen the tip of the iceberg."

"You don't know me like he does. You don't know what I'm really like."

Patrick throws the bag of ice in the trash, flushing with irritation. "What the hell do you mean? You're Will Patterson, the good guy with a big, stupid heart on your do-gooding sleeve, and when he's not around, you know that. Stop letting him take that away from you."

Will blinks at him, his face blotchy and near tears. Patrick still hates that he finds Will so hot when he's about to cry. It undermines his righteous rage.

"I'm only going to say this one more time. You're a good person. You don't deserve to be made to feel like you aren't. You're the *last* person in the world who should ever feel like that. And I'm absolutely sick of it, even if you're not."

Patrick stalks over to the bathroom door. He looks back. Will is hunched over the sink, staring down at the drain. He waits to see if

Will has anything to say, but there's only silence.

"I'm getting a drink. I'll see you out there." He swings the door open, but stops at the last second. "Why on earth do you still care about that jackass?"

Will only looks over at him, blinking back tears.

Patrick pushes past Will's mother, who's waiting outside the men's room door. "Ms. Patterson."

"Dr. McCloud, are you okay?"

"Nothing a shot of whiskey won't cure."

He heads to the bar and orders another bag of ice for his head and a shot of whiskey for his pride. He turns around to see Will be accosted by his mother outside the bathroom.

Everyone is staring at him.

"Oh, for God's sake, don't you have lives?"

He keeps his eyes on Will, wrapped up in his mother's embrace. He throws the shot glass back and swallows it down.

"Baby, what was all that about? Why did Ryan hit Patrick?"

Will sighs. "I think Ryan's just having a hard time accepting my marriage."

His mom purses her lips. "Well you can't really blame him, can you?"

Can't he though? Ryan broke up with him and started a relationship with Hartley before he even knew about Patrick. Will glances toward the bar and sees Patrick watching him.

"I don't know. Things haven't been right with me and Ryan for a long time."

"Oh no, honey! This is just a temporary glitch. It'll all be sorted out soon enough and, once it is, I'm sure you can make up with Ryan."

"You know what, Mom? He's with Hartley now. He dumped me

for Hartley. And after the things he's said, and what he just did to Patrick, I don't think he's the guy I fell in love with anymore."

"Oh, Will." A sadness darkens her eyes. "You can't mean that."

"I do. I really do." He squeezes her hands. "It's my life, Mom. And I'm going to live it my way."

"Will—"

"Listen, why don't you go talk to Uncle Kevin. He's waving you over. I'm sure he wants to know what's going on."

"Baby, are you sure you're all right?"

Will smiles reassuringly. "I'm sure. Besides I need to check on Patrick."

His mom nods uncertainly but leaves him alone, and that's what he wants most.

As he crosses the room, the punch replays in his mind. Ryan's arm drawing back, his eyes going steely and cold, as violence erupted from him without warning. Punching Patrick without remorse. And for what? For wanting Will when Ryan didn't?

And God, Patrick's face as he'd crumpled to the floor! Shocked, vulnerable. Will's first urge had been to protect Patrick, to follow him down and cover him. And his next urge, one that had blindsided him with its intensity, had been to beat the hell out of Ryan for hurting his man.

There's no denying it now: there's more than one way to knock a person down. Ryan may have never used his fists on Will, but he'd beaten him up all the same. Will takes a deep breath. His stomach is tangled in knots and he wants a drink. No, he wants a dozen drinks. He takes another deep breath, taking command of the urge.

"Here," Patrick says when Will reaches him. He thrusts a glass of seltzer water into Will's hands.

"Thanks." Will takes a long swallow before placing it on the bar.

"You okay?"

Is *he* okay? Not really. "I'll be fine. I'm worried about you."

"I'll be fine too." Patrick frowns at something across the room.

Will follows his line of sight to where Kimberly is talking to a small court of people: Kevin, Scott, Caitlin, Jenny, Andy, and his wife, Martina. They're obviously talking about Ryan's punch. The whole group keeps casting long looks over at them with way too much interest and, in the case of Caitlin, a little glee. Jenny breaks free as if she's going to come over, but Patrick shakes his head, and with a small frown she drops back into the group.

"Are you okay?" she mouths.

Patrick winks at her and makes the okay symbol with his fingers.

"At least they're staying on their side of the room?" Will says.

"Do you want to get out of here?" Patrick presses the bag of ice back to his temple.

Will exhales. "I really do. What's the time?"

Patrick checks his watch. "It's just seconds until midnight. We should stick around for that."

"Keep up appearances," they both say in unison.

Patrick puts down the bag of ice and wraps his arms around Will. The blue heat of his eyes burns away at the shame and sorrow in Will's gut. How can he deserve that expression? How can Patrick want him? After everything?

Patrick slides his fingers into the hair at Will's nape, making him shiver. "It's going to be okay, puddin'-pop," he murmurs soothingly.

"Ten!"

"Nine!"

"Eight!"

The countdown rings out. Will glances around the room as his friends and family prepare to welcome the new year. Balloons shudder in the air around them, and the shine from twinkle lights shimmers in Patrick's auburn hair.

"About before, and being sick of it? You're right. I am." Will leans into Patrick's embrace.

"Of course you are. I'm always right." Patrick chucks Will's chin up. His eyes linger on Will's mouth.

"Two!"

"One!"

"Happy New Year!"

Noisemakers squawk and the room fills with the sound of people shouting. But in the midst of the craziness, Will's heart thuds, and suddenly it's the only sound he can hear. *Thump, thump, thump.*

Patrick's kiss is soft and sweet, but Will wants more. He pulls Patrick tight against him and licks at the seam of his mouth. When he opens, Will falls headlong into hot, hungry want. Patrick moans quietly into his mouth. His fingers tangle in Will's hair as their heads tilt and the kiss deepens. Shuddering, Will clutches Patrick's arms. His pulse races and his cock thickens as Patrick whimpers urgently, and they cling together.

When Patrick breaks the kiss, he pulls back and their gazes meet. The room swirls around them, out of focus, and roaring with music, laughter, and cheers. Will smiles goofily, his heart tumbling wildly and his entire body buzzing. Patrick strokes at the cleft in Will's chin. They stare into each other's eyes.

"Take me upstairs," Will whispers.

"I must have a concussion after all. I'm hearing things."

"I mean it. I want you."

"Well, damn. Happy New Year to me."

Will kisses him quickly, and then takes his hand, leading a dumbstruck Patrick out of the party.

Chapter Twenty-One

THEY DON'T TALK on the ride up to their room. As soon as the door is shut behind them, their clothes come off and Patrick takes control, sending blood rushing to Will's cock.

Patrick presses Will onto the bed, climbs on top of him, and kisses him deeply. Will scrambles at his back, feeling the slide of skin under his palms, and the tight, taut movement of muscles. Patrick groans, humping his hard cock down against Will's, and the hot slick of his pre-come takes Will's breath away.

"Wait," Will pants. "Stop."

"What?" Patrick ceases the roll of his hips. "Why?"

"It's going a little fast. Let's go slow."

Patrick laughs, burying his head in Will's neck.

"What?" Will runs his hand up and down Patrick's back, his heart tripping madly.

"Puddin'-pop, we've been married for over a month. I'm afraid to know your definition of slow."

Will laughs too, and when Patrick lifts up to gaze warmly down at him, Will can't stop himself from going in for another kiss. It's painfully arousing, and Patrick's mouth is deliciously hot, slippery, and firm.

"I wanna be inside you," Patrick whispers. His voice is raspy and raw, desperate and wild. Will kisses him again, sucking his tongue in, needing to get closer. He cups Patrick's head in his hands and they move together. Hard cock pressing on hard cock. Will feels like he might come from this alone. "Or," Patrick says. "You fuck me. I don't care who fucks who, Will. I just want to be with you."

Will's cock twitches, and he fists his hands in Patrick's hair, moaning as Patrick sucks down his neck and then back up to his mouth. Another searing kiss, and Will pants hard, his lungs burning. The slide of Patrick's skin against his, the friction of their cocks channeling next to each other in the hollow made by their heaving bellies, and the intimate scrape of their stubble as they kiss and lick and rub together has him spellbound, poised on the edge of coming.

"Will you?" Patrick kisses his mouth. "Will you please?"

"Will I what?" Will asks dumbly.

Patrick pulls back, his face looking so open, so needful that Will slides his hands to Patrick's ass to grind him down again.

"Fuck me." Patrick's eyes widen. "Or have you never…"

"Yeah. I have."

Once. But Ryan didn't like it any more than he'd liked being the one on top, and he sure as hell never offered himself up to Will as easily as Patrick just has.

"So?" Patrick says breathlessly, still moving against Will in a mind-numbingly good way. "Are we doing this or what?"

Will blinks.

Patrick's hard, and he's horny, and he wants Will. He *wants* Will. And Will wants him too.

This is what honesty feels like.

Will spreads his legs so their dicks press together more tightly. They both moan as Patrick grabs Will's wrists and holds them down against the bed by Will's head.

"Nuh-uh," Will whispers, so turned on he's surprised he can speak. "I'm in charge."

Patrick raises one eyebrow and grins. "Prove it." Will flips Patrick over easily, shoving his wrists up over his head. Patrick's eyes glint.

Will thrusts sharply against Patrick, drawing a gasp. "Do you like that?"

Patrick squirms and grins. "You know I do."

"Yeah?"

"Hell yeah."

Will leans forward, still holding Patrick's wrists, and presses their mouths together again. As the kiss turns wild, he releases Patrick and grabs fistfuls of hair instead, rolling their bodies together as they suck, lick, and softly bite. Patrick scrabbles at Will's back, and Will breaks the kiss long enough to sit up and stare down at the man below him. Pink nipples, flushed chest, and blood-red mouth from kissing.

"Beautiful."

Patrick runs a hand down Will's sternum, his fingers tracing along Will's chest hair and nipples. "Who? You?"

"You." Will strokes his hands over Patrick's pecs and abs, grinning as stomach muscles quiver under his touch.

Patrick grabs the back of Will's neck, pulling him back down for another kiss. As they rut, Will moans, gasping against Patrick's mouth, and Patrick swallows his noises, pliant underneath him, letting him set the pace.

Breaking apart again, Patrick moans. "Tell me what you want now. Anything. I'll give you anything."

Will's head spins and he touches Patrick's kiss-bruised mouth. "I want you to suck me." Then he remembers. "Nevermind. Your head is hurt—"

"I can do it."

"Are you sure?"

Patrick nods quickly. "I want to."

"Tell me if you change your mind?"

"Get your fat dick up here, puddin'-pop," Patrick rasps, shifting so that he's angled perfectly on the pillows.

Will straddles Patrick's face.

When Patrick nods his head, opening his mouth wide, Will grips his own dick and slowly feeds it to him. Patrick sucks hard. Biting down on his lip, and thrusting in until he feels the back of Patrick's throat work around him, Will trembles all over. Slowly, he slides back out, relishing the slick pull of suction. "Oh my God," he whispers. "I'm gonna come so fast."

"S'okay," Patrick murmurs, and then he latches his mouth back on Will's dick, and it's too good to keep his eyes open. Will grips the headboard and fucks into Patrick's mouth slowly.

Patrick slides his hot hands everywhere, stroking the base of Will's cock, gently squeezing his balls, skimming down his crack and teasing at his hole. Will throws his head back and groans.

"Oh God," he gasps, tightly gripping the headboard and opening his eyes to stare down at Patrick's lips stretched around him. "I'm going to come."

Patrick slides off the shaft and swirls his tongue around the head of Will's cock a few times before sealing his mouth around him again and jacking him quickly.

"Oh!" Will groans, nipples tingling and balls jolting. A moment later he's convulsing, crowing in pleasure, and spilling onto Patrick's tongue.

Trying to catch and swallow every spastic pulse and burst of come, Patrick chokes and sucks greedily.

Popping free of Patrick's come-covered lips, the air feels cold on Will's still-twitching dick. He flops onto his back, trying to catch his breath. Patrick slides up beside him, fitting into the crook of his arm. He flicks the tip of his tongue against Will's mouth, and Will opens up for him, tasting himself in Patrick's kiss.

It's amazing. Warm, sweet pleasure flows under his skin. It's better than anything, better than cake, better than alcohol. Better than being drunk. Rolling onto his side to see Patrick licking stray come from the corner of his mouth, his blood heats back up. He wants more. A lot more.

"Let me—" Will says, reaching for Patrick's leaking dick.

"Let's take it slow," Patrick murmurs, leaning in to take Will's mouth again. "Take our time."

They make out like teenagers, rolling around on the bed. Patrick's dick smears pre-come all over Will's stomach and hips. As they touch and rub, hump and kiss, Will's cock surges back to life.

"Lube?" Will asks, reluctantly pulling away from Patrick's mouth. "Condom?"

Patrick blinks and clears his throat. "Bedside drawer," he says, turning on his side to open it. Will takes the opportunity to admire the long lines of Patrick's body. His lean back, slim legs and his firm, tight ass. "I've been hoping my husband might put out. Wishful thinking, I told myself, but hey, quitters never win, and winners never quit, or something, and for Christ's sake where are they? Oh, good, here they are."

Patrick produces the supplies and settles on his back.

"Are you sure about this?"

"I'm not a virgin and this isn't a romance novel." Patrick's voice is tender as he trails his fingers up to Will's mouth and touches his lips reverently. "Will, I want you to fuck me. That's what I *want*."

Will swallows hard and nods. He can barely breathe as he slicks up his fingers and presses one against Patrick's pucker. Patrick spreads his legs wide, planting his heels on the mattress and bearing down so his hole opens up for Will's fingers.

"Oh, wow," Will murmurs. Patrick is tight, but he makes encouraging noises as Will works him open. "Feel good?" Patrick nods, sweat dotting his forehead. "Do you like this?"

"I love it." His cock leaps when Will touches his gland, and his eyes go dark and wide. He stares up at Will when he presses there again, and then he twists on Will's fingers, a moan breaking between his red lips.

Will grins, pressing a quick kiss to Patrick's mouth.

"Do it," Patrick whispers. "Don't make me beg."

"The great Dr. McCloud begs?"

"For this?" He rubs his hot hands over Will's shoulders. "Absolutely."

Will withdraws his shaking fingers and has to concentrate hard to quell his tremors enough to roll a condom onto his own straining cock. "How should we…do this?"

Patrick hesitates a second before rolling onto his elbows and knees.

Will's thighs jump and quake taking in the sight of Patrick offering himself up like this: vulnerable muscle and flesh, his tight pucker beckoning between his spread cheeks. Will shivers and slicks his cock with extra lube before lining up and pressing for entrance to Patrick's body. The initial resistance sends a flood of too-sweet sensation through his gut, and he pauses, shifts from knee to knee, and pulls back.

Patrick glances over his shoulder before dropping down to his elbows, his forearms resting against the mattress. He spreads his legs even wider. "C'mon, puddin'-pop. I'm ready. Make me come for you."

Will groans as he thrusts forward, pressing inside Patrick's body in one long, firm push.

"Yes!" Patrick yells.

Will stares in awe as he slides in deep, his balls slapping solidly against Patrick's ass as the thickest part of him squeezes into Patrick's tight body. Pleasure is mindless and consuming. He grips Patrick's hips to steady himself—and to keep from passing out.

"So good," he grits out like a half-sob. "It's so good."

Patrick breathes harshly, cheek pressed against the bed, and his eyes and mouth wide open as he spasms around Will, muscles twitching in his back. Will rubs his hands over Patrick's lower back, trying to see through the haze of lust gripping him. Patrick's ass is tight like a vise around the base of Will's cock and he feels like he's going to blow his load now, immediately, if he doesn't move hard, and if he doesn't move soon.

"Fuck," Patrick gasps. He reaches back and grips Will's thigh. "Wait."

Despite his driving need to shove Patrick down and nail him to the mattress, Will takes deep, steadying breaths and keeps rubbing his hands over Patrick's back, down his trembling thighs.

"You're big," Patrick whispers, taking a halting breath.

"I'll go slow."

Patrick shifts his knees and Will bites down on his lip as little involuntary noises leave Patrick's mouth, small whimpers of pleasure.

"Okay?" Will asks.

Patrick shudders, chills break over his ass and back, and Will moves his hands over them, rubbing them away.

"Not yet," Patrick mutters. "I need a second."

Will struggles to obey as he stares at Patrick's hole stretched around the thickest part of his cock. "Oh God," Will murmurs.

Patrick's noises as he struggles to open for Will are so different, so defenseless. Will feels possessive of them. He wants to own them and keep them somewhere safe from harm. He senses when Patrick's body relaxes, but he waits for a signal.

"Go slow." Patrick taps Will's leg.

Will pulls almost all the way out before sliding back in, building up a rhythm as Patrick starts moving too, meeting Will's thrusts with his own.

"Oh, yes," Patrick slurs, his back twisting as he grips and pulls with his hole, riding Will's dick. "Give it to me. Fuck me, yes."

Will drops down against Patrick's back, breathing in the sweet scent at his sweaty nape, and loses himself in the fuck. It's beautiful and honest, and he takes it greedily: the hot, tight grip of Patrick's ass on his cock, the perfect, relentless pounding, the cries of pleasure and the litany of grunts. He shifts a little, changing angles, looking for that place inside Patrick that will make him come undone, and when he hits it, Patrick scrabbles at the bed and shouts.

Will snaps his hips, aiming for it with every stroke, and Patrick bites the pillow, gripping the sheets in his hands, until he loses control and throws his head back, shouting. His back muscles bunch and flex, tight and wiry, and his neck cords at the sides with the strain of his hoarse cries.

"Gonna make you come," Will grunts. "Want to feel you squeeze my dick."

"Yeah. Make me come for you."

Will snarls and digs in harder, faster, thrusting until the room is filled with the sounds of pleasure. He's flying high, strong and happier than he's ever known. Fucking Patrick is joy; it's truth. It's letting go of the terror he's felt his whole life about being gay.

"Yes!" Patrick's asshole spasms. "Fuck, Will! Harder!"

Will clutches Patrick's hips, hungrily taking in the view of his cock fucking in and out of Patrick's clenching ass. Below him, Patrick jerks himself off. His arm moves in time with Will's hips, and his noises are different now, all deep grunts and low growls as he rushes toward his climax.

Will plasters his chest against Patrick's sweaty back and they move together. He latches onto Patrick's neck with his mouth, sucking and worrying the skin with his teeth, wanting to leave a mark, wanting to see the evidence tomorrow.

Patrick groans. "You're gonna—" His hand on his cock speeds up. "Make me—" And he comes, shuddering, clenching and barking, "Ah—God," in a hot, deep voice. Will's rhythm falters for a moment, but he puts his hands on Patrick's shaking shoulders for leverage as he fucks hard into Patrick's ass, over and over, until he can't hold out another second.

"Patrick!" he shouts, shooting hard and burying himself deep. He convulses and collapses, twitching helplessly in the throes of bliss.

When he reluctantly pulls out, Will ties off the condom and drops it into the trashcan by the bed before flopping down on his back next to Patrick on the bed. The room fills with the sound of their panting breath and the scent of sex.

Will glances at Patrick. His eyes are closed and he's lying boneless on his stomach, his body sated and relaxed. *I did that. I made him look like that.*

His eyes open. "What?"

Will shakes his head. "Nothing." He grins. "Just feel good."

Patrick snorts. "Yeah, this time *I'll* be the one limping all over town."

"You—you liked it, right?"

Patrick lifts his eyebrows. "You couldn't tell?"

Will shrugs, some of the old self-doubt creeping back in now that the endorphins from his orgasm are receding. "I mean, it seemed like you did, but…"

"I liked it," Patrick says simply.

Will smiles again, his confidence restored. "I liked it too."

"Good."

Will turns on his side, trailing his fingers down Patrick's back. "But you know what I like even better?"

"What's that?" Patrick pries open one of his eyes.

"I like it when *you* fuck *me*."

Patrick grins, sliding across the sheets. He bends down close and whispers in Will's ear, "Roll over. I know what you like most of all."

"Oh yeah?"

"Yeah."

Will does as he's told, and as soon as he's settled on his stomach, Patrick spreads his ass cheeks open.

"Ready?"

Will squirms and spreads his legs farther apart. "Ready," he gasps.

Patrick licks his way down Will's crack, stiffens his tongue and spears it against Will's hole. It takes a long time, but eventually Will comes from Patrick's hand on this cock and his mouth on his ass, proving his point extremely well.

Chapter Twenty-Two

THE NEXT MORNING, they wake up tangled together as usual. But this time is like their very first morning, and they're naked and covered in the remains of sex. Will slides out of Patrick's arms, going into the bathroom to urinate and check his blood glucose. When he comes back into the room, Patrick sits up, calls him over, and drags him back down into bed.

"C'mere," he murmurs against Will's hair. "What's the rush? We've got time."

Will relaxes into Patrick's arms, his balls tingling and cock rising. Patrick slides his hand down to cup Will's erection. "Insatiable. What am I going to do about this?"

Will arches into Patrick's touch, already aching for the sweet oblivion of orgasm delivered at Patrick's skilled hand. But a nagging thought surfaces before he gives in completely. "Aren't you going in today?"

"In you? I'm ready if you are."

"Into the hospital." Though Patrick getting inside him sounds like a much better plan.

"Oh, yeah. The hospital." Patrick nuzzles his neck and slides his thumb through the pre-come beading at the slit of Will's throbbing dick. "Yeah, but not until eight."

Will glances at the clock. "It's nine."

Patrick jolts up, gripping Will's cock almost painfully. His eyes are wide and all the languid warmth he'd exuded before is gone in a flash. "What? How?"

"I think we were a little distracted." Will thrusts his hips up, pushing his dick against Patrick's palm. "We forgot to set the alarm."

Patrick's eyes dart from Will's hard, throbbing dick in his hand to the clock and back again. "Let's make this fast, puddin'-pop. I want you to come for me, got it? Now. Not ten minutes from now. *Now.*"

Will shivers. "Bossy."

"I'm in charge. And late." Patrick's hand moves quickly, hitting an undeniable and relentless rhythm. Will's hips roll with the squeeze and grip, but he can't seem to hit the crest. Shaking, he slides one hand up to play with his own nipples, and the other down to join Patrick's tugs.

"Yeah," Patrick mutters. "That's right. Get yourself off for me." He releases Will's cock and crawls between his legs, sucking two fingers into his mouth and sliding them down Will's taint to his cleft. "Spread your legs. Like that. Good."

Heat rises in Will's face as Patrick watches him jerk off. "Do you like this?"

Patrick's grin is feral. "Love it." He shoves one of Will's knees up, exposing his hole. "Mmm. Fucking hot." He rubs his wet fingers over Will's asshole, massaging and tickling his taint with his thumb. "Come for me now. Show me what I want to see."

Will groans, his balls tightening, and he spasms. "I'm close."

"Look at me."

Will drags his eyes up from his hand flying over his cock and meets Patrick's urgent, blue gaze. "Come," Patrick grits out. "I want to see you shoot."

Digging his heels into the mattress, Will flings his head back as his white-hot orgasm pumps through him. Strings of come land on his chest and neck. "Oh! God!" He trembles, arching and shaking, losing his place in the world as his body collapses into spasms that go on for a long time.

When he stops shaking, Patrick's kneeling by his side, one hand gripping Will's jaw and the other flying over his own cock. Will blinks up at him. "I wanna come in your mouth," Patrick mutters. "That okay?"

Will nods, and Patrick's grip on his jaw tightens until Will's mouth is held open. "Fuck!" Patrick's head falls back, his throat exposed and pulse pounding in his neck. "Yeah. Here it is. Now."

Will lurches forward, pulling out of Patrick's grip to suck the head of his cock in, swallowing salty spurts of come while Patrick's hands clench in his hair, his thighs trembling under Will's palms.

Patrick pops his dick free of Will's mouth and sits back on his heels, eyes glazed and breath coming in a fast rush. "Three minutes. Not bad. Not bad at all." He kisses Will's mouth quickly and then rolls off the bed.

Will lolls back into the pillows, admiring Patrick's naked ass as he strolls into the bathroom without a glance back. The shower turns on. Will reaches for the phone and orders room service, letting them know there would be an extra tip involved for delivering it in the next ten minutes.

He waits until the shower turns off and then heads into the bathroom for his turn.

"Give the guy an extra five for hustling when our breakfast arrives," Will says as he steps into the wet tub.

Patrick is shaving so quickly Will worries he might cut himself. "Did you test your blood yet?"

"Of course."

"Don't forget your insulin this morning."

"I never forget, Patrick."

Patrick shoves back the shower curtain, looks Will up and down, and then says curtly, "Stop being hot."

"I can't help it? I'm just showering."

Patrick runs his finger down the length of Will's soft cock. "Damn. Well, whatever. I've gotta get dressed." He turns and leaves Will to wash alone.

When Will steps out of the bathroom, scrubbed clean and feeling like a pin cushion after his insulin injection, he finds Patrick chomping on the last of a peanut-butter covered bagel and packing up his medical bag. The swelling on Patrick's temple has gone down, but the bruise has morphed from red to purple.

"Your breakfast is over there," Patrick says as he fires off a text to someone. Probably his new assistant, Stan. "Promise me you'll eat well and keep a close eye on your glucose today. Sex changes things. Uh, in your body, I mean."

"I'm fine, Patrick."

He nods and sends another text. "You'd think I was the chief of staff. They can't do anything without me."

Will smiles softly, eats his breakfast, and dresses while Patrick places a call to Stan telling him that if he doesn't do his job then he'll have to find a way to steal Hunter from his old office in Atlanta.

"Charming," Will says when Patrick disconnects.

"I don't have time to deal with him when I'm already running late." Patrick pulls on his boots and coat. He pauses and looks up at Will where he's leaning against the dresser. "But I do have time to deal with you."

"Do I need to be dealt with?"

Patrick smiles, his eyes soft and warm. "Do you?"

"I'm not freaking out about last night if that's what you're worried about."

Patrick nods brusquely and grabs an armful of snacks and a water bottle from the minibar. "Good Works is closed for New Year's Day, right? You got other plans?"

Will runs his eyes up from Patrick's boots to his neck. He remembers Patrick's head flung back this morning, his hand flying over his cock. Shameless. Liking what Will had given him. Coming for Will.

Patrick's eyes flicker a little, a subtle change that Will thinks is a flash of worry, but then it passes. "Puddin'-pop? Plans? Got 'em?"

"Oh, uh, yeah. I'm meeting my uncle at the farm to help with the kids today. We're taking them riding."

Patrick grabs his bag. "Yeah, well, everyone should wear helmets. I don't want any of your idiot family to be my New Year's Day head trauma." He pauses in front of Will and touches his chin. "Or you."

Will's heart clenches.

Patrick goes up on his tiptoes, roaming his hands over Will's shoulders. "Are we good?"

"Yeah, we're good. Happy New Year, Patrick."

The kiss is fast, but Patrick pulls back with a dreamy smile on his face. "I'm already late. I could cancel this surgery. Get you back in bed."

"I'm pretty sure someone with a brain tumor is waiting for you to perform a New Year's miracle. As nice as going back to bed with you sounds."

Patrick slides his hands down to Will's ass, squeezes, and then busses him again quickly. "Okay. If you're sure. I gotta go. I'm late enough as it is."

Will bites his lip as Patrick walks across the room, his gait obviously affected by their activities the night before. Will reaches down to adjust his suddenly hard cock to a more comfortable position.

Patrick pauses by the door, his fingers tapping his thigh. "I'll see you this afternoon."

"All right."

"Maybe we can revisit your request from last night?"

"What was that?"

Patrick's smile glints. "That I fuck you, of course."

Will swallows thickly. "I can't wait."

Patrick hitches his bag on his shoulder and struggles for words a moment before saying, "Last night was great, didn't you think?"

Will smiles. "I think you're going to be late."

Patrick nods and shuts the door firmly behind him.

Collapsing to the bed, Will presses his face to the sheets, taking in the scent of them together. He rolls onto his back, stares up at the ceiling, and smiles goofily.

THE WEATHER'S DROPPED to below zero and the wind is whipping, nixing the family's plan to ride. Instead, Uncle Kevin takes them all out to the barn to muck stalls and generally clean things up. When there are groans and moans from Caitlin, Olivia, and Connor, Uncle Kevin launches into an encouraging speech about starting the new year as you plan to go on.

"Let's make everything nice for the horses. It'll be our pledge to them to keep things just as nice the rest of the year. Sound good?"

Will snorts a laugh and crosses his arms over his chest as Caitlin rolls her eyes and stomps off toward her favorite mare Ginger's stall. Will knows she'll probably just huddle back there and text her new beau long, whiny messages about how life is super unfair.

Olivia gets straight to work, though, grabbing a shovel and heading back to her pony Blimp's stall. Her readiness to do her duty isn't unexpected, and Connor, who's still young enough to think that maybe mucking stalls can be fun, scrambles after her to help.

Uncle Kevin gets the tack and saddles down, laying the pieces out on a blanket on the ground. "Connor can oil and clean these. We'll let Caitlin pout in the back with Ginger, and Olivia can deal with Blimp. You and I will handle the heavy mucking. Okay with you?"

"Sure." Will helps him lay out the tack, fingering the supple leather of an especially nice bridle. He hasn't been around the farm much in a long time and he's missed the scent of hay. He glances toward Manny's stall, remembering Christmas and the glow in Patrick's eyes as he'd looked at Will.

He touches his medic alert bracelet and feels heat crawl up his back. He closes his eyes and licks his lips, remembering the expression on Patrick's face as he'd come for Will that morning: commanding, yet vulnerable and wild. And the night before! The way his body had been so strong and hot beneath Will, and inside he'd been a furnace. Had he ever called Patrick cold? He'd been an idiot. No, Patrick was burning up and Will could still feel the heat.

"That sure was something last night," Uncle Kevin says, taking the bridle from Will's hand.

Will jerks his eyes open and flushes so hard his thighs sweat. "What?"

Uncle Kevin's brows lift. "Ryan punching Dr. McCloud."

"Oh, yeah. That." He clears his throat. "It was something. Yeah." He can't think about Ryan right now. Not with his heart hammering and his hands clammy with the memory of what he's shared with Patrick. What he's willingly offered up.

Uncle Kevin doesn't seem to notice. "I know you two aren't together right now."

"No, we're not." Will waits for the crushing pain. It doesn't come. Instead, he feels like someone sewed wings onto his back overnight, and he might run out of the barn and take flight, wide blue winter sky taking him up into the new year.

Uncle Kevin gazes sincerely at Will, reaching out and gripping his forearm reassuringly. "I think he must still have feelings for you to go that far. Jealousy can drive a man to violence. Believe me, I remember the feeling too well sometimes."

Will doesn't want to think about Roy's indiscretions and how they led to his eventual death. Will's not following in Roy's footsteps. No matter what he's done with Patrick, it's still miles from Roy's level of habitual infidelity. And he's not following in Kevin's footsteps either. Will isn't going to continue pledging his fidelity to Ryan, no matter what Ryan says or does, or if they are even together.

He loves—or loved Ryan, but he can make another choice. He can let himself enjoy whatever this is with Patrick for what it's worth, for as long as it lasts, and he doesn't owe an explanation about it to anyone.

"Jealousy isn't an excuse for violence." Will reaches out to grab more tack from the wall, running his fingers over the smooth, comforting leather. "Ryan should be glad Patrick isn't going to press charges for assault."

"Maybe. But you and Ryan had something special. He'll figure out that this new young man isn't half the person you are and come back to you. He loves you."

Will doesn't think they should talk like this here where Caitlin, Olivia, or Connor might hear. "I don't know what Ryan feels for me. AA tells me that his opinion of me isn't even my business. But I'll say this: I'm not sure he ever loved me."

Uncle Kevin puts his hand on Will's shoulder. "Don't think like that. Ryan always kept you safe and protected you from your baser instincts. You'll find your way back to each other. If it's meant to be, it will be."

Will makes a face. "That's the thing. I don't think it's meant to be anymore. Don't think it ever was."

"But you were lovers."

Will scoffs. "Barely."

Kevin tilts his head. "You lived together."

Will clears his throat as Olivia stomps by with horse blankets in her arms. "We did. But that's over."

"It can't be. You won't let it be," Kevin says with confidence. "You need him."

"Do I?"

Connor comes running from the back of the stable with Olivia's favorite farm dog Rupert loping after him.

"To keep you—"

"Don't say safe. I can keep myself safe."

Kevin stares at him with an expression that tears at Will's heart. He can only imagine how it ripped Roy apart to see it and know he'd caused it. Will wonders what it will take for that pain to ever go away.

"It's okay, Uncle Kevin. I'm going to be okay."

Olivia yells from the hayloft, where she's climbed to take some blankets for storage. "Don't, Connor! Uncle Kevin, Connor's trying to climb up here!"

Uncle Kevin tears his eyes from Will's face. "Connor, get down. You know you're not allowed up there without a grownup."

Will watches to make sure Connor climbs down and scurries back toward Ginger's stall to bug Caitlin, Rupert at his heels. "Uncle Kevin, not every relationship works out. Look at Mom."

"Yes, look at your mother."

Will swallows the bubble of shame that presses in his throat. "And this whole thing with Patrick is complicated."

Uncle Kevin gives a small, closed mouth smile before striding over to his work cabinet and pulling out rags and oil for Connor to use. "Well, with any luck your grandmother will be able to work that out for you."

Will nods, scratching at his ear. He remembers the small noises Patrick made as he'd struggled to take Will's cock, and the expression on Patrick's bruised face this morning when he'd touched Will's chin. It's a lot to process. He's still full of so much want, like he didn't come three times last night and get off this morning. He clears his throat, his cheeks hot, and feels his uncle's eyes back on him.

"Will, what's going on with you and Dr. McCloud?" Uncle Kevin looks around to make sure the kids aren't listening. "Does Ryan have a reason to be jealous? Did Patrick deserve that punch?"

"Patrick's a great guy, and I know you and Mom are really confused about him and how everything happened, and I get that. But Ryan left *me,* and anything I do with Patrick isn't his business. And one last thing: Patrick sure as hell didn't *deserve* to be punched. No matter what Ryan feels or thinks about me, or what Patrick and I have done together."

Uncle Kevin zeros in on the last sentence. "You've done things with Patrick? Since you returned to Healing with him?"

Will lets out a long breath. "I'm not going into this with you."

Uncle Kevin studies him carefully and then concedes. "You're right about one thing, no one deserves to be hit. But if something's changed between you and Patrick—"

"No, no, nothing's different."

Kevin eyes him. "I feel like you're not being entirely honest with me, Will."

Will's phone beeps, announcing a text, and he pulls it out, relieved for a moment's break from his uncle's inquisition. He blinks. The text is from Patrick. His stomach coils in a nervous twist, and he clicks to read it.

Between my bruised head and ass-sore limp, I'm getting lots of stares today. Patient asked if my wife beat me up. Told him it was my husband's boyfriend. Good times.

Will chuckles.

"Good news?" Uncle Kevin asks.

Will shrugs and shakes his head. "Just a friend."

Uncle Kevin doesn't look convinced, and as Olivia climbs down from the hayloft, Will decides to head it off at the pass. He nods toward Manny's stall. "Listen, I know you love me, but I can handle my own life."

"I know you can."

"Then I'll just get to work."

He can feel Uncle Kevin watching him as he grabs a pitchfork and opens Manny's gate.

"Connor," Kevin calls. "Come here! I need your help with the saddles and tack, buddy!"

Will pats the stallion on the nose, talking to him softly so that no one will hear. "Hey, guy." He leans the pitchfork against the wall and grabs a brush, deciding to pamper Manny a little before turning him out while he mucks his stall. "So, Be Your Own Manny," he whispers. "Got any advice for me?"

The horse shifts into the brush Will runs down his side. "Well, I'm working on it, you know. Being my own man. Standing up for myself. Doing what I want for my own reasons. It's kind of hard. I'm not sure I'm any good at it."

Manny looks at him solemnly and then tosses his head.

"Yeah, I hear ya. Shake it off." He sighs. "I want to."

Will gives Manny a nice rub down, and then leads him out to the corral to wander a bit in the fresh snow while Will clears his stall. He's only dumped one small load from the wheelbarrow when his phone beeps again. It's another text from Patrick.

Don asked if I'd visited the pharmacy for painkillers because I looked 'happy.' Told him the term was 'fucked out.'

Will's heart soars and his face prickles with heat. How can he feel happy and embarrassed and full of pride all at once? He's still trying to reconcile those feelings when he gets yet another text.

Donny told me: "I remember how it was. In the beginning the honeymoon just goes on and on." I don't want to imagine him having a honeymoon. Don naked. Ew. Kill me.

Will laughs and he tries to stifle it when Uncle Kevin comes around the corner to check on his progress. He suddenly feels sixteen again, hiding in an empty horse stall with Jack Linton's cock in his mouth.

"Going okay back here?" Kevin asks.

"Great. Do you need help with Summer Solstice or Pennsylvania's stalls?"

Kevin smiles at him like he's trying to read Will's mind and failing. "When you're done, sure."

"Okay." Will tosses another few pitchforks full of shavings to the side, using the shavings fork to remove the dung for the wheelbarrow.

What are you doing? Patrick's next text reads.

Mucking stalls. Too cold to ride.

There's no reply to that, and Will puts his phone away after a few minutes of waiting. He looks up to see that Uncle Kevin's leaning against the gate watching him.

"Sure you don't need help?" Kevin asks.

"I'm sure." Will smiles, but it feels weird, and he goes back to mucking.

During the family meal later, Kimberly announces that despite attending the New Year's Eve party with Mark Walton, she's been secretly dating Jason Kirkpatrick, her employee at the tack shop, for a month now. "We've kept it very quiet. He's a really good man. Very kind to me."

"This is why you've been staying late at work," Olivia says.

Kimberly smiles. "You all know and like him. I'm sure you see why he's—"

"I swear to God I will move in with Grandma Betty and Uncle Kevin if you marry him. No, I'll move in here at the farm if you even bring him *home*," Caitlin announces.

Will touches Olivia's hair and smiles down at her reassuringly as the shit hits the fan. It's another hour before everyone has calmed down enough for Will to make an exit. Kimberly has huffed out to the stable, Caitlin has stomped to the guest room Grandma Betty reserves for her, and Olivia's back out in the tent with Rufus. Making sure Connor is comfortably watching a Nickelodeon show, Will goes back into the kitchen to kiss his grandmother goodbye and wrap up some leftovers for Patrick.

Uncle Kevin pulls him aside. "Will, you're right about one thing. You're an adult now, and you can make your own choices in life. But I just want to tell you…well, I hope you're making good ones. I think you really need to consider what you're doing with this doctor."

Will bites his cheek to keep quiet.

"There's nothing wrong with…well, any of that," Uncle Kevin goes on to say, looking constipated at his allusion to sex. "But just make sure you've both got the same end in mind." He squeezes Will's shoulder. "Start as you mean to go on. And if you don't mean to go on with him, then maybe it shouldn't start."

Will turns Uncle Kevin's words over and over in his mind on the drive to the Tallgrass. How many times has he watched his parents start something they don't intend to finish—with each other, with lovers? How many times has he told himself he isn't that kind of person? And now here he is, aching to get back to the Tallgrass so he can get Patrick naked and suck his cock until salty-tangy semen floods his mouth. All he wants is to push Patrick back on the bed, lift his legs—and, *God.*

Will presses the heel of one hand to his right eye, trying to shake loose from the lust. But all he can think about is Patrick's expression as he comes.

When he pushes open the door to their hotel room, Patrick's there, taking off his jacket and turning to greet him. Will's eyes catch on the bruise on Patrick's temple, the purple hue of it against his auburn hair and light skin. Will leans with his back to the door, trying to keep from reaching out.

"Hey," Patrick says. "You look clean for someone shoveling crap all day."

"Showered at the farm," Will gets out around his lust-thick tongue.

Patrick starts on the buttons of his shirt, a long stripe of skin showing as he goes. "Lock the door. Get your clothes off."

Will takes a shaky breath. *Start as you mean to go on.* "About last night," he manages.

Patrick's face shifts, shutters a little.

Will forces himself to say the rest. "Maybe it shouldn't happen again?"

Patrick's hands drop to his sides and he stares at Will, his eyes intense and penetrating. Will's breath comes in short, deep pulls, and his cock is so hard that it hurts confined in his jeans, and he's shaking all over from holding back. He hears a high-pitched broken noise, and he realizes it's from his own throat, and Patrick's eyes go soft and so, so hot.

Will shoves off the door and thrusts his hands under Patrick's shirt, finding skin, grabbing tight, and whimpering into a hungry kiss that burns through him.

He gives in to it, and just like the night before it's better than alcohol, better than a bottle of whiskey. It's empowering and good, and he's strong, so strong as he takes Patrick's cock in his ass, and jerks himself off, and flips onto his back to take it again.

"This new year is getting off to a great start," Patrick declares.

"It is."

Patrick clutches Will's chest hair, and Will arches up into each thrust.

Despite everything, despite how stupid it might be, Will's happy, and Patrick is too. Will can see it, and damn going forward. It doesn't matter how he means to go on, because he wants this right now.

The consequences can wait.

To be continued...

Tune in to the continuation of the *Wake Up Married* serial!

Wake Up Married, Episodes 4–6

Episode 7, Will & Patrick's Endless Honeymoon, is now available!

Gay Romance Newsletter

Leta's newsletter will keep you up to date on her latest releases and news from the world of M/M romance. Join the mailing list today. letablake.com

Leta Blake on Patreon

Become part of Leta Blake's Patreon community in order to access exclusive content, deleted scenes, extras, bonus stories, rewards, prizes, interviews, and more.
www.patreon.com/letablake

Other Books by Leta Blake

Any Given Lifetime
The River Leith
Smoky Mountain Dreams
The Difference Between
Heat for Sale
Stay Lucky
Stay Sexy
Omega Mine: Search for a Soulmate
Bring on Forever
Angel Undone

The Home for the Holidays Series
Mr. Frosty Pants
Mr. Naughty List

The Training Season Series
Training Season
Training Complex

Heat of Love Series
Slow Heat
Alpha Heat
Slow Birth
Bitter Heat

'90s Coming of Age Series
Pictures of You
You Are Not Me

Co-Authored with Indra Vaughn
Vespertine
Cowboy Seeks Husband

Co-Authored with Alice Griffiths
The Wake Up Married serial
Will & Patrick's Endless Honeymoon

Gay Fairy Tales
Co-Authored with Keira Andrews
Flight
Levity
Rise

Audiobooks
Leta Blake at Audible

Free Read
Stalking Dreams

Discover more about the author online:
Leta Blake
letablake.com

About the Authors

Author of the bestselling book Smoky Mountain Dreams and the fan favorite Training Season, Leta Blake's educational and professional background is in psychology and finance, respectively. However, her passion has always been for writing. She enjoys crafting romance stories and exploring the psyches of made up people. At home in the Southern U.S., Leta works hard at achieving balance between her day job, her writing, and her family.

<u>Alice Griffiths</u>

A long-time reader of romance novels, Alice Griffiths finally took the plunge into writing, teaming up with best-selling author Leta Blake for the 'Woke up Married' serialized comedy. A lover of tropes, Alice enjoys mining old ideas and putting a fresh, funny spin on them. Formerly working in the newspaper industry, Alice is now an art curator. She lives in Sydney, Australia.